SECRETS

VERA COWIE

SECRETS

COLLINS
8 Grafton Street, London W1
1989

William Collins Sons & Co. Ltd
London · Glasgow · Sydney · Auckland
Toronto · Johannesburg

First published 1989
Reprinted 1989

BRITISH LIBRARY CATALOGUING IN PUBLICATION DATA

Cowie, Vera, *1928*–
Secrets
I. Title
823′.914[F]

ISBN 0-00-223430-0

Photoset in Linotron Galliard by
Rowland Phototypesetting Ltd,
Bury St Edmunds, Suffolk
Printed and bound in Great Britain by
Butler & Tanner Ltd, Frome and London

FOR LAURA LONGRIGG

CONTENTS

PART ONE: Claire   9
PART TWO: Jake   151
PART THREE: Rory   403

Part One

CLAIRE

'I clothe you in the colours of my longing'
W.B.YEATS

CHAPTER ONE

'You look absolutely beautiful, darling,' her mother said tremulously, stepping back from the long gleaming train.

Claire regarded herself in the pier glass, a shimmering figure glowing with the lustre of a pearl, her grandmother's diamond tiara glittering through the smoke-like translucence of her pure silk tulle veil. 'I feel it,' she answered softly. 'I feel . . . exalted, somehow.'

'Not – nervous?'

'About marrying Rory?' Claire's laugh rang with confidence. 'Never! It's all I ever dreamed about.'

'There is more to marriage than dreams,' her mother pointed out gently.

'Oh, I know that. But with Rory – how could it be anything else?'

'He is only a man, you know, like other men.'

'Of course he's not! He's Rory! There's no other man like him!'

'All brides think that way.'

Claire turned to her mother, her whole being giving off light, radiant with all the confidence and anticipation of a bride on her wedding day, her beauty enhanced by her happiness. 'They may think,' she said, 'but I *know* . . .'

Her mother sighed. 'You are so young . . .' she said, half to herself.

'As old as you were when you married Daddy.'

'Ah, but that was another world . . . just after the war. Times were hard and so were we – from necessity, not choice. I don't think I ever was as *young* as you are now . . .'

'I know what I'm doing, Mummy. I know what I want.

And what I want is Rory.' Her smile was brilliant. 'The unholy miracle of it all is that he should want me!'

'It's obvious you are in love.'

'Utterly, absolutely, devastatingly – for ever and ever, amen.'

There was a tap on her bedroom door and Logie, the family butler, came in. 'I beg your pardon, milady,' he said to Claire's mother, 'but there seems to be some dispute as to the champagne to be served for the toasts.'

'But I gave them explicit instructions,' Lady Margot Drummond said crossly. 'The vintage Dom Perignon – the non-vintage stuff is for afterwards, when nobody will be in any condition to tell the difference . . . I suppose I must come and spell it all out again. Why is it that people seem to lose all their wits at weddings?' She turned to her daughter. 'You have twenty minutes before you leave for the church. I'll send your father up just as I leave.'

'Not to worry,' Claire said serenely. 'I'm all ready.'

'Allow me to say, Miss Claire, that you look quite breathtaking,' Logie said to her, with all the paternal fondness of a privileged servant.

'Thank you, Logie. You are going to dance at my wedding, aren't you?'

'With the lightest of hearts,' he assured her.

No lighter than mine, Claire thought, turning to her reflection once more. I do look good. Happiness does wonders for one's looks. Under the mist of her veil, her vintage-Burgundy hair glowed, dressed so that the Drummond tiara, a delicate filigree of first water diamonds and teardrop pearls woven into a design of lover's knots, could nestle comfortably and securely in its soft waves. Her dress was a confection of yards and yards of rustling faille; not white but a rich cream, infinitely flattering to her matt skin and dark-red hair. It had a heart-shaped neckline which showed to advantage the diamond heart dangling from a triple row of seed pearls – Rory's engagement present. The sleeves were elbow length, tied with lover's knots of crisp ribbon; and the fabric fitted closely over her breasts and waist until just below her hips it fell away into a twenty-foot train. Her veil was a cloud of pure silk tulle, its border continuing the theme of lover's knots. It would cover her face when she went down the aisle of her family church with her father: it would be thrown back when she returned on the arm of her husband.

Her flowers were roses and camellias, with white heather for luck, and she had something old in the shape of the cream satin shoes her grandmother had worn at her own wedding in 1922 – bar-strapped with Louis heels; she had been as petite as Claire was now, and they fitted perfectly Claire's size three and a half feet. Her lingerie was brand new, from Janet Reger, and she had borrowed her tiara from her mother, to whom it belonged, while on her right leg above the knee she wore a frilly blue garter.

Rory will be proud of me, she thought, as she surveyed herself. I want him always to be proud of me. I am not going to give him any cause for complaint. She laughed softly. Complaint! Not where Rory was concerned. With Rory as her husband she confidently expected the untroubled path she had walked for twenty-one years to continue for however many she still had coming. She was not a religious girl, though her father had insisted his children be given religious instruction, but now she closed her eyes and folded her hands and said fervently: 'Thank you, God, for bringing me Rory. I don't know what I have done to deserve it but I promise I will do my best to live up to it.'

Her bedroom door opened and Caroline de Beaumont, her chief bridesmaid and best friend, rustled in, also wearing stiff cream faille but this time cut straight across the collar bones with long tight sleeves to the wrist. 'I've brought you a nerve-steadying glass of champagne,' she announced.

'I'm not nervous,' Claire said. 'Look . . .' She held out a hand. It was rock steady.

'Well I am . . . I've got those two hellions your nephews to keep an eye on, remember.'

'They're not hellions! They're sweet.'

'Well, they do look cute in their kilts, but it's Rory I can't wait to see. He always looks good enough to eat but I'll bet in full Highland rig he looks positively consumable.'

'Down girl,' giggled Claire. 'He's spoken for.'

'Well, I rather fancy that best man of his.'

'David Grant? Yes, he is nice.' Claire sipped her champagne.

Caroline prowled around her. 'Well, it may have cost the earth but it was well worth it,' she pronounced finally. 'You look absolutely fabulous.'

'Just so long as Rory thinks so.'

'Oh, come on. He only had eyes for you from the moment he picked you up out of the snow.'

Claire smiled. 'I know . . . that's the magical thing about it all. I still can't quite believe it.'

'You had better believe it because he will be demonstrating his ardour in not too many hours from now.' Innocently: 'Unless you already know all about that.'

'That's what I mean about it being magical. In spite of his reputation – and I still think a lot of sour grapes went into *that* murky brew – he's been a latter-day perfect gentleman. Honestly!'

'Golly!' marvelled Caroline. 'It must be love then.'

'It is,' Claire told her simply. 'I knew it the moment we looked at each other . . .'

It had been a year ago last December; she had been in Gstaad with her 'group': four girls who had been friends since school, and four boys, staying in the family chalet of one of them and with no thought but to enjoy themselves. They had been high-spirited, given to high jinks and not a little horse-play. It had been during a snowball fight that Claire, having been hit with one right in the face, put up a hand to wipe away snow and dropped her glove. Bending to pick it up she had not realized that she was precariously balanced on the edge of the slope they were about to ski down, or that she was facing the wrong way. As she straightened, the movement pushed her backwards and before she knew it she was sailing down the slope at ever-increasing speed. There were shouts of laughter which changed to shouts of alarm as they saw that she was not pretending and that her cries of fright were genuine. The boys pushed off, but before they could get to her, a figure swiftly flashed in front of them, did a perfect turn and stopped dead, right in her path. She careered into him with such force that they both fell over. Claire was not hurt, only winded, and she felt herself picked up, righted and held by the arms. 'Are you all right?' a man's voice asked.

'I think so . . .' She brushed more snow out of her eyes and then looked straight into another pair as blue and as deep as the waters of her native lochs. She had never seen such blue eyes; they held her helpless and drew her into their depths. She stared into them, mouth open slightly, feeling their impact like a physical blow.

'You look a little shocked.'

I am, she thought dazedly, but not by the fall. Her rescuer was physically electrifying. Six feet four and built to scale, with a deeply tanned skin and the classically handsome face of the young Apollo. His smile, when it came, buckled her knees and she fell forward.

'Are you all right, Claire?' Simon Maitland asked anxiously.

'Yes, no bones broken . . .' she managed shakily.

'Thanks awfully, sir,' Simon said politely, and Claire looked at her rescuer again. Sir! she thought. He can't be more than thirty. As their eyes met for a second time she felt a wave of heat scorch her body.

'I'm afraid it was the only way to stop you,' he said, on another million watt smile.

'I'm glad you did,' she assured him.

'I thought you were having us on,' Caroline giggled nervously. 'You sailed backwards like a kite!'

'I lost my balance . . . I hadn't realized I was more or less teetering on the edge.' And have fallen over, she thought.

'Thank you very much, Mr . . . ?' she said in her best, Nanny-taught manner.

'Ballater, Rory Ballater.'

Claire felt a quiver of shock. I don't *believe* this, she thought.

'Small world,' she said shakily. 'I'm Claire Drummond.'

'Good God!' The blue eyes swamped her again. 'Not Hamish Drummond's little sister?'

'The only one he has.'

'Well I'll be damned . . . Last time I saw you, you were a skinny brat in pigtails kneeling on the floor of a butt.' The dark voice seemed to melt her bones. 'You have grown up, and no mistake.'

As they looked at each other the world seemed to recede, enclosing Claire in one that was all blue, blue, blue. She felt her skin prickle as another wave of heat left her trembling.

'Darling!' a woman's voice called, impatient, sharp, and Claire looked to where a blonde, stunningly dressed in the most elegant, zingingly scarlet ski-clothes, was frowning across. 'Do come along . . . we shall be late for lunch.'

'Coming . . .' Rory Ballater turned back to Claire. 'How is Hamish these days? I haven't seen him in years.'

'Fine. He's with the British Embassy in Washington.'

Rory Ballater laughed, and Claire once again shivered. 'He always was diplomatic.'

'You haven't been back home for a long time,' Claire remarked lightly.

He shrugged. 'I've been travelling . . .' The blue eyes seemed to darken. 'Scotland holds little for me any more, I'm afraid . . . or it did, anyway, until today . . .' This time, Claire found herself blushing furiously. He smiled again. 'We must have a drink, talk over old times. Where are you staying?'

'We're at the Bruningens' chalet,' Caroline volunteered.

He raised his eyebrows. 'Are you now. In that case you can invite me for a drink.'

'Of course,' Claire said quickly. 'It's the least I can do.'

'Rory!' called the woman, imperiously.

'I must go . . . I'll give you a ring,' he said to Claire, leaving her in no doubt that he would. He flipped a salute and then, turning his skis with the expertise of a professional, pushed himself off and schussed down the hill to the waiting woman and her group.

'Wow!' Caroline breathed reverently. 'That is prime male . . .'

'Caroline!' snapped Simon.

'Well, he is! Oh, don't be so stuffy, Simon. Honestly, you can be so boring at times!' She turned to Claire. 'You actually know him?'

'He's a neighbour of ours. He was at Eton with Hamish.'

'Rory Ballater . . .' Charles Bingham-Smith said thoughtfully. 'Bit of a rotter from what I've heard.'

'Do tell!' Caroline urged, her eyes sparkling.

'Far too experienced for a child like you,' he retorted. 'That blonde is more his type . . .'

'Did you see her outfit?' Charlotte Wigram sighed enviously. 'Designer stuff if ever I saw it.'

'Designer clothes, designer men,' Caroline purred silkily. 'You will invite him for a drink, won't you, Claire?'

'Of course I will.'

'Good. I need to get in some practice with *real* men . . .' She shrieked as Charles rammed snow down her neck and another riotous fight developed.

'Are you sure you're all right, Claire?' Simon asked concernedly.

'Yes . . . yes, of course . . . no bones broken.' But I think my heart has been badly damaged, she thought.

She did not see him during the rest of the day and he did not call that evening, or the next day. She was beginning to think she had imagined that look in his eyes when, as she was dressing for a chalet party the following night, Caroline came bursting in: 'It's him!' she announced dramatically.

'And not on the phone either – here!'

'What?'

'Downstairs, large as life and absolutely twice as handsome!'

'You're joking.'

'I am not – see for yourself.'

She seized Claire's hand and whisked her to the top of the cantilevered staircase. Peering over the swiss-clock carving of the banister, Claire saw Rory Ballater in chestnut cord trousers and a heavy clotted-cream Aran sweater, standing in front of the big fire; examining the portrait of Helga Bruningen. Her daughter Sissy had invited Claire and the rest of their group to stay at the family chalet, but on their very first day she had fallen and broken an ankle, and her over-anxious mother had whisked her away to Geneva to see a bone specialist. 'You must stay and enjoy your holidays,' she had told the rest of them with kindly largesse, before taking Sissy away in one of the family helicopters.

'Isn't he just *gorgeous*,' whispered Caroline besottedly. 'And off the leash.'

'What do you mean – leash?' Claire snapped.

'The blonde . . . he's "staying" with her. She owns that huge place further up the mountain – the one with the turrets. She's French – Madame Hector Chevreau. Her husband is an industrialist – and safely back in Paris.'

'How do you know?'

'I made some enquiries, as they say,' Caroline replied airily. 'She's his mistress.'

'That's none of your business,' Claire hissed angrily.

'If he is making you his then I want to know the ins and outs. You are such an unworldly little thing.'

Caroline was the 'fast' member of the group. Much more worldly wise than Claire or Charlotte or even Sissy, she had already had three stepfathers and her mother was in the throes of providing her with a fourth. Like her mother, Caroline also believed variety was the spice of life.

'And he does have a reputation,' she went on, with an 'I told you so' air. 'He's had more women than you and I have had hot dinners.'

'Don't be vulgar,' Claire told her coldly.

'He's thirty-two – that makes him twelve years older than you, but when it comes to experience he is as old as Methuselah.' Her flippant tone turned grave. 'Watch yourself, Claire. You're not used to men like him.'

'And you are, I suppose?'

'I've met more of them, that's all. My mother's second husband was a Rory Ballater. They come expensive.'

Claire brought Caroline's mother to mind: a rather hard-faced, daggers-drawn, elegant woman who had enough money to brook no kind of opposition from anyone; who had descended on Heathfield at school gatherings like a movie star, swathed in sable or stunning couture clothes, utterly extinguishing the other mothers in their sensible tweeds or Aquascutum coats. Caroline lacked for nothing except her mother's interest, and she had already acquired the first coating of shellac which would eventually come to be the glossy armour her mother wore. But she had a kind heart and she had always been Claire's best friend at school. When Caroline had been left at a loose end come holidays, with her mother in New York or Hong Kong or Sydney, Claire had taken her home to Scotland, and Caroline was grateful. Claire's home life was stable, solid, old fashioned and filled with love. She didn't, Caroline thought now, looking at the heart-shaped face dominated by its melting pansy-purple eyes, begin to know the half of it. She glanced downstairs again. Rory had seated himself in one of the big sofas, ankle on knee, and was leafing through a copy of *Paris–Match*. What are you after, Rory Ballater? she wondered.

Claire, when she eventually went downstairs to join him, neither knew nor cared. He had kept his promise, he had come, he was interested in *her* – that was enough. As he stood up to meet her, he smiled, and again she had that feeling of being plucked from her world and into his, where nothing was familiar but everything was exciting. Her experience of men as against boys – for that was what Charles and

Simon and Anthony and James were – was nil; against Rory
Ballater, a professional mercenary in the battle of the sexes,
she presented no challenge. He moved in and took over
without a shot being fired.

'So, tell me about yourself,' he invited, as they were sitting
alone later, the others having gone to the party, 'What do
you do with yourself? Where do you live?'

She told him of the London flat she shared in Cadogan
Gardens with the three girls with whom she was sharing the
chalet. It was Sissy's flat, but her mother, ever over-
protective, had refused to let her live in it alone and vulnerable to predatory men – which meant as many flatmates as the
bedrooms would run to and additional convoy protection in
the way of Maddi, Sissy's nurse, 'who looks like Heidi thirty
years on and sixty pounds heavier', Claire said ruefully,
making Rory laugh delightedly.

'And what do you do with yourself all day?' He had a way
of focusing himself on you with those incredible eyes which
Svengali'd you into confessing all. He made Claire feel that
he had never met anyone like her; that he was the one being
enchanted.

'I work for de Lisle's – the estate agents? I take our
customers to the houses we have for sale or on lease, show
them round –'

'And charm them into paying the earth?'

Claire blushed.

'You could, you know,' Rory said, with a seriousness that
had her swallowing hard.

'And what else are you good at?' Rory asked, refilling her
glass. Caroline had appropriated a bottle of champagne from
the enormous Bruningen cellar – Krug Premier Cru. 'You
don't give a man like Rory Ballater a can of Coke!' she had
said scathingly.

Now, sipping the deliciously dry, tinglingly chill wine,
Claire was not sure if it was that or Rory Ballater which was
making her blood sing.

'Well, I learned French and Italian and how to cook, and

then I took a Pitman secretarial course – and learned to ski, but not very well, as you saw.'

'Let me teach you.'

Claire swallowed. Rory Ballater was a champion; he had cups and medals and had once skied for Britain in the Winter Olympics. 'Would you?' she asked breathlessly.

'With the greatest of pleasure. We'll start tomorrow.'

'I should like that,' Claire said, making the greatest understatement of this or any year.

'And do you go home to Scotland often?'

'About once every six weeks or so. I usually spend my weekends with friends.'

'Who are they? Perhaps I know them.' Which would not be surprising; Rory Ballater moved in Claire's world, where weekends in the country, shooting, fishing, riding, were as much a part of life as washing the car was to others. He had been at Eton with her middle brother, but for some years now he had not been home much, paying only the occasional visit to Ballater House. The family home was an enormous Victorian pile built by his great-grandfather in the 1880s, when Ballater's Best, a superb single malt, and later Ballater's Blend, which was developed when the opening in the market had been spotted by that shrewd old man, had made their fortune. The Ballaters had once been enormously rich, that much Claire knew, but according to local gossip Rory's father had spent recklessly, and with such energy that he had been forced to sell the company to pay his debts. All that was left was Ballater House and ten thousand acres of some of the best shooting in Scotland.

He told her he had just come back from Kenya where his older sister – 'You remember Margaret' – lived. Before that he had been in Australia. 'I like to travel, don't you? I hate the thought of being tied to one place, one kind of life.'

Claire, who knew only France, Italy and Switzerland, nodded earnestly, though she had been brought up in a part of Scotland that was, in many ways, still feudal; the 'locals' who lived in Glen Drummond all worked, in one way or

21

another, for the family who owned it. Her father was a reserved and formal man of the old school who, though he loved his children dearly, always shook hands with his sons on meeting and did no more than kiss his daughter on the cheek. Claire had been brought up along traditional lines: always eat whatever is placed in front of you, never speak with your mouth full, never interrupt when another person is speaking, always shake hands when being introduced and always keep your bedroom neat and tidy; but she had been surrounded by love. Her mother, unlike her father, was a woman who showed her feelings and though it was always to Sir John that people deferred, Claire had soon come to realize that it was her mother who ran things; it was to her people came for help and advice. Sir John was respected, but Lady Margot Drummond was loved.

Rory Ballater, on the other hand, was the product of a wastrel father and a mother who was notorious for her affairs. Once her husband had run through his fortune she had left him, when Rory was just a small child. When his father had married again it had been to a widow with three children of her own and no time for a boy she knew resented her. She had at once taken matters in hand; Ballater House was let every August, for as much money as the traffic would bear, to rich Americans willing to pay for the honour of blazing away at the grouse which infested the Ballater acres. She had turned, according to Claire's mother, to hotel-keeping, even to advertising Ballater House in certain Texas shooting periodicals, coming down heavily on the fact that it belonged to a Baron (leaving out the fact that it was only in the fourth generation, the title of Baron Ballater having been bestowed on Rory's great-grandfather by Queen Victoria, because Ballater's Best was her favourite tipple), and managing to arrange a shrewd bargain with the company's new owners to serve nothing but Ballater whisky to her guests. The fact that the family fortune had been founded by Angus Ballater, a crofter with an illicit still, was never mentioned, and as she was a pushy, self-assertive woman, she always managed to provide other guests with lineages as long as the Amazon and titles glittering enough to dazzle men whose petrodollars had no history at all. Claire knew that Ballater House and its house parties were regarded by the neighbours as more than *infra dig*, but as she had heard from her mother not long before that Rory's father had died – and not in his own bed – she surmised that Rory had come back to claim his title and what was left of his inheritance.

'Will you be going to Scotland?' she ventured.

'I've only just come from there,' was all he said, giving no hint as to what had transpired.

He said very little about himself, but he encouraged her to talk about herself in a way that was insidiously flattering and ego-boosting, and by the time he left, having arranged to come and collect Claire next morning, she was helplessly and hopelessly in thrall.

He dominated the rest of the holiday. She did not see him every day, and she spent those when she didn't in a daze of ecstatic anticipation. She had never met anyone like him before; he was effortlessly co-ordinated, a superb sportsman who was a great skier and a daredevil on the Cresta run. She never saw him in the evening; but true to his word he gave her invaluable instruction and her skiing improved no end. She was not up to the black runs he dominated so easily, but neither was the woman he was with; her interest was in appearing on the slopes every day in a different outfit, all stupendously chic. But whenever she encountered Claire she inevitably displayed to her an attitude that proclaimed Rory as her property; it was in the way she laid a bejewelled hand on his arm, or waited for him to light her cigarette. In the dining-room of the Palace Hotel, where Claire and her friends were taken one night by Mrs Bruningen to celebrate her birthday – she had returned with a despondent Sissy plastered to the knee – Claire saw Rory and his companion engaged in a low-voiced tête-à-tête, her hand resting possessively on his. Claire felt a blast of jealousy which ruined her enjoyment.

On her last day she told Rory she was returning to London, hoping desperately he would say: 'Give me your number and I'll give you a ring.' But he didn't. All he said was a casual: 'I'll be there myself sooner or later. Perhaps we'll run into one another again.' But he smiled at her in a way that seemed to suggest he would make sure they did.

She heard nothing from him her first week back, and she found it hard to settle back in the rut, to extol enthusiastically the virtues of six bedrooms *en suite* or a genuine Adam fireplace or the latest in state-of-the-art security systems. She refused to go out at night in case he called, and when at the end of her second, miserable week she went up to Scotland, it was, for the first time in her life, with great reluctance. All she could think of was Rory. When her mother said, at the breakfast table one morning, her father having already left it, 'I hear you ran into Rory Ballater in Gstaad,' she answered, 'Literally,' as casually and lightly as she could. She tried to make the story of how it had happened amusing, adding at the end, 'He said he had been up here.'

'Indeed he has . . . the glen is full of it. A head-on collision with his stepmother. It seems he has given her notice to quit. His father had little to leave but what he had has gone to Rory. She has been told to take herself off. I gather the rafters rang with the name calling! If he has put rout to Jennifer Ballater he is indeed a man to be reckoned with. That woman never bothered about wearing the velvet glove on her mailed fist.'

'All the better to clobber you with,' murmured Claire.

'Well, he probably needs the money – he has inherited his father's propensity to spend, spend, spend – and whatever else that woman was she certainly made Ballater House into a going concern. It is thanks to her the place is in a much better state of repair. Whatever she made she did not spend on herself. Rumour has it that she expected her late husband to leave it to her – there is no entail – but she made a mistake

24

there. James Ballater loved money but he hated her turning his family home into a Scottish Alamo.'

Her mother poured more coffee for herself. 'Whatever, rumour has it that Ballater House is all that Rory has inherited, and the land, of course. I expect he will sell. I heard that one of the big hotel groups was interested in acquiring it. That way, he will at least have more to live on than his wits. He went to Kenya under a cloud: something about gambling debts.'

'I think you are warning me off, Mother,' Claire said, tilting her chin. 'There is really no need. I have neither seen nor heard from him since I left Switzerland.'

'Good,' her mother returned calmly. 'He is too old, too experienced, too much, for a girl like you. You could never afford him.' Which was what Caroline had told her only a day or two before. 'He always has an eye out for the main chance,' she had said.

'How do you know?'

'I asked Mummy. She moves in his circles. That woman he was with? She was paying his way. All his women pay his bills. He hasn't any money.' Caroline had been picking through the invitations littering the mantelpiece. 'Mind you, if I could afford him I wouldn't decline the opportunity . . . Are you going to Chantry this weekend?'

'No. I'm going home.'

'Like a good little girl,' mimicked Caroline. 'You realize that's why he didn't pursue? Good girls aren't his scene . . .'

That morning, Claire went riding, and the first thing she did once she was out of sight of the house was turn her horse's head in the direction of Ballater House. It was twenty miles from Castle Drummond by road; less than half that distance across the moors. She came out of the trees on the hill above the small valley where it stood, among acres of lawn and a formal Italian garden transplanted, root for root, from Tuscany. It was a vast Victorian pile, on the lines of Balmoral, and though Claire had never been inside it she knew, from her mother's description, that its interior was in keeping with the massive grandeur of its façade. There was no one to be seen, but then, if Rory's stepmother had gone . . . She urged Tam, her placid five-year-old bay gelding, down the hill. She was curious to see where Rory might, she prayed, live in the future – which was for her coming, more and more, to revolve around him.

She tied Tam to a statue of Diana the Huntress and went cautiously across the gravel drive, where she peered through one of the enormous leaded windows. She could see gargantuan furniture, a fireplace big enough to roast an ox in, heavy, gilt-framed pictures.

Then somebody said, 'All you had to do was knock and I'd gladly have shown you round.'

She whirled, to see Rory Ballater, big and beautiful in a superbly cut tweed hacking jacket and cavalry twill trousers, regarding her with a smile.

'Oh!' she said breathlessly. 'I didn't know you were here . . .'

'No. But I knew you were.'

'Oh,' said Claire again, feeling her stomach flop.

'I rang the flat and was told you'd come up here for the weekend. I was about to call on you.' The blue eyes went over her in a way that had her senses whirling. 'It seems we are two minds with but one thought . . .' He took her unresisting hand. 'Why don't I show you round?'

'It's big, isn't it?' Claire said, her wits having deserted her, conscious only of the hand holding hers, sending rills of molten fire all the way up it and through her entire body.

'Yes, isn't it?' Rory said, amused. It was all gilt and scarlet; designed, Claire thought shrewdly, to impress. 'All my step-mother's work,' Rory said sardonically. 'All these acres of fitted carpet are her idea; she covered up a superb parquet floor. I intend to change all that.'

'You – you're going to live here?'

'Of course. I am Ballater now. This is my home . . . I left it because –' a shrug. 'It's no secret that my stepmother and I did not get on.'

26

He showed her the vast dining-rooms, the billiard-room, the library, the gun-room, with its racks of Purdeys and Hammonds locked in their cases. He showed her the bed-rooms – again all deep-pile carpet, draped four-posters and adjoining bathrooms. 'At least she knew what Americans are willing to pay for,' Rory said drily, as he indicated a tap that said Iced Water.

'Will you carry on – the shoots, I mean?'

'Yes, but I shall do it differently. Ballater House will become what it was originally: the house of a Scottish landowner, not some characterless hotel.' There was more than a trace of bitterness in his voice. Of course, Claire thought tenderly, he was born here. He has his pride. He is, like me, a Scot.

'I'm sure you will do it well,' she said sincerely.

He raised his other hand to touch her cheek. 'Sweet,' he said, in a way that had Claire once more drowning in the incredible blueness of his remarkable eyes.

She rode home in a bemused daze, but said nothing to her mother. Least said, she thought, soonest mended, and as luck would have it, at the luncheon table her father said: 'I hear that fellow Ballater is back. Turfed out That Woman and intends to take over the place. Bad blood, the Ballaters. Feckless, the lot of them. Take out but never put back. Archie Muncrieffe tells me that Ballater is going to sell off some of his acreage to the Scottish National Tourist Board for a Highland Park! Next thing we'll be having coachloads of tourists tramping through the Glen.'

'I expect he needs the money,' his wife said placidly.

'The Ballaters don't know how to handle it, that's their problem. Jamie Ballater went through ten times what I had from my father, and from what I hear his son is tarred with the same brush.'

Claire said nothing, concentrating on eating her lunch. Rory had asked her out to dinner in London the following Monday night.

And it was not to the Poule au Pot or the Santa Croce,

27

where Claire had always paid her share; Rory Ballater took her to Waltons. He took her to San Lorenzo, where they sat at a table next to Warren Beatty. She went with him to polo weekends at Cowdray Park – Rory was a six goal man, but not being able to afford his own string of polo ponies ('A good one fetches £20,000,' he told her) he rode those belonging to syndicates. He took her to the ball Lord Cowdray gave, and under his encouragement she splashed out on a glorious Belville Sassoon paper taffeta ballgown of a deep violet to match her eyes; it cost more than all the skirts and sweaters she had bought from Benetton or Fiorucci. He took her to Goodwood, they went to Annabel's, they attended first nights, gallery showings, cocktail parties where the guests were suave, cigar-smoking men and bejewelled, maquillaged, clothes-horse women with hard drawls and cold eyes. They spent weekends at country houses and castles and Claire gladly trailed after him, wading through mud in her green wellies and waiting patiently while he outshot everybody there.

Every time she went home to Scotland she said nothing, even though her mother, by casual things she said, made it plain that she knew what was going on. Her father, thank God, had no idea. She knew he would not have approved. An obedient, well-brought-up girl, Claire had never thought that she would willingly and deliberately deceive her father, who rarely went to London, being happiest on his own acres, a country gentleman content with his life, his dogs, his horses, his tenants. But she was by now so desperately in love with Rory that had he asked her to run away with him then and there, she would have done so.

Now and then he would say: 'Have to go away for a while, but I'll be back, never fear.' And he would disappear for a week or ten days, sometimes longer, leaving Claire to mope, impatient with the scrupulously shared dinners at her former favourite restaurants, the high spirits and, she now thought rather superiorly, the high jinks that had once seemed such good fun. Charles and Simon and their ilk seemed gauche and childish. Rory was a *man* – and such a man. She longed with an increasingly desperate desire for him to make love to her, but he never did. He kissed her – oh, how he kissed her – into mindless submission, but he never went further. The gossip that said he never bothered with any woman unless she was willing to pay for the pleasure was obviously a lie. Never once had he expected her to pay for anything. And he always seemed to have money. He had bought her a bracelet of amethysts carved into violets hanging from a fine gold chain 'to match your glorious eyes', he sent her flowers, he came with her when she bought clothes and she, who had been brought up to spend thriftily, now spent recklessly on designer dresses and sumptuous ballgowns.

And then, before she knew it, it was August and he was going up to open Ballater House. True to his word, the fitted carpet was gone from the hall, which now gleamed from industrious polishing of its original parquet.

With her organizational skills, Claire helped him compose the guest lists over the coming weeks; how many the party would contain, whether they would bring their own guns, the quantities of food needed – and here Claire suggested that if he was going to make it truly Scottish instead of international, he should serve his guests the cuisine of the country. Good porridge – but made with cream – and bannocks and oatcakes for breakfast with marmalade made by Mrs MacAllister, whose recipe invariably won first prize in every competition; mutton pies, Forfar Bridies, thick beef sandwiches and steaming barley broth on the shoots. She suggested he limit the party to twelve – his stepmother had crammed in every paying guest she could – and she came up with the idea of providing every guest with their own picnic box, of silver, of course, and engraved with the Ballater crest. He already had a portable fridge which could be plugged into one of the Land Rovers, and a hot cupboard. And a plentiful supply of whisky. Rory's manservant Wilkie, a surly individual whom Claire did not like, was always along to dispense the drinks.

29

'Darling, you have worked magic,' Rory told her enthusiastically at the end of the first shoot. 'The last drive before lunch was done in double quick time. You should have seen the speed at which they moved down the hill. As soon as they saw the trailer they forgot to pick up the birds and made a beeline for the food!' He picked her up and whirled her round. 'What would I do without you?' Then he sobered, and a serious look came into the vivid blue eyes. 'I mean that,' he said gravely. 'I have come to realize it more and more . . . I *can't* do without you, Claire, and that's the truth of it. Marry me.' A look of desperation which totally undermined her came into his eyes. 'Please . . . marry me.'

'Oh, you idiot . . .' Claire said, tearful with joy, 'as if I could say no!'

Her father was both hurt and horrified. 'Ballater!' he exclaimed. 'My daughter marrying a scoundrel!'

'Not any more, Daddy,' Claire said, facing him squarely, every bit as stubborn as he was. 'He told me all about his past; he left nothing out. I know what he was – it's what he intends to become which concerns me.'

'He will always be what he is,' her father said angrily. 'A wastrel and a scoundrel. Why, the man lives off women! Mark my words, it's your money he's after! You are twenty-one in two months' time and that's when the money your grandmother left in trust for you is handed over – that's what he's after! What can a man like him want with a girl like you?'

'He loves me,' Claire said proudly, 'and I love him. Very much, Daddy, more than I have ever loved anyone or anything. I mean to marry him, and I am old enough to do so with or without your consent.'

Her father regarded her sadly. 'I never thought to hear my daughter say that to me,' he said heavily. 'The man has bewitched you.'

'He has made me very happy.'

'You are not his wife yet. I dread to think what will happen once you are.'

'You don't know him,' Claire said angrily, 'and therefore have no right to say such things.'

'I knew his father, and from what I hear, it is very much a case of like father, like son. James Ballater was a bankrupt, he gambled away his inheritance, his mother is nothing more than an adventuress and her son has been living off women ever since. He has not a penny to his name and he has no job, no income –'

'He is making a lot of money from the shoots.'

'And I don't approve of that, either! We have his appalling stepmother to thank for that. But then, she was a Sassenach and knew nothing of how things should be done.'

'You married an English girl!'

'With Scottish blood, and Ballater blood is bad blood. Always has been, always will be. They have never amounted to anything: rags to riches to rags in just four generations. Wastrels, the lot of them. No sense of responsibility. They know how to take but expect other people to do the giving. This is not what I wanted for you, Claire. He is not the kind of man I expected to welcome as a son-in-law.'

Claire met her father's hurt and angry eyes with sadness but determination. 'I'm sorry, Daddy. But he is what *I* want. I love him, more than I believed it was possible to love someone. I can't visualize life without him.'

His quick temper slipped its leash. 'Then I wash my hands of you!' he said angrily, and left her.

'Give him time, darling,' her mother counselled wisely. 'He will come round. All I want to ask is one question: are you quite, quite sure you know what you are doing? Love loosens everyone's nuts and bolts; under its influence people do things they later regret. You hardly know him.'

'Mummy, I've known him for the past eight months.'

Margot Drummond bit her lip. The confidence of youth, she thought. Eight months . . .

'I know his reputation; he's told me everything. Nobody

31

knows the real Rory, but I do. He had a father who ruined the family fortune and a mother who was exactly what Daddy says she was – an adventuress. He was brought up by servants. He has no idea what it is like to be loved, as I have been. Is it any wonder he went wild? You and Daddy brought me up to realize my responsibilities: if Rory's parents regarded them as excess baggage, then how can you expect him to even know what they are? Yes, there have been women – he told me about them. None of them ever meant anything to him. I think that in some way he was using them to get back at his mother.' Margot Drummond hid her surprise at Claire's perception; many women twice her age did not possess it. 'But he *loves* me; he wants to settle down, to stop racketing around. He needs me, Mummy. And the thought of life without him is something I cannot bear to think about.'

Gently: 'He is thirty-two, darling. Are you so sure he can change?'

'If I help him, he can.'

Oh dear, thought her mother, seeing the light of the zealot in her daughter's eyes: the legions of women who have thought that *they* could change a man set in his ways.

'I only want you to be happy,' she said finally.

'I will be. If I didn't think Rory was capable of making me the happiest woman in the world I wouldn't even consider marrying him. And I mean to, Mummy. With or without your blessing, not to mention Daddy's.'

He has bewitched you, Margot Drummond thought, yet she was impressed by the firmness in Claire's attitude. She had always been such an obedient little girl; eager to please, happy to oblige, anxious for approval. Rory Ballater had uncovered a Claire who was every bit as stubborn as her father and every bit as purposeful as her mother. Perhaps she can handle him, Margot Drummond thought. Perhaps she is what he needs. A steadying influence. She wondered if Rory really had told Claire the whole truth and nothing but the truth.

'He made full confession, then?' she asked casually.

'He told me everything,' Claire answered simply. And he had, honestly, unflinchingly, and in a way that only served to enslave her even more.

'I know I've been a doubtful prospect, darling,' he had told her, 'but all that racketing around was because I had no safe harbour to run to, no anchor to keep me from being washed away. When I met you I thought you were just another pretty girl and a nice one. I never expected that you were the one I had been looking for all this time: that safe harbour I had despaired of finding. You are so steady; you don't flap and you don't nag and you believe in me. Nobody ever did that before; they only believed of me – the worst possible things, and I don't deny I gave them good cause. But all that is finished. I want to leave it all behind and start afresh. I can't do that unless I have you with me. I need you, Claire . . . you have no idea how much I need you . . .'

'Oh, darling, you have me, all of me, now and for ever . . . I'll help you give up gambling. I'll help you every way I can.'

He had cupped her face between his hands.

'You are so young,' he said, troubled.

'Almost twenty-one. And I'm quite old for my age really.'

He had laughed exultantly, gathered her in his arms. 'You are a marvel,' he said. 'I don't deserve you.'

'Well, you've got me,' Claire had told him lovingly. 'And you will find I am not so easy to get rid of.'

'He needs me, Mummy,' she repeated now. 'In ways you just don't understand. You married a man who was rock steady even when he was young; I know Rory has a reputation for wildness and unsteadiness but all that is going to end – has ended. This year's shooting season has been the most successful ever. He has made a lot of money, and I won't let him gamble it away. Together we will make Ballater House a profitable enterprise. I have so many ideas . . .'

But not one where the real Rory Ballater is concerned, her mother thought. She knew better than to say so. The more she argued, the harder Claire's resolve set. You are much stronger than I gave you credit for, she thought. Perhaps it will work out. Perhaps a strong woman is what Rory needs. But you will need all your strength, my darling. I only hope that it runs as deep as it seems to.

And it was with this thought in mind that she set out to convince her husband who, where his wife was concerned, was always amenable to persuasion. In the end he gave his blessing, albeit reluctantly, and the engagement was announced. Rory gave Claire the Ballater sapphire which his mother, on being told her son was getting married, had sent to him in a surprising gesture of generosity. It was a ten carat marquise-cut solitaire surrounded by cabochon diamonds.

'She *is* coming to the wedding, isn't she?' Claire asked, turning her hand this way and that.

'With my mother, anything is possible. If she does come it will be out of curiosity, no more.'

The bitterness in his tone only served to convince Claire that she was right in thinking that it was his mother who lay at the bottom of Rory's previous attitude to women. He had seen her desertion as a betrayal for which he had been punishing the rest of her sex ever since. He has never really been loved, she thought, but I will change all that.

Now, turning from the mirror on her wedding day, she resolved once more that she would give Rory that sense of self-worth she was sure he lacked, and when someone knocked at the door she called: 'Come in, Daddy,' expecting her father. But it was her future mother-in-law.

'See you in church,' Caroline said hastily, before whisking herself out.

'It is a mother-in-law's privilege to see the bride before the ceremony, is it not?' Davina Ballater asked lightly, with the charm her son had inherited in full measure. 'If it isn't, then I am instituting it.'

'Of course,' Claire said warmly. 'I'm so glad you came. It means so much to Rory.'

Davina Ballater raised her exquisitely plucked and shaped eyebrows. 'Does it now?' she murmured. Then she smiled. 'You look positively spectacular.'

'So do you,' Claire replied honestly.

It was a winter wedding, late January, and there was still snow on the ground, but Claire knew that there was a great log fire roaring away in both fireplaces in the Great Hall downstairs, where the reception would be held, and the church was now centrally heated thanks to her father, who had hated shivering during services. Davina Ballater was swathed in Russian sable; and her hat was a devastatingly chic affair of silk organza and coq feathers. She had to be at least fifty, but careful surgery had resulted in a face entirely free of wrinkles and still exquisitely beautiful, but in the manner of a wax dummy. Too perfect, Claire thought, too unreal.

As always, Davina's bluebell eyes went straight to the pier glass from which Claire had just turned. 'One does one's best to keep the ruins in a decent state of repair,' she sighed.

'I only hope I present such a ruin in time,' Claire said smilingly.

Davina turned to pat her cheek. 'Sweet child . . . no wonder Rory is so besotted. I had wondered . . . you are not his sort at all.'

How would you know? Claire thought, then felt uncomfortable as Davina proceeded to confirm her diagnosis.

'I suppose you think I have been a most peculiar mother,' she said. Claire said nothing. If she said yes it would be bad manners, if she said no it would be a lie. 'I married far too young . . . seventeen. I was eighteen when I had Rory and he was such a demanding brat . . . greedy from the word go. They wanted me to feed him but I couldn't stand it . . . he was absolutely voracious. I wasn't ready for him and I hated this freezing, God-forsaken backwater. Nor – unlike you – was I in love with my husband. I married him because my mother more or less made me. The Ballaters were enormously rich, then, and we had sod-all. I stood it as long

35

as I could and then made a bolt for it. And in case you think I am justifying myself to you, let me make it plain that I have never regretted it.'

'Not even Rory?' Claire asked quietly.

Davina shrugged her sable shoulders. 'I am not cut out to be a mother. The maternal instinct is one that was left out of my make-up, and that's all there is to it.' Then she smiled, and it was Rory all over again. It bathed you in such radiant warmth that you forgot the cold hard words. 'But I am glad he has found you. The Drummonds have a reputation for probity and steadiness. Quite unlike the Ballaters.' She turned to peer at her reflection again. 'But then, you know all about them, don't you? I didn't send a wedding present; I've got something much more to Rory's taste.' She opened her alligator handbag, one of Hermes' best. 'I am giving it to you because you will take the better care of it. Rory is his father's son. Money burns away his pockets like sulphuric acid. If you take my advice – and it comes from hard knowledge – you will put it where it can stay until you need it. And don't tell Rory. He won't expect anything from me. He is never backward in coming forward to say he has never had anything from me anyway.'

Claire took the envelope Davina held out. It was not sealed. Inside was a cheque drawn on Coutts for one hundred thousand pounds. Her jaw dropped.

'I always choose rich men,' Davina advised her with a cynical smile. 'And my present husband has more money than even Rory could run through. But take my advice, sincerely offered. Tuck it away.' She gave herself a last once-over in the mirror. 'Well, time to go downstairs and run the gauntlet of all those old biddies who earnestly pray each night that I will get my come-uppance. By their lights I should be repenting on my knees, but instead, I thought I would give them the satisfaction of confirming their opinion of me as the Scarlet Woman.' She held open her coat; under it was a dress, so simple, so plain, so perfect that it must have cost the earth, of bright scarlet pure wool crêpe, and on one shoulder, a diamond sunburst that dazzled. 'In keeping with my image, don't you think?'

'You really don't care, do you?' Claire found herself asking.

'Only about things that matter.' She came forward, placed one smooth cheek against Claire's, enveloping her in a cloud of 'Arpège'. 'Good luck,' she said, and then swept out.

Claire stood with the envelope in her hand. Not tell Rory? Never. She was not starting on married life with a lie. Of course she would tell him. He would be pleased. But temporarily she placed it in the bottom tray of her jewellery box.

When her father came to collect her, Claire thought with a pang that he looked worn and old. Yet he was only sixty-five. A professional soldier for the first half of his life, he had been badly wounded at El Alamein and as a result had only one lung and that damaged. Always a fit and active man, he had not taken kindly to the ensuing curtailment of his activities, and this had had an adverse effect on an already irascible temperament. He had been strict with his three sons, expecting from them the virtues instilled in him by his own father; thrift, probity and honour. But to Claire, his last child, separated by six years from her youngest brother, he had always been more indulgent. Now, she knew he was still not wholly reconciled to her marriage, but like her mother, though it had taken longer, he had come to accept that Claire's resolve was that of a true Drummond; she would not be shaken free from convictions firmly held.

Now, he took his daughter's hands and she saw his eyes fill. Not a man given to parading his emotions, Claire bit her lip at this proof of his feelings.

'Well, daughter,' he said. 'Are you ready?'

'Yes, Daddy. I'm ready.'

'You look beautiful,' he said. 'Almost as beautiful as your mother was on our wedding day.'

'I hope I am as happy thirty-five years from now.'

His steel-blue eyes regarded her searchingly. 'Time will

tell,' he said finally, 'but if wishes are any help, then all you hope for will be given to you.'

'Please try not to worry, Daddy. I am very happy. I love Rory very much and he loves me. I shall not be far away – just across the valley – and we shall see each other often.'

'I hope so,' he said. Embracing her, he kissed her tenderly. 'Now, shall we go?'

The servants were in the hall, along with those tenants who had come to wish her good luck. There was a chorus of good wishes, and Claire smiled round at them all radiantly. 'Thank you,' she said.

'You're a bonnie bride, Miss Claire,' Mrs Mckinnon, the cook, said proudly, having known Claire almost all her life.

There was another chorus of 'Aye, that she is,' and everyone crowded round to see her bestowed in the big black Rolls.

It was only five minutes to the church, which stood on Drummond land; it was small, and as Claire entered, a quick glance showed that it was packed, with many people standing at the back. Her father had been scrupulous in his invitations to those people whose lives were bound up with that of the Laird and his family; there were as many people from the village and the Glen as there were guests from London and Edinburgh. Her mother and Caroline were waiting to arrange her train and, as they did so, Claire looked down towards where Rory, splendidly handsome in full Highland dress, awaited her with his best man, also wearing the kilt. She still could not quite believe it; this virile, sexy man, who could have any woman he wanted by crooking a finger, actually wanted *her*. I will be all you want, Rory, she promised. You will not regret a moment of our marriage. I will make you happy. This I swear.

Her mother slipped away to her pew, and Caroline came to arrange the folds of the veil over Claire's shining face. She slid her arm through that of her father, the organ started up the wedding march, and head up, smile wide, Claire began her walk down the aisle.

CHAPTER TWO

They honeymooned in the Bahamas, on the yacht of one of Rory's many rich friends. Claire had been disappointed and dismayed when she found that they would not be alone, but part of a group of twelve, of whom ten were strangers. They had the main stateroom which the yacht's owner, a Brazilian industrialist, had insisted they occupy. He and his current mistress – a girl of about Claire's age with a sumptuous body and not a brain in her head – moved into another cabin.

'But I thought we would be on our own,' Claire protested. 'This is our honeymoon, Rory.' She knew she was sounding petulant but she couldn't help it. This was not what she had expected. No wonder he had told her that their honeymoon destination was 'a surprise'.

'Darling, this is not costing us a penny. And Bruno is a valuable man to know. He can do me no end of good, steer me in the right direction, the one where money can be made. We can't exist on what I make at Ballater House; too much has to be ploughed back. And I want to enlarge, go on to bigger and better things. Bruno can help me. How many brides get to spend their honeymoon on a yacht this size? Look at this stateroom. How much luxury can you take? Have you seen the bathroom – a sunken bath, yet – and those taps are solid gold! No one will intrude, they know this is our honeymoon . . . Bruno is being kind; he doesn't make a gesture like this to just anybody.'

That night, they ate dinner alone in their stateroom – and the food was superb, like the wine. Through the open window they could hear the sound of the local steel band Bruno had brought on board, playing soft, sensuous calypsos. The breeze was perfumed and the yacht, at anchor off one of the more remote islands, rose and fell gently on the calm sea. The moon rode high, and it was a far cry from the snow-bound day of her wedding, after which they had left for Inverness where they flew to Heathrow, changing to a 747 for the long haul to Nassau.

They flew first class and drank champagne and were given star treatment by the cabin staff. A car had met them and driven them to the yacht. And she had to admit that Bruno de Souza had been charming, greeting her with obvious pleasure and assuring her that the yacht was hers to command. If she and her husband wished to be alone they were at liberty to remain so; if they felt like joining in they would be warmly welcome. Whatever she wanted only had to be asked for. He was hers to command. And he had kissed her hand. She had not then been introduced to everyone. 'Later,' Bruno had said on a smile. 'I know you two will want to be alone . . .' Claire had had a blurred impression of bared shoulders, deep tans, gold jewellery, island-chic fashion.

Now, sitting across from Rory, her hair taking fire from the light of the candles, the air heavy with the scent of the tropical flowers: bougainvillaea, jacaranda, hibiscus and poinsettia, wearing one of her trousseau dresses, a cloud of rose pink chiffon, her diamond heart at her throat, Claire looked across at her husband in his white dinner jacket, a scarlet carnation in his buttonhole, his blue eyes regarding her with a look that had her heart thumping, and thought: I am a bitch to complain . . . This is wonderful. How many women get to spend their honeymoon on a luxury yacht where anything they want can be supplied? He did it to surprise me, and he *does* mean to get on; if this man Bruno can help him then I must do all I can to back him up. She reached across and took his hand. 'Thank you, darling, for all this . . . I'm sorry if I sounded ungrateful. I really was taken by surprise . . .'

'In a little while, I intend to take you in an entirely different way,' he said softly, in a voice which had her trembling.

When they had finished dinner they went outside to their

40

private veranda, where Rory drew her down on to one of the deeply cushioned steamer chairs, she lying half on him, while he caressed her with the tips of his long fingers, as delicate as feathers but deeply disturbing to her equilibrium. He had done this when they were engaged, but tonight she knew he would not stop, with that regretful but firm sign which told of a self-control strained to its utmost, just as she was ready to beg. Now, there was no need for him to say: 'No, darling, this is not like all those other women. With you, I want a proper wedding night; I want you all virginal and unspoiled; I want to know all the traditional pleasures of a husband, and that includes being the very first man his wife has ever had . . .'

Now, taking the champagne flute from her unsteady hand he proceeded to kiss each of her fingers; she could feel his strong white teeth nibbling gently. He pressed his warm mouth to her palms and she felt his tongue. She looked down at his bent head; the dark-red hair so clean and shining which grew into a widow's peak at the nape of his neck. She put her own mouth to it. In a trice he had changed her position; she was leaning against the cushions, he above her, kissing her shoulders and throat. 'You smell like a rose garden,' he murmured. 'And it is going to be roses, roses all the way, darling, I promise you . . .'

She arched with a gasp as his teeth closed on the fleshy lobe of her ear. She felt him laugh. It compounded her delirium. 'I knew it . . .' he murmured softly. 'Oh, you are going to make such a willing pupil, my darling . . .'

She had seen how deft he was. He had perfect physical co-ordination in all things; now he proceeded to handle her body in a way that rendered her helpless. As his mouth neared her own, his hand slid up into her hair, holding her fast. His lips explored behind her ears now, her temples, her jaw, places she had not realized could be so sensitive, causing deep and uncontrollable rills of pleasure deep in her belly, a fluttering sensation which made it hard to breathe. When at last he covered her mouth with his own it opened under his with a hunger that was as greedy as a child's yet as passionate as he could have wished for. She ceased to be passive, and returned his deep and searching kisses without restraint. Getting to his feet he swept her up in his arms, took her back inside to their sumptuous bedroom. But he did not deposit her on the bed; instead, he laid her down on the fur rug – it was chinchilla – before switching off all the lamps but one, which shed a soft glow through the swathed chiffon shade. Then he proceeded to take off her clothes, his mouth following his hands, hers aiding and abetting his own stripping. But it was not frantic; every movement flowed into another. Claire had often wondered about the undressing part; it was the one part of lovemaking which always seemed to her to be awkward. Not with Rory; before she knew it they were both naked. He leaned on one elbow to study her, his eyes going over her as his hands had, with delight.

'You are an odalisque,' he murmured. 'Small but perfectly made . . .' Then he fell to kissing her again. She had not known it was possible to receive so much enjoyment from another mouth; she felt dizzy with pleasure. His hands fondled her shoulders then slid to her breasts, which were small but full. He picked her up, turned her round so that they were sitting, she between his thighs, his erection hot and pulsating against her buttocks, his hands cupping her breasts. She felt his mouth on her spine, it went down, then up again to her nape, which he bit playfully, making her jerk convulsively. His fingers played with her nipples, which hardened almost painfully, and again she felt that strange, heavy fluttering in her belly. She could feel the moisture between her thighs, and as if he knew she was ready, she felt his fingers steal down her hips, caress her inner thighs, parting them, and then she felt them probing her. She shuddered violently, thrust against the fingers until he turned her once more so that she faced him, pulling her close, her breasts pressing against the wall of his chest. Then he began to kiss her again. Her mind clouded; she was incapable of thinking, only feeling. Their mouths were as juicy as ripe fruit; they breathed each other's breath, they inhaled each other's scent. Then he bent her back and his mouth left hers to slide down her throat to her breasts, where he took a nipple into his mouth and sucked. A spasm of pleasure so pure shook her violently and she cried out; she lay back helplessly against his strong arms while he lapped first at one breast then at the other, his fingers tweaking and caressing one while his mouth teased its twin. She thought she would faint with pleasure; her breath was roaring, her heart pounding, her body trembling. With consummate sensuality he proceeded to drain her will, until her breath was coming in gasps, her head twisting from side to side as the heat he was generating melted her insides.

Then once again he laid her down, but this time he spread her legs wide, and still caressing her breasts he began to kiss and nibble her toes, sucking each one, causing quivers of sensation to zing from them to the juncture of her thighs, stabbing her there, making her jerk each time. Slowly his mouth progressed up her legs, her thighs, and then he buried his face in the tangle of soft red curls and she felt his tongue unerringly find what it sought. She climaxed at once, body arching, head strained back, but he did not stop. Again and again he brought her to wild, bucking orgasm, her hands scrabbling desperately in the silky softness of the rug, her throat making raw, wild, guttural sounds, her body straining upwards to that flicking, licking, caressing, lascivious tongue until she was bathed in sweat. After half a dozen tumultuous orgasms he drew her into his arms, smoothing her tangled hair, kissing her damp face and closed, exhausted eyes.

'Touch me, Claire,' he commanded in a low voice, 'caress me . . .' She had never touched a man's penis before; she had not known it was so silky, so hard, so delicately tender. 'Yes . . . gently . . .' His voice was hoarse. 'Yes . . . that's right . . .' As her fingers explored, sliding up from its base to its sensitive tip she felt the groan which welled from him. She rotated her fingers there, felt the sticky substance oozing from it.

In another of his rapid movements he had her legs up over his shoulders and she had a fleeting glimpse of his bobbing penis before it was nuzzling, pressing where his mouth and fingers had been, then there was a glorious sensation of being filled as he thrust into her. She came instantly, and then once again. She lost count of the times he brought her to total and almost unbearable fulfilment. The hoarse sounds that came from her were ones she did not recognize; she wrapped her legs tightly around his waist and rose to meet his thrusts, circling her hips, making him gasp as she ground herself against him, tightening her internal muscles around him as he penetrated as deep inside her as it was possible to get. Their sweat-soaked bodies slapped like the water against the hull of the boat, her hands seized his flat buttocks and pulled him ever deeper into her as they seemed to spiral upwards in a frenzy of eroticism that turned her into a snarling animal. Her eyes were wild, unseeing as she strained for the ultimate. She heard his breathing change to harsh panting as his thrusts quickened; they strained against each other desperately and then she felt him spill into her; hot and copious. For a moment their bodies locked in a spasm of ecstasy that was almost agony, she heard him shout, heard her own answering cry and then, for a few seconds, she lost consciousness. She came back to herself to find him sprawled heavily against her, chest heaving, breath rasping in his chest, his face pressing into her throat. She could feel his sweat trickling on to her. Then, after a while, Rory raised himself on one elbow to kiss her closed eyes and lax mouth.

'I was right about you,' he whispered. 'You were made for it . . .'

'I thought I was dying,' Claire said dazedly.

'That's why the French call it le petit mort.'

'Yet I have never felt so alive . . . my whole body is singing.' She kissed him with passionate gratitude. 'Oh, thank you for making it so unbelievably glorious.'

'Worth waiting for?'

'Oh, yes, yes . . .'

'Good. Then I'm satisfied – and I mean that. You were incredible . . . so utterly responsive. I knew you would be.'

'I didn't. I had no idea . . . I've learned about sex, my darling, but I've also learned about myself . . .'

'And this is only our beginning.'

They had a shower together, which ended in another bout of glorious lovemaking under the roaring fall of four different shower heads, then Rory opened another bottle of champagne before carrying her to the big eight-foot-wide bed where he made love to her once again. They did not leave their cabin for three days.

When they appeared, on the fourth night, to join the rest of the guests for dinner, their appearance in the main salon, all glitter and gold, was greeted with applause which had Claire blushing furiously but left Rory unperturbed. The way everybody was smiling made her aware that they knew exactly what she and Rory had been doing, but their host was affable and kind and sat her next to him at dinner. Claire was glad that she could flaunt a ring every bit as good as the ones liberally decorating the elegant hands of the other women, and that her dress was up to the mark; a Zandra Rhodes of white tulle embroidered with mauve thistles composed of tiny crystals and pearls.

Afterwards, there was dancing, and then everybody emptied their glasses before heading for one of the launches which took them ashore to Nassau and the gaming tables.

'But I thought you weren't going to gamble any more?' Claire eyed Rory in dismay.

'Darling, I can't very well refuse . . . it would be churlish of us to act the prude and drop out. It isn't serious,' he said laughing at her. 'It's just fun . . . you had better bring some money with you.'

But the fun included Rory coming to her to ask her for the money she had brought, becoming irritable when she said uneasily: 'I think we should call it a day . . .'

'Oh, don't be stuffy,' he cajoled. 'We are on our honeymoon. Don't be kirkish about it for heaven's sake. Besides, I might win this time . . .' And it was with elated satisfaction that he stuffed what he had borrowed back in her evening bag. 'See . . . I told you. I've come out ahead . . .' Claire had not played; she had watched, been aghast at the piles of money carelessly laid on the green baize tables, betting on the turn of a card or the spin of a wheel. But she could tell that Rory loved it; he had that blazing look in his eyes, the one he wore when in the throes of lovemaking. With her father's strictures ringing in her ears, Claire felt both uncomfortable and guilty. Even when her father played bridge the stakes were pence rather than pounds. These people were gambling in hundreds, even thousands.

But when they got back, Rory was high on his success and once more made such mind-bending love to her that next day, when he got up to go water skiing, she stayed in bed, exhausted and not a little sore, sleeping almost the whole day away. Rory did not come back until late afternoon, and that night, after dinner, it was back to Nassau once more. But the days were glorious; they swam, snorkelled, sun-bathed; she tried her hand at water skiing and wind-surfing, and one night there was a party, with people coming from the mainland. More hard-faced, glamorous women and rich, elderly men. Another night they went to an island disco. Claire was a good dancer, she loved it, and was never off the floor. It was on going to the powder room that she heard two of the women discussing her.

'A sweet little thing, but quite out of her depth,' she heard one woman, a blonde always hung with first water jewels, say. 'Not his type at all.'

'Very pretty, though, quite lovely in fact.'

'Rory always did go for the lookers.'

'I hear her father owns thousands of Scottish acres so he hasn't acted entirely out of character.'

They both laughed, then the blonde said: 'I wonder how long it will take her to find out what that really is?'

They went out, leaving Claire sitting frozen in the lavatory cubicle in which she had been hidden while they talked. 'Bitches,' she spat out loud. How dare they talk about Rory like that? That was the old Rory. He had promised her to become a new one. How *dare* they surmise that he had married her for money? He had done well from last year's shooting season; every week booked and at five thousand pounds a gun the final total in the ledger had been entirely satisfactory. He doesn't need my money, she thought proudly. And we still have his mother's cheque . . . about which she had, as yet, said nothing, intending to surprise him later.

When she went back into the disco Rory was nowhere to be seen, but her host came up and asked her to dance and he was so attentive and charming that she forgot her earlier disapproval of him: a man his age – he had to be at least fifty – with a girl thirty years younger as his mistress. When they went back to the table, Rory was still missing; so was the hard-faced blonde with the jewels.

A member of the crew – the one who drove the launch – came across and bent to whisper in the ear of her host, who tapped his glass with a spoon before announcing: 'I am informed that there is a storm on its way. We must return to the yacht at once and move her to safe anchorage.'

Claire rose to her feet, her hand groping for her wrap. 'But Rory isn't here . . .'

'He cannot be far . . . I will have him looked for.'

'I'd much rather wait for him.'

'I cannot allow that,' protested her host jocularly. 'He would much rather you were safe on the yacht. I will send the boat back for him, never fear . . .'

But the storm came up very quickly; the yacht had only just anchored inshore in the lee of the nearest sheltering bay when it struck. The rain was like their four-head shower, and the lightning was bright enough to read by, while the thunder growled and roared with such ferocity that Claire hid her head under the bedcovers.

Fortunately it did not last long; the wind dropped, the rain stopped, and the heavy swell calmed. Claire was dozing when she heard the sound of the launch. She ran to the veranda, from where she could see it come alongside. She felt weak with relief when she saw Rory, and was about to call his name when she saw him turn to hand up someone else. It was the hard-faced blonde.

She saw Rory flip a salute before striding off towards the stern, and their cabin on the upper deck, while the blonde headed in the opposite direction, but as Claire stood, frowning, she saw a man detach himself from the shadows and plant himself in the blonde's path. She could not hear what he said, but it was obvious he was angry. She recognized him as an amiable Irishman who spent most of his time reading bloodstock periodicals; he was always good natured, always cheerful, and he had always been avuncular towards Claire. Now, she saw that he was furiously angry, and as she watched, he lifted a hand and struck the blonde a vicious swipe across her right cheek, following it with an equally vicious backhander to her left. She staggered back against the rail. The man turned on his heel and stalked away, leaving the woman cowering, one hand pressed to her cheek. Hearing Rory in their adjoining sitting-room, Claire whisked herself back inside and just managed to scramble back into bed before the bedroom door opened. He came across to where she lay, pretending to be asleep, and bent over her. She stirred, as though sensing him.

'Oh, you're back,' she said, feigning drowsiness. 'Where on earth did you get to?'

'I ran into Monty Glenalver – you know Monty, don't you?'

'Isn't he the man that bought the Carcraigan estate?'

'That's him . . . we got to talking and I had no idea you'd all gone back to the yacht until they came looking for me . . . You know how it is when you run into someone you haven't seen in an age . . . He's got a nice slice of one of the casinos on Paradise Island, doing extremely well out of it . . .' He chattered on as he undressed, flinging his clothes any old where – Rory was hopelessly untidy; invariably always hung his clothes on the floor. He did not mention the blonde, so Claire said on a beautifully staged yawn: 'That blonde – what's her name – the one with the jewels – she was missing too. I hope she got back all right.'

'You mean Vanessa Carlyle?' Rory chuckled. 'She's in trouble. She came back on the launch with me, and in fear and trembling, I might add. That storm was her bad luck. Did you notice Johnnie Gallagher stayed on board tonight? She took the opportunity to do a bit of catting around; she hadn't counted on the rest of you not being able to find her when the time came. Johnnie will have noticed she wasn't present and correct when the roll was called and he'll punish her accordingly. He might even decide to kick her out, but knowing Vanessa – and I do – she won't be short of a bob or two to tide her over until the next big fish comes along.'

He slid into bed, fitting his body against hers, cupping her breasts in his hands and nipping the back of her neck with his teeth. 'Did you think I was playing the tomcat with her?'

'Of course not!' Claire answered indignantly. The heat and strength of his erection pulsating against her spine was proof of that. No man who had been tomcatting would be so hard and so ready; not even Rory, who was capable of making love to her several times in a night, she told herself firmly.

'Are all the women on this ship mistresses of one sort or another?' she asked, thinking of the slap, the humiliation, the naked display of power.

'No . . . just most of them. Do I detect a note of coven-anter disapproval?'

'Well, it is a strange place to bring a bride.'

'Why? If these women had the chance of marrying these men they'd break the three-minute mile to get to the altar. Don't you realize they're all green with envy? You've got me, legally bound and tied. Besides, Bruno is enormously taken with you. He says it is a pleasure to see you enjoy yourself, because you make the smallest kindness or sign of attention seem an act of enormous significance. I told him it was no more than good Scots manners.'

Claire turned round so that she could put her arms about his neck and press herself against him passionately. 'I am so lucky to have you,' she said in a voice equally as passionate. 'Sometimes, I think it all must be a dream.'

'Good. That's how I wanted you to feel. I wanted this to be a honeymoon to remember.'

'Oh, I shall never forget this, never!' Claire swore fervently.

'Well, it's not over yet. Tomorrow we sail for Bermuda, calling at Barbados and Trinidad and –' Her mouth stopped his words.

'Just so long as I am with you.'

'I will always be with you . . .'

When they reached Barbados, he took one of the little Hobie-Cats and they searched for and found a deserted bay that had nothing but trees and sand, where they swam and sunbathed naked, and ate a picnic of cold roast squab and drank the bottle of champagne which came packed in its own special insulated bag. And that night, they dined *à deux* at an intimate candle-lit table at the lovely Bagatelle Great House, with its thick stone walls and glorious sea view. Then they walked, slowly and lingeringly, along the water's edge, where Claire slipped off her high-heeled evening sandals, tucked up the long skirts of her thin summer silk and trailed her feet in the warm water of the Caribbean.

'I think I must have died and gone to heaven,' she said dreamily.

'Good God, I've gone and married a lapsed nun!'

'No, that's the marvellous, unlooked-for glory of it all – you have married *me*! You could have any woman you wanted –' her smile was a demure tease, '– *have* had any woman you wanted.'

'Exactly – had. Now, I only want you.'

She stopped, turned to face him, her lovely face grave but her eyes shining. 'Thank you for choosing me,' she whispered adoringly.

He cupped her face with his hands, a slight frown marring his classic forehead. 'You are an intense little thing, aren't you?' he said, sounding both surprised and uneasy.

'I never knew I was – until I met you.'

Rory kissed her thoughtfully, then they strolled on once more. 'I never had much to do with love before,' he said after a while. 'It was something I was careful to avoid. I saw what it did to my father when my mother left him . . . he was finished. He got into the clutches of that mercenary bitch, my stepmother, and she wrung him out and drained him dry. I swore no woman would ever do that to me.' He smiled down at her. 'Then I met you . . . you're not like the rest of them. You're honest and true and so incredibly giving.'

'I could deny you nothing,' Claire said simply.

Again he frowned down at her and again his voice was uneasy when he said, somewhat roughly: 'I'm not perfect, you know. For God's sake don't make me into a plaster saint.'

'I don't want one. If you were made of plaster you couldn't make love to me the way you do.'

Rory laughed, good humour restored. 'And you like that, don't you . . . how you like that.'

'I've never known anything like it,' Claire told him seriously.

'Then let me see if I can't show you another thing or three . . .'

And he had her there, up against a palm tree, her dress up around her waist, the rough bark scraping her bare shoulders but not even noticed in the whirl of ecstasy into which he could always plunge her, a vortex that drew her down and down yet at the same time up and up so that the leaves of the palm seemed to spin in the star-blaze of the night sky. There was no one to hear her, so she cried out her passion to the sand and the sea, sobbing incoherently, her body jerking with each stabbing thrust and then exploding with a violence that had her slumping limply in his arms afterwards.

They returned to London after six glorious weeks, both deeply tanned, both deeply contented. People looked at Claire and saw she was now wearing the glow of a woman well and truly sexually satisfied. 'What else?' they asked each other. 'It is Rory Ballater, after all . . .'

They moved into the flat in Thurloe Place which had been their wedding present from Claire's parents; it was all ready and waiting down to the last teatowel. Then Claire went back to her job while Rory began his, obtained through her father's influence, at an upmarket stockbroker's. Both allowed them plenty of time for the social round.

They had returned in time for Cheltenham — Rory liked racing; then Claire took him to the Chelsea Antiques Fair where he bought her a lovely little Worcester cupid. They attended all the balls: the Horse and Hound, the Rose and, naturally, the Caledonian Ball at Grosvenor House, where Rory outshone all the men in his kilt and Claire wore her own Drummond tartan draped across her left shoulder and fastened with a seventeenth-century silver plaid brooch, behind which she sported a sprig of holly, the clan plant of the Drummonds.

They also threw a series of dinners to which they invited all their friends. Claire did the cooking. 'Why spend good money on something I can do as well as they can?' she asked practically, when Rory was all for having someone in. She discovered he did not like her doing housewifely chores. They were for servants. 'Darling, I can't leave everything to Esperanza' — this was their Spanish maid of all work — but his attitude was that her job was to entertain the guests, looking lovely and being gracious. Rory, she discovered, was a snob. The fact that he was the 4th Baron Ballater was very important to him. He lectured Esperanza, whose

English was basic, about the niceties of English forms of address. 'Not madam,' he said, enunciating slowly and loudly as if she was deaf, 'my lady.' But when he was not there Claire was quite happy to be called 'señora'.

She also discovered, from bills crammed into his desk drawer, that he was still gambling. She was horrified at the sums involved. He owed an East End bookmaker more than £10,000.

'Are you mad?' she asked him in hurt reproach. 'We can't afford this sort of thing!'

'Oh, now Claire . . .' This was his invariable reply. A groan and a sigh of 'God, here we go again' resignation. 'We aren't short of money. There is my job, your job – not to mention the income from your trust fund – and there is the shooting season to come.'

'We shall need every penny for that; we have to supply our guests with what they are paying – and through the nose – for. And it's not only the gambling . . . we're spending at a rate of knots.'

'We have to keep up standards,' he reminded her, which was his way of saying appearances. She had discovered that they were important to him too. 'Besides, the bets I made were supposed to be sure things. Otherwise I wouldn't have lost so much.'

'What language were the horses speaking?' Claire snapped acidly. 'Rhyming slang? And why haven't you paid your bills?'

'Because I haven't any money! What I made on Ballater last year is tied up just the way you wanted. I can't get at it until we need it.' Pause. 'But yours isn't . . . Besides, you have a trust fund that makes mine look like chicken feed.'

'And the income I get is commensurate with the amount invested. If I spend capital that income is naturally reduced.'

'By some niggardly amount. For God's sake, you've got half a million pounds in gilts.'

'Fortunately!'

'Oh, don't fuss, there's a good girl. My little man is happy to carry me. I'm the only Lord he's got on his books. It probably gives him kudos and attracts more customers so he's probably gaining more than I've lost.' Which is no doubt why you opened an account with him in the first place, Claire found herself thinking sourly.

'You *promised* me no more gambling,' she said.

'And I won't, honestly.' He kissed her and cajoled her and for a while was as loving and attentive and passionate as she could wish, so she withdrew twenty-five thousand pounds of capital and paid not only that bill but others which were long outstanding – from before the wedding, in fact. Claire had been brought up that debts were dishonourable, unlike most of the people she knew and whom Rory emulated, who let bills run on for years.

Then, in April, when they had gone up to the Grand National, Rory's horse fell at the first fence and once again, Claire paid the bill. 'It's not as though you can't afford it,' he flung at her angrily, when once more she remonstrated. 'You're turning into a shrew and a nag and if there is one thing I won't stand for it's a tongue-lashing wife. Christ, you count every fucking penny!'

'If we're going to buy that place in Sussex we *need* every penny. That will have to come out of capital too because what we make on the shooting season is already spoken for. We can't spend, spend, spend without putting back, Rory. Surely you see that.'

'All I see is a wife who begrudges me every last bit of enjoyment I get.'

'I don't, but I do worry that you seem to have no idea how to handle money. *Please*, darling, if you get any more of these hot tips, do test the temperature first!'

But the flat season was a cumulative disaster. Rory lost large amounts on every single one of the big races, from the 2,000 Guineas to the Derby, and it was Ascot which precipitated the first crack in the foundations. There had been increasingly frequent arguments and always about the same thing – money. Rory could not understand Claire's unease. She had a fortune sitting there – and if she would only let him handle her money he could make her far more than the 'safe' if regular quarterly cheques she received. 'You have to speculate to accumulate,' was his favourite aphorism, but Claire had been raised to regard speculation as dangerous. She was glad now that she had heeded his stepmother's advice. Rory had no idea that the £100,000 she had given them was safely invested – in their joint names – with her own trustees. It was the plug she used to stop the drain on her own capital which would be needed for the 'little place in the country' Rory was keen to buy. He scorned her 'book-keeper's mind' which kept household accounts and details of every penny both received and spent, and her stubborn resolve to balance them. When sarcasm failed he took to sulking, and Claire discovered yet another facet of his character which came as a disappointment. He could sulk for days. He did not speak, he did not touch her, he withdrew the passionate lovemaking which Claire, by now, had come to need, and left her frantically currying his favour, even as some part of her blushed for shame. *She* always had to apologize to *him*; only when she had would he relent, but in such a way that she lost a little more of her independence, both of mind and body. It was unwittingly asserting that independence that did for her at Ascot.

First of all he rendered her speechless by telling her he had taken a box and invited a party of eight, every one of them, in Claire's opinion, aiders and abetters of Rory's fatal – but only in *that* regard, she told herself devoutly – flaw.

'A whole box! But they cost the earth nowadays. Why couldn't you find someone to share the expense?'

'Ballaters never "share",' he told her loftily.

'Are you intent on losing yet more shirts – like the dozen new ones you bought from Turnbull & Asser and which have not yet been paid for? Like your three new suits from Gieves and Hawkes, and your new polo gear. We shall have to provide the champagne, order the food from Fortnum's. It will cost a fortune.' She was near to tears.

'Christ, all I need is a snivelling moaner. I've got some really hot tips this year. I stand to make a packet.' And I know of what, Claire thought stonily.

Then, when he saw what she proposed to wear for Ascot week he threw yet another tantrum. 'You've been seen in every single one of those dresses. This is Ascot. Get yourself to Caroline Charles or Gina Fratini for something suitable for my wife to be seen and admired in.'

'We can't afford it. These are hardly worn . . . I don't suppose I've had them on more than a couple of times each.'

'That's twice too many. I'm not appearing at Ascot with a wife dressed like a novice in a downmarket handicap,' he roared. 'I'm sick and tired of your bloody parsimony. You are your father's daughter, all right. Everybody knows he won't spend a penny where a farthing will do.'

'That isn't true!' Claire flared angrily. 'Just because I was brought up to handle money responsibly – you run through it like a field of . daisies.' And a fat lot I see of yours, she thought resentfully. Another facet of her husband's increasingly disturbing character was that he regarded what was his as his and what was hers as ours.

Dear God, she thought, as she took herself off to spend money which would mean drawing yet more capital. Am I mean? She asked this of Caroline, who went with her to choose dresses for Ascot for herself.

'Well . . . not mean, darling, just good Scots canny, that's all. You always paid your way in the flat, and were ever generous with loans when one of us overspent our allowance – usually me. I can't recall a single instance when you did that. We all thought you were an absolute magician with money.'

'I wish I was,' Claire sighed lugubriously.

'Well, darling, you knew Rory was less than careful with lolly when you married him. Mummy said he was frightfully expensive.' She made a *moue* at the sight of Claire's face. 'Sorry, darling . . . that's all past now, I know. Everyone is marvelling at the way you've brought him to sexual heel.

Never looks at another woman these days. Oh well, they say there is no man so prudish as a reformed rake.'

'Rory is no prude,' Claire murmured.

'So what are you complaining about? Rein him in gently, don't bear down on the curb.'

And taking a taxi home with her new dresses, anxious to try them on and display them to Rory, Claire resolved to curb her own inclination to worry about every penny spent. They still had slightly less than half his mother's wedding present left, though with what she had spent today and the expense of Ascot . . . Stop it! she scolded herself. He never stints on you, does he? Whatever you want you can have. Some women have to beg for every penny. It's not only Rory who has to try and change, my girl.

But as luck would have it, the very next day she ran into a friend of Rory's on her way back to the office after having shown an enormously rich Lebanese round a super de luxe house in The Boltons.

'You are looking delectable, as usual,' he complimented her, eyeing her Rive Gauche suit and polished chestnut brown shoes and handbag. 'Rory is a lucky devil. I can see it is true when they say lucky in love unlucky at cards . . .'

Claire felt a stab of shock. 'How unlucky?' she managed to ask lightly.

'Oh . . . about ten thousand I should say. Plunging recklessly . . . hadn't seen him at the Claremont in an age . . . thought maybe he'd taken the pledge or something.' Seeing her dismay and realizing he had dropped a clanger, he consoled her hastily, 'Don't worry, luck's bound to change. Always does, you know. Law of averages and all that. Probably do better at Ascot. Awfully nice of you to ask me, by the way. And taking a whole box! So old Rory can't be doing too badly . . . Must rush . . . See you next week. Bye.'

Lucky in love, Claire thought numbly, as she walked on, seeing nothing but the fact that Rory had dropped ten thousand pounds at a gambling club. He promised me, she agonized. He *promised*. Why doesn't he realize he's unlucky at cards?

Well, aren't you lucky in love? she asked herself with asperity. That, at least, had not changed. She still loved Rory, was still desperately anxious not to drive him away. He had awoken something in her that was now filled with raging, clamouring need. I suppose I'm hooked on him, she thought, pausing at the lights. Every time he apologized: 'I know I can be a shit at times, darling, but bear with me. I can't change overnight. It has to be done gradually . . . don't take any notice of my bad moods. I have a lot on my mind right now . . . I need to know you will always be there. I don't know what I would do if you weren't . . .' she was only too happy to be mollified in the only way he knew how, even knowing she was becoming dependent on it. But afterwards, when the roseate glow had dulled, she would begin to worry again. *Why* did Rory need to gamble? What was it that made him fling money away like a used ticket?

She had mentioned the matter to her mother the last time she was home, attributing Rory's failings to someone else, because the last thing she wanted was for her parents – more especially her father – to know that Rory was behaving in exactly the way he had predicted.

'Gamblers, like alcoholics, have some fatal weakness in them; they are both now regarded as illnesses, I believe,' was her mother's opinion.

'But curable, surely.'

'Well, it takes active participation on the part of the invalid and a great deal of careful therapy.' Which, Claire realized with a sinking heart, Rory would never undergo because he flatly denied that his gambling was out of control. 'It is only a bit of harmless fun,' was his argument. That that same harmless fun had lost both the family fortune and the company on which it was built Claire was careful never to mention. Rory was very thin-skinned where his father was concerned. His name was never mentioned. Claire knew that in Rory's eyes his father had betrayed his heritage. Because of him the Ballater fortune – which had been considerable – no longer existed. Claire could not understand how Rory wasn't able to see that he was fitting his own feet into every footprint his father had left, but she knew instinctively that it would not do to ask him. It was all to do with his insistence on living in the manner he had been born to; on spending as though the Ballaters still had their millions; on being treated as the fourth Baron Ballater, able to hold his own in the circle of his peers. He was very quick to spot a slight, and woe betide anyone not sufficiently well-bred or known who claimed the slightest familiarity. Rory could charm the birds off the trees; he could be light-heartedly and effortlessly all things to all men – and all women – but at the first signs of what he took as not being accorded due deference, he froze. Well, thought Claire. If Princess Margaret can do it, why not a mere Lord?

She had no doubt, however, that this thin-skinned pride was the reason why, at Ballater House, there was nothing to remind him of old Angus Ballater, whose croft had disappeared decades ago; it was his son whose portrait by Sargent held pride of place, along with the letter and signed photograph from Queen Victoria, extolling the virtues of Ballater's Best.

Poor Rory, Claire thought with tender sympathy, deep down he is so insecure. In some strange way it only made her love him more; showed her his vulnerability, but also that pride which burned with a dangerously fierce flame. Which was why, when she badly dented it, he went, as Caroline had been wont to say, bonkers.

He approved wholeheartedly of her dresses and the hats to go with them. 'Now you look the thing,' he said proudly, before proceeding to give her instructions as to her behaviour, her attitude to this one and that. The people he had invited were once more the hard-faced women – which is no doubt why I had to put in the right appearance, she thought – and affable yet even tougher men, and it was from one of them, a mild-mannered man with a weatherbeaten face and an Australian accent, that she gained knowledgeable insight into the right horses to back.

'I wish you'd tell my husband,' she joked.

'He is welcome to any information I have, but he backs hunches rather than form.' And he went through the card for the entire week, ticking off those he thought had a good chance. Many were unfancied, a couple rank outsiders. Claire took to studying Rory's form books, which he regarded with indulgent amusement, and without telling him placed a small accumulator bet of £5 on six horses, all running in the smaller races except for one – the King George V and Queen Elizabeth Stakes. When the first one came in ahead of the field Claire was delighted, but kept her knowledge to herself. Rory's horse was fifth. When the second and third of her horses won she swallowed hard but still thought – no, I won't tell him. There are still three more to go. By the time it got down to five runners on the trot she was jumping with nerves.

Just before the all important sixth of her races, on which all depended, the Australian suggested they take a walk down to the paddock to see the jockeys mount up, and she agreed with alacrity. Her nerves were getting the better of her and she did not want Rory to wonder why she was in such a state of high excitement.

'That's the one,' the Australian, whose name was Charlie Cochran said, pointing to a small bay horse whose jockey was wearing red, blue and green.

'The Drummond colours,' Claire said excitedly. 'Oh, do you believe in omens?'

'I'd much rather believe a good bloodline and a stopwatch.'

'Is that how you know which horse is going to win?'

'I like to check out their speed and stamina as well as their antecedents.'

'Do you visit the stables, then?'

'I watch them work out,' he replied easily.

Claire watched the horses at close quarters as they walked

round the ring, stayed to see the jockeys mount preparatory to riding out on to the course.

'He looks awfully small,' she said doubtfully.

'A big horse has a longer stride, but that doesn't necessarily mean it has the edge.'

'You know an awful lot about horses.' She sighed. 'I only wish my husband was as scientific as you are.'

The Australian looked into the lovely face with the wide violet eyes and red hair under a hat composed mainly of creamy yellow roses. All your husband knows about horses you could write on a stamp, he thought. All flash and filigree. Thinks he knows it all but in reality has not the slightest idea . . .

'Some people like the element of risk,' he shrugged. 'Too much knowledge takes the edge off for them.' Except Rory Ballater's skill in picking horses would not cut butter.

Claire nodded, her mouth dry and her effort to stop trembling holding her almost rigid. If she won for the sixth time she had made a small fortune . . . A godsend, she thought, considering the way Rory had been losing all week.

All around them grey toppers and frothy hats thronged, the summer silks of the women making a glorious mélange of colour against the brilliant green of the grass. She had spotted lots of faces she knew – it had taken them all of twenty minutes to get to the paddock from the box – some of whom had been surprised at her companion, who had the look of an ex-jockey himself; not much taller than Claire and brown as a walnut. He positioned them as close to the winning post as possible, which meant that they did not see much of the race itself, but they had a head-on view of the horses as they came up to it, and when they saw the red and the green in among the leaders Claire seized her companion's arm. 'It's there,' she shrieked, beside herself with excitement. 'Oh, come on Bluebird, come on . . .' She was jumping up and down with excitement. She held her breath as the announcement came over the loudspeaker. When the winner was named, she gasped. 'Oh, my God . . .' she said, sounding

61

both terrified and transported. 'I've won . . . I've actually gone and won!' She flung her arms around the Australian. 'Oh, thank you, thank you . . . you are a genie. Do wave your magic wand again some time, won't you?' Eagerly: 'Do I collect my winnings now or later?'

'If you hang on for a while, we can take your loot back to the box with us.'

'Where've you been?' Rory barked, and she saw at once that he had lost again.

'Collecting my winnings.'

'Your *what*?'

'My winnings. I had six horses spread through the week and I – what did I do?' She turned to the Australian. She knew exactly what she had done because it had been explained, but something told her it would not do to spout facts and figures at Rory right now.

'Some were doubles, some were trebles, and there was an accumulator overall. Everything she won previously went on this last race.'

Rory stared. 'You told her which horses to back?'

'I gave her my opinions.'

Somebody laughed. 'Charlie Cochran's opinions are other people's holy writ when it comes to horses.'

Rory swallowed. 'You are Charlie Cochran?'

'We were introduced,' murmured the Australian, but Rory had dismissed the small, nut-brown man, obviously not comfortable in his morning dress and topper, as a nobody. He had been brought along by one of the other guests, also a man from Australia.

Rory turned to Claire. 'How much did you win?' he asked, in a tight voice.

'Something over eighteen thousand pounds.'

Rory went white. 'Well done,' he said, in a tone so odd that people looked, while Claire's heart sank. What he said and what he thought were two different things. Behind the praise he was absolutely furious. Amidst the congratulations, the opening of several more bottles of Krug, Claire felt the dawning of terror. She knew that look. It meant she would suffer for it.

It turned out that Charlie Cochran was a famous Australian trainer and yes, he had once been a jockey who had won every big race there was all over the world.

Rory ignored Claire for the rest of the afternoon; it was not until they were driving back to London in the back of one of the Rolls he had hired, the glass dividing them from the chauffeur safely closed, that he turned on her to snarl, in a voice which unnerved her: 'How *dare* you do that to me?'

'Do what?' Claire asked stupidly. 'I only spent five pounds . . .'

Rory's eyes blazed. 'Five bloody pounds to win almost nineteen thousand! You never thought to come to *me* to tell me that Charlie Cochran had given you some red hot tips.'

'But you were introduced to him, as I was . . .'

'Your duty was to come straight to me; tell me what he had said. Don't blame me for your own shortcomings.'

Claire's mouth was open. She could not for the life of her understand why he was so angry. She had won, hadn't she? A lot of money for a very small outlay.

'I didn't really believe for one minute all six horses would win,' she protested. 'He was nice and he seemed to know what he was talking about . . . you know I know nothing about horses. I just asked him, as you do of people who do know, what he thought was worth having a small flutter on.'

'You ask Charlie Cochran – *Charlie Cochran* – what to back and you sneak off together and he advises you not only what to bet but how, and you never say a bloody word to me? Christ, what sort of a damn fool does that make me?'

'It doesn't make you look a fool. I told you, I asked his advice . . .'

'But never thought to give it to me.'

'You know you never took any notice of any suggestions I made all week.'

63

'They weren't coming from Charlie Cochran.'

'I didn't know who Charlie Cochran *was*. He was just a rather nice man.'

'Liar! You knew who he was, all right, and you used him to show me up. By God, if you want me to stop gambling this is the wrong way to go about it, you spiteful bitch!'

'At least I have recovered every penny you lost – and more!'

For a moment she thought he was going to hit her. His arm rose, then, with a glance at the stolid back of the chauffeur it was lowered again, but with an effort. She had never seen him so angry. He terrified her.

'You are making a perfectly innocent bet seem like a Borgia plot,' she protested nervously.

'Conniving with that bloody Australian – and I shall have a word with whoever it was brought him in the first place because *I* didn't invite him – is as dirty a plot as ever I came across. I shall never forgive you for showing me up like this – never!' And he threw himself back in his corner and sulked all the way home.

Claire was dumbfounded. How had she shown him up? He had always smiled indulgently when she suggested a horse. 'What did you do, pick it with a pin?' he had teased. 'Leave this sort of thing to me, darling, there's a good girl.' She was not to know Charlie Cochran was a former jockey. He had not been introduced as one. Yes, she had thought him knowledgeable, but Ascot always had its fair share of them. She had only bet £5 because she honestly had not expected to win. Never a six horse accumulator. It had been – she had thought – a bit of fun, no more. And she had made enough to cover every penny spent on the day. What was humiliating about that? I don't understand him, she thought helplessly. Worse, I don't know him at all . . .

When they got home he slammed into his dressing-room, came out having changed, then slammed out of the front door. She did not see him for two days and nights. The first night she cried herself to sleep. She had known Rory's pride to be a hot-house plant which needed all the tender loving care she could lavish on it, but that he should be so thin-skinned as to resent her winning a great deal of money was beyond her. Had she deliberately set out to show him up she could not have demonstrated her skill so ruthlessly, but she *hadn't*. A pleasant little man had seen her studying her programme and asked her what she fancied, to which she had laughingly replied, 'To back a few winners, naturally,' whereupon he had said casually: 'Well, if you would like me to point you in the right direction . . .'

It had been no more than what Rory was so intent on having – a bit of fun. When the Australian had explained to her what was possible, according to the odds and the complicated way he arranged her bets, she had – again laughingly – said: 'Chance would be a fine thing,' not believing all her horses would win for one single moment. Now, instead of being glad for her, for them having come out in credit rather than in debt, he was mad as hell. Her tears gave way to anger all during the next day, but when she got home that night there was still no sign of him. Only clothes lying on the floor to show he had been back to change.

She spent another miserable night, missing his warmth, his body, his lovemaking – for he never let a night go by without bringing her to gasping, ecstatic, grateful fulfilment – and spent the next day in a state that hovered between frantic worry that he would never come back, and fear as to what would happen when he did. She found herself praying: let him come back to me, please God, let him come back. I need him, I can't do without him. Her body burned for him. She hid her head under the covers at the thought of life without him. In spite of all he was – and was not – she was still deeply in love with him. He was, she realized with something akin to panic, her life. All right, so he wasn't perfect, she had been naive to expect perfection. He was a man, no more, and a complicated one, with his fair share of faults and idiosyncrasies. And I *have* harped on about money, she thought guiltily, but we shall never see eye to eye on that subject. Rory is a spender and I am a saver. I shall just have to keep my savings under cover, that's all. And I won't nag. I must not nag, she repeated. Only let him come back and I will never nag him again – about anything, never mind money. I'll save my quarterly cheques from the trust fund and we will live on our salaries. We can do it if I am careful and he doesn't start in on the gambling again. I'm good with money. I have to be if he is going to be so bad. Face it, she told herself. Rory is a spendthrift. It's up to you to see that he doesn't end up in the bankruptcy court, but don't let him see. He still doesn't know about his mother's cheque. How well she knew him. How right she was to advise me as she did.

When Rory finally did come home, she saw at once that he was in a better mood, so that when she apologized, as humbly as he could wish, he said to her sternly: 'No more public humiliations. Do you understand?'

'I didn't realize you would see it that way –' began Claire.

'See it that way! How else am I supposed to see it? You connive with an ex-jockey who is now a famous trainer to place bets that are absolutely sure things without so much as a hint to me! Your duty was to come to me before placing them.'

'Darling . . .' Claire protested lightly, but with steel in her voice, 'I am not your slave.' In spite of her resolve her reaction was instinctive: her own pride surfacing in revolt.

'Nor are you supposed to make me look like a fucking amateur in front of all my friends.'

'If they are laughing at you, then they are no friends of yours,' Claire retorted, only to see his face darken. 'I'm sorry,' she said hastily. 'Me and my quick tongue.'

'Something else you had better take in hand. I have no use for a wife who is a ball-breaker. I've seen enough of them, thank you. Those awful American wives who are on their third husband by the time they are thirty, and he, poor sod, being nagged into leaving the field clear for her fourth.

Your tongue is razor sharp at times, Claire. Be careful how you use it in future.'

'I promise,' Claire said guiltily.

'No wife worth her salt shows up her husband in public,' he lectured her. 'Which is not to say that I will allow it in private either,' he added sternly. 'Your duty is to support me at all times.'

'I'll try,' Claire promised meekly.

'Then we will say no more about it,' he allowed magnanimously.

So they made it up, and the rest of the year passed, if not in the unalloyed bliss of the first half, then in a state of truce. In August, they went up to Scotland and the ensuing season was so successful that Rory was jubilant when Claire was able to show him the accounts she kept so scrupulously and display the splendid profit they had made, once all expenses were accounted for.

'I'll say this for you,' Rory told her admiringly, 'you are a born manager. You haven't stinted on anything yet we've come out much further ahead than I had even hoped for.' The thought of all that lovely money waiting put him in a good mood for the Boxing Day Shoot at Castle Drummond, an annual event attended only by family and friends. Christmas had been spent with Claire's family, and the Christmas spirit was still uppermost, though the men were only too pleased to escape from the household of relatives and small children. Those youngsters deemed old enough always made their début with a new 20-bore at the Boxing Day Shoot.

Claire proudly displayed her neat ledgers to her mother when she came over for tea next day.

'Well done, darling,' her mother praised.

'I had a good teacher,' Claire said lovingly. 'Besides, we will have to plough most of it back. I want to keep on the extra ghillies. Robbie Lovat can't do it all by himself and the more care we give the moors now the better for next year's season. Daddy always says that what you get out always depends on what you put in.'

'Don't get your father started on the question of moor management,' warned Margot Drummond.

'Well, I did ask his advice. And grouse stocks are all important if we are to keep this little enterprise going.'

'Is Rory pleased?'

'Absolutely delighted. He says I'm a born manager.'

'I should hope so. You are my daughter. Just so long as you never let him see you managing.'

Claire frowned. 'That's what I don't like. I *am* a good manager. Why should I pretend not to be just to avoid denting my husband's pride?'

'Because your husband is a man whose pride is important to him.'

'What about mine? I am a person, I have my own pride.'

'You know what happens when two stags lock horns; sometimes they are unable to free themselves and they both starve to death. Better to allow some leeway; there is plenty of grass for you both.' At her daughter's frown: 'You cannot have a marriage with two proud people. It will be a battle-ground. Sometimes, you can win by using other methods. All that matters, where men are concerned, is that they are *seen* to win. But there is nothing to stop you, in your turn, being the one to arrange it.'

Claire stared at her mother. 'Is that what you do with Daddy? I always thought he called the shots, as our American guests have it.'

'Yes, but I pulled the handle.'

Claire looked at her mother's calm face and burst into laughter. 'Why, you shocking fraud,' she said.

'Your father is a proud Scot too, and was brought up in the Highland tradition. I, on the other hand, am a devious Sassenach.' Margot Drummond patted her daughter's hand. 'Let them *think* what they like,' she advised. 'It's what we *know*, that matters.'

'I suppose one has to compromise,' Claire said slowly.

'To a certain extent, but not to that of blending in so well that you lose your individuality.' Margot Drummond smiled.

68

'It takes time and experience. You can, as yet, only notch up one year. That is always the difficult one in any marriage. That's when corners get knocked, edges rubbed. And Rory is that much older than you; was independent for so much longer. Many men find it difficult to adjust to their loss of freedom.'

But Rory hasn't deemed it necessary to adjust, Claire thought rebelliously. I am the one who has to do that. I am the one who is expected to conform, accept, obey.

'High ideals are all very well, and I think you went into this marriage with yours at an impossibly lofty setting. Life is about practicalities not ideals. What one would like and what one gets are two very different things.' Shrewdly, she finished: 'As, I think, you have already discovered.'

Claire's smile was rueful. 'Yes, I have.'

'Then learn from what you have discovered. Everyone makes mistakes but only fools make the same one twice.'

Claire took her mother's advice to heart. She was careful not to tell Rory what he should do about ploughing back profits into the Ballater Estate. She merely suggested, and without telling him, she added to the amount put at the service of the estate from his mother's cheque. She also had a quiet word with Rory's factor who, only too happy to have the money he so badly needed, entered into the conspiracy with willing compliance.

They returned to London in perfect charity with one another. Rory had worked hard and Claire had redeemed herself in his eyes. He had money to spend and she had left the estate in good hands and deep in the black, with enough money to pay for the conservation of the moors and its resident grouse, snipe, blackcock and – further up the mountain – the ptarmigan.

Only once had there been a slight groundswell which Claire prayed would not turn into a Force Eleven gale. It had been at the dinner table, where Rory was, as usual, magnetizing the wives, two of them on this particular occasion, who had accompanied their husbands to Scotland.

Neither shot – not guns anyway – but both were their respective husband's umpteenth wife and were leaving no opportunities open for yet another change. Betty Jo Rawlins had started life as an air hostess and looked like a Marilyn Monroe clone: three pairs of false eyelashes and designer nails. Patricia Lorrance had begun her career in the chorus line at the Sands in Las Vegas; she was a dead ringer for Jane Russell. Both were deadly when it came to protecting their own interests, but Claire posed no threat while Rory, well, as Betty Jo said to Patricia – nobody *ever* called her Patty any more – 'He's so gorgeous he tempts me – almost – to break my vow.'

'Not of celibacy, surely!'

'Huh? No, I mean not to sleep with any man who can't put up a million dollars! He's broke, as the British say; only this place and all those acres.' She giggled. 'And whatever is beneath that pleated kilt . . .'

Now, this night, she turned her baby blues in Claire's direction to ask breathlessly: 'Is it true, Lady Ballater, that you are actually descended from three Kings of Britain?'

'Me and several thousand others,' Claire admitted lightly.

'Oh, come now, darling,' Rory purred silkily. 'My wife is too modest. Her ancestry is so blue-blooded it's nearly purple. On her father's side she is descended from that same King Duncan of Scotland who was murdered by Macbeth, and also from King James the First and Sixth – that is Sixth of Scotland and First of England – while on her mother's side, she is descended from my very favourite of all the English monarchs: King Charles II.'

'Does that make you royal?' breathed Betty Jo.

'Not in the least,' Claire told her briskly. 'Any royal blood I have has been well diluted over the years.'

'Six hundred of them,' Rory added helpfully. Claire's hand was steady as she lifted her glass but her heart was fluttering. She knew that tone. Rory sarcastic was Rory in a snit. She held her breath when the expected question came: 'And do you have royal blood too, Lord Ballater?'

70

'No. But I've no doubt it still contains a high proportion of best Scotch.'

Betty Jo giggled delightedly. 'Bubba says he is taking as much back home to Dallas as he can carry. Isn't that right, honey?'

'Damned tootin' it is. I guess we are both descended from self-made men, Lord Ballater. My own granddaddy wildcatted all over Texas before he struck it rich. We don't have titles back home, but the Rawlins have been in Texas nigh on a hundred years so I guess that makes us as near royal as you can get back there.'

Claire knew Rory was still burning when, as they were undressing for bed, he said: 'Nigh on a hundred years,' in an acutely accurate drawl. 'God, I'm sick and tired of pandering to these rednecks who think money entitles them to assume the purple.'

'The Rawlins are a nice couple,' Claire defended.

'The only nice thing about them is the ease with which they will pay their bill. Dear Bubba is worth a conservative two hundred million dollars!' Rory's voice was savage.

'Well, he is paying a fair proportion for his ten days here,' Claire consoled.

'Chicken feed, as he keeps saying. At this rate it's going to take years to get anywhere.'

'It depends where you want to get to,' Claire offered cautiously.

'I don't see myself acting as mine host for the rest of my life.'

Claire read the signs like the expert tracker she had become. Rory was bored. Well, she thought, it has been six weeks.

'I can't wait to get back to London,' he went on restlessly.

'We shall be, soon,' Claire soothed. 'But we can't afford to cut the season short.'

'I'm sick and bloody tired of "can't afford".'

Claire bit her lip. She knew these friable moods by now; they meant he was ripe for any mischief, and sure enough, the next night, instead of the usual bridge, he suggested they try poker. 'Now you're talkin',' Bubba said happily, only to be seconded by Hub Lorrance. Patricia, who had graduated from chorus line to pit boss, agreed guilelessly: 'It would give a little edge to things . . .'

'Count me out,' Betty Jo said. 'It's bad enough being bawled out for my bridge. I'd never survive poker.'

Claire did not play either. Neither did the Japanese, but the Germans were happy to sit in. By the time Claire went up to bed, only the three Americans and Rory were at the green baize card table, and Rory, from the good-humoured way he was acting, was ahead.

Don't lose too much, Rory, Claire prayed silently. I know you hate the fact but we really can't afford it. But when he came up to bed he was whistling. A good sign.

'Does your fine fettle mean you won?' Claire asked, feather light.

'It certainly does! Why is it that Texans think they invented the game? It must have to do with all those John Ford westerns.' Rory laughed. He was exultant. 'I cleaned them out! I showed them that there's still something I can do!'

He emptied his pockets on to his tallboy. Piles of twenty- and fifty-pound notes. 'A perfect end to their stay,' he gloated.

Claire felt uneasy. The last thing she needed was for Rory to get the reputation of a card sharp. She made a point of mentioning it next day, and though Bubba Rawlins shrugged it off she could see that he was not pleased.

'Your husband could get a job as a pit boss any day,' Patricia Lorrance drawled, and Claire met her suspicious eyes with a confidence she was far from feeling.

'I should have warned you,' she said lightly, 'Rory is rated a very good player.'

'He had the devil's own luck,' grumbled Hubbell Lorrance.

But the goodbyes were affable and their booking for the next year not rescinded. Claire stood until the Rolls-Royce had moved off down the drive then went back inside to speed the departing Japanese and Germans. It was later, when she was accompanying Mrs Forbes, the housekeeper, round the guest suites, making sure nothing had been left behind, that she heard Rory talking to Wilkie. 'I showed them a thing or two,' he was saying. 'Every one of the things you taught me . . .'

'And they didna suspect?'

'Not a thing. You taught me too well. I thought at one time that dear old Bubba had rumbled but he wasn't sure enough to say so.'

'Well, be careful. Once is no bad thing as long as ye dinna do it too often.'

'He got my goat,' Rory said sullenly. 'Always talking about this well and that and how many barrels a day he gets and how much he sells it for. And it isn't as though he can't afford it. I took quite a few thousand off him and serve him damn well right. It makes me feel that much better.'

They moved off and Claire glanced at Mrs Forbes, but she was stripping beds and piling linen and clicking her tongue at the lipstick stains on the pillows.

Rory was cheating, Claire thought, surprised at the calm she felt. And Wilkie taught him how to do it. She was so shocked she was almost in a trance. I can't say anything, she thought. I daren't. But neither can I let him do it again. Oh, Rory, just when I thought everything was going well.

Fortunately, the Americans in the next houseparty were not Texans but wealthy easterners from Philadelphia. 'Gentlemen, by God,' Rory exulted, and it was back to bridge again.

But the last party of the season included Bruno de Souza, and he came as Rory's guest. 'My chance to repay a little of the hospitality he showed us on our honeymoon,' Rory explained, and he and the Brazilian spent a lot of time together, Rory fawning over him in a way that gave Claire the creeps.

And when he left, Claire heard Rory say heartily: 'See you in London, then.'

73

'I shall look forward to it.' Bruno de Souza turned to Claire.

'A most enjoyable ten days, Lady Ballater. Thank you.'

'I'm glad you enjoyed it.'

His companion this time had been another young girl about Claire's age, who spent most of her time painting her nails, and appeared at dinner staggering under the weight of her jewellery, most of which Claire recognized as having been worn by the girl who had been *maîtresse en titre* on the yacht. He probably makes them sign a receipt, she thought.

And sure enough, when they returned to London, Bruno de Souza became almost a lodger. It was Bruno this and Bruno that, and Bruno says or Bruno thinks. So that one day, when Rory returned one evening, Claire was not surprised when he said: 'I'm chucking in my job.'

Claire took a deep breath. 'Why?'

'Bruno has offered me a much better one – and guess where – in Paris.'

'Paris!'

'Isn't that marvellous? I was fed up here anyway, have been for some time. I'm not getting anywhere; low man on the totem pole as Bubba would say. Bruno has offered me much, much more.'

'Doing what?'

'Working for his import/export firm.'

'And what does he import and export?'

'Oh, just about everything . . . food, wine – he has several vineyards in Bordeaux – he has interests in many companies.'

Claire was silent, then: 'What about my job?' she asked.

'You can jack that in too. You won't need to work any more because I'll be making more than enough.'

'And this flat?'

'We'll sublet. I've already had a good offer from one of Bruno's friends.'

'You've got it all arranged, then?'

'Even down to where we live in Paris. A house Bruno owns . . .'

74

Like he owns you? thought Claire.

Sensing that she was not exactly delirious with joy, Rory snapped: 'You might show a little enthusiasm.'

'I'm trying to, but it's something of a shock.'

'You'll soon get over it,' Rory said carelessly. 'This is my chance, poppet. There is no limit to how high I can go with Bruno.'

And what happens when he lets you drop? thought Claire. She neither liked nor trusted the Brazilian any longer. She did not like the way he looked at her, did not like his friends, did not like his attitudes.

'Oh, come on, darling,' coaxed Rory. 'It's the chance of a lifetime. I'm not getting anywhere here. And Paris – think of it! Paris!'

'When?' asked Claire.

'As soon as everything is squared away. You can give in your notice tomorrow.' It was easily said, but it was an order.

Her mother said: 'Paris! But how exciting.'

'Yes, isn't it,' Claire said.

'Do I sense that you are not best pleased?'

'Well, it did come out of the blue.'

'So did the bluebird. Perhaps Rory will do better there. And you will be back from time to time, and for next year's shooting season, of course. I might just pop across and see you myself. Any excuse to visit Paris!'

'But I was just getting everything together here,' Claire protested. 'And I like my job . . . Nor do I relish the thought of strangers living in my lovely flat.'

'It would be stupid to leave it lying empty. Think of burglars and that sort of thing. And you will have a nice little nest egg to come back to.'

But Claire discovered that the arrangements with the sub-lessee included a quarter's rent in advance paid into their joint account and at once withdrawn by Rory.

'Travelling expenses,' he said airily, when she queried it.

75

And when she checked the statement, as she always did, there was no sign of Rory's poker winnings being paid in. He's gambled it away, she thought despairingly. Oh God, why did we have to meet up with that awful man again? He's a bad influence. I shall just have to bring mine to bear, she thought. And she once more thanked her lucky stars that what was left of Davina Ballater's cheque was where Rory could not get at it.

Who knows, she thought, as she packed. Perhaps it will be good for Rory. He always does better when he's happy.

She ignored the little voice that murmured: But what about you?

CHAPTER THREE

Paris was fun. Paris was a tall, narrow house on the Île de la Cité, overlooking the Quai de L'Horloge and the right bank: just the right size and furnished with an eclectic mixture of ancient and modern: Louis XIV furniture and thirties art deco; Aubusson carpets and Laura Ashley fabrics; huge gilt mirrors and stencilled chrome, but all mixed to a perfect blend that was, Claire was assured by Rory's friends, *très chic*. It was not to her taste, but Rory was so pleased with it she had not the heart to tell him so. He was the old Rory: gay, light-hearted, passionate, in control – as he needed to be, she now understood, at all times. She supposed it was because of his parents' marriage, in which his father had been utterly under the influence of his mother. She now trod carefully; it was important to Rory that he was seen to be deferred to, though she knew she must give no sign that it was anything other than instinctive: the natural female response to god-given male rights. And when she got it right he was so loving, so anxious to please, she thought fondly.

One day, shortly after they had settled in, he said to her, 'Look, darling, I've been thinking. I have been lucky enough to fall on my feet here. I now know people who know everything there is to know about making money, and that, my sweet, is what your trust is not doing right now. You are getting a niggardly return on your investments. Oh, I know it is "safe": all that gilt edged stuff, but with just a little more flair and knowledge I can double your income.'

Claire was careful not to let him see her sudden unease. Rory's enthusiasms and the final results often failed to meet at the designated spot, but she sensed that he was anxious to make up for what had gone before; to put back what she had taken out to pay his debts.

'What did you have in mind?' she asked cautiously.

'Not me – Bruno. I asked his advice. There is nothing he doesn't know about making money work. Look how rich he is! I've asked him to have a word with you.'

And it all seemed too good to be true. When Claire – unbeknownst to Rory – checked up in both the *Financial Times* and the *Wall Street Journal*, the stocks Bruno had mentioned were indeed riding high. He had talked about venture capital – 'but the right venture, of course.' And had told her about some of them; he talked about floating issues, anticipating trends – even instigating them. Claire asked for time to think it over.

'But not too long,' Rory advised. 'Every day lost is a chance gone the same way.' And checking every day she saw Bruno's predictions coming true.

'What did I tell you?' Rory asked. 'You can salt back every penny you make and that way I will feel better about all that money you spent on me. You do understand, don't you, that I won't feel right until you have recovered every penny.'

And it was to allay his insistent concern that she finally agreed and wrote to her trustees telling them to sell her portfolio and transfer the funds into a Swiss bank account.

'You won't regret it,' Rory told her vehemently. 'I'll see to that.' And from the way he kept handing her two-inch-thick bundles of thousand franc notes – 'proceeds from a very profitable little speculation' – she was both grateful and relieved that he had not been sold another of the flawed pups he had bought so often back in London.

To her parents she wrote that Rory was now doing very well: she also gave the impression that he was doing what he was doing with her blessing, though in reality she still had no idea what, if anything, he was doing at all.

Then, her conscience clear, she was able to enjoy the lush life into which Rory ushered her. Dinners at Maxim's, nights at the opera, shopping in the Rue de Rivoli. She was able to buy her clothes from Yves St Laurent, Karl Lagerfeld, Sonia Rykel. She shopped for linens at Porthault and arranged exquisite pure silk flowers from Trousselier in Lalique crystal vases, she bought food from Le Comptoir Gourmand and several silk scarves at a time from Hermes. It was there that Rory bought her a 'Kelly' bag, the famous Hermes padlock bag with the false bottom in which to keep her jewels. Rory had insisted she send to the bank for them: 'You are, after all, the wife of an English *Milor* and I want you to look the part.' The twenty-inch-long strand of pearls that had belonged to her maternal grandmother was much admired, as was the delicate Victorian setting of the diamond and pearl necklace set *au tremblant*. She wore them for the Grand ball and dinner she attended in celebration of *le Quatorze Juillet*, where they embellished the magnificent liquifaction of pale-grey satin made for her by Balmain. Maud Frizon made her a pair of satin shoes of the same material, their heels studded with pearls and brilliants. Over it she wore the chinchilla wrap – all six feet of it, which Rory had presented to her earlier that evening.

'Darling, it's fabulous!' she had cried excitedly as he draped it about her shoulders. 'But – it must have cost a fortune.'

'Well, aren't I making one?'

She took a chance. 'Everything is – going well, then?'

'Everything is going perfectly. I told you Bruno would come up trumps.' He put his hands on her shoulders. 'Isn't this better than London? That poky flat, my dead-end boring job, you having to work at all. I can't cope with having to live on a shoestring. It – well, you know how it makes me.'

Yes, Claire thought on a shiver, she did. Here, with no money worries, he was as devoted, as passionate, as she could wish, but the more she had of him, the more she found she wanted.

'You are insatiable,' Rory would tease her after she had collapsed, vibrating like a twanged guitar string.

Claire knew that she had no control over herself where sex with Rory was concerned; sometimes, even in the midst

79

of her delirium, some part of her uneasily recognized in Rory's smile the power of one who knows he is a Supreme Being, holding total dominion over her. But their time in Paris so far had been unalloyed bliss, all she had so naively expected at the beginning. Except now she knew she had to work at it. Rory had to be 'handled'; she could read his facial expressions and body language by now; knew when to approach and when to back off; but as the former occasions far exceeded the latter nowadays she counted herself lucky.

She had tried to analyse, for she tended to introspection, what it was about Rory that held her so magnetized. The dark-brown voice, the dazzling smile, the power and passion of his lovemaking, the saturation of his blue, blue gaze. She could not rationalize it. She only knew she wanted him – needed him by now – and that she could not visualize life without him. Sometimes, her euphoria was such that she felt nervous; whoever it was who dealt your hand in life, they never gave you a winning hand all the time. Then she would scold herself for doubting. Rory was living up to his promise. He showed her papers which confirmed that her trust was back to its original figure and more, he lavished gifts on her, he never did more than raise an indulgent eyebrow at her own now lavish spending.

'Money is meant to be enjoyed,' he shrugged. 'We are young and the world is ours . . . and I intend to keep it so.'

Now, sipping champagne, eyeing the dazzling room, the glittering crowd, the silks, the satins, the jewels, she did not doubt him for a moment.

Suddenly, somebody knocked her arm and she just managed to keep her glass steady. 'Ooops . . . sorry . . . it's this damned dress. I keep tangling my feet in the skirt.'

Claire turned to see a big, Junoesque woman wearing a fortune in emeralds and a black velvet dress that revealed a pair of superb shoulders and a decolleté that drew the eyes. She had a rather commonplace face and an accent Claire could not quite place, except it was northern. She was what Rory would term as N.O.S. – not our sort.

'I didn't make you mark that glorious dress, did I?' the woman asked anxiously.

'No, it's all right.'

'Thank God for that.'

Claire found herself smiling into a pair of warm brown eyes. There was something refreshingly down to earth about them; so different from the calculating smiles of the women she had met through Rory, whose eyes did a quick scan while their internal computer totted up the total cost of the dress, the jewels, the attitude, before adjusting their own accordingly.

'I hate these bashes,' the woman said bluntly, 'but an appearance is obligatory when your husband is with the British Embassy. I'm Mollie Hoare-Brown.'

'Claire Ballater.'

'I know . . . you and your husband are making quite a splash. *Tout Paris* is talking – in the most complimentary terms, of course.'

'Thank you,' Claire said, amused.

'My feet are killing me – shall we sit down?'

'Why not?'

'It's good to talk to a compatriot. My French still leaves a lot to be desired.'

They found a sofa against one mirrored wall and Mollie Hoare-Brown sank down on it with a thump, making it creak alarmingly.

'Oh, what a relief . . .' Her grin was cheeky. 'I'd take off my shoes but Clive would kill me if I did. He's a stickler for the rules.'

'Have you been in Paris long?'

'Eight months.'

'You sound as if you would rather be somewhere else.'

'I would. I don't go a bundle on the French, I hate their food and I think their prices are horrendous. This –' She plucked at her black velvet. 'I could have bought half a dozen dresses at Fenwick's for what this cost.'

'I've had the occasional bargain from there myself.'

'I'll bet that was the one in Bond Street. I'm talking about the one in Northumberland Street, Newcastle.'

'I thought I detected a northern accent.'

'I'm a Geordie and proud of it.'

'I'm a Scot.'

'Well, I was born not far south of the border so that makes us almost compatriots.'

Mollie waved away the liveried footman who proffered a silver salver laden with flutes of freshly poured champagne. 'What I wouldn't give for a good cup of tea.' Her grin had Claire smiling back. There was something very likeable about this blunt, northern woman.

'You must get bored with this sort of thing, your husband being with the Embassy.'

'I do, but I've been doing it for long enough now to know the drill. I always fortify myself with a thick hunk of Stottie cake and a cup or two of Hinton's best before I come to one of these things.'

'What is Stottie cake?' Claire asked, fascinated.

'A flat kind of bread we make back home. I make my own. The tea I have sent in the diplomatic bag.'

'You are an experienced Embassy wife, then?'

'Well, this is my third foreign posting. First one was Spain – I quite liked that – Spanish was easy to learn because of my Geordie accent, same flat A – then we went to Vienna and now we're here. Clive is keeping his nose clean in the hopes he will eventually get Washington.' Mollie sighed. 'If only it was the one back home . . . That's where George Washington's family come from. We had President Carter there a few years ago . . .'

'But you do get home from time to time, don't you?'

'As often as I can – more now since my father had his first heart attack. I've told him to retire but it's like talking to a brick wall. His business is his baby now that Mam is dead and I'm married. God knows he doesn't need the money. He's a self-made man, my Dad. Started off with a bike and the skill of a born motor mechanic back in the fifties. We lived in Hebburn then, just above the river. Now he has a nationwide chain of garages, a taxi fleet, a coach-hire firm and another fleet of hire cars – Rolls-Royces and Mercedes and such like. I worry about him living all alone in that big house in Morpeth . . .'

'I miss my family too,' Claire said, 'but we shall be going back home in August.'

'Murdering all those poor grouse, I suppose.' Mollie saw Claire smile and acknowledge the bow of a man who walked by with another man. 'That's Bruno de Souza, isn't it?'

'Yes.'

'I don't know him but I've heard of him. Dodgy customer.'

'In what way?' Claire asked casually.

'Not quite kosher, as they say. Got his fingers in a lot of juicy pies with questionable ingredients, but always several steps ahead of the law.'

'You mean he's a crook?' Claire found herself asking calmly.

'Bent as a croquet hoop. Ah, I see they're making a move to what they laughingly call dinner in these parts . . .' Mollie heaved herself up from the sofa. 'I wonder what messes they're giving us tonight. What I wouldn't give for mince and dumplings . . . Oh well, duty calls . . . I'm to be taken in by some Military Attaché or other . . . ah, there he is . . . see you later, I hope.'

'Yes, of course . . .' Claire saw her own dinner partner, a member of the Diplomatic Corps, coming towards her.

She was down the table from Rory, who had taken in the wife of the German Ambassador. Bruno de Souza was opposite her, seated next to a woman Claire did not know but who was as thin as a pencil and stupendously elegant in a dress that seemed to have been painted on; stripes of zinging poison green and silver paillettes which left one shoulder bare.

When he was bending towards his companion Claire studied him. Strangely enough she had not been surprised when Mollie had told her he was a crook. She had, she now accepted, always distrusted him. Too suave, too – watchful. Yet it was through him that Rory was now doing so well. What worried her was that it might be by illegal means. Rory was so easily taken in, she thought, glancing down the long table at him, obviously charming his companion out of her mind. I will have a word with him, warn him . . .

At the ball later, when the rest of the guests arrived, Claire did not get to talk to Mollie again. She was on the dance floor too often. When she danced with Bruno he said: 'So, things are going well for you, I hope.'

'So far,' Claire agreed.

'Always the pragmatic Scot, eh?'

'Enough to know that in this world, there is a price to be paid for everything.'

'Not by beautiful women such as you,' he assured her gravely. 'They travel free.'

Something in the way he said it, the way he held her, made Claire move a little further away from him. She became aware that Bruno de Souza desired her.

'I prefer to pay my own way,' she told him ringingly.

'And can well afford it, the way your "investment" is paying off.'

'I have been meaning to ask you,' Claire took the opportunity offered, 'to explain to me just exactly how that is. Rory has told me very little . . .'

'I thought you understood that your money was being used as venture capital.'

'Yes, but what kind of ventures?'

'Property – land is always valuable and the right land even more so. A holiday complex in Sardinia, a security-conscious development of some half a dozen *de luxe* villas in the hills above Nice; things like that.'

'I should like to see them,' Claire said.

'And you shall . . . once construction begins. Right now there is only the land . . . But I do have the architects' plans for the villas. The very latest in state of the art, computer-controlled security for people who are slightly

84

paranoid about being robbed or mugged. They will sell for around one hundred million francs each . . .'

He saw her eyes widen. 'But that's –'

'Ten million pounds. Your share will, of course, be commensurate with your investment, but it will be considerable, I assure you.' Sensing he had her undivided attention: 'It will not be realized until all the villas are sold, of course, but there are already firm offers for three of them; a famous pop star, an oil sheik and the lady who owns the biggest cosmetics company in America. All of them very, very rich and in need of an absolutely secure bolt hole away from everything.' He pressed home his advantage. 'By the time the development is finished, your four hundred thousand pounds will be in the region of four million.'

Claire blinked. 'Four million . . .'

'In time . . . you must be patient, you understand. We have not long bought the land. Construction of such marvels with all their electronic devices will take at least a year . . .' A shrug. 'In the meantime, there are other, shorter-term investments which are already producing their dividends . . . as you have obviously realized.' His eyes went to the tightly fitted bodice and enormously puffed sleeves of her ballgown.

'It all seems too good to be true,' Claire said at last, and somewhat disbelievingly.

'But it is. Fortunately, I have well-placed friends in the necessary section of a certain *département*, and from whom I learn the occasional advantageous fact.'

At a price, Claire thought but did not say. Perhaps that was what Mollie Hoare-Brown had meant: bribes. But that was not against the law, surely, and this was France . . . Brought up by parents who had instilled a strong moral sense into their children, Claire found the thought of bribery somewhat repellent, but to make such a profit it was obviously necessary. I just won't say anything to Mummy and Daddy, she thought, that's all. In fact I need not tell them anything. I mean, four million pounds . . .

85

She saw Mollie briefly as she went for her wrap at the end of the evening. 'Here's my number,' Mollie said, pressing a slip of paper into Claire's hand. 'Give me a ring. I'm at a loose end a lot of the time and it was lovely talking to you. Maybe we can lunch or go shopping some time . . .'

'That would be nice,' Claire said, resolving to use Mollie to find out as much as she could about Bruno de Souza. In spite of herself, she still felt faintly uneasy about the smooth explanation, the careless use of astronomical figures.

So when, a couple of days later, Rory said: 'I'm going down to Nice with Bruno for a couple of days,' she answered lightly: 'Going to look at the villa site?'

'That's right. Bruno told me you had been asking him questions.' He took hold of her shoulders. 'I thought you trusted me,' he said on a headshake, while his smile did not quite hide the coldness in his voice.

'Only to always do the right thing,' she returned, still light and airy.

'This *is* the right thing. Thanks to Bruno's contacts we are on to a fortune.'

'Another one?'

'I am doing nicely thank you, but not as nicely as I want. I'm greedy. I want it all. I want to prove to everyone, your parents included, that you have not made the mistake they were – probably still are – sure you made.'

'I don't think so and that's all that matters.'

She slid her arms about his neck. He did not respond as he should so she pressed against him, kissed him. She felt him tense, then he put his own arms about her and kissed her back. Eyes tightly shut, mind whirling, lips and tongues probing, licking, she lost herself in him as always.

'Miss me,' she murmured huskily.

He fondled her sensually, touching, cupping, stroking, tantalizing her beyond bearing. 'I can promise that with my hand on my heart,' he murmured.

'I love you,' she said. What was love if not a constant desire to merge with a certain person; to become part of them, lose your identity in them, become one glorious ecstatic whole? He was not perfect, she knew that now, but then, neither was she. And what he was she needed. 'Take me with you,' she pleaded softly.

She felt him withdraw. 'Can't. This is strictly business. But when I come back I will make you my business . . .'

'Promises, promises . . .'

But she saw him go with a light heart because she had his return to look forward to. Meanwhile, she would look for birthday presents for her twin nephews Hamish and Jamie, the children of her eldest brother, who were about to celebrate their fifth birthday. On impulse, because she had formed an instant liking for her, she rang Mollie Hoare-Brown and asked if she would like to accompany her on a foray to *Le Main Bleu* in the rue Saint-Honoré to buy some toy soldiers, a speciality of the famous toyshop. Mollie was delighted to accept. 'I want to go to *Jeux D'Aiguilles* anyway,' she said. This turned out to be the famed needlework shop. Mollie was a needle-point fanatic. 'It helps pass the time,' she explained. She bought herself one of the one-of-a-kind handpainted designs, after which they strolled back to the rue Royale where they spent a pleasant half-hour among the crystal and china of Lalique, and Claire bought her mother one of their bird figurines; a kingfisher. Then they lunched at the nearby Au Grand Comptoir. Claire had a four o'clock appointment at Alexandre – she had taken enthusiastically to the French custom of visiting the hairdresser three times a week.

'You are certainly living it up,' commented Mollie. 'I go to a little hairdresser on the corner of our street which our *concièrge* recommended to me. A quarter of the price and every bit as good. These places rook you something terrible. Tell you what, though, come to me for dinner. Clive has some meeting or other so I'll be on my own. I'll cook you something that will stick to your ribs.' Claire agreed happily, and went off to Alexandre to have her hair done by a young man with three gold hoops in one ear.

True to her word Mollie, who lived in a rather grand apartment in the Avenue Foch – 'Belongs to some French marquise who charges the earth and won't let us so much as move a thing' – was busy in the kitchen when Claire arrived. 'Sit yourself down – if you can find somewhere.' The salon was full of exquisite furniture including a dozen small tables crowded with bric-à-brac and family photographs.

'I'd rather watch you cook.'

'Come on then . . . just let me get us a drink.' Mollie made them both a powerful gin and tonic and then they went into the old-fashioned French kitchen. 'This is my favourite room. That old stove reminds me of the kitchen back home and my mother blackleading ours.'

Mollie was making pastry; she did not weigh anything, merely threw handfuls of flour and equal size pieces of what looked like lard and margarine into the mixing dish. 'I know the French always use butter but I find that too rich. I make my pastry the way my mother taught me and her mother taught her and I'll bet you won't taste better anywhere.'

'What are you making?'

'Mince pie – an old Geordie standby. Do you cook?'

'I was taught how to at school.'

'So was I, but I had the best teacher in my mother and she was the best cook who ever lit an oven.'

'How come you are a diplomatic wife?' Claire found she was consumed by curiosity because Mollie Hoare-Brown did not fit the bill at all.

'I don't look the part do I? Don't play it either. Clive comes from my part of the world except his people once owned a great deal of it. Now, the times have changed, the fortunes reversed. The Hoare-Browns are the new poor while the old poor – the Armstrongs, that's my family – are the new rich. I married Clive because my dad wanted me to make a good marriage, as they say. He educated me to be a lady and that meant that none of the men I knew felt at ease with me. The silly old bugger has dreams of me one day being an Ambassador's lady.'

'All fathers want things for their daughters that those same daughters don't usually want.'

Mollie threw Claire a shrewd glance. 'Same boat, eh? Except your father didn't haul himself up by his boot straps like mine did. I've seen him go out at 2 a.m. in the pouring rain to see to a car that had broken down. But it stood him in good stead. The bike became a van and then he bought a lock-up garage. That was forty years ago. Now he's a millionaire who owns his own company. If he went public – which he absolutely refuses to do – he could be even richer, but he says he already has more money than he knows what to do with, God love him. Mam died before she could reap the benefits and he was determined I wouldn't go the same way; worn out at forty. So he sent me to expensive schools and had me made into a lady.' Mollie's smile was wry. 'Trouble is, I'm not. I'm Mollie Armstrong from Hebburn and proud of it. Mind you, when Clive married me he had to contend with his family looking down their pinched noses, but I was making it worth his while so he took no notice.'

Claire stared into her glass, somewhat embarrassed by Mollie's frankness.

'Truth to tell I married Clive to please my Dad, and because the man I loved wanted children and I can't have any. A malformation of the uterus, they said, which means I could never carry a child to full term. So I mother Clive instead. What I was really meant for was to be wife to a hard-working man who came in off his shift dead tired, ready for a plateful of pot pie and a bottle of brown ale, but it didn't work out that way. Clive doesn't mind about the children, you see, because he never expected to have any in the first place.' Pause. 'He likes men.' A shrug. 'And I never could see what there was in all this sex stuff. It is meant to conceive children and if I could have had them . . . well, then I'd have put up with it. But it suits me the way things are.'

Claire was by now staring fixedly into her glass.

'Oh, don't mind me, pet,' Mollie grinned, totally buoyant. 'I tend to call them as I see them, as an American embassy friend of ours is wont to say. And Clive is very careful up front. Not a breath of scandal; he can't afford it in his job. I provide the perfect wife and he provides my Dad with no end of pride. And we get along fine. I'm very fond of Clive and he of me. We understand one another. Most people would regard it as no marriage but it's a damned sight better than a lot I know. Clive is the best friend I'll ever have and I'll give friendship pride of place before sexual compatibility any day.'

'You are very strong, aren't you,' Claire said, simply stating a fact.

'I told you. I'm a Geordie. You have to be tough to survive where I come from.' She was rolling out pastry with quick, skilled hands.

'But – is sex really not important to you, then?' Claire found herself asking disbelievingly, contrasting attitudes.

'No, and never has been. I suppose by today's standards that makes me as queer as Dick's hatband but really the plain truth is I was born with an almost – no, not almost – a non-existent libido. I'd have liked children and I'd have done what was necessary, but I have never been able to see what all the fuss is about, myself.' She glanced at Claire's face. 'Obviously you don't agree with me.' The brown eyes twinkled. 'I've always thought that whoever designed the human body had a very mischievous sense of humour. I mean, it is all so ludicrous, if you think about it. I tend to laugh and that ruins everything.'

Claire shuddered at the thought of what would happen if she laughed at Rory, except that laughter was the last thing on her mind when he began his mesmerizing, senses-shattering lovemaking. Poor Mollie, she thought pityingly. Her trouble is that she simply has no idea . . .

'Mind you,' Mollie went on po-faced, 'I've never had a Rory Ballater.'

Claire looked up sharply but at Mollie's expression she had to laugh, though her voice was sympathetic when she said seriously: 'Perhaps, if you had . . .'

'Perhaps is a deserted village on the road to no-where.' Another smile. 'But that is not in your direction, is it?'

'No. Rory always has a destination in mind.'

'Well, if he is travelling with Bruno de Souza then he should watch out for highwaymen.'

'Is he – dangerous?' Claire asked carefully.

'What he does is. Rumour has it that he owns a couple of *maisons de rendezvous* that are clearing houses for all kinds of information: that he has friends in very high places who keep him happy because he has information about them which could make them just the opposite. Clive says he would not trust him as far as he could throw the Eiffel Tower.'

Glancing at Claire's face: 'I said rumour has it,' she repeated. 'Nobody has ever come up with any proof, and you know how people are where unbridled success is concerned. The knives come out before you can say Jack Robinson, and Bruno de Souza is very successful.'

So is Rory right now, Claire thought. Dear God, what has he gone and got himself mixed up with?

Well, Mollie thought, glancing once again at Claire's troubled expression. Clive said I should warn you and I have. I can do no more . . . As she had taken to Claire, so she had not taken to her husband. A proper Flash Harry had been her first thought on being introduced to him; the kind that will do anything for money. Absolutely sure that everything he wants can be got, no matter what the price, and that for him, it will be a special one anyway. Before she had married, Mollie had kept her father's books and her shrewd mind had quickly recognized the non-payers; the ones who relied on their charm to blind you to the fact that they were con men. In her eyes, Rory Ballater had con man written all over him. She had wondered why Claire did not see it, until she realized that Claire saw everything through her husband's dazzle, with the result that her vision was distorted. Nutty about him, had been her conclusion.

'Enough about me,' she said chattily, 'tell me about yourself. I've never met a Laird's daughter before . . .'

The mince pie was delicious; the pastry melted in the mouth and the filling was redolent with onion and juicy, finely ground beef. The carrots glistened with butter and the mange tout were young and crisp, while the tiny potatoes had been coated first in butter and then in finely chopped mint picked from the herb garden Mollie kept on the kitchen windowsill. With it they drank a bottle of claret.

'Clive is a wine buff and has made me into one,' Mollie said. 'So much so that I've invested in a vineyard in Bordeaux.' She laughed. 'Makes a difference from the parsnip and beetroot wine my granddad used to make.'

Mollie was so easy to be with, Claire thought; as comfortable as a pair of shoes in which you could walk for miles without limping. There was an almost disembowelling honesty about her, and Claire knew that whatever she was told would be kept where nobody else would ever get at it. Of all the people she had met so far during her time in Paris, Mollie Hoare-Brown was the only one Claire would trust unreservedly. She reminded her of her father's ghillie and long-time friend Dougal McKie; the same straight-from-the-shoulder candour, the being unimpressed by title or position and judging by deeds and character; the giving of one's best and expecting to receive the same. I have made a friend, Claire thought, of the kind that are hard to come by. One she knew would help her get to the truth of things. Like exactly what Rory had done with her trust fund. She told Mollie of the plan forming in her mind.

When Rory came back his mood was sunny, so Claire seized her chance.

'Mollie Hoare-Brown has invited me down to Bordeaux

to have a look-see at the vineyard she owns. I thought I might accept.'

Rory raised an eyebrow. 'Why not?' he said judiciously. 'A vineyard, eh? I've heard she's a very rich lady.' Indulgently he went on: 'I'm glad you've made a friend, poppet. She tends to call a spade a bloody shovel but with her loot she can afford to be – different. Run along and enjoy yourself. I shall be rather busy over the next few days anyway.'

Doing what? Claire thought at once, only to castigate herself for her suspicions. You're becoming paranoid, she warned herself.

The next day, Mollie and Claire left Paris, but they did not take the N9 for Bordeaux; they drove to Orly, from where they flew to Nice. At the airport they picked up the car Mollie had hired, and which she drove, French-style – 'You've got to beat the bastards at their own game,' she said ruthlessly – while Claire navigated. All she had to go on was the name of a small town or village she had spotted on the plan Bruno had showed her, which had looked to be just north of the proposed development. But when they got there, though the town was lively enough, for it was a market town, there was no development to the north, nor to the south either. And when they tried east and west it was the same story. No sign of any building work, either announced to commence or just starting to. There was nothing but empty countryside.

'You are sure this is the place?' Mollie asked, knowing damn fine it was but aware that Claire was becoming increasingly alarmed.

'Yes, I memorized the name.'

Mollie thought. 'The logical thing would be to find out from the offices of the local *commune* but at this stage I think it is better we don't ask questions.' Coming to a decision: 'I'll ask Clive,' she said.

Claire sat in shocked silence on the journey home, which Mollie did not disturb. Rory was out when she dropped Claire at their house.

'Don't say *anything*,' Molly warned. 'It could well be that work has not started yet. These things do take time, you know. French bureaucracy is a joke.'

'I don't think work will ever start,' Claire said tonelessly. 'I think that the money was never invested at all. I think that what we have been spending so wildly and recklessly was my money; I think Rory needed to put on a show; to be accepted. Appearances count for so much, with Rory. The image is all . . . He moves with a crowd who regard conspicuous consumption as the only way to make an impression.'

'Your husband does not need money to do *that*. He seemed to bend over backwards to be nice to me.'

'Yes, Rory can give that impression. He can give you his undivided attention in such a way as to make you feel singled out . . .'

A classic sexual adventurer, thought Mollie; a libertine who enjoyed the chase and the conquest, afterwards discarding the kill once it had been brought about. Any marriage with a husband like that was bound to cause havoc where the wife was concerned. She had heard one or two things but said nothing to Claire, who obviously had no idea. Claire, she surmised from what she had told her of her background, was a well-brought-up girl from a somewhat straight-laced family. There was an aloofness about her; the first time Mollie had seen her she had been reminded of the classic virgin princess. She had been astounded to learn that she was Lady Ballater, the wife of a man whose reputation had preceded him like an advance circular, but there had been a wistfulness, a certain lost-lamb air, that had appealed to Mollie's motherly instincts. At thirty-eight she was old enough to be Claire's mother.

Married his wife for her money, they had said. Not his type at all, they had said. Old Scots family – which had served Claire well in a country that still cherished fond memories of Mary Queen of Scots – whereas his is new. He had to marry well in order to survive, they had said. What better than a virginal little rich girl, dazzled and blinded by a sexual expertise which was legendary. It won't last, they had said. Nothing lasts with Rory Ballater . . .

So, after dropping Claire off, Mollie drove home to the Avenue Foch. Clive was in his study, working on some papers. Whatever else he was, he was a conscientious worker.

'Well?' he asked, sitting up and taking off his glasses.

'Sweet bugger-all,' Mollie answered bluntly. 'Not so much as a billboard.'

Clive knew where they had been. Mollie had told him. Clive had a somewhat pedestrian mind but it was a scrupulous one and he too had taken to Claire when he had met her, which was why he had warned Mollie to put Claire right about Bruno de Souza.

'I did some checking today,' he said now. 'The *département* has no knowledge of such a development so I went down the chain to the commune and it was the same answer. The whole thing is a figment of Bruno de Souza's imagination. Like the drawings he showed Lady Ballater. Probably good for no more than framing.'

'Damn,' Mollie swore softly.

'I did a little more spadework elsewhere,' Clive went on. 'A man I know in the Palais de Justice. Bruno de Souza is suspected of involvement in drug running.'

Mollie's breath hissed as she drew it in sharply. 'If Lady Ballater has "invested" in a scheme of Bruno de Souza's then it's probably a shipment of heroin or cocaine. It comes in via Marseilles, which is not too far from where the "development" was to take place. I think you should warn your friend, my dear. There is trouble ahead.'

'I'll tell her tomorrow.'

'Tell her to go home to Scotland – immediately. And if she has any sense she will take her husband with her.'

'Sense doesn't come into it,' Mollie said gloomily. She sighed. 'I'll try, but she still thinks that her husband is God's gift to her for being a good girl.'

*

But Mollie did not get to tell Claire anything. She was awoken at 2 a.m. by a telephone call from her father's housekeeper. He had suffered another coronary and was in intensive care in the Royal Victoria Infirmary in Newcastle. By 4 a.m. she was flying out of Paris in a chartered plane, headed for her dying father.

CHAPTER FOUR

In the distance, the beating line could be seen moving slowly down the glen. The sun was warm, there was the smell of heather after the light rain of early morning, and the drowsy hum of insects. As Claire watched through the glasses, the flash of a flanker's flag dispelled the somnolence and against the deep-blue haze a cloud of black dots rapidly materialized into fast-flying grouse, skimming the contours of the hill. At once there was a concerted raising of twelve-bores like a guard of honour outside a church, and birds began dropping out of the sky to bounce among the heather. Thank God, Claire thought from her vantage point alongside the purpose-built trailer. Rory had promised another double-gun day. It was worth while sinking so much of last year's profit into the estate, she told herself happily. Far more than Rory realizes, but absolutely the right thing to do. Every day of the past three weeks had provided superb shooting and their guests – mostly Americans again – were full of praise. Ballater House was fully booked all season. And needs to be, Claire thought now, since what we get from it is the only income we have.

The glory that was Paris had collapsed like the houses built of cards Rory erected when he was bored. Choosing her moment, Claire had tackled Rory about the development. At first he had been evasive, tended to bluster, but when he saw that she was angry he had turned defiant. When she mentioned Clive he admitted the truth.

'All right, so the import/export was drugs,' he snarled. 'It made us money, didn't it? More money than you've ever seen.'

'Evil money; money made out of other people's pain and suffering and vile dependence.'

'Oh, for God's sake don't be so bloody sanctimonious.'

'I want you to stop it. I want you to stop it *now!*'

'I will – after this shipment. I stand to make too much money. After this one we'll go back home . . . it's almost time anyway. And I'll have more money to make even more improvements to the estate. Just this last one,' he pleaded.

'It always is just this last one with you,' Claire said bitterly. Her revulsion was in her eyes, her face, her voice. 'How could you *do* it?' she asked. 'Drugs!'

'It offered a quick, incredibly high return. I wasn't going to stay in the business for ever, it's far too risky, but I've done very well and sunk every penny I made into this last big one, the biggest yet. I'll be rich, really rich, at last.'

But because Mollie, in her haste to get to her father, had forgotten all about warning Claire, they were left with very little time to make their escape when the shipment was intercepted by the French police.

They were having, for once, a quiet, almost silent dinner alone, when Rory was called to the telephone. He came back at the run, white-faced and in a panic.

'We've got to leave. You've got exactly thirty minutes to pack what you need.'

'What?' Claire's voice rose as she got to her feet.

'The shipment has been intercepted. There's not too much risk of me being discovered because I'm too far down the chain but Bruno says to get out. He's sending a car which will take us to a small plane which will fly us back to Scotland.'

'But –'

'No buts, just go and pack some things. *Go on!*' he shouted. 'Thirty minutes, I said.'

Claire fled for her bedroom. Hastily she seized a case, began cramming clothes into it; no time for careful folds in tissue paper; she stuffed, pushed, crammed as much as she could into the one bag which was all Rory said they could take, weeping silently. First of all she had discovered that her husband cheated at cards – because he had, in spite of her telling herself that poker was a game of bluff and all he had done was bluffed his opponents; now she discovered he was involved in drug-running.

Rory was slamming drawers, swearing, making an awful lot of noise in his panic-stricken efforts to pack his own bag. He put his head round the door to shout: 'The passports, where are our passports?'

'In the top drawer in the *bureau de plat*.'

'Have you any money?'

'A few thousand francs . . .'

'Good, because I haven't.'

When he saw she was packed before him he ordered her to go and stand by the window and look for the car.

'What's the use of running?' Claire asked him despairingly. 'They will only come after us.'

'I'm not giving them the chance. Besides, I wasn't involved in the actual running of the stuff. I only invested in what it cost to buy the cocaine. Bruno saw to the processing and the sale. Besides, there are a dozen people between him and the men on the street. He is no fool, is Bruno. He won't be caught and neither will we.' He was reassuring himself rather than talking to her. 'He's a good friend, is Bruno. He'll see us safely away.'

In case you talk, Claire muttered to herself. He knows you as well as I do. Look at you now, in a blue funk, terrified out of your wits. She stared out of the window at the rain; it was pouring. Then she sniffed, turned. Rory was at the grate, burning papers.

'Oh, God,' she gasped disbelievingly, 'you haven't got things in writing!'

'Letters from Bruno, that's all . . . but better be safe than sorry.'

'I don't feel safe but I certainly am sorry – sorry I ever married you!' she screamed at him.

He took no notice. She saw that his fingers were trembling

so much he could hardly sweep the ashes into the fire-shovel, which he brought over to the window. Opening it wide he tilted the shovel so that the wind and the rain caught the ashes and blew them away. As he did so a car came round the corner of the street and drew to a stop outside the front door.

'That's us . . .' Rory said, voice cracking with relief. 'Come on.' He seized both cases, leaving Claire to follow, and the manservant who, with his wife, cooked for and looked after them, stolidly cleaning the table and taking absolutely no notice. Of course, Claire thought hysterically as she fled out the door and down the stairs. They come with the house, and that was supplied by Bruno de Souza . . .

The car was a Mercedes 450E and its rear doors were open. Rory threw in the cases, bundled Claire after them then got in himself. It moved off before he had time to close the door. The driver did not speak; he drove fast, but not fast enough to attract the attention of the police, and soon they were out of Paris, heading Claire knew not where. They drove for about an hour, then turned off a tree-shrouded lane on to a rutted track where Claire saw a small plane waiting in the field beyond, its single engine idling. Once again Claire was bundled in; with the bags and Rory's big frame it was uncomfortably crowded, but she made herself as small as possible to allow room for Rory's long legs.

They took off at once and such was her nervous exhaustion that Claire fell asleep, waking only as the plane descended, to land in a flat, desolate spot on the moors with no road and nothing but the mountains in sight. As soon as they were out it took off again and vanished in the now full darkness.

'Now what do we do?' Claire asked wanting to laugh hysterically.

'We wait. We will be collected.'

Within minutes headlights appeared over the hill. 'Good old Wilkie,' exulted Rory, for it was he, at the wheel of one of the Range Rovers.

'We're near home?' Claire asked disbelievingly.

'Too dark to recognize, eh? We are at the far reaches of my own moors – an hour or so and we'll be safe at Ballater House!' He put Claire in the back with the bags while he sat in front and held a low-voiced conversation with Wilkie which Claire could not distinguish.

Claire went straight up to her room as soon as she entered the house where she dropped on to the side of her bed and stared at the floor. She felt numb, cold, tired. And in utter despair. After a while she dispiritedly opened her case and began to take out those clothes she had packed; not even a tenth of all she had bought so happily. Still hanging in the big armoire of her bedroom in Paris were all her evening dresses, her splendid ballgowns, her chic suits and elegant dresses, nearly all her shoes. All she had brought, she realized, were the clothes she had taken with her. She had spent a fortune and had absolutely nothing to show for it. She began to laugh, and the laughter spiralled, finally ending in an outburst of weeping which left her exhausted.

When Rory came up, a little while later, she was sprawled on her bed, fast asleep. He took off her shoes, covered her with a quilt, put out the light and left her.

She had been awake for some time, lying in the cold aftermath of the earthquake which had destroyed her belief in her husband when the door opened and he came in, carrying a breakfast tray. She turned her head away, unable to look at him. She felt him set the tray down over her legs, then take one of her cold hands.

'I'm terribly sorry, poppet.'

'You are always sorry, Rory, but it never prevents you from repeating your mistakes.'

'I did it for the best.'

'Whose best? Yours, of course. Everything you ever do is for *your* best.' Now she did look at him. He was drawn, tense, obviously in the grip of some great nervous strain.

'I know you're angry with me,' he said very low, 'and you have every right to be, but –'

'No more buts, please!' Claire said violently, as she flung his hand away.

'I did it for *us*,' he repeated. 'Not just for me. I wanted to pay you back – and I would have with this one last deal. I stood to make every penny you had invested and that much again. It was a sure thing –'

'They always are sure things.'

'Don't turn your back on me now,' he pleaded, and his voice was shaking. 'You are all I have left . . . I need you.'

'Why? I have no more money left.'

She saw him wince. 'That's unfair –'

'No, only true.' But she also saw that he expected her to stand by him in his adversity. That he took it for granted that he would be able to persuade her as usual. It was in the calculating look underlying the hurt in his eyes.

He was over his first fear of apprehension by the police and the ensuing scandal. They were safe now; they were back home, and should anyone ask he would say – and Wilkie would corroborate – that they had returned a few days ago to ready Ballater House for the shooting season due to commence in a couple of weeks' time. Now he had to make sure of her.

'Don't worry,' she told him calmly, 'I won't say anything to anybody, especially my family. Do you think I want them to know that I am married to a man who traffics in drugs?'

He ducked his head as though to avoid blows and she saw him chewing his bottom lip. 'God but you're cruel . . .' he said in hurt tones.

'*I* am cruel!' Claire laughed. 'Dear God, if ever a pot called a kettle black –'

'I wanted to make money quickly and easily,' he shouted at her. 'I was sick and damned tired of watching pennies, counting coppers. Somebody blabbed, that's what went wrong. We had absolutely no trouble with any of the other shipments –'

'I don't want to know,' Claire cut in with decisive coldness.

'But it was *your* money; *you* gave it to me –'

Claire stared at him. 'You wouldn't dare . . .' she breathed.

'When you've got your back to the wall you will dare anything. I need you to stand by me right now. I need for us to appear as though nothing has happened, so that anybody looking in our direction will see nothing, assume nothing. But if they do, I shall have to tell them that it was your money, that you gave it to me . . . knowing for what purpose.' Claire looked at the handsome face, the ugly twist to the sensual mouth, the scowl that lowered the brow, the suddenly marble cast to the eyes, and wondered with cold curiosity how she could ever have, so hopelessly and help-lessly, loved this man, struggled so long to justify all that he was not, never would be. Her sense of unreality had her enclosed in a transparent bubble of disbelief; she could see, she could hear, she could even touch, but she did not believe. She could look into the blue eyes, see how hard they could become when the deliberate charm was not being exercised, the flat rage that warned her he would not stand for having *his* wishes contravened and he was not about to stand any of her goddamned nonsense. She should know by now the swiftness with which he could fly into a rage when she did not come to heel quickly enough. But as she stared at him she realized that her long, measuring look had him confused. She saw his hardness shift to a mixture of threat, fear and pleading.

'Don't make me do that, Claire,' he said reproachfully.

'*Me* make *you?*'

'I want us to stay together. I don't want to lose you.'

'You have lost me, Rory. You have lied to me, stolen from me, involved me in the filthiest of trades. You never loved me, only what I could bring you, the thing you really love – money. Well, you have had it. I have nothing left to give, but know that if I had, I would not let you have it.'

'Oh, now Claire . . .' She knew that hurt tone, forced herself to meet the eyes that were now fully switched on; that sea of blueness which distorted her inner vision. 'The one thing you can believe is that in all this, the last thing I meant to do was hurt you.' He was bending every effort to sway her, touch her where she was most vulnerable, tighten and weld the bond she was intent on breaking. 'I did it for you,' he said huskily, and she was astounded to see moisture in his eyes. 'I wanted to show you that I could do it, make money, provide for you, care for you. It seemed such a heaven-sent opportunity. It was just an investment like any other. Import/export, as I said. I bought in, Bruno sold and I got my share of the profits. What was so wrong in that?'

Claire shook her head. 'If you don't know by now, Rory, then it's a waste of time my explaining it to you.'

'Then you force my hand,' he said sadly. He put his hand in his pocket, brought out a folded paper. 'I didn't burn everything last night,' he said conversationally. 'Something made me keep this back.' His laugh was confident. 'The old instinct was working after all . . .' He unfolded the paper and Claire could see it was a letter which bore, she saw as he held it in front of her face, her own signature.

'This is the letter to the bank in Switzerland authorizing them to pay to Senhor Bruno de Souza the sum of four hundred and sixty-two thousand pounds, signed, sealed and delivered by you.' Claire said nothing, but she had tensed, waiting for the worst. 'If you leave me, make me look a fool in front of everyone, I shall show this letter to your father and tell *him* why we left Paris in a hurry.'

'You couldn't!' It was a cry of agony. 'It would kill him!'

Rory's smile was so smug as to be callous. 'Exactly.' Then his face hardened. 'I am not having you run out on me, Claire. *Nobody* leaves Rory Ballater. Do you understand me?'

'You would destroy my father to preserve *your* so-called reputation?'

'I will make it clear that his daughter invested money in a drug-running operation, with a man who ran a string of brothels, who conducted a flourishing blackmail operation, who –'

'Stop it!' shouted Claire.

'Your father is such an upright man. His honour is his

life. So proud of the unbesmirched name of Drummond. Told me I was not good enough for you. I was only a Ballater, not long out of the croft, whilst you were a Drummond.'

'He would not believe it of me; of you, but never of me.'

'He would the way I would tell it.' Softly: 'And you know I can, don't you?' He smiled at her. It was so cold it made her shiver. 'You are not going to leave me,' he said. 'I will not allow it. You are my wife. You will stay with me, go where I go, live as I live. Do you understand?'

'Hating you all the while!'

'Just so long as you are careful not to give that impression in public. If you do . . .' His voice trailed off and he shrugged. Then, in the same hard voice: 'Now you will get up and dress and you will take up your duties as mistress of this house. I am going to invite some friends to dinner on Saturday night; to announce our return, so to speak. Old friends together before the pressure of business forces me to put it before pleasure. You will preside.'

'Wearing what? I left everything behind in Paris.'

'Your clothes are being sent on, along with mine. I spoke to Bruno this morning. The police have arrested several people but they have not made a move towards me. Bruno, of course, is protected. He has powerful friends.'

'And will he return my money?'

Rory's hand came up in a lazy arc before hitting her hard across her left cheek. 'Mind your tongue,' he said icily. 'That shipment is lost, but there will be others. We will stay here as usual until the end of the year; we will have an even better season than last time, then we will take what we have made and I will invest it as before.'

He waited for her to speak. When she did not he said: 'I take it, then, that you have made your choice.'

'No,' Claire answered dully. 'You have made it for me.'

Now, she turned back to the van as the last of the grouse disappeared over the skyline. Time for lunch; to play the gracious chatelaine, to dispense food and wine and the right kind of conversational charm, knowing that Rory would be watching her, especially today because her father was one of the guns. Rory had set to work to charm him into coming; to show him how successful his daughter's marriage was. It was for Claire a slow crucifixion. Her father was so frail now. Her mother had told her that he tired very easily these days, that his irascibility was worse, as if he knew his hold on life was slipping, which fact had made Claire even more determined to hold out for as long as it took for her father to be safe. Safely dead. It was emphysema in his remaining lung. He could not walk far, and today had been driven as close to the butt as possible by her mother, in the old pony cart. Claire could see her now, urging the placid old pony on at the trot. Her father would be ready for his lunch. Something hot; he could not abide cold food on a shoot, even in summer. So she had a heated jar of mutton broth, his favourite, for him. For the others she had a choice of beef bourguignonne, steak and kidney pie and a casserole of grouse. For those who preferred something cold she had a salmon mousse, cold game pie and salad. Wilkie would see to the wine. Wilkie, her jailer. When Rory was not around he watched her, and now that he no longer had to mind his p's and q's the contempt and hatred he felt for her showed plain. Claire had not been able to account for it until it came to her one day, watching Rory and Wilkie together; the possessive familiarity of the servant to the master gave Claire the clue she needed. She had known at once that Wilkie despised women: now she saw that he hated her because he was jealous. He had accepted her while she was a necessary evil; now that the masks and the gloves were off he showed his contempt openly.

No matter what horrors lay behind the façade, Rory kept up those appearances which were so important to him. There would be no gossip. In front of their guests he was the loving, attentive husband; he joked, teased, gave abundant evidence of his abiding love for his wife, his pride in her. So many of the wives gushed: 'You make the most perfect couple,' and Rory would beam and Claire would smile, screaming silently inside, because when the guests had gone he would not even look at, never mind speak to her, and he had moved out of their bedroom. It was this, to Claire's shame and despair, that hurt the most. Knowing what he was in her mind, still her body craved him. She despised herself for her weakness, but he had made her his creature in the one way she could not fight. He had awoken her sexuality and created appetites he now assiduously proceeded to starve.

The worst times were when they saw her parents. More than once she saw her mother eyeing her pensively, but her father was not so perceptive, and he was rapidly growing very old as his physical weakness overtook him, so that he saw nothing but the perfectly presented picture Rory was so careful to draw, and was happy. When he said to her: 'I am glad to have been proved wrong, daughter. It has relieved my mind greatly,' she wanted to howl, weep, scream at him that it was all a lie. That she had never been so unhappy in all her life. But she only smiled lovingly and kissed him. 'I'm happy that you are happy, Daddy.' She knew that the very fact of her being even on the fringes of what had happened would strike him a mortal blow. Rory might have tricked her, but to her father, the undeniable fact that he had not stood out against the marriage, had allowed it to take place against the grave misgivings he had made it plain he possessed, would have hastened his decline. He too was a proud man, and the reputation of the Drummonds was a responsibility he had impressed upon his children. To have his only daughter involved, no matter how innocently, in the sale of what he regarded as an abomination, the most morally reprehensible of trades, would have struck at the very heart of him. He longed for only one thing now; to see Claire's children.

'We are doing our best, sir,' Rory told him with a resigned smile, giving the impression that it was not his fault.

Her mother was more direct. 'You look tired, darling,'

she said concernedly. 'You're working much too hard. You've done wonders already. Surely you can ease off a little.'

'Once the season is over, I will,' Claire lied easily. 'Don't worry, Mother. Hard work never hurt anyone.'

And work she did. She kept herself busy, involved herself in every aspect of the estate, saw that their guests got their money's worth, but the praise she received only made Rory worse. When they were alone he would subject her to a torrent of abuse, made all the worse by the low, icy voice in which he gave it. He denigrated her abilities, criticized her performance, complained that she took too much upon herself. She was no more than a lovely clothes-horse, there to shine her light on him as he stood centre stage. Any compliments she received were to be redirected to him. He proceeded to demolish, piece by deliberate piece, the edifice of her pride and self-respect. He taunted and tortured her, the more so when she had just seen her father, with casual threats about revealing the truth, but she knew him well enough by now to be quite sure that he would not do it unless he had no other recourse. Yet there was always the possibility; his mood swings were unpredictable, and it would only take one careless slight to send him over the edge.

It was Wilkie who prevented him from going over. He could always talk Rory round. It struck Claire with hideous irony that the one man who would gladly see her go to the wall was the same man who did all he could to prevent it, because Rory's 'perfect' marriage had done so much to redeem his former reputation amongst those who mattered. Rory wanted to be accepted; Rory wanted to become part of the tightly knit, often sober-sided Highland society; he wanted to return to the fold and thus erect and maintain a new reputation as a reformed rake, behind which he could hide while he conducted his real life. Claire came to realize that she was his passport to that world. She was a Drummond; all that Rory longed to be, with a long lineage and an ancestry of which she could be proud. She was known to be *pur et sans reproche* with a father who epitomized all that was meant by the word 'gentleman'. Claire was unconsciously what so impressed their American guests: a lady. For Rory, she provided the perfect cover.

Now, she once more slipped into her part, informing one envious American guest where she got her perfect tweeds, and another of the best shop in Edinburgh to buy them. She dispensed food on the Crown Derby china Rory insisted she use – 'There will be no paper plates on a Ballater shoot while I am its host.' The accompanying heavy Georgian silver cutlery came wrapped in a heavy linen napkin. The glasses Wilkie filled with choice wines were crystal. 'Luxury and an old-style shoot is what they are buying and that, by God, is what you will give them,' Rory had ordered her curtly.

Now, she saw him smile proudly as another guest said admiringly: 'You sure know how to do things in style, Lady Ballater.'

On the Friday night David Grant arrived. Claire was happy to have one friend of Rory's whom she liked.

'I'm so glad you could come,' she told him affectionately.

'Well, a weekend is all I can manage, but it's better than nothing.'

'Is that fraud case still being heard?'

'And will be for another six weeks at least. It's complicated.' His smile, which changed his undistinguished face into something instantly likeable, appeared. 'And it makes me a nice fat fee.' He walked to the edge of the balustraded terrace at the back of the house where they were having pre-dinner drinks. 'Oh, it's good to be back . . . I may be only a Lowland Scot, but you always make me feel like an honorary Highlander.'

'Go on with you, you Lowlanders think you're the salt of the earth.' Her smile was warm. 'And in my eyes, you are.'

She had often wondered what had made David Grant,

quiet, soft-spoken, honourable, make a friend of Rory, and had finally asked him.

'He took me over at school . . . He was so grand, so – dominating. I was small and shy and inclined to be bullied. Once he took notice of me the bullying stopped. Nobody took Rory on. Not then, not now . . . He was a great swell and the best athlete the school had produced in an age. There was nobody like him at cricket, and as for running . . . I was lucky enough to be made his fag.'

'Lucky!'

'I mean that.' David was serious. 'He didn't bully me or beat me, ever. He protected me.' While you worshipped him, Claire had thought. Rory would never have been able to resist that. 'I know he is – was –' David had corrected himself, 'wild, but there was nobody to check him; nobody who cared enough about him.' He had looked at her gravely. 'That's why he's so lucky to have you.'

Oh, David, Claire thought now in anguish. If only you knew . . . But she could never tell him. He would understand, he would be concerned, he would be deeply upset, but she could still never tell him. She could never tell anyone. It was more than her life was worth. And more and more she was coming round to the point of view that it was not worth anything.

'You and David seemed to be having a sentimental re-union,' Rory sneered that night, when he came into her bedroom as she was undressing. He now slept in the adjoining room.

'We're good friends. I was glad to see him.'

'Just so long as you continue to be no more than that.'

Claire looked at him contemptuously. 'David is your friend,' she said. 'I am not capable of such treachery.'

Once again his hand snaked out, caught her hard on the cheek. 'Mind your tongue,' he warned coldly. 'While we are at Ballater there must be not one breath of suspicion about anyone, most of all my wife.'

'If there is ever any suspicion about anything it will not

be because of anything I have done.' She met the hard stare head on.

Rory laughed in another of his abrupt changes of mood. 'I'll say one thing for you,' he observed. 'You don't lack for courage.' His smile made her flinch. 'We'll see how long that lasts.' On another laugh he sauntered out.

Claire was careful around David after that. She wanted to give Rory no cause for grievance.

'I haven't offended you, have I?' David asked on the Sunday evening as they waited for the car to come and drive him to Dalcross to catch his flight to London.

'Good heavens no. What makes you think so?' Claire replied quickly.

'I've hardly had a chance to talk to you. I had the impression you were avoiding me.'

'Of course I haven't! But I do have guests to see too. I'm now a professional hostess,' she said lightly.

'And it's going well, I can see. You've made this cheerless barracks into a haven of hospitality.'

'Into which you are welcome *any* time.'

'Still friends, then?'

'I look on you as my friend as well as Rory's.'

'Good. Remember that, won't you? If ever you need a friend, I mean.'

Conscious of Rory's eyes Claire said flippantly: 'It shall be engraved in my memory.' She called to her husband. 'Come and say goodbye to David, Rory. He's just leaving.'

'Oh, Rory is going with me to Dalcross,' David said.

'Oh?' Claire was surprised.

'We haven't had much of a chance to talk either.'

'Don't worry, I'll be back for dinner,' Rory said carelessly. 'Hold the fort till I get back.' He turned to David: 'If you can tear yourself away from my wife,' he said jocularly.

'Goodbye, Claire.' David kissed her as usual. 'It's been a lovely weekend.'

'We are here for a few more weeks. Come again if you can.' She kept her tone light and easy, that of a woman

III

talking to her husband's oldest friend, but she was not surprised when, lying in bed that night, making out a list of supplies to be ordered for the next influx of guests, Rory came in from his bedroom. She had expected a tongue-lashing for not, in his eyes, conducting herself as his wife should, and for showing him up by paying too much attention to his friends. But she had not expected that he would be naked or that he would be fully erect and obviously intent on having sex with her.

'To what do I owe the honour?' she found herself asking boldly.

'You are my wife.'

'Who or what has made you realize it?'

'Why I want to fuck you is of no concern. All that matters is that right now I feel like it,' he said with brutal coarseness.

'Well I don't.' She made to get out of the other side of the bed but with his fast reflexes he had her pinned down before she could do so.

'Maidenly modesty at this late stage?'

'Modesty has nothing to do with it. I just don't want to sleep with you – now or ever.'

'I don't give a damn. Haven't I made it plain that it's what *I* want that matters?'

She struggled against the powerful hands; her papers slid off the bed into a heap on the floor as he held her down with one splayed hand while he roughly stripped her of her nightdress with the other.

'Your father keeps dropping hints about a grandchild and it has occurred to me that a baby is all we need to complete the picture of the perfect couple.'

'I want no child of yours!' Claire spat at him.

'Were you perhaps thinking you would prefer one by David?'

'I wouldn't do that to you, even now, and you know it!'

Rory laughed. 'As it happens I believe you . . . David is that rare thing, an honourable man.' Then, conversationally: 'You know he is in love with you, don't you?'

'Don't be ridiculous,' Claire said, as coldly as she could, but she suddenly knew why she found his eyes on her whenever she turned to look at him, why he touched her as often as he could, even if it was only her hand.

'Quite desperately, poor bastard. But, being David, it will never come to anything. His Sir Lancelot scruples will hold a hell of a lot tighter than those of the original.' Rory laughed again. 'He regards you as some sort of Virgin Goddess . . .' Another laugh. 'Married to me two years yet he still sees you through rose-coloured glasses. I wonder how he would feel if he knew what a lascivious little thing you are when in the throes of passion . . . of what you like doing, what you like having done . . .'

He had her naked now, and was exploring her body. In spite of herself, Claire jerked as the old electricity coursed through her veins. 'All these weeks of abstinence . . . you must be ready to explode . . .' The long fingers smoothed, caressed, probed; a moan broke through her clenched teeth. He knew where she was most vulnerable; knew that her body's clamouring hunger was straining to break free. She felt terrified; not of him, but of herself. He was about to consume her like some cannibal and while her self-respect fought him, her still raging desire for him undermined her resolve like some insidious fifth column. As always, he reduced her to a mindless, greedy animal; drew her into a Nirvana of climax upon climax. Sweat poured from her like rain; he had her this way and that, from the front, from the rear, he laved her with his tongue, but there was no love in any of it. He was giving a performance as he conquered her body, subjugated her mind, took her without tenderness, without care, without love. He used her, but it was usage her body had longed for even as her mind writhed in shame.

Only when she opened her eyes because she felt a sudden need to see his face did the ultimate realization of what she had become hit her. His eyes were brilliantly blue, shining with a fierce, hard light, yet they were cold; inhumanly cold in a way that froze her fevered heat as a blast of arctic wind will turn a fragile flower into an ice sculpture. The planes of his handsome face were those of a carved idol yet were rigid with intensity. But not on her. On himself. He was in her, merged with her, supposed to be one, yet he was totally apart, totally immersed in himself.

So it was, she realized numbly, as the last fragments of her self-esteem crumbled, and so it always had been and would be. To Rory Ballater, the only reality was himself. He had come to her tonight not because he wanted her for what she was, the woman she was, the *being* she was; he had come to her to demonstrate his hold on her, because another man had made him aware that she was still desirable.

Rory, she realized, in the grip of a pain that obliterated all feelings of sexual satisfaction, was a user. To him she was his property, marked and labelled: Rory Ballater. His wife.

Something in her died then, even as the passion he had aroused withered in the icy blast of his self-absorption. When at last he left her, without a word, the first thin coating of what was to become an ice sepulchre had begun to shroud her in emotional numbness.

CHAPTER FIVE

There was a doorman in the pink marble lobby of the expensive apartment house, and while he called to check that Mollie's arrival was expected she looked round at the closed-circuit television cameras keeping a watch on her.

They *must* be doing well, she thought relievedly. Rents in highrise blocks like these also tended to reach for the sky.

The doorman turned from the telephone and came round the desk to precede her to the bronze doors of the lift. 'Milord Ballater has the penthouse,' she was informed grandly before the door slid closed.

Rory was waiting for her amidst a plethora of mirrors, crystal chandeliers, a profusion of greenery and wall-to-wall carpeting into which her feet seemed to sink up to the ankles.

'Hmmm, nice,' Mollie said, dry as dust, and Rory laughed.

'It does go over the top but I took it for the view. You can see for miles in all directions.'

Mollie repressed an acid comment. Be thankful you have found Claire again, she told herself. Now she could apologize for running off and leaving without a word. It had been almost six months since she had made her dash back to Newcastle, to find her father on a life-support machine and not expected to live. What he had needed for a long time now was a heart transplant, but the months had gone by without a suitable donor being found. There were still, she had reflected bitterly as she sat at his bedside, willing him to hang on, things that even all the Armstrong money could not buy.

And he had held on; forty-eight hours later he was still fighting, and it was that night that a young man was brought in with terrible head injuries, having totalled his Kawasaki against the side of a forty·ton juggernaut on the Newcastle bypass. He died without ever regaining consciousness but in the pocket of his leather jacket they found a donor card. His mother, blank with shock, gave her permission and within minutes George Armstrong was being prepared to receive a twenty-year-old heart to replace the one he had worn out with fifty years of unremitting hard work.

It had been a time of great joy for Mollie, watching the grey face take on colour, the feeble impotence change to gathering strength which in turn, as he returned to the world, became tinged with impatience. Within a week he was booming like Souter Point Lighthouse and making plans to return to work.

'Get away man,' Mollie told him scathingly. 'If you think I am going to allow you to return to sixteen-hour days and meals eaten on the run you had better think again. We are getting a Manager. Somebody half your age with twice the strength. He's out there somewhere and I intend to find him.'

It had taken three months, and at the end of them her father was chafing at the bit.

'Look, pet, there isn't anybody,' he told her impatiently. 'We're wasting time. I'm a new man now. I can cope. I've been at work since I was fifteen. What will I do all day if I can't run my own business?'

'Watch somebody else do it.'

And Mollie finally found what she was looking for. He was thirty-three, voraciously ambitious and as sharp as they came. He had been managing a small engineering factory on the Team Valley Trading Estate and had turned it from a strife-ridden battlefield into a thriving concern with full order books. He would control the day to day running of Armstrong Motors; her father would dictate policy and act as a consultant.

She stayed another three months while the manager was run in; Mollie knew the business backwards and by the time she returned to Paris, so did her pupil.

Clive took one look and said: 'You look worn out. What you need is a long stretch of rest and recuperation. I've got extended leave due. We'll go south and lie around in the sun for a month or two.'

They stayed at the delicious villa belonging to the man who had been Clive's closest friend at Oxford. The villa had originally belonged to Cléo de Mérode, the famous *horizontale* of the Belle Epoque, and it had been designed by the man who built the Paris Opera House.

'This is exactly my idea of a whorehouse,' Mollie said, as she inspected rooms as extravagant as an ice-cream sundae complete with nuts, whipped cream and a cherry on the top. But it had superb gardens, an attentive staff and it was just down the road from Monte Carlo, where the Monaco Grand Prix was due to be held in the coming week.

Mollie spent the first few days lying on a sun-bed wearing a bikini. 'For once I can get into one!' she exclaimed joyously. She had always had a weight problem but the months of worry and hard work had fined her down, in spite of the fact that when she was tense she turned to food for comfort. Not even the large amounts she had shovelled down had been able to compete with the constant gnawing of fear, and she had lost more than a stone.

While she sunbathed, Clive told her all the latest *on dits*, like the fact – mentioned in his letters but now amplified by what detail he knew – that the Ballaters had quit Paris in a hurry. Bruno de Souza had likewise departed for Brazil. A massive shipment of cocaine had been intercepted at Marseilles by the French police and several arrests had been made, but they had been the men involved in the actual smuggling. Rory Ballater and his co-conspirator had been the money men but this fact could not be proved conclusively.

'The cocaine had a street value of twenty million francs,' Clive told her. 'Ballater must have been on to a fortune had he received his share of the profits.'

'Well, Claire certainly spent one. Her clothes were fabulous and so were her jewels.'

'I wonder if she still has them?'

'Not for long if Rory is broke.' She sighed heavily. 'I feel responsible, somehow. If only I had been able to warn her.'

'They got away, didn't they?'

'Yes, but I can't help feeling that she must be feeling I let her down by not getting in touch since. I did write to her at Ballater House but she never replied.'

'They may not be there any more.'

'God knows where they are,' Mollie sighed again, 'or what they're doing. But I feel it in my bones that it won't be anything she approves of.'

'I never could understand what a sweet girl like Claire was doing married to a man like Rory Ballater. She's years younger than him –'

'You're ten years older than me.'

'But she's so – so young, so – innocent. I always thought there was something fresh and pure about that girl.'

'Beauty and the Beast?'

'Rory Ballater is no beast, if his attraction to women is anything to go by.'

'I mean beast by nature. That man was all surface and no depth. Claire had character, even if she was so "young".'

Clive smiled. 'You know what I mean.'

'Yes; that quality of – integrity. A girl you could trust and you knew had not a malicious bone in her body.'

'And far too idealistic.'

'What makes you say that?'

'Oh, things she said, her attitudes, her vision of life. That is why I say I do not understand her marrying Rory Ballater. He is self-seeking, corrupt, a born opportunist.'

Mollie nodded her agreement. 'Men like him expect too much – from women, I mean. They know they are good but expect to be worshipped for it.'

'As Claire did?'

'Yes . . . She was mortally hurt when she found out about the non-existent development. I think she suspected, down where she would not have to confront it, and the fact that I was there when she found out only served to complete her humiliation.'

'Yet she went back to him.'

'I know – he's got her right where he wants her.' She heaved herself up from the sun-bed. 'And right now I am going to see if that is at Ballater House . . .'

But a surly Scots voice informed her curtly that Lord and Lady Ballater were travelling on the Continent and no, he did not know where, or when they were expected back.

Where are you, Claire? Mollie thought. What is that husband of yours up to? She could not rid herself of the feeling that something was wrong, had done since her letters – and there had been two, not one as she had told Clive, went unanswered. That was not Claire. She was scrupulous about things like that; always punctual, always there if she said she would be. A couple of times, if she was going to be even five minutes late for an appointment with Mollie, she had telephoned to explain. The girl Mollie had known would have regarded not answering one letter as bad manners; two as the height of rudeness. Mollie could think of only one explanation. Claire had never received them. I wonder, thought Mollie. Then: why not? Claire had given her the number, told her that any time they were in Scotland she would be hurt if they did not either call or visit. So she rang Castle Drummond, asked to speak to Lady Drummond.

Claire's mother was delighted to hear from Mollie. 'Claire told me so much about you, what a good friend you were to her.'

'Which is why I want to re-establish contact.' Mollie explained her hurried departure.

'I know the feeling,' Margot Drummond sympathized. 'My husband has not been well for some time now, otherwise I would have gone across to see Claire. I haven't heard from her for several weeks, which is not like her. Normally she writes to me regularly and often.'

I knew it! thought Mollie, then asked casually, 'Where are they now?'

'I have no idea. They never seem to stay long in one place. First it was Rome, then Milan, then Cannes, and the last letter I had was from Nice. My son-in-law has itchy feet, I'm afraid.'

'Well, perhaps I might run into her,' Mollie said cheerfully. 'The Riviera is quite a small place, really, and what the magazines call The Beautiful People tend to congregate in certain places.'

'If you do, do remind her that she still has a family who would love to hear from her,' Margot Drummond said lightly.

'I'll sit her down with pen and paper,' Mollie promised.

Margot Drummond laughed. 'She told me you were very strong-minded.'

'Go on,' Mollie joked comfortably, 'you can say bossy, I don't mind.' What a nice lady, she thought, when she had rung off. You can tell the real ones a mile off – a thousand miles off. And she's worried. That came across too. At that, it isn't like Claire to forget to write to her mother. Those two are as close as I am to Dad. What is that bloody man up to now? she thought irritably.

And then, leafing through a copy of *Jours de France*, she came across a picture of a group of people at a cocktail party at the Monte Carlo Country Club during the Open Tennis Tournament, only the month before. Among the smiling faces, which included Boris Becker and Princess Stephanie of Monaco, was that of Rory Ballater. His wife was not present.

Bingo! thought Mollie, reaching for the telephone. But the Ballaters were not staying at any of the hotels in the principality, nor were they expected, and in any case, all the hotels were full because of the forthcoming Monaco Grand Prix, due to take place the very next week.

That's it! Mollie thought. That's Rory Ballater's chosen territory. And sure enough, at a cocktail party graced by the Monegasque royals, to which Clive, at her urging, obtained invitations, a glittering affair held at the Hôtel de Paris,

Mollie found him. He was part of another laughing, glossy group, the men wreathed in cigar smoke and expensive aftershave, the women in designer dresses and lavish jewellery. Claire was not among them.

Eyeing him from across the room, Mollie had to admit she was not the only woman doing it. He drew the gaze. So much so that the woman he was with adopted a predatory stance and turned a malevolent stare on any woman who tried to muscle in. He looked glossy, burnished, in the money. He smiled a lot, laughed continually. Even from this distance the blue of his eyes flashed like high voltage electricity. Well, I'm glad you're happy, Mollie thought. But where is your wife? She determined to find out.

She waited, manoeuvring herself nearer and nearer, so that when his gaze, which constantly roved the room, came her way, he could not fail to see her. For a milli-second she saw his smile congeal, the eyes flicker, and then he was coming in her direction, unleashing a dazzler, hand out-stretched.

'By all that's holy, Mollie Hoare-Brown,' he said pleasurably.

'Long time no see.' Mollie smiled broadly, shook hands.

'Not since last year, in Paris . . .'

'Yes, I had to leave in rather a hurry, I'm afraid.' That drew no response; his look of attentive enquiry in place. 'My father had another heart attack.'

'Oh, I am sorry . . . I hope he made a full recovery?'

'When I left he was full of the joys of spring,' Mollie assured him. 'But I was sorry not to be able to tell Claire I had to go home *tout suite*. She must have thought I had deserted her. Where is she? I'm dying to see her again . . .'

She saw Rory's glow dim. A tiny frown marred the bronzed smoothness of his brow. 'Claire is not at all well, I am afraid. Has not been for some time . . .' He studied her thoughtfully, seemed to come to a decision. 'Actually, I'm glad I met you. I could do with some of your northern common sense and practical advice.'

'Anything I can do,' Mollie told him truthfully.

'Let's sit down,' he said. 'Over there . . .' He put a hand under her arm, moved her to a massive sofa upholstered in champagne-gold silk.

'What's wrong with her?' Mollie asked anxiously.

He met her concerned eyes and his own mirrored her feelings. 'Claire has been in a state of deep depression for some months now. Ever since she lost the child she was carrying.'

Mollie's intake of breath came from the stab of pain which lanced her. Unable to have her own children, a miscarriage was, to her, the deadliest of blows. 'Oh, no . . .'

Rory nodded sadly. 'No apparent reason . . . she was well, happy – we both were. It was what we wanted.' His voice was bleak, bitter. 'They called it a spontaneous abortion; they happen, we were told. Often for no apparent reason.' He sighed. 'Which is where the trouble lies. Claire has been searching for a reason ever since and the only answer she can come up with is that she did something wrong; that she is to blame. That the whole thing is her fault.'

Mollie was silent, but she was keening inside. Oh, my poor Claire, she thought, her compassionate heart aching.

'I've had her seen by endless doctors – some of the best in their field, but nothing seems to work.' His voice was filled with suffering when he said: 'They are now talking of having her taken into a nursing home for nervous diseases. They think that she needs long and careful therapy . . .'

'Oh, dear, I am sorry . . .' Mollie, in her compassion, laid a hand on his arm. He covered it with his own, obviously distressed.

'She doesn't seem to care for anything any more. She hardly speaks, she won't eat, she isn't sleeping . . . I don't know what to *do*, Mollie.' He bit his lip. 'Worst of all, she regards me as her enemy . . . she seems to think I am persecuting her for losing our child.'

'Miscarriages are mysterious things,' Mollie said sadly.

'I've seen women sink into the blackest depression after one of them. They seem to lose all interest in life.'

'That,' Rory said heavily, 'is what is happening to Claire. I can't get rid of the terrible fear that she is losing her mind.'

'Why haven't you taken her back home?' she asked tentatively.

'She won't go. Flies into the most terrible rage when I suggest it. I think she is ashamed. The Drummonds are all well hung with children; Iain now has a daughter in addition to his twin sons, her middle brother Hamish has four children – she feels she has failed and is deeply ashamed.'

Mollie frowned. 'But – what about her mother?'

'She has enough to do with Claire's father on her hands. You know he is going downhill fast?'

'No. I had no idea.' Lady Margot's words had been to the effect that her husband had not been well for some time, not that he was dying.

'Besides, if she won't go home, I might do more harm than good if I brought her mother over.' His sigh weighed a ton. 'It is very difficult to know what to do for the best.' He seemed to hesitate then said: 'We have to be very careful, you see, in case she tries suicide again.'

'Suicide! Again!'

'Yes . . . she once managed to get her hands on a bottle of aspirin and took the lot. Fortunately her nurse – I have a full-time nurse looking after her – was on the spot and we got her to hospital where they pumped out her stomach. Now, we watch her round the clock.'

Dear God! Mollie thought, almost stupefied with shock. Can this be Claire we are talking about? She had come to realize that her friend was a sensitive, vulnerable woman, but suicidal? Never! thought Mollie. She had far too much good Scots common sense. Yes, she told herself, but she also had a miscarriage. We women are penalized by our own bloody biology.

'This is the first time I have been out in months,' Rory

said. 'I usually spend all my time with Claire. It's no fun when you're worried about someone you love.'

Mollie twisted the diamond and ruby bracelet on her left arm. First time in months? What about the Monte Carlo Open?

'Having an invalid on your hands is very restricting,' she agreed sympathetically. 'I spent every night with my father when he was convalescing. That's why we have come down here, to give me a rest. We only arrived today.' She did not know why she lied. She only felt it was best he did not know they had been here a week; that she had been trying to run him down.

Be careful, she told herself. Remember this seemingly unhappy man is the same man who ran drugs; who got out of Paris one step ahead of the police. Who lied to his wife. Who invested her money in a non-existent property development that was in reality the purchase of a shipment of cocaine. And it *had* been him in that picture in *Jours de France*. Nobody looked like Rory Ballater except Rory Ballater. His good looks were instantly recognizable. And from the way he had been acting earlier, he was about as worried as a man who had just come up on the pools.

'Would it help if I saw her?' she asked, throwing down the gauntlet, but the way his face lit staggered her.

'Would you? Claire liked you so much . . .'

'Of course I would. I will do anything I can to help.'

Now she felt guilty. You and your instant prejudices, she scolded herself. Perhaps he's telling you the truth. Find out before you condemn him for a liar.

'I've taken a penthouse on the Promenade des Anglais at Nice. Glorious views and Claire lies out on the balcony – it's glassed in so she can come to no harm. Where are you staying? I can see if Claire is up to receiving visitors and give you a ring.'

'We are staying at a friend's villa.' Mollie gave him the address and phone number.

'I'll call you, then.' He pressed her hand warmly. 'Thank

you, Mollie. I'm sure Claire will be pleased to see you – if she recognizes you, of course. Sometimes she doesn't even know me.'

'We can but try,' Mollie told him staunchly.

'Bless you,' he said, then went back to his friends.

'Well?' asked Clive, when he came across. 'You seemed to be having a serious conversation.'

'We were.' She gave him the gist of it.

'Oh, dear,' Clive said gravely. 'That sounds bad.'

Rory called her two days later. 'Could you come this afternoon?'

'What time?'

'About four. I won't tell Claire; we'll surprise her . . .'

Now, as he led her across to an ornate double door: 'I hope the surprise isn't spoiled,' she asked innocently.

'No. The doorman spoke to me. Claire has no idea you are coming.' In the foyer he closed the door then said bluntly: 'Don't be too shocked when you see her. She has – changed physically as well as mentally.'

Filled with foreboding Mollie nodded and followed him through to a large room filled with sunlight from a bank of windows at the far end, overlooking the sea. Lying on a chaise longue in front of them was a figure with a light coverlet over her legs. Her head was turned to the windows. As Mollie approached, went round the foot of the couch, she saw that Claire's eyes were closed. She bit her lip on the jolt of shock which almost made her cry out. She was looking at a death's head. The cheeks were sunken, the eye sockets so dark a grey as to be almost black. The hands that lay limply on the coverlet were well kept and manicured, but they were fleshless, like the claws of a scrawny chicken.

Rory bent over her. 'Claire . . .' His voice was gentle, almost a caress. 'We have a visitor . . .'

The eyes opened and once again Mollie received a shock. They were lifeless; the lovely pansy purple Mollie remembered was filmed as if by a layer of dust. They looked at Mollie without recognition.

'Hello stranger,' Mollie said in broad Geordie. Claire continued to stare dully. 'It's Mollie . . . you remember Mollie, don't you?'

'Mollie.' Claire's voice was empty, merely an echo.

'Back again like the proverbial bad penny. Come to say I'm sorry I had to leave you without a word, but my Dad had another heart attack and I had to go and play Florence Nightingale. The patient made a full recovery so here I am to see if I can't do the same for you.'

Claire's gaze was intent now. Mollie had a sense of interior struggle. Rory had set a chair by her couch and when Mollie sat down she picked up one of the lax hands; it was weightless.

'You daft bugger,' Mollie scolded softly, 'don't tell me you've forgotten Mollie? Blaydon Races, remember? Newcastle Brown Ale? Stottie cake?' She reached for her handbag, brought out a paper bag. 'I made some this morning . . .' She unwrapped a triangle of round flat bread. 'It's still warm and I piled on the butter . . .' She placed it in Claire's hand, wrapped the long fingers around it. 'Go on, give your tastebuds a treat.'

She raised the hand to Claire's mouth. She saw Claire sniff the aroma of fresh bread then the teeth bit into it. Chewing was obviously an effort, but as the taste percolated, Mollie saw the dull eyes begin to clear. This time, Claire took another bite of her own volition. Her smile was that of a delighted child. 'Mollie . . .' she said.

'No wonder you are worried,' Mollie said to Rory as he walked her to the lift half an hour later. 'I have never seen such a drastic change in anyone.'

'She was not much company, I'm afraid.'

'No matter. Clive always says nobody else can get a word in anyway, once I start. What matters is that she knew who I was.'

'Yes,' Rory agreed, 'she did, didn't she.'

'All she did was look at me and smile, but it's a beginning.'

126

'I knew you would do her good.'

'When can I come again?'

'Give me a ring tomorrow. We have to take it from day to day and never know how she will be.'

'All right.'

It was three days before Mollie was told she could come again, and this time, Claire did not know her at all. She stared blankly, did not touch the Stottie cake, lay with her head turned to the window all the time. She seemed to have tuned out the world.

'I thought I had got through to her,' Mollie said unhappily.

'That's how she is, I'm afraid.'

'There must be *something* we can do!'

Rory regarded the seemingly lifeless figure of his wife. 'It looks,' he said heavily, 'as though there is only one option open. She must go into a nursing home. She needs professional help. I have done all I can and I'm not getting anywhere. I don't want to send her to strangers but what else can I do?'

'When?' Mollie asked.

'Probably next week.' Rory smiled at her warmly. 'But come back again as often as you can until then. I know it's probably a waste of time but I want Claire to have every chance.' He paused. 'As a matter of fact – I've been invited to watch the Grand Prix with some friends. They have a flat overlooking the course. I would feel so much better if you stayed with her in my absence. Nurse Defarge will be here, but –' A shrug.

'I'll be here,' promised Mollie.

He pressed her hand. 'You are very kind.'

Claire was in her usual place when Mollie arrived next morning. She was carrying a big, floppy tapestry bag. 'My embroidery,' she explained. 'I can talk and sew at the same time . . .'

She looked towards Claire. 'How is she today?'

'In one of her remote states. She also sleeps a great deal. The doctor says it's a means of escape. When you sleep, you don't have to think.'

'She does look as though she has gone beyond our reach.'

'I think she has, finally,' Rory said sadly. 'Just sit with her, talk to her. Nurse Defarge will see to the rest.'

He bent over Claire, brushed her forehead with his lips. 'Don't worry, darling. I will see that good care is taken of you.'

Mollie would have sworn his eyes were wet. I misjudged him, she thought guiltily, as she took out the chair cover she was busy on. I cannot fault his care of her. She lacks for nothing except the will to live. Well, he'll *have* to tell her mother now, she thought.

It was when Nurse Defarge came to give Claire her pills, which she took every four hours, that Mollie noticed that the nurse looked pale, that her eyes seemed to have difficulty in focusing.

'Are you all right?' Mollie asked.

'A migraine . . . I suffer from them.'

'Oh, you poor thing . . . Why don't you go and lie down. You can't function with a migraine and Claire needs no looking after. Here, I'll see she takes her pills. You go and get into bed . . .'

'If you are sure . . .'

'I'm positive. I'm an old hand around sick people. Go on, get yourself to bed.'

'Thank you, Madame.' Nurse Defarge was obviously dying to lie down in a darkened room, and lost no time in doing so.

'Right . . . now, a glass of water.' Mollie poured it from the pitcher which stood on the trolley by the wall along with the carton of pills. The name meant nothing to her. It was in French, but she understood the rest of it. Two tablets every four hours.

But when she went back to Claire she was lying with her eyes open. More, they were no longer dull. They were bright with intelligence and recognition.

'Claire!' Mollie was both dumbfounded and delighted.

'Shhhh . . .' Claire lifted a finger to her lips.

'It's all right; she's gone to lie down. Migraine.'

Claire smiled. 'Good. Talk.'

'But I thought –'

Claire chuckled at Mollie's amazement.

'What the hell is going on here?' Mollie demanded in a vibrant hiss. 'Here – before I forget you're supposed to take these pills.'

'No!' The word was like being hit by a bullet, making Mollie jump and spill water. 'Bad. Make me sleep. Not able to think. No pills.' Claire dug a hand deep into the squabs of her chair and came up with a wadded pack of tissue. She held it out to Mollie. 'Take . . . throw away.' Mollie peeled back the layers; in the centre were at least a couple of dozen pills.

'Make me confused; tongue not work, hands shake . . . none since you came. Put under tongue, spat out. Need to talk. Tell you.'

Her voice was hoarse, unused; she struggled to form words, like someone learning a foreign language.

'They are keeping you sedated, is that it?' Mollie asked grimly.

'Yes. Want me go nursing home – bad place. Never come out.' Claire licked her lips.

'Would you like a drink?'

'Tea . . . love tea.'

'You shall have as much tea as you like, just let me check on nursie first.'

Nurse Defarge was on her bed, room darkened, in the third bedroom Mollie tried.

'Just came to see if there was anything you needed,' Mollie whispered.

'Nothing – just sleep. It is the only thing . . .'

129

'Then you sleep as long as you like. I'll stay with Lady Ballater. I've just given her her pills.'

'Thank you . . .'

'Right,' Mollie said briskly, shutting the sitting-room door. 'We are safe for an hour or so. Tea coming up.' She found a box of Jackson's Breakfast Blend and used twice the normal quantity. When she poured out the hot liquid it was a dark golden brown. Claire's eyes gleamed as Mollie held the cup to her lips, and she sipped thirstily.

'Could you eat something?'

'Stottie cake?' Claire asked.

'I almost didn't bring any . . .' Mollie produced a thick wedge, heavily buttered, and Claire fell on it greedily. She emptied the first cup and Mollie poured a refill. This time Claire managed to hold the cup herself, though her hands shook uncontrollably. 'Pills take away appetite,' she said. 'More?'

'I only brought the one piece of Stottie cake but there's a lunch tray in the kitchen. Probably for me. Chicken salad, fresh fruit and cheese.'

'Please,' Claire said.

She managed almost all of it, especially the morning-fresh bread thick spread with Normandy butter. 'Good,' she mumbled through a full mouth.

'Right,' Mollie said, pouring herself a cup of tea. 'I'll ask the questions, you give me the answers as best you can.' Claire nodded her agreement. 'What exactly is wrong with you?'

'Not ill.'

'Then why do you look it? Thin as a rake and so terribly weak. Rory told me it was depression.'

'No. Pills – drugs. Make dopey, confused, take away appetite. Pretended to be worse so Rory would go race. Wouldn't go unless he was sure it was safe.' Claire's smile was livid. 'Fooled him.'

'Why? What is going on here, Claire?'

'Rory punishing me. Wants me dead.' Claire stared hard into Mollie's shocked eyes. 'Killing me by kindness.'

'Kindness!'

'Seems to be.'

'But why?' Mollie's expression changed. 'He's punishing you for the miscarriage?'

'Not miscarriage.' Claire's voice was strong suddenly. 'Abortion.'

Mollie's mouth hung open. '*You* had an abortion? He made you?'

'No. My idea.'

Mollie was appalled. 'In God's name why?'

'Rory's child. Could not have Rory's child.' Claire's eyes were glittering in a way that made Mollie shiver. She had never seen such naked hatred in eyes that had never shown anything more than the occasional dislike. 'Not possible suffer nine months' hell.'

'He didn't want it, then?'

'Didn't know about it till it was done.'

'Oh, my God . . .' Mollie was perceiving levels of emotional violence that terrified her.

'More tea . . . helps loosen tongue.' Claire held out her cup. Now Mollie's hand shook as she poured. She felt out of her depth, even more out of her class.

'When was this?' she asked, subdued.

'What month now?'

'May.'

Claire thought. 'January,' she said.

'And he's been feeding you drugs ever since?' Claire nodded. 'Do you know what they are?'

She saw Claire struggling to form the word. 'Tran – tranq –'

'Tranquillizers?' Claire's nod was vigorous. 'But they can be addictive.' Again Claire nodded violently. 'But why? In God's name *why*?'

'Punish.'

'*Punish!*'

'Long story. No time.' Claire's eyes implored. 'Tell Mother. Please, tell Mother.'

131

'Of course I will, but what can she do? Rory is your husband.'

'Mother will know.' A small smile. 'Mother always knows.'

'I'll call her as soon as I get back to the villa.'

'Tell her come soon. *Soon*,' pleaded Claire, becoming agitated. She was also exhausted. It had taken all her strength to communicate in her disjointed way. Her face was very pale and there was a fine film of perspiration on her forehead and above her mouth. But she struggled to make one last plea. 'Tell Mother,' she whispered. 'Come for me. Soon . . .'

'I promise,' Mollie vowed. 'Now you rest. I'll go and check how Sleeping Beauty is doing.'

She was still dreaming. Claire also slept, for a little over two hours. When she awoke she was again thirsty. Mollie made more tea. The pills, Claire explained in her disjointed way, made her dry-mouthed all the time, but for some reason they kept her short of liquids.

'Probably to intensify the action of the drugs on your system,' Mollie said shrewdly. 'Does your nurse know what is going on?'

'Think so. Sleeps with Rory.'

Mollie shivered. 'Who is your doctor?'

'Friend of Rory. Not a good one. Nurse not real nurse.'

'God almighty!' Mollie was horrified. 'I've never heard of anything so hideous in all my life! Where I come from people don't even know about such things!' Anxiously she asked: 'Are you sure you can keep up the pretence until your mother gets here?'

Claire nodded. There was a resolution to her face that told Mollie she was utterly determined to outwit her husband.

'Won't take any more pills. Pretend to be doped.'

'Well, if I call your mother tonight she could conceivably be here tomorrow.'

Claire's face was transfigured by hope. 'Yes, *yes!*' Her smile was the one Mollie remembered; bright and shining and full of love and confidence. 'Knew you would help.' Her hand reached for Mollie's. 'Good friend. Strong. Not fooled by Rory.'

That's what you think, Mollie thought. If your nurse had not had that migraine I would still be under the influence.

'Stopped taking pills after saw you. Only way. Had to tell you. Made up mind.'

Mollie squeezed the claw-like hand. 'I'm not the only strong one around here.' She shook her head. 'I could never have an abortion in the first place, never mind have it entirely on my own.'

'No choice,' Claire said, and her eyes were bleak, turned inward to horrors which Mollie was glad she could not see. She already knew too much for comfort, and there was still Rory to face.

'Never mind,' she comforted. 'We'll get you away from him.'

'Had no hope,' Claire said. 'Had no help. Then you came. Changed things. Changed me.'

'By God it did!' Mollie agreed fervently. 'I got the shock of my life when you looked at me with those eyes of yours and I saw them filled with life. I thought you'd really become a zombie.'

Claire said flatly: 'Almost did.' Her smile was proud. 'Not now.'

'You're a clever girl,' Mollie praised.

'Had to be. Married to Rory.' The hatred filled her eyes and her voice when she said: 'Not for much longer.'

'A complete sentence!' They smiled at each other in delight. Then Mollie checked her watch. Four o'clock. 'I'd better go and check your jailer again.' It was as well she did. The bed was empty, but Mollie could hear the sound of running water. She scuttled back to the sitting-room.

'She's up. You go into your act and I'll clear these things away. I'll tell her I've just given you your pills.' Hastily she took two from the bottle, shoved them in the pocket of her linen skirt, left the water-filled glass in plain sight.

When Nurse Defarge came back, Mollie was in the kitchen

rattling dishes, having cleared away the evidence, and Claire was lying with her eyes closed, ostensibly out for the count.

'Better now?' Mollie asked brightly.

'Yes, thank you. I am grateful, Madame.'

'No trouble. Claire has been asleep most of the time. I gave her two pills at four o'clock. Was that right?'

'Quite right.' Nurse Defarge checked her patient's pulse, frowned.

'She was a little restless,' Mollie lied glibly. 'Didn't want her pills.'

Nurse Defarge nodded, satisfied. 'That is often the way.'

Mollie threw herself into her role. 'Poor Claire. It breaks my heart to see her so – lifeless. It's like talking to a china doll. And she was such a lively, happy girl . . .' She picked up her capacious bag. 'Tell Lord Ballater I will ring him tomorrow.'

'Of course, Madame, and thank you again for being so kind.' She was much more affable now. Decided she can trust me, Mollie thought derisively.

She bent over Claire. 'I'll be back, all being well,' she said softly, and she pressed Claire's shoulder in a way that said: Hang on.

She thought over what Claire had told her, during the drive back to Cap-Ferrat. It was all so fantastic she still could not quite accept it. Why would Claire wish to abort her husband's child? Why was he so obsessed with punishing her? What terrible things had been happening during all the months Mollie had been away? There was no doubt that Claire's feelings for Rory had undergone a hundred and eighty degree reversal. There had been no mistaking the hatred that had glittered in those sunken eyes; it had also curled the edges of her voice, as a naked flame will curl paper. Last time I saw her she thought the sun shone out of his aspect, Mollie thought. I saw how it hurt when she discovered he had lied to her. She hated what he had done but she was – not then anyway – capable of driving straight on northwards, by-passing Paris for Calais and a ferry home.

Since then, something had gone terribly wrong; something so awful that it had turned the bright, shining flame of her love into ashes and dust in the mouth.

It was the abortion that threw Mollie. She would not have believed Claire capable of aborting the child of a husband she had worshipped. What would drive a woman like Claire to do such a terrible thing? Or should that be who? Mollie asked herself.

She told Clive everything, including her own feelings. 'I don't understand it,' she told him, utterly baffled. 'Claire is no monster. She always struck me as a warm, loving person and I know she loved children. She told me reams about her twin nephews and how her brother and his wife were hoping for a girl and she was to be godmother. What on earth has happened to change her?'

'Rory Ballater?' asked Clive.

Mollie had given him the pills so that he could have them analysed. She also asked him to investigate the location of homes for the mentally sick. 'I don't think it can be too far away. It has to be within easy access because if he took her on a long journey, that would entail special preparations and I've got a feeling that he doesn't want too many people to know.'

'And take up too much time,' Clive agreed. 'He has to get Claire spirited away and into electroshock treatment so that when her mother does see her there is no possibility of Claire blowing the gaff.'

'Well, I'm going to call her right now . . . the sooner she gets here the better. Claire seems to think she will know exactly what to do. I hope to God she does.'

Margot Drummond was very glad to hear from Mollie so soon, and when Mollie said bluntly, 'It's not good news, I'm afraid,' she said merely, in a calm, controlled voice: 'Tell it all to me, please, no matter how bad.'

Mollie gave it to her straight, and she was full of admiration at the way the calm voice became brisk and businesslike. 'I will leave tomorrow morning. I should be with you some time in the early afternoon. Give me your telephone number so that I can ring you back with details of my flight. I cannot leave tonight because my husband would find it strange and I do not wish him to know anything at this stage. I will ring you back within the hour.'

Mollie was waiting when Lady Margot walked through into the arrivals lounge at Nice Airport, and she recognized Claire's mother at once. Claire was her image. Only the hair was different; well-polished pewter instead of red, but the large violet eyes were the same, as was the heart-shaped, fine-boned face. She was of middle height but gave the impression of being much taller because of her carriage. She was simply but superbly elegant in a trim navy silk suit – perfect for travelling – and carried only one small bag. Mollie recognized her instantly as a lady to be reckoned with; saw why Claire had told her confidently, 'Mother will know.'

'Lady Margot?'

'Mrs Hoare-Brown?'

'Mollie to my friends.'

Margot Drummond's handshake was firm. 'I cannot tell you how grateful I am to you for alerting me. I had been of the opinion that all was not well for some time. Have you any further news?'

'I called your son-in-law this morning. Claire is not up to receiving visitors today. No point, he said. She has retreated into one of her silences.'

'Good girl,' Lady Margot said with brisk finality. 'It will be easier to keep up the pretence that way.'

'What do you intend to do?' Mollie asked, as she turned the car on to the Grand Corniche.

'Take Claire away. It must be done fast; no hesitation. Rory has a devious mind but men like him are often caught wrong-footed by a straight-forward frontal attack. I have a plan. I worked it all out last night. My youngest son, Fergus, is at present in Gibraltar on route to Portsmouth after a round the world voyage. I spoke to him last night. He has been granted special leave. He will arrive here this evening.'

'How did you manage that?' Mollie asked, impressed.

'I pulled every string I could find. I have a cousin who is rather high up at the Admiralty.'

'Ah . . .' Mollie said. 'The famous Old Boy network.' All it takes is a quiet word, Mollie thought, but it has to be in the right ear. More and more she was coming to see Margot Drummond through her daughter's eyes.

'I have also arranged for a private plane to be standing by, and for a private ambulance to take Claire to it, once we have her safe. I also happen to know the British Consul here . . .'

Mollie had to laugh. 'And I wondered how on earth you were going to pull it off,' she said resignedly.

'I do not wish to create an avalanche. If I know Rory, he will be of like mind. Appearances are all important to him. That is what I intend to capitalize on. It is therefore vital that you somehow get to see Claire tomorrow, and that you tell her to be ready. If I surprise her it might – upset her equilibrium.'

'Hmmm. I don't think we can count on another tête-à-tête. We were damned lucky to have the one that turned up yesterday.' Mollie chewed on her lip. 'I could perhaps slip her a note?'

'No. Too dangerous. It has to be done in a way that will arouse no suspicion.' She looked directly at Mollie. 'There is a way, but it will be tricky.'

'I'm all ears.'

Mollie rang Rory later that evening, and was told she would be welcome to see Claire.

'Can we make it tomorrow morning?' Mollie asked. 'I have the hairdresser at two.'

'That will be fine. About eleven?'

'See you then.'

'All set,' she reported back to Clive and, by phone, to Lady Margot.

When Rory let her in next morning she was loaded down

with a sheaf of magazines, a large bunch of flowers and a big box of pralines – Claire had a weakness for them, and Mollie had had Fauchon send her down a kilo.

Claire was lying in her usual place, eyes closed, but as Mollie bent over her one eye opened; it was alert, focused, bright with lucidity and intelligence. As Mollie stared into it it closed in a wink.

'Brought a present for a good girl,' Mollie said heartily. 'Look, Fauchon's pralines. Remember?' She busied herself opening the exquisitely wrapped box. 'How has she been?' she asked Rory concernedly.

'She has been very withdrawn.'

'Well, perhaps the pralines will have an effect. The Stottie cake did, didn't it? . . . and speaking of that, I'd love a cup of coffee.'

'I'll see to it,' Rory said obligingly, as she had hoped. Quickly, Mollie took a praline from her pocket, unwrapped it and popped it into Claire's mouth saying loudly: 'There now, wrap your taste buds around this . . .' at the same time holding up the wrapper, on which was printed in tiny but clear letters: 'Mother here. Coming 2 p.m. today. Play doggo.' She saw Claire read it rapidly then nod. Mollie screwed up the paper and put it in her pocket, hastily unwrapping another praline and putting its paper into the ashtray then shaking the box to reassemble the contents. Then she unwrapped another one so there were two papers in the ashtray. 'Heaven on the tongue, hell on the hips,' she mumbled to Rory when he came back. She held out the box. 'Help yourself . . .'

Claire seemed to be chewing blissfully. 'See . . . she always had a weakness for them,' Mollie confided.

Rory was obviously not going anywhere for he drew up a chair opposite Mollie's once the coffee was brought. No chance of a conspiratorial confab today, Mollie thought, but at least I've passed on the message.

Claire played her part perfectly. She lay with her eyes closed, seemingly enclosed in that world of her own to which, Rory said, she was now retreating more and more. Liar! Mollie thought virulently, looking at the handsome face, seemingly so concerned. You think you have covered all eventualities, don't you? Got me along as a reliable witness. Good old commonsensical Mollie Hoare-Brown. You can't pull the wool over her eyes. If she says Claire was away with the mixer then she was, all right. An unimpeachable witness to flourish at anyone who expressed doubts. That was why he had allowed her access. You have such an opinion of yourself, don't you? Mollie thought. God's gift. Think you can get away with anything – up to and including murder, and Claire would have to go because she had dared to think and act for herself.

Mollie had often wondered why it was that Claire seemed to have no friends other than those of her husband. Only me, she thought, and that, if I am any judge of character, because I was loaded. Rory Ballater will overlook anything provided that what towers beyond is a mountain of money. But obviously he was not able to overlook the fact that Claire had aborted his child. No, she thought, that would dig at the very heart of him: his overweening masculine pride. God love her, she thought, glancing at Claire's closed, blank face. For her to do such a thing she must have been desperate beyond my imagining. She gulped coffee as though in an attempt to wash away the awful picture that her imagination had painted.

'You'll stay to lunch, won't you?' Rory asked genially.

'Thank you, but I have to be gone by one-thirty. I have the hairdresser at two.'

'Another social occasion?'

'Yes, yet another cocktail party.'

'It's always the same during Grand Prix week.'

They fell to discussing the social season on the Riviera, but Mollie was thinking about what was to happen at two o'clock. That was when rescue, in the shape of Claire's mother and brother, was supposed to arrive, and she had been told to be gone by then.

'You have been an inestimable help and support, but it is best that you play no part in what must be done. My son-in-law is a vindictive man with a long memory. I would not like you to go through the rest of your life looking over your shoulder,' Lady Margot had said.

'Nasty piece of work,' Fergus had agreed. He had dark-red hair like his sister but was a good foot taller. 'If I'd been at home I'd have told Claire a thing or two about him. Sister of a friend of mine killed herself because of Rory Ballater.'

'Nothing was ever proved,' his mother remonstrated.

'Oh, come on, Ma! He'd been seeing Aisla for months, and the post-mortem showed she was pregnant, didn't it? She took that overdose not three days after he had swanned off to Kenya. If that isn't proof I don't know what is. She was absolutely nuts about him and couldn't take it when he dumped her.'

'I take it Claire didn't know this?' Mollie had asked.

'She was at school in Switzerland when it happened.'

'Can't see how she couldn't have known,' argued Fergus. 'The Blairs lived not ten miles away. It was the talk of the Glen.'

'She wouldn't have believed any talk,' Margot Drummond sighed. 'She believed only in Rory. I am afraid he roused impossible expectations in her; she idealized him as some sort of god. In reality he is only too human, and a badly flawed one at that. Claire was too young . . . she was always an idealistic little girl; no man could have fitted the specification she drew up for herself, because it was created out of her dreams.'

'She always seemed to me not only to give of her best but to expect the same from others,' Mollie said tentatively.

Margot Drummond smiled. It was tender with memories. 'Yes . . . Claire was always bringing home stray cats, lame dogs. Other people's hurt hurt her. She thought she could change Rory, because he led her to believe he was willing to try. What has happened is that he has changed her.' A deep sigh. 'Just how much I am almost afraid to find out.'

Mollie had wondered if she ought to explain about the change in Claire's physical appearance but decided not to. The shock would, she reasoned, be more of a help than a hindrance. There would be no need, once Margot Drummond saw her daughter, to pretend other than what she felt.

Now, Mollie turned her gaze to the limp figure on the chaise-longue. All your dreams turned into a hideous nightmare, didn't they? Of a pragmatic, practical turn of mind herself, she had nevertheless realized that there was a spirituality about Claire which endowed her with that radiance which had first struck Mollie at the fourteenth of July ball in Paris. Yet there had been a sadness about her too; as though the first tear had appeared in her shining bubble. Mollie had often watched her gazing at her husband. There had been no denying the adoration she felt; Claire Ballater was a woman deeply and passionately in love with her husband. At the same time, there had been something wistfully disconsolate about her. A sort of: What do we need all this for, Rory? We have each other.

And now you have nothing, Mollie thought with a pang. Not even your child.

Nurse Defarge returned not long after Mollie's arrival. She had evidently been shopping, for she went straight into the kitchen.

'Don't tell me she cooks too?' Mollie joked.

'It isn't worth while hiring domestics. I have to be out a great deal – I have a job to do – and Claire eats so very little. Nurse Defarge is, like all Frenchwomen, a dab hand in the kitchen.'

The lunch she produced for Claire was simple but beautifully prepared. A clear soup, followed by a fluffy omelette. It was uphill going, though. Claire kept turning her head away, clamping her lips.

'Would you like me to try?' Mollie asked practically.

'I am well capable –'

'Let Mrs Hoare-Brown try,' Rory commanded, and it was enough for Nurse Defarge to obey instantly.

'Now then,' Mollie said, tucking the napkin under Claire's chin. 'Let's pretend, shall we? Like this soup being a bowlful of my split pea soup, simmered with best bacon bones, grated carrot and a little onion.' She saw the glimmer of amusement which flickered in Claire's eyes as she opened her mouth.

Nurse Defarge watched in stony silence as Mollie coaxed Claire to empty the soup bowl.

'Now then, what shall we make this omelette into . . . I know; a helping of my pot pie; lovely chunks of beef, simmered until tender as a baby's bum, then put under a suet crust with a handful of juicy lamb's kidneys and creating the most gorgeous gravy you ever tasted.' Claire ate the omelette.

'You are a magician,' Rory praised. 'How do you do it?'

'I had to do this sort of thing to get my Dad to eat hospital food. I won't tell you what he called it. Invalids tend to be fractious: you have to humour them.'

Claire looked meaningfully at Claire's coffee cup. 'Thirsty?' Mollie asked. 'What have you got that's long and cool?' she asked the nurse.

'Madame is not supposed to drink too much —'

'Well I think she's thirsty. She drank all the water I gave her with her pills.'

'Bring my wife a glass of barley water,' Rory said, pleasantly, but again it was an order obeyed with alacrity. Claire drained it. Then she smiled drowsily, lay back and closed her eyes.

'She'll sleep for hours now,' Rory said. 'I haven't seen her eat so much in an age.'

Probably because she never got the chance, Mollie thought. No wonder she is skin and bone. You are starving her of everything she needs.

'I'll gladly come back and do it any time you want,' she offered.

'I wouldn't dream of putting you to so much trouble,' Rory declined, but in such a way as to make it seem genuinely grateful.

You missed your vocation, Mollie told him silently. You are a born actor. The little clock on the marble mantelpiece chimed the hour.

'Oh, my God! Is that the time!' Mollie gazed aghast at her watch. It said 1.35. She held it to her ear. It had stopped. 'Damn . . . the battery must have gone dead. I'm going to be late for my hairdressing appointment . . .' Bloody hell, she thought in dismay. Now I've gone and done it. She made a scramble for her bag. But she was too late. The door bell rang. Buggered! thought Mollie.

Nurse Defarge went to the door. Rory had risen to his feet: as alert and watchful as a pointing setter. Mollie had a sudden sense of danger. Obviously, the Ballaters had few visitors; an unexpected one sounded his alarm. Still watching him, Mollie saw his face change as she heard a voice, high, clear, pleasant yet utterly commanding, say: 'No, do not announce me. This is intended to be a surprise . . .' Obviously she had got past the doorman. Margot Drummond appeared in the doorway on the last word, Fergus close behind her. Mollie saw Rory's chest swell, as if he had drawn in a furious, calming breath. She became aware of a murderous, terrifying rage, then he was smiling, moving forward, hands outstretched.

'My dear Rory . . .' His mother-in-law accepted his embrace, his Judas kiss on both cheeks. 'I know you do not like surprises, as a rule, but this one offered itself so irresistibly. Fergus's ship is in Gibraltar but the poor boy is not due back in Portsmouth for another month so I thought I would fly down and see him then I ran across Honoria Stewart – you remember Honoria – at the Farqhuars' the other night and she told me she had seen you down here at some cocktail party or other – you do know Honoria, don't you? The Stewarts have that place over by Ardnacarraigh – no? I was sure you did, well, no matter, she knows you –' A dimple appeared. Where the hell did she get that from? Mollie wondered. But it was all in keeping with the performance. Pure dragonfly. Skimming the murky waters of Rory's displeasure and giving an artless display of gurgling charm. 'But then, doesn't everyone? Anyway, as I was in the vicinity, so to speak, I thought what better than to drop in here and see how you both are. I haven't heard from Claire in an age . . . I suppose the ceaseless round of gaiety in which you two engage leaves no time for letter writing.' A reproachful yet painful flick of disapproval stung her final: 'But we are on the telephone, you know . . . ' Her glance fell on Mollie, standing just behind and to one side. 'Oh, I didn't realize you had a visitor . . .' Margot Drummond moved forward. 'How do you do. I'm Margot Drummond.'

'Mollie Hoare-Brown.'

'Claire's good friend? Oh, this is fortuitous! She has told me so much about you. I am so glad to meet you at last. This is my youngest son, Fergus.'

He had nodded affably at Rory, now he shook Mollie's hand as though he had not discussed strategy with her the night before. 'Mrs Hoare-Brown.'

'It has been so long since we heard from you,' Margot Drummond was chiding. 'I know the Riviera is the flesh-pot *par excellence* but I still think that even a postcard would not have gone amiss. Claire is usually so regular with her letters . . .' She was smiling in her most light-heartedly charming way, at the same time stripping off her fine-as-silk leather gloves. 'Now, then, where is Claire? I am absolutely dying to see her.' She looked round and caught sight of the chaise-longue at the far end of the room, in its usual place by the windows. Mollie saw her smile fix, a frown mar the smoothness of her brow. The afternoon sun was casting a nimbus of light around a head of instantly recognizable red hair.

'Claire . . . ?' Just the right amount of puzzled doubt, then she was moving swiftly down the room before Rory could stop her. 'Darling . . . ?'

'She hasn't been well – ' Rory said swiftly, rapidly follow-ing, but not fast enough to prevent his mother-in-law from bending over the still figure.

'Claire – Claire!' She bent closer, and when she straightened her face had changed for the worse. The look she threw at Rory had Mollie flinching.

'What is the meaning of this? Why is Claire in this semi-conscious state? How long has she been like this? What is wrong with her? Is she being attended by a doctor? If so, what is the nature of her illness?'

The questions hit Rory like a hail of bullets, and each one scored a bullseye. 'She didn't want you to worry – ' he began placatingly.

'Not to worry! I do not hear from my daughter for weeks on end and when I do see her I find her comatose and obviously very seriously ill. Why have you not informed me of this appalling state of affairs?'

Mollie watched this awesome display of total command with rapt fascination. Now I see how Margaret Thatcher terrorizes her cabinet, she thought. No wonder Tory ladies have the reputation they deserve.

Margot Drummond flung out a dramatic hand, gesturing to her daughter in a manner worthy of Bette Davis. 'My daughter is *ill!* It is obvious that she has been ill for some considerable time yet you have not seen fit to inform me, her own mother, of this deplorable state of affairs. I had thought to make a surprise visit, Rory – I had not expected to be the one to receive a very considerable shock.'

'A doctor is treating her,' Rory mumbled defensively.

'Then kindly have him brought to me. I wish to know what kind of treatment he is giving her.'

Rory threw a hunted glance at Nurse Defarge, who had positioned herself by the door as though for a quick exit.

'Nurse,' Margot Drummond called imperiously. 'Perhaps you will kindly inform me of the nature of my daughter's illness?'

'Milady Ballater has been suffering from depression.'

'Brought on by what combination of events?'

'She had a miscarriage.'

'A miscarriage!' Rory went first red and then white. He reminded Mollie of nothing so much as a recalcitrant school-boy being carpeted by his Head for breaking a window in the dorm. With icy quiet she went on: 'Why was I not informed of this either?'

Rory squirmed. 'I told you . . . Claire did not feel you should be worried. She thought that you had enough to cope with –'

'Since when have I not been able to cope with anything anybody cared to throw at me?'

'She wanted to spare you –'

'Spare me!' Margot Drummond drew in a lungful of quivering breath. 'What I am being spared of here is the truth! *What has been going on here?*'

She turned to her son. 'Fergus, ring the Consulate. Ask Robert Fellowes to send along the best doctor he can find – immediately.'

'Now look here –' blustered Rory.

'I *am* looking. And I am dismayed. I am shocked.' The voice was quiet but it had Rory leaking blood. 'I am appalled, that you should allow my daughter to sink so low and not have the common courtesy or decency to inform her family. This is not what I regard as the care and attention of a loving husband. She does not know me, she does not respond to me! Look at her!'

Rory did so. Mollie slid her eyes to the floor, clasped her hands to keep from shuddering. My God, he does hate her, she thought hysterically. For a moment, there had been a flash of the most malevolent evil. But Margot Drummond kept up the assault and Mollie suddenly saw how right it was. What a strategist! she thought admiringly. She is not giving him time to bring his own guns to bear.

Margot Drummond turned hers in Mollie's direction. 'What can you tell me about this?' she asked. It was a command.

'Claire has been like this since I first saw her – what?' She turned to Rory. 'Six days ago now? She did recognize me but most of the time she seems to retreat beyond anybody's reach.'

'And what attempts are you making to bring her back?' Margot Drummond demanded icily of her son-in-law.

'I have done and am doing all I can.'

'To do what? It is obvious that my daughter belongs in a hospital. Why is she not in one now?'

'I don't trust French hospitals,' Rory said sullenly.

'There is an American hospital in Nice, is there not? Why did you not trust it? Really, Rory, I cannot understand how you have allowed this appalling situation to get so far, my daughter to sink so low.'

'Doctor on his way,' Fergus reported, coming back from the telephone.

'Good.'

'Now hang on a minute –' Rory tried to assert his authority.

'My daughter appears to me to be hanging on to life,' Margot Drummond blazed.

'You are exaggerating . . .'

'I do not think so. This – this rag doll is not my daughter and well you know it!' Again she bent over Claire, laid a hand on her brow, raised an eyelid. Then she whirled on Rory again. 'What have you been giving her?'

'Only pills the doctor gave me.'

'Let me see them please.' Lady Drummond held out a hand in the manner of a consultant surgeon expecting the proper instrument to be slammed into it. It was Fergus who picked up the bottle of tranquillizers, set it on his mother's flat palm. The fingers closed round it, read the label. 'What are these?' she demanded of Nurse Defarge.

The nurse jerked as though touched by a whip. 'Tranquillizers.' Her voice was a mutter.

'Tranquillizers . . . I see . . . From the looks of it, massive doses. You are aware they can be addictive? How long has this been going on?'

Rory did not answer, neither did the nurse. 'It's five months now, isn't it?' Mollie asked him helpfully. 'I'm sure that's what you said . . .'

'Five months!' Margot Drummond advanced on her son-in-law. 'I am taking my daughter out of here.'

'You have no right –'

'Right!'

'Claire is *my* wife; *my* responsibility, not yours. It is precisely because I knew you would take over that I did not send for you. Claire is a Ballater now, not a Drummond. *I* will say where she goes and what is done.'

'What has been done here is callous neglect! You have forfeited your rights, Lord Ballater. You have deliberately kept your wife's parents in total ignorance of their daughter's mental and physical collapse, and in my opinion, through deliberate malice aforethought. I warn you; do not take on the Drummonds. I think you know that we wield considerable influence where it matters – especially to you. I am taking my daughter out of here and it will be in your best interests *not* to stop me.'

Standing by watching Margot Ballater raining verbal blows on Rory Ballater was an education, Mollie thought. No wonder we once ruled half the world, because almost every one of the men who did so had a wife like Margot Drummond behind him.

The doorbell rang. 'That will be the doctor,' Fergus said, making smartly for the front door.

He was not alone. 'Sir Robert . . .' Margot Drummond said gratefully to the British Consul.

'This is Dr McLellan.'

'A fellow Scot! Thank you so much for coming so promptly. It's my daughter . . .' Lady Drummond led the doctor over to Claire.

Mollie did not know whom to watch. Rory, fists clenched, seeming to sway with the seething boil of the rage he was struggling to contain. A vein stood out on one smooth temple, and his mouth was working. Why doesn't he stop her? Mollie wondered and then saw why. Rory Ballater was afraid. Like all bullies, he was a coward. No wonder Claire had wanted her mother. Rory Ballater was afraid of Margot Drummond. Nurse Defarge was trying to blend in with the walls: Fergus leaned against the door to the kitchen, arms folded, seemingly no more than an interested onlooker, yet Mollie saw that his eyes never left his brother-in-law; that his body was poised, ready for swift action. Sir Robert Fellowes stood politely yet alertly by. Lady Drummond and the doctor conferred in low voices. Mollie saw the bottle handed over. Then the doctor straightened.

'Your daughter must be removed to hospital at once. Certain tests must be made. She is dehydrated and I am concerned about liver damage. I have a car downstairs . . .'

Is there *anything* she has forgotten? Mollie marvelled.

'Now look here,' Rory said frantically.

Margot Drummond ignored him. 'Fergus! Carry your sister down to Dr McLellan's car.'

Fergus sprang away from the wall to lift his sister as if she was an empty bag. That she actually did feel like one was evident from the look he threw his brother-in-law. It bored a hole between his eyes.

'You have no right –' Rory tried again.

'Do not talk to me of rights,' Margot Drummond told him, soft with menace. 'Yours have been forfeited by your callous disregard of my daughter's illness. You have not heard the last of this, but be assured that your relationship to this family is terminated as of now! What you have done is unforgivable. I was prepared to make every allowance in spite of the misgivings I had about your marriage to my daughter; that you should stand by and allow her to sink into a state of living death calls for allowances of a size and quantity beyond even my resources! Now stand aside. I do not wish to spend a moment longer in your presence than is necessary.'

149

That made Mollie look at her watch. She was utterly confounded to see that less than five minutes had passed. As long as he does not realize, she thought; that the doctor, the Consul and the car had been round the corner, near a public telephone. That a pre-arranged signal of three long rings had alerted them. That this whole thing was a deliberately created whirlwind designed to give him no time to think. One punch after another had kept him off balance. Now, they had to get away before the effect wore off.

'May I come with you?' Mollie asked hastily, feeling the need to explain why she had not been long gone.

'Of course. I am glad that Claire had one friend who cared enough to be concerned for her.'

Lady Drummond followed her son, who had disappeared with his delicate burden, along with the doctor and the Consul. Mollie brought up the rear. She did not say goodbye. She left Rory Ballater standing in the middle of the floor, Nurse Defarge in a similar state of shock, and the debris of an emotional earthquake. Not willing to disturb the precarious silence, she closed the door very quietly behind her.

Part Two

JAKE

'Love is, sooner or later, the beginning of all suffering'
WOLF DEITRICH VON RAITENAU,
17th-century Archbishop and Regent of Salzburg

CHAPTER SIX

'What do you think?' Mollie asked. 'Should we tell him to go and do the necessary?'

Claire pursed her lips. 'The salary he is offering is a great deal more than a successful commission salesman earns – and we get our own sizeable commission.'

'But three! Come on, Claire. The man has got to be an eighties version of Jack the Ripper.'

'Isn't that how the City regards him? The *Financial Times* called him *the* corporate raider.'

Mollie scowled down at the open file in front of her. 'His millions have obviously gone to his head. What is it with the mega-rich? They think their money will buy them anything.'

'He is buying the best there is.'

'Which is what we sent him. The cream of our particular crop. What more does he want?'

'Me?' asked Claire.

Mollie frowned. 'Very funny . . . no, seriously, Claire. There isn't anybody else.'

'Yes there is,' Claire said calmly. 'Like I said – me.'

Mollie eyed her askance, then her expression changed to one of alarm. 'You're not serious!'

'Yes I am.'

'He'd eat you for breakfast!'

'I'd give him indigestion. It's time I went back into the world again, Mollie. I've vegetated long enough.'

'The doctor told you – one whole year – '

'Which is on its last legs . . . I'm ready, Mollie. Good and ready.'

'That is only your opinion.'

'To which I am fully entitled,' Claire said gently.

Mollie shuffled uncomfortably. 'Look, you hit rock bottom, and nobody is happier than I am to see how marvellously you've managed to climb out of the pit. But standing on your own two feet is one thing. Kneeling before some American tyro who wants what you, in my honest opinion, are not yet up to giving him is quite another. This is a very demanding job. He wants your single-minded devotion to him and his interests.' Pause. 'I would have thought you had had more than enough of that kind of slavery.'

'I have. This will not be *emotional* slavery.'

'No, more like penal servitude. I vote we tell him to go look elsewhere.'

'I disagree,' Claire answered with a flat calm that clearly showed the rocks of her stubbornness just beneath the surface.

'Look, he has gone through our three best girls like a knife through butter! So perhaps Jennifer Carberry and Diana Forbes were a little too young; Shuna Meredith isn't. She's handled the most nit-pickety *nouveaux riches* and brought them right into line but even she balked at this Jake Burns. You remember what she said? The man is a slave-driver. He wants a house – she shows him a dozen from the very top of the range, all exactly as specification, and what is his reaction? 'Not quite right.' He hands her a list of people he wants to meet which include those you have to be vaccinated to see and then gets surprised – no, not surprised, downright shirty – when she reports difficulties. The man expects to be given entrée to 10 Downing Street and Buckingham Palace and all because he is who he is. And just who is he anyway?'

'A very, very rich American entrepreneur. *Forbes* has him in its top one hundred.'

'I've got him on a list of my own,' Mollie snapped darkly. 'You are out of your tiny if you think I'm letting you into his lion's den.'

'That's all in the past. I'm over it now, ready to start again.'

'At the top? That isn't the place to start.'

'Why not? I fit the specification. Listen – '

'I know it by heart.'

Claire paid no attention. ' "Impeccable conversational skills mandatory, plus the necessary educational background to enable second-nature handling of upper echelon situations. Languages essential, particularly French. Accomplished socially. No ties. Able and willing to travel, often at a moment's notice. Capable of acting as hostess and holding own in any social situation. Well read, well bred, well connected. Age limit 35", that gives me ten years, "knowledge of good food, wine and restaurants", and haven't I a whole store of that. "Must be more than presentable", I think I can still say that I am, "but able to live out of a suitcase", haven't I just. "Dress allowance provided. Hours – as and when needed." '

'Exactly,' Mollie capped. 'Which means twenty-four hours a day if need be. You aren't up to that and you know it. Not yet. It's only seven months, after all.'

'Since I came to work for you. For three months before that I wasted time at home doing nothing – '

'And for the six months before that you were being treated for a nervous breakdown! All right, so you have come on, and a long way from the wraith you were, but Jake Burns does not lie in your direction. Maybe, in another six months . . .' She's got guts, Mollie thought, and she really has pulled herself up in handfuls, but she is still stuck together with spit. One clash with Jake Burns and it will be pick-up-the-pieces time all over again.

'I won't know if I can handle him until I try,' Claire was arguing. 'This is a job, Mollie. All the man wants is a social secretary.'

'With the looks of Catherine Deneuve and the social clout of the Princess of Wales!'

'He's willing to pay handsomely for someone who can put him in touch with people he would not otherwise ever get to know.'

'You will be expected to entertain, act as his hostess. That will mean late nights. You've seen the list of places he wants entrée to. With that schedule you will need eight hours every night and ten at weekends.' Mollie leaned forward. 'Look, if you want an assignment, what about Sir George Benham? Three days a week and no strain: just someone to help him through the three days he spends as Consultant Emeritus to his merchant bank.'

'That is just what I don't want. That wouldn't offer me any kind of challenge. I would be exchanging one featherbed for another. I have to know I'm not going to fall apart at the first signs of strain, and the only way I can do it is by taking it on. I can't go around the rest of my life with you and Mother on either side of me like seeing-eye dogs.'

'Have you told your mother?'

'I mentioned it.'

As Margot Drummond had mentioned it to Mollie, the last time she and Clive had spent a weekend at Castle Drummond.

'She's becoming restless. But I regard it as a good sign. She's flexing her muscles, so she must feel they've got their strength back.'

'You don't think it's too soon?'

'We must give Claire credit for knowing whether or not she is ready.' Margot Drummond smiled. 'I always say that the hardest part of having children is knowing when it's time to let go.'

Mollie grinned. 'Mollie by name, Mollie-coddle by nature?'

'If you had not been there to "mother" Claire I would not have seen her go off to London with you. She needed you then, and you were there.' Thoughtfully: 'I think she has finally arrived at that stage on her journey back when she has reached a very important crossroads. Either she continues on the road to find herself on her own, or she goes along with us, always hovering to make sure she doesn't trip or encounter a waiting mugger. I too, want to protect her; she has suffered so much, lost so much. But only she knows what she needs to find in order to become, once again, the whole, rounded Claire Drummond.' Her smile was proud. 'And she has come so far already, hasn't she?'

True, Mollie thought now, looking at the determined face.

They had expected, once they got Claire away, safely into the private nursing home situated on the banks of a loch tucked away in a fold of the Cairngorms, that it would only be a matter of time before her physical deterioration was made good by careful nursing. What they had not expected was that once beyond Rory Ballater's reach, she would suffer a complete nervous collapse.

'Why?' Mollie had asked, stunned. 'Why? She fought as hard as anyone.'

'That was what kept her going,' Claire's doctor said. 'The struggle. Now that it's over, so is her resistance.'

'But this – this silence and withdrawal. This is not the pretence I recognized when I visited her. This is real.'

'It's the only way she can deal with her guilt.'

'Guilt!'

'At her failure. To be the wife her husband wanted, not to have realized that she never was that kind of woman. What he wanted her to be and what she knew she was were at odds with each other. She narrowed her focus so that she saw only him, as he wanted, and then could not square that with her desire to be herself. She is tormented by the guilt of not being the woman – the kind of woman – her husband would have loved, as she loved him. Beautiful, obedient, ever loyal, unquestioningly trusting. I think she suffered mental and physical agonies in her struggle to conform – that her endurance, her unfailing struggle to justify her love, became too much for her. When she knew that her husband was deliberately trying to destroy her spirit she had something on which to concentrate that obliterated all other considerations: her stubborn refusal to allow him to destroy her. Now that struggle is over, she is once more confronted by those unresolved conflicts, the unanswered questions.

Why had she failed? Where had she gone wrong? Why had she ever loved him in the first place? I think she saw him as some kind of imaginary hero; someone who had been badly wronged, someone she could put right, and she was young enough and idealistic enough to be convinced that she could do it. When she failed, she began to question her own competence. The truth, of course, is that her husband made demands she found impossible to meet, but her explanation of this is that *she* was the one at fault. Hence the guilt of failure.'

'Oh, my poor Claire,' Mollie said with an ache in her voice.

Lady Margot, who had been sitting by quietly, now asked: 'What, then, is to be done?'

'An act of exorcism, if you like. She must be brought to see that the fallibility was not only hers; that she was expecting too much not only of her husband but of herself. We must bridge the gap between myth and reality; make her see that the criticisms she could not help but make, of a man she thought would never give her cause even to make them, were valid; that all that has happened was *not* her fault. That given the type of woman she is and the kind of man he is, the marriage never could have worked. She must be helped through what is, after all, a period of mourning for a marriage that died.'

It took months of patient therapy and the unfailing support of family and friends. Mollie went up to Scotland as often as she could, and gradually, as time went on, she saw the blurred outline that was Claire Drummond reappearing, as the carapace of ice in which she had protected herself melted. The withdrawn remoteness tentatively drew nearer to the life from which she had fled in self-lacerating fear and hatred; she began to read the books and magazines they brought, to play Scrabble again, to watch television. To eat. There was no more of the silent figure staring out of the window seeing nothing but her own failure. She began to gain weight and the skeletal frame slowly rounded out. But the hollows beneath the high cheekbones were to remain, as was the wariness in the eyes. They did not laugh any more, or light up with eagerness or joy. Even when the doctors pronounced her well enough to go home, Mollie knew that the woman who had survived the holocaust of her marriage was no longer the girl she had first met. She was older, wiser, and worst of all, so much sadder.

After the nursing home she spent three months convalescing at Castle Drummond, though there had been initial reluctance on her part to go there. Too near to Ballater House, her mother said wisely, and made it plain that Rory had not set foot in Scotland since Claire's flight. The divorce papers had been served, originally on the grounds of Intolerable Conduct, which, under Scots Law, meant that the defender in the suit had behaved in such a way that' the pursuer could not reasonably be expected to live with him. But then Rory fell into another pit of his own digging. Fergus, having seen what the Riviera had to offer, had gone back there with a group of friends on a further weekend leave, his ship being required to stay in Gibraltar longer than had been anticipated. They had done the rounds of the fleshpots, and it was when they were in Cannes for the film festival that Fergus had spotted Rory asking for his key at the desk of the Carlton Hotel. Once Rory had disappeared into the lift, he had gone across to the desk to enquire if Lord Ballater was a guest. Yes, he was told, Lord and Lady Ballater were occupying a suite for the duration of the film festival.

My God, the man has to be off his rocker, Fergus thought, as he hastened to a telephone to call his mother. Either that or doped to the gills. *How can he be so stupid?* The Drummond lawyers had at once instituted enquiries and subsequently the grounds were changed to adultery.

They were astounded when Rory, who had entered a defence against the Intolerable Conduct charge, offered none to the accusation of adultery.

'What else?' Lady Margot had asked wisely. 'Intolerable Conduct is something he would regard as the blackest stain on his character while adultery is entirely in keeping with it. He is Rory Ballater, after all. What matters is that the suit will not be defended. Claire will be free much quicker than we thought, and since Rory is offering no defence, it means, under the new Divorce Laws, that there is no need for the thing to go to court. It can all be done by way of sworn statements.'

She went with Claire to Edinburgh, where Claire gave her statement or affidavit to a Notary Public. He then prepared a minute which was lodged with the Court of Session. The judge was obviously satisfied because the decree was granted, in Claire's favour, in a very short time.

'You see?' Lady Margot asked at the celebratory dinner that night. 'No washing of dirty linen in public. Rory would have hated that.'

Claire's father knew of the divorce, but that was all. He never once said 'I told you so' to his daughter. He merely patted her hand and said feebly, 'I am happy to have you home again, daughter.' He was now a very sick man, on oxygen most of the time, and bed-ridden. True to his code, when he died, about six weeks after Claire had gone home, they found that he had left his estate in apple pie order. Castle Drummond was not entailed; he left it to his wife for her lifetime along with a hefty settlement; from her it would go to his eldest son, Iain.

Hamish, who flew back from Washington with his wife, was left a considerable sum of money and various personal mementoes, as was Fergus. Claire received outright the sum of one hundred thousand pounds, 'to grant her independence'.

The funeral was attended by the entire Glen, because Sir John had been a much respected man. Afterwards, Mollie took Claire down to stay with her father at the big house just outside Morpeth, where George Armstrong, now bluff, hale and hearty, made her welcome, and Mollie cooked up a storm. She also cooked up an idea, which she presented to Claire one morning along with her bacon and eggs.

'I am going to start an upmarket employment agency now that we're based in London. Clive was telling me how difficult it is to find superior secretarial help. I don't mean your average shorthand-typist. I mean well educated girls of good family who know the ins and outs of things your average girl would have no idea how to cope with. I am going to call it the Crème de la Crème. How would you like to help me run it?'

'I know nothing about running an agency,' Claire demurred.

'No, but you know where to get the girls. You've got the "in" I need; acquaintance with *Debrett*, not to mention *Burke's Landed Gentry*. Clive has a lot to do with visiting American high-fliers and they keep asking him where they can find the "right" English girl to steer them through the minefields of English society. I think that between us, we could supply them.'

'You would need offices, equipment, there would be advertising . . .'

'I can do all that. I know how to run a business; I kept Dad's books for years. But I don't have your contacts.'

'It would cost . . .'

'Money is the least of my worries. Dad made me financially independent years ago. What I need is your know-how, where to find all that lovely double cream.'

Claire laughed, but Mollie saw a gleam of interest in her eyes. 'If I came in, it would be as your partner. We invest fifty-fifty.'

'Done!' Mollie agreed with alacrity.

'All right. When do we start?'

'You use your estate agent connections to find us the right offices. Where we set up our stall is important; our clients won't want to use an agency situated in Kennington or Clapham or somewhere out at the back of beyond. It has to be Mayfair, Knightsbridge – the right postal district.'

'Leave it to me,' Claire said.

She found them a suite in New Bond Street, not far from Asprey's. An entrance area where the receptionist/telephonist would sit, with comfortable sofas, a coffee table with the latest magazines, plus a supply of freshly made coffee; a large room big enough for two desks, the requisite filing cabinets, drinks cabinet *et al*; a third, smaller one behind for the secretary they would share. Claire decorated it. Not aggressively modern, but a blend of eighties tech and English country house comfort. 'We have to make it immediately apparent what we are selling.'

'And not cheaply, either.'

Claire consulted a school friend whose husband ran a successful Head Hunting agency for high-fliers, and he offered succinct and helpful advice. Claire then made it her business to see that the right people heard about them, and Clive furnished them with their first customers, both Americans. Then followed a goodly selection of Germans, Italians and other Europeans. Within three months of opening, they had a steady but select clientele. Their girls were strictly temporary, but invariably, the men they worked for asked them to make the post permanent.

'We are losing girls at a rate of knots,' Mollie grumbled, as the latest came to inform them that she was accompanying Mr Lee Chung back to Hong Kong to help him run his varied companies.

'Not to worry,' Claire told her confidently. 'There are lots more where they came from.'

And then, one day, they had a call from a man called Jake Burns, who was in Europe for approximately six months and wanted a social secretary – he had brought his own commercial secretary along with him – to guide him through the unknown waters of English society. It was his commercial secretary who came along to the agency.

'To interview us,' Mollie said indignantly.

Her name was Cora Sue Mennenger and she obviously disapproved of the whole ridiculous scheme. She was short, stout, inviolably prejudiced against all things unAmerican. She had a sniff that expressed disapproval in more ways than *Webster's Dictionary*, and she obviously resented the very idea of 'Mister Burns' wanting some fancy pants English girl to hold his hand while he hobnobbed with Barons and Earls. When she told them what she wanted, she sniffed and said sourly. 'If you can match that paragon of all the virtues then my name isn't Cora Sue Mennenger.'

'Normally, we prefer to interview the client himself,' Mollie countered.

'Mister Burns is a very busy man. He doesn't have time to waste on hiring help. *I* do that.'

'Nevertheless, Mr Burns will want to see our applicants, surely.'

'After me. He told me to see to it and that's what I aim to do. I know the way his mind works. Have done these past twelve years. Knew him even before I worked for him. We come from the same town.'

'And where might that be?' Mollie enquired sweetly.

'Cimarron, Oklahoma.'

'I thought that was a musical,' Mollie wondered innocently. The sniff was graphic. It described, in detail, the despised ignorance of the British concerning all things American.

'Would you like a cup of coffee, Miss Mennenger?' Claire interposed tactfully.

'English coffee? No thank you.'

'That's the West, isn't it?' Mollie asked. 'Indian territory?'

'There's a goodly number.' Proudly: 'I've got Indian blood myself. Most Oklahomans do.'

'Does Mr Burns?'

'No. He's English on his pa's side and Swedish on his ma's. But there's been Burns in Oklahoma more than a hundred years now.'

'Heavens,' marvelled Mollie, in a way that produced another sniff.

'And just exactly what is it that Mr Burns is looking for?' Claire asked.

'A fancy English lady who can introduce him to the right people. He's got a whole slew of letters of introduction. First off he wants to know if they are any good.'

'Is this his first time in England?' Claire asked.

'Yes. We've been in Australia for a year – just come back from there – and we were in Canada for a while and then we spent a time in Hawaii before going Down Under. Now we're here.'

'And what does Mr Burns do?'

This time the sniff was one of pride. 'Makes money.'

'How?'

'Whichever way he gets the chance. He's what you call an entrepreneur.'

Mollie looked across to Claire. 'One of those,' her expression said.

'Like T. Boone Pickens?' Claire asked.

Cora Sue looked surprised. 'You know about Boone? Well, apart from the fact that he's from Texas – right next door you might say – I guess that's as good a comparison as any. They've both got more money than Fort Knox.'

'And what does he intend to do in Europe?' Claire asked.

'Make more money.'

'Ask a silly question . . .' Mollie murmured. 'Why don't you give me a job description, Miss Mennenger. Then we know what we have to look for.'

'I told you. A fancy English lady – and if she's got a handle to her name so much the better – who can steer Mr Burns right on how things are done over here. Knows her way around the top drawer. The best hotels, the best restaurants, oh – and a house. We've got a suite at the Dorchester but Mr Burns wants a house. At least six bedrooms – there'll always be people to stay – plenty of bathrooms, a room he can use as an office plus one for me, double garage, grand dining-room, a modern kitchen, a big room for cocktail parties and such, and all furnished. Cost is whatever it takes.

And it has to be in the right neighbourhood. What you call Mayfair.'

'The English equivalent of the Upper East Side?' Claire asked. Another sniff. 'I guess. Whatever, this girl has to know just the right place.'

'Anything else?' Mollie asked wide-eyed.

This time the sniff almost lifted her out of her chair. 'She has to be good-looking. Well dressed. With one of those fancy English accents. And between twenty-five and thirty-five with no ties. She has to be able to devote her time to Mr Burns and he is liable to take up an awful lot of it. He's the kind of man as works hard and plays hard.'

'And when will Mr Burns be available to see these girls?'

'You call me. I'll arrange it.' And pick the plainest one you can find, Claire thought amusedly. There was no doubt that Cora Sue Mennenger was shooting for bear.

They culled three of their best, sent them along. The first picked was Lady Jennifer Carberry, a ravishingly pretty girl whose family went back to Henry II and who possessed all the other qualities Jake Burns had obligingly listed. She lasted a week.

'I'm sorry, Miss Drummond,' she had said flatly, burning anger at a fast rate, 'but it is just not on. He demands the impossible and that awful secretary of his is always hovering, stick to hand to shove it between your spokes. I am sorry, but I am not Superwoman. I wish to be re-assigned.'

Next in to bat was Diana Forbes, who had once been married to the son of a Duke until he found her playing footsie with one of his grooms. She was sharp, sophisticated, cool as a well-iced Pimms. She came back, icily furious, after two days.

'Impossible man, appalling woman,' was her verdict. 'I have neither the time nor the patience to put up with a professional cowboy and a sexually frustrated spinster.'

Shuna Meredith, at thirty-two the eldest of the three, was last. She was the widow of a Guards colonel killed in the Falklands, and had a son at his first, expensive, prep school.

She was not easily flustered, she was a lovely looking woman, and through her marriage had impeccable connections. She herself was the daughter of a former Archbishop. She stuck it out the longest: a fortnight.

'I'm sorry, Miss Drummond,' she said in her soft, reasonable but decision-made voice. 'I am afraid that what Mr Burns needs is beyond my capabilities. It is not a social secretary so much as a wife that is needed here, except that it would be a true marriage of convenience. Always that of Mr Burns. It is not that he is selfish, you understand. More that he is single-minded. And Miss Mennenger seems to think that it is her job to protect him from the machinations of English women who are willing to go to any lengths to ensnare a naive, unsophisticated American.' Shuna had smiled. 'Whatever else Mr Burns may be – and he is a combination of a great many things – he is neither naive nor unsophisticated. It merely suits him to be thought so. But neither am I, Miss Drummond, the right person for this particular position.'

That was why, now, Claire had entered her own name. What she had heard intrigued her. Jake Burns, she realized, was Challenge with a Capital C. If she could meet it, rise above it, then she could say she was herself again. Not the self she had been: that had been razed to the ground. In its place was a much sturdier edifice: designed to withstand earthquakes; furnished with the bare minimum of illusions, protected by extra sensors and alarms so that the minute a predator crossed the invisible boundary every alarm went off. This self had intensified air-conditioning on all emotional levels, allowing for an even, if somewhat cool, temperature at all times. This self had an entrance lobby guarded by an ever alert and rigorous sentry. This self was as well-protected from emotional attack as it was possible to be. There would be no threat from Jake Burns in that direction. All three candidates had been of more than average attractiveness and desirability; all of them had reported that they might as well have looked like the bearded lady. Diana Forbes had been most informative about what she derided as 'Burns blondes'. 'He has a harem,' she had told them. 'Every one of them a Marilyn Monroe clone. He changes them with his sheets.'

Which had prompted Mollie to observe shrewdly: 'I think it's time we changed her. She's narked because she wasn't offered the chance to slip between them.'

Jake Burns was not looking for a woman, Claire surmised. He wanted the latest in state-of-the-art, high-tech, laser-operated, trouble-free machines. What he needs, she thought, is me. He is the perfect test-bed for the new model Claire Drummond. If I can handle him I can handle anything. She bent all her energies to convincing her partner of that fact.

'This is what I need, Mollie. Good, hard, honest work, and you know that specification fits me like a Jean Muir dress. Let me try it on. If I find that it doesn't really suit me then I'll get rid of it.'

'It's too soon,' Mollie maintained stubbornly. 'Besides which, you are forgetting something of vital importance.'

'Such as?'

'You will be set smack bang in the middle of a world I thought you no longer wanted any part of. He wants to get in with the very people you hated when Rory made you part of their scene.'

'Wrong,' Claire said. 'What Jake Burns wants is someone to steer him past the pilot fish and into harbour; Rory married me for the same reason but in spite of that he never really quite made it. They accepted him because of me and he knew it and hated me – and them – for it. Jake Burns is willing to pay. Strictly business. And if he has to find out that in this country, money is *not* the key that opens all doors, then it is a lesson he must learn. He's had the plutocracy; now he wants the aristocracy. Why shouldn't I avail myself of the fantastic salary he is willing to pay in order to prove my point.'

Mollie stared, feeling a chill at the cold rationality; the sense of things being looked at through a microscope. Well, she thought, when you've been lucky enough to survive a deadly disease you make sure from then on that you don't run the risk of contamination. But she made one last try.

'I thought you were happy, working here with me.'

'I have been. Happy and grateful. You have already given me back a great deal of self-worth, but what I need to fill the last empty space, you can't give me. I need to face and surmount a challenge. To see if I can not only fill the specification but improve on it. I'll not only get him into harbour, I'll get him tied up to the very best berth.' She saw that Mollie's common sense agreed with what was being said, even if her emotions were feeling more than slightly sea-sick. 'The agency is off and running. Our reputation is established. We are what our name implies, and we can easily fill any gap I leave.'

'Where will I find another you?'

'I'll be in the perfect position to look for one – and to tout for business, so to speak. People who have not, as yet, come our way.'

'Your mind is made up, isn't it?' Mollie sighed.

'Absolutely.'

'Well, I can't stop you if you are so determined, but you still have to get round your mother.'

'She won't stop me.'

'She has her own guilts about not stopping you before, and look what happened. And it was her that sprung you from jail, wasn't it?'

'Yes, I knew she would, once she was aware what was going on. My mother always likes to know what's going on. Only that way can she see what has to be done. In this instance, she will see that this is something I have to do.'

Mollie spread her hands in a gesture of *fait accompli*. 'I'll say this for you,' she said, 'you've got guts. Me, I'd not enter the lions' den until I was sure they had all been tranquillized. You're no coward.'

Oh, but I was, Claire thought. I was a coward and a slave. Enslaved by a man I loved beyond all reason but discovered too late I could not trust. A man who was a product of my own imagination. I made Rory Ballater into what I hoped he was. Didn't I tell my own mother on my wedding day that he was a dream come true?

What she had not told her – not told anyone but the kind and patient man who had, day after week after month, helped her to come to terms with herself; to confront her demons, admit her failures, accept that she was not the one to blame; that she had not failed a man whose tendency was to regard any misfortune that befell him as someone else's fault – was how that dream had turned into a terror-filled nightmare.

It had begun shortly after they had once again left Scotland as soon as the shooting season was over. They had not returned to France but had gone to Italy; first to Rome, then north to Florence, ending up in Milan. Once again Rory had taken up with his kind of people; the ones who lived life in the fast lane and used up great quantities of money in doing so. What they did not know, Claire thought, as she observed but did not take part, (which incurred Rory's increasing displeasure), was that they were themselves being used up. She soon realized that Rory was again looking for an 'in'; that he was eager to avail himself of the fast profits to be made. He was controlling the money now. Claire had to ask him for every penny. All they had made during the season was being eaten up as Rory looked desperately for the right connection; yet again, it was Bruno de Souza who offered it.

Rory came in one evening and ordered her to pack. They were leaving for Nice.

'I thought France was out?' Claire had asked.

'Not any more. Bruno says it's quite safe. They have nothing they can use against either of us.'

'This time.'

'Do as you're told,' had been his peremptory reply.

What he did was invest, once again, in the shipments of cocaine which Bruno de Souza imported from Colombia.

Worse, she soon understood that not only was he a dealer, he was a user. His mood swings became more and more unstable under the influence of cocaine. She never knew from day to day, often hour to hour, how he would be. He could go out sunny and smiling, return snarling and vicious. He took to taunting her, revelling in his power over her. And at last, he openly began bringing women back to their flat. Too late she found out that there had always been women, ever since the beginning; that on their honeymoon, on the night of the storm when he could not be found, he had been on the damp sand of the beach not far from the casino, engaged in sex with Vanessa Carlyle. He had laughed contemptuously when he told her that.

'You swallowed it, hook line and sinker . . . I hadn't been talking to Monty Glenalver – he wasn't even there. I'd been fucking Vanessa. She was ripe for it; desperate for it. She couldn't have enough. That Irishman was no good in bed and she's a lady that can't do without it. Nothing she won't do, either.' And he had insisted on telling her, in great detail, what she had done, what they had both done. 'One of the best I ever had, Vanessa, but no use because she's as broke as I am. We both had need of a backer. She hooked up with Johnnie Gallagher while I had the great good fortune to run across you. So, what more natural than we should get together again to celebrate our mutual good fortune?' His laugh was more a drugged giggle. 'And your bad luck.'

He told her in great detail about the women he had had. During weekends at Cowdray Park, other weekends in the country – 'everybody played musical beds except you. Little Miss Prude. Did you know that was what they called you?' Another laugh. 'No, of course not. You were so bloody innocent it wasn't true. I think if I had sat you down and made you watch you would have found some excuse for me. You and your bloody excuses! Do you have any idea how sick and tired I am of those cow eyes of yours looking up at me like some dumb kewpie doll? I thought your innocence was sweet, at first; touching, somehow. Until it began to bore me. Christ, how you have bored me!'

And on, and on and on, her silence infuriating him even further. 'Christ, you make me sick! You and your bloody good breeding. The saintly Drummonds, far too good for the rest of us.'

'That was why you married me, wasn't it? Because I was a Drummond and you hoped some of my respectability might rub off on you?' That brought a backhander which sent her sprawling.

'I've told you before, mind that tongue of yours. The only conversation you make is the kind that's intended to humiliate me. So bloody superior, all your stiff-rumped family, looking down on me because I was the great grandson of a crofter, while you, you were descended from fucking kings.' He savagely mimicked a Texan drawl as he fluttered his eyelashes to squeal: '"Is it true, Lady Ballater, that you are descended from three kings of Britain?" Kings of Britain! Jesus Christ!'

How that had obviously rankled, Claire thought, nursing her aching cheek. She had known he had been resentful of the comment, but that he should have such total recall many months later was proof that no matter how hard he sucked, the thorn was still embedded in his pride.

Which was no doubt why he did his best to humble hers. He brought women back to their flat, sometimes one, sometimes two, once there were three, and he made Claire watch while they engaged in every sexual perversion known to man. But the sight of her, sitting there, looking yet not seeing, only infuriated him more and he screamed at her to get out of his sight.

When, one day, she asked reasonably: 'Why don't you let me go, Rory? You don't want me. You don't even like me. Let me go. We have no marriage. We have nothing. If I make you so unhappy why do you keep me around? Isn't it better that we end it?'

'You will go when I tell you to. Nobody leaves Rory

Ballater. Nobody, do you understand?' He raved on for some time, which was when Claire finally realized just how twisted he was. Bitterness, rage, envy and self-pity had warped his personality to the extent that it was now hopelessly bent out of shape; had been even when she was falling helplessly in love with him. She had sat unmoving, silent. It was liking screaming at a ghost.

'Nobody rejects me!' he was almost gibbering with rage, but Claire knew that it was not his wife he was denouncing. It was his mother, who had abandoned a small boy too young to understand why. That rejection had scarred him for life. His father had rejected his inheritance by squandering it, leaving Rory nothing with which to salvage an already badly damaged pride.

On and on he went, threatening, cursing, accusing, denouncing, and when finally her silence got through to him he took it as an accusation and his hand arced through the air to slash her across the face; once, twice, then again a third time. There was blood trickling from her mouth when she picked herself up from the floor. 'Get out of my sight,' he hissed.

And then, one weekend, David Grant came down. Rory did another of his lightning quick changes, played the uxorious husband, attentive, devoted, tender. But David was no fool; the icy remoteness with which Claire conducted herself made it plain that all was not well. He was kind to her, thoughtful, protective, and she was grateful.

'If ever you need a friend,' he said to her when it was time for him to go back to England, 'remember me.'

'Thank you, David. I will.' And it was true. Hitherto he had been no more than David Grant, Rory's oldest friend; quiet, nothing to look at, shy and reserved and out of his depth in Rory's bottomless waters. Now, as he took her hand, pressed it, kissed her cheek, he said in troubled tones:

'It's these damned people he has taken up with. A rotten lot. Not worth a light. I never could understand that about Rory; how he always equated wealth with moral worth. Get

him away from them if you can, Claire, but if you can't –
then remember me.'

His glance was filled with meaning as he turned and waved
one last time as he got into the car that was waiting for him,
Rory at the wheel.

It was that night that Rory repeated his assertion that
David was in love with her.

'Haven't you noticed him hanging on your every word?
Mooning over you like some lovesick puppy?'

'He has had no encouragement from me.'

'Not good enough for you either? Surely not, he's a Grant.'

'He is also your best friend.'

Rory laughed. 'That's *his* version.'

'Then why do you bother with him? Because he admires
you? Hero-worships you?'

'It suits him – and it suits me.' He came over to where
she was sitting, sat down beside her. 'If you want to have a
little fling, for God's sake pick somebody worth your while.
I wouldn't be at all surprised to find that David is still a
virgin, and after all I have taught you he would be a terrible
disappointment.' He began to play with a curl at the nape
of her neck. 'I wouldn't mind, you know, if you did have an
affair. It would not be natural not to wish to play tit-for-tat.
Have you ever been so inclined?'

'No.'

'Why not?'

'I take my marriage vows seriously.'

Rory laughed. 'More fool you.'

But he kept returning to the subject; more and more he
kept insisting he would not mind if she found 'consolation'
elsewhere. 'Just because I don't want you any more is no
reason to go without. And you have come to need it now,
haven't you? Tell me, how long has it been, now? You must
be ready to burst with frustration.'

And he would kiss and caress her stiffly resisting body,
which would invariably betray her. He still had the power
to press all her switches, and he would rouse her to the brink

of screaming need and then get up and brutally leave her; aching with desire and hollow with the lack of fulfilment.

Then he asked David down again. Claire knew very well what he was after and made up her mind to issue a warning.

'I know, I've seen the change in him. He's on drugs, isn't he? He's acting very strangely.' David sounded perturbed.

'Be careful, David. He's not to be trusted. He's throwing me at you deliberately. He has some fiendish plan in mind. It's best we give him no cause for complaint.'

'Leave him, Claire. Come away with me. I know I can make you happy and would give everything I have for the chance. I've loved you ever since I saw you coming down the aisle to marry Rory but you couldn't see anyone but him. I know you're unhappy. I went back last time wishing I had said something. Leave him, come away with me. He isn't safe any more. These damned people he runs around with are spiritually and morally bankrupt and I can't bear to see him ruin you.'

His spaniel brown eyes had pleaded, but for some reason they had irritated her because she knew Rory was right. David Grant was not the man for her. He had no idea of what Rory was capable of; never would comprehend in his decent, upright, honourable way.

'No, David. I wouldn't do you the disservice of incurring Rory's hatred.'

'I don't give a damn for Rory. All I can think about is you.'

Claire shook her head. 'No. I made my own bed. Now I must lie on it.'

And it was in bed that night that David came to her. She saw at once that he was high; that Rory had finally managed to persuade him to join in the general inhalation of the lines and lines of cocaine, laid out like spills on the glass surface of the coffee table. He was not a big man, being only of middle height and slight build, but he was high on coke and ravenous with sexual deprivation. He came at Claire like a tiger and such was her despair, her sense of hopelessness, that she put up no resistance. She let him take her. It was loveless, joyless and over very quickly. Afterwards he wept. She could not comfort him. She lay on her back in the darkness, feeling used, spent and unutterably weary. Finally, he got up and crept away.

Claire stayed in her room next day, pleading a headache. She did not see David again because next morning, when she got downstairs, he had gone.

That night, Rory came to her bedroom, asked her without preamble if David had run away because she had turned him down. When she denied it he began hitting her. 'You drove him away, didn't you? You sanctimonious, holier than thou bitch! Couldn't even put yourself out for my best friend.' He then proceeded to cross-examine her.

'What did you say to him?'

'Nothing.'

'Liar! I saw the way he looked. You broke him, didn't you, just as you've been trying to break me, you ball-breaking bitch.'

'I did nothing to him. I said nothing to him.'

'Liar!' This was accompanied by a blow. He would not leave it alone. He raged at her, threatened her, until she thought her head would split.

'Tell me what you did to him,' he roared at her, shaking her like a rag doll.

'I did nothing!' she screamed at him. 'It was he who did it to me. He came to my room, high as a kite, and he forced himself on me. Is that what you wanted to know? And I let him! I lay back and let him because I don't care any more. Please, Rory,' she sobbed, 'let me go . . . please . . . I can't take any more. Send me away if that is how you want it to look. Tell everyone it was my fault, but let me go, I beg of you.' She had her face buried in her hands, body heaving with the convulsions of her sobs. It was not until she felt something cold pressing against her fingers that she opened her eyes. He was holding a gun to her head. She heard him cock the hammer.

175

'Now tell me the truth,' he said very softly. 'You seduced him, didn't you? You invited him to your bed, didn't you? You made an assignation with him, didn't you? Tell me the truth or I'll shoot you, do you understand? I will put a bullet through your brain. The truth. You invited him into your bed, didn't you?'

Claire was terrified; her mouth was dry and her heart was beating so hard she thought she would faint. She knew he meant what he said. There was a manic look in his eyes which told her how close he was to the edge. He pressed the gun closer. She felt the cold circle of its steel pressed against her flesh.

'The truth,' he commanded, still very softly. 'David couldn't force himself on anyone if he tried . . . you know it and I know it. There is only one way he could have you: by invitation. Right?'

Claire knew he would believe nothing but what he wanted to hear. What do I care? she thought dully. It would end all this wretchedness. Sudden death would be better than the slow one he is inflicting on me. But something in her would not roll over and die.

'I will not lie to suit you,' she said as firmly as she could, though her voice was wildly out of control and she found it hard to breathe. 'He was high on cocaine and he was – not himself. He forced himself on me. But yes, I let him. I just lay back and let him. Is that what you want me to say?' She felt deathly tired, closed her eyes and waited. But what she felt was the gun taken away. She opened her eyes. He was sitting on the bed. The gun was still in his hand but it was no longer pointed at her.

'Tell me,' he said conversationally, 'what was he like? Was he any good? As good as me? Better than me? What did he do to you?' His voice was calm, interested, but there was a look in his eyes which brought out the gooseflesh all over her body. He is mad, she thought. Dear God, he is stark, staring mad!

'I told you to take a lover, didn't I?' he asked, sounding

pleased with himself. 'Now tell me – tell me everything.'

He cross-examined her at length. She was terrified, shaking, but she answered as best she could. He nodded, smiled. 'Poor David . . . I knew he wouldn't be much between the sheets but I thought, with all that I've taught you, it would be an experience for him.' He got up from the bed, the gun hanging limply from his hand. 'Well,' he said, still conversationally. 'Now we know, don't we?'

He turned and walked out. He even shut the door quietly behind him. Claire ran for the bathroom where she was violently sick. She spent the rest of the night crouched on the tiles, resting her folded arms on the rim of the bath, shivering violently and making plans to escape. She knew now that her husband was insane.

Next day, when she tried to leave her bedroom, she found it locked. He kept her there for twenty-four hours. She had no food, only water from her bathroom. She huddled on her bed and waited. She must have dozed, came awake with a violent start as her door crashed open.

'Well, well,' Rory said in a voice that had her retreating to the far side of the bed. 'If it isn't my faithless wife. My worthless, faithless wife.' Then he sprang. He gripped her by the hair, forced her head back and proceeded to call her every vile name he could think of. She had betrayed him, he said. She had cuckolded him. And with a spineless wimp like David Grant.

'How dare you do this to me? Didn't you realize I was testing you? Proving your love for me? You dare to allow a cretin like David Grant – *David Grant* – access to your body after me! If you had taken a man – a real man – I would not have minded, but no, you had to humiliate me with a spineless creep! You did it deliberately, didn't you? You had to give yourself to somebody beneath my contempt so as to show your contempt for me!'

Claire stared at him, utterly confused and befuddled. Her

dazed mind could not follow his twisted reasoning. 'You told me to be kind to him,' she faltered.

'*I* told you! That's your excuse, is it? "I was only following orders, sir," ' he mimicked savagely. Then in a calm voice: 'Nobody will believe him, you know. Not David Grant, who couldn't say boo to a frightened goose. People will laugh at him – and at me!' His voice rose to a scream. 'People will laugh at *me*, you bitch.' He drew a deep breath. 'Well, I shall have to punish you for that, won't I? *Won't I?*' He let her go, and his hands went to his waist. She saw him unbuckle his belt.

'No, Rory – no!' She scrabbled frantically away from him.

'Yes, Rory, yes!' He caught hold of a wrist, flipped her over on to her stomach, shoved her nightdress up to her waist, revealing her small, rounded buttocks.

'You always had a nice bum,' he said, fondling it. 'Round and juicy, like a peach. Did David like it?' His laugh had her struggling madly, but he had her hands above her head in the grip of one large, powerful hand. 'I'll deal with him later,' he said, 'you first . . .'

He hit her with the belt until she was unconscious; left her lying on the bed, her flesh criss-crossed with weals that were oozing blood. This time she was alone for three days.

Then he came in, and while she tried to crawl across the bed on her stomach, he said: 'There, there . . .' as though soothing a fractious child. 'Rory make it better now . . .' And he proceeded to bathe her cuts with warm water and antiseptic, afterwards applying a soothing salve. Then he exchanged her bloody nightdress for a clean one, laid her tenderly on the day-bed – on her stomach – while he changed the bloodied sheets. Then he placed her back in the bed, a pillow in the small of her back to raise her buttocks from the pressure of the mattress before feeding her a bowl of hot beef bouillon. Finally, he handed her a glass of water and two tablets. 'Here, these will take the pain away.' Terrified, utterly at a loss, not knowing what to do or say, Claire did as she was told.

'You do understand, don't you, that I had to punish you? People who do bad things must be punished.' His smile made her shudder. 'Now you won't ever do anything bad again, will you?' When she did not answer, he repeated, 'Will you?' his voice hardening.

'No,' Claire whispered.

A smile. 'That's a good girl.' He bent to kiss her and she had to force herself not to shrink from his lips. 'Sleep well,' he said sunnily before going out. She heard him turn the key in the lock.

She put the constant nausea which plagued her down to the constant state of terror in which she lived; it was not until, in the bath, soaping herself, that she realized her breasts were tender. Her period must be due. Her body always gave her warning. Then it hit her. Getting out of the bath she ran naked into her bedroom, seized her handbag to take from it her pocket diary, in which she logged her monthly periods. Her mother had advised her to. 'That way, as soon as you miss one, more importantly two, you will know exactly when you became pregnant.' Riffling the pages Claire searched backwards. The last letter P was marked for the 20th October last. They were now in late January.

'Oh, my God . . .' She sank on to her bed, her dripping body soaking it. I'm pregnant, she thought. Dear God, I am pregnant with Rory's child. She knew it had to be his, rather than David's. That little episode had been only three weeks ago. No. This child was the result of Rory's rape back in Scotland. And she had stopped taking the Pill when Rory had stopped sleeping with her. They tended to make her gain weight and she had seen no reason to take drugs she no longer needed. She sat staring at nothing, conscious only of a paralysing shock, which eventually gave way to an even worse sense of fear. He won't believe me, she thought. Not in his present manic state of mind. He will believe it is David's. And then, you know what he will do . . .

She swallowed, found herself wishing it *was* David's, because she knew, instinctively, passionately, ice-cold bloodedly, that the last thing she wanted was Rory Ballater's child. Getting up, she went to get her Hermes 'Kelly' bag. In the safety-box bottom, under the suede lining, she kept what money she had managed to acquire from Rory. Every night, before undressing for bed, he emptied his pockets on to the top of his tallboy; piles of notes and loose change. Claire had taken to filching the occasional note. It had been easier when they shared a bed; when he moved out it had been necessary to get up very early and tiptoe through to his room. Fortunately, Rory asleep was Rory concussed. He could sleep through anything. She never took more than one note, the occasional few loose francs. And he had never twigged. Now, locking her bedroom door, she spread the money on the bed and counted it. She had a little over ten thousand francs. A thousand pounds in English money. Surely that will be enough, she thought. But just in case, I must get more . . . In the meantime, she had to take an enormous risk.

A whole week later, in Paris for a few days, Rory gave another of his parties. Claire was always supposed to attend, but normally, by the time the party turned into an orgy, she had withdrawn to its fringe, eventually to slip away unseen, for by that time Rory was too busy to notice anything. This time, she stayed. She had lain, dry-eyed and sleepless, coldly and clinically reviewing her options, and had finally decided on a course of action. Her terror of the alternative drove her forward. Never had her mind been so clear, her will to survive stronger, her aim more positive.

She waited, biding her time, until she judged the time was right, and seemingly drifting round the large room, from group to group, managed to merge with the one containing Denise Theroux, a high-priced courtesan who had started out as a member of the line at the Folies Bergère and made her way up the ladder by stepping on the backs of a pyramid of rich protectors. Her current paramour was a business partner of Rory's; equally involved in the smuggling of drugs. He was a Corsican, and reputed to be a member of one of Marseilles' most feared gangs. Denise was hard as nails but she had been surprisingly kind to Claire, so long as that kindness provided no threat to her own security. She was always exquisitely dressed, her long legged, lushly breasted body presented as a jeweller will present a fabulous jewel.

Now was the moment, under cover of the general hum of conversation. They were enjoying pre-coke drinks, relaxing before the main business of the night started, when clothes would come off and couples would disappear into one or other of the four bedrooms (when they were filled then the couches or cushions on the floor or even the carpet, would serve as places for their frantic, greedy, mindless 'liberating' coupling. Claire murmured softly, 'I would like to talk to you. Alone.'

Denise did not falter in her seemingly riveted attention to a man who was telling a long, involved – and obscene – story. 'Where?' she asked without moving her lips.

'Over there; by the windows.' Claire knew it was not safe for them to withdraw from the gathering. Rory was as yet still observant, still constantly monitoring her attitude and behaviour. If he saw her standing by the window, chatting to Denise, being as pleasant as he had ordered her to be, he would take it as a sign of her obedience. And under the hubbub of conversation – there were some two dozen people present – it would be possible to have a private conversation.

With a smile, Claire drifted onwards, eventually made her way to the floor-to-ceiling windows which opened on to the balcony, high above the street. She opened the windows, spread them so that fresh air flooded in; cool and sweet to lungs choked by heavy cigar smoke and the clash of several expensive perfumes.

'Oh, good, fresh air . . .' Denise said, drifting across in her turn. She had the perfect smile on her face; polite but not wholly covering a boredom she saw no point in concealing. All the women regarded Claire with a sort of condescending amusement, tinged with pity; a woman out of her depth in shark-infested waters. Now, she asked:

'Well?'

'I need your help.'

'How?'

'I need the name of your abortionist.'

Denise lifted her ever-present cigarette, always in a long jade holder, to her lips, drew a deep drag, exhaled a stream of blue-grey smoke which the night breeze swirled away. Her eyes met Claire's head on. 'Well, well,' she said softly. 'Still waters do run deep after all.'

'I heard you discussing abortions once. I know you have had several. You were saying how good he was; how quick, how thorough, how skilful.'

'How expensive?' murmured Denise, wielding her own hammer.

'How much?'

'Depends how far gone you are.'

'Ten weeks.' They were standing smiling at each other, two women exhanging party conversation, no more.

'Ten thousand francs minimum,' Denise said.

'I want you to introduce me to him. Fix an appointment.' Denise looked into the large, violet eyes. They were clear, bright, and very hard. She moved her bare shoulders as if she found the night air chilly. 'As soon as possible,' Clare said, her mouth smiling, her eyes not.

'Naturally,' murmured Denise. She smiled one last smile. 'I will be in touch,' she said, before drifting back to the party.

Claire turned her back on it, stood staring out over the city, silvered by the moon. Well, I've done it, she thought. I have put myself at her mercy. If I have read her wrong then I'm done for, but if I don't take the chance then I'm done for anyway.

'Why did you not want your husband's child?' her analyst had asked her, much later.

'I did not think of it as a child. I could not afford to. I thought of it as an extension of him, and the idea revolted me. I was also terribly afraid. I knew that if I told Rory he would at once assume that it was David's child; that nothing I could say would change that conviction. Nor could I face the thought of seven months of hell far worse than anything I had experienced previously. I wanted – needed, to be – exorcized, I suppose, as well as excised. It was an instinctive reaction. As soon as I realized I was going to have Rory's child I knew that it was the last thing I wanted. I hated and feared him; how could I ever love any product of that evil, twisted, psychopath? I wanted him dead and I wanted his seed dead too. That's how I thought of it. As a bad seed. Something which had to be destroyed. Having it would have destroyed me. So I trusted Denise.' A faint, wry smile appeared. 'And she came up trumps. She did get in touch, but not with me, with Rory, to say that I had asked her to introduce me to the "little woman" who made her dresses; all superb copies of pirated *haute couture* models. Denise told her lover that they were originals and pocketed the difference. When she went to the collections she memorized designs, then drew them for her dressmaker who produced the most incredible duplicates. She had worked in the *atelier* of Hubert de Givenchy for many years and then left because somebody else was given a promotion she thought she deserved. Making copies was her revenge.' The wryness became livid. 'Having the abortion was mine. Rory was talking about children, you see. He had told me – no children for at least two or three years. First, we play . . . But then he began to talk of a child, a son, of course; one with Drummond as well as Ballater blood. Something, he said, to keep me occupied, and, at the same time, earn my keep.'

'He looked on me as a brood mare – with the best possible blood lines, of course. He joked about having me "covered", went through an obscene charade of wondering who he would get to act as the "teaser".' Claire's voice had been flat, devoid of expression, recounting a message given and received. 'But he had not touched me in months: not since the night he raped me.' She had looked at the doctor and the still deeply shadowed eyes were glittering, like ice. 'It was not conceived in love, you see; only contempt and hatred. He used me. The conception was a by-product, no more.'

She fell into a silence that brooded. The analyst waited then prompted: 'So Denise called Rory?'

'Yes. He was surprised but pleased. Said I was showing some sense at last. Denise came and collected me, told him we would be back for dinner, and drove me to the abortionist. He was a young man; a gynaecologist with a large practice, but his main income came from abortions. Still being illegal in France, they were expensive, but there were many women like me who were unable to make the trip to London to have it done for very much less. Denise left me there. Said she would return later that afternoon. The doctor examined me, confirmed that I was two and a half months' pregnant and then asked me for the money. Ten thousand francs. Then a nurse took me into a sort of operating theatre where I was anaesthetized and given a D&C. Afterwards I was made to rest for a couple of hours while they checked on me every thirty minutes. Then, at five o'clock, Denise came back and collected me. The doctor gave me painkillers, told me I would bleed for several days but that there should be no complications. He advised that I rest. So when we got back, Denise told Rory that I had fainted at the dressmaker's, recommended I rest for a while. He was on his way out and not really interested. Denise made me a cup of tea and I went straight to bed, where I stayed for the next twenty-four hours. Then I got up and life —' again the wry smile — 'went on as usual.'

'How did you feel, afterwards?'

'Relieved.'

'Not guilty?'

'No. Not for that. Never for that. I did what I had to do. It was not knowing what to do that made me feel guilty; my trying to be the woman Rory wanted and would love, and failing every time. I could not have had Rory's child. It was as simple as that. The idea revolted me, much more than

184

aborting it did. What I had done, I reasoned, was to have a cancer removed to save my life.'

'And that is still how you see it?'

'Yes. If I have sinned then God will punish me – if there is a God.'

'You told me you were brought up to believe there was.'

'Rory disabused me of that idea. Heaven, like love, is an illusion, but hell is real. I know. I lived there. Hell exists, and it is man made.'

'Why did you tell your husband?'

'Revenge. *My* punishment of *him*. He could not conceive – ' again the livid smile – 'that any woman would deliberately abort *his* child. It was the worst possible kind of blow to his self-esteem. That is why I delivered it.' The livid smile once more settled back into the familiar death's head. 'I knew he would never forgive me.'

'You did not wish to be forgiven?'

'Not by him. I did not want anything from him any more. But I wanted to be able to forgive myself. Aborting Rory's child was the price I saw I had to pay for my own self-redemption.'

'But that led to more punishment.'

'I expected it. What I had not expected was the form it would take.'

'What did he say when you told him?'

'He just stared at me. I could see he was totally shocked. He had not believed that I could be so cold-blooded. He had thought I was still so in love with him that I could not bring myself to rid myself of his child – *his* child. Then, when he asked me why, I told him.'

'Because I hate you,' she had said, drawing on its bottomless reserve. 'I loathe the sight of your face, the sound of your voice, your very presence. I loathe the sound of your step, the careless way you slam doors, your overweening ego, your smug self-satisfaction, your assumption of rights you have no right to exercise. For months now, I have broken out into a cold sweat at the thought that you might want to exercise those rights.' Her eyes blazed at him with the coldness of a laser. 'But you being you, it will not occur to you that this – transformation – is in any way your fault. Nothing is ever *your* fault. That you have systematically and selfishly killed my love is why I killed your baby. You murdered all I felt for you by your self-obsessed self-everything! I despise you for your lies, your greed, your thievery, your countless betrayals. You *used* me; you took away my identity, made me into your chattel, your – your *thing* – to be used as and when and how you saw fit. You never saw me as a human being, and as for being a woman – I was just one of many. All you ever wanted of me was the money I could bring. Well, I'm free of you now. No matter what you do, how much you beat me, I am free of you. I have got down on my knees and prayed that you would get rid of me; throw me away as being of no further use. I have refused to join in your fun and games because I hoped that you would tire of the one you were playing with me. Well, I have won this game. I have got rid of your child and I am rid of all feelings as far as you are concerned. I knew what I was doing, when I had that abortion; I did it deliberately. The thought of giving birth to your child made me sick!'

As he stared at her, he must have realized that she was utterly indifferent as to whether he was suffering or not; that she had arrived at a point where he could no longer reach her, either by physical pain or verbal abuse. She was, as he had somehow always known but refused to recognize, a much stronger character than he: in personality, in will, in the strength to survive. He could beat her senseless but he would not be able to destroy her spirit. He had turned and walked out.

'It was after that,' Claire said to her analyst, 'that he began his campaign to destroy my mind.'

'You knew he was giving you drugs?'

'Yes. At first, he must have put them in my food. I began to feel listless, woozy, confused. I lost track of time, spent most of it sleeping or just lying semi-conscious, unable to think clearly. I tried not to take them but he forced me; he would open my mouth, drop them in, make me drink the water to wash them down. Later, when he had me reduced to total helplessness, he brought in Nurse Defarge. She was sleeping with him. They used to make love in front of me, but I didn't care. When they were asleep I used to crawl to where the water was kept, drink as much as I could to see if I could wash the drugs from my system. Then they got wise and never left it within reach. I had given up, accepted that I was truly finished, when Mollie came ... She was my chance, so I took it, and stopped taking the drugs. I put them under my tongue, swallowed the water and then spat them out when they were not looking. Rory punished me for Mollie, until he saw that she too could be used. One night, he came to me and he had the gun again, but this time he said he would use it on himself. I had destroyed him, he said. He could not live with what I had done to him. He had written a note, telling the world what I had done. How I had humiliated him in a way no man could bear. I couldn't speak – my tongue would not work – but I could look.' Once more the livid smile. 'He read my expression, saw that I would like nothing more but that he should be dead ... That was when he started doubling the dose, except when Mollie was present. I spat them out too. I had been surviving on hatred: Mollie gave me hope and that gave me strength.'

'Why do you think you collapsed, then, once you were free?'

'Reaction. I needed time to restore me to myself.'

'And you think you are getting there?'

'Don't you? We are talking about it, aren't we? I'm telling you things I swore I would never tell a living soul.'

'And has it helped?'

'Yes. I see things so much more clearly now.'

'Tell me what you see.'

'A whited sepulchre. My husband's dazzling exterior was

just that. Inside he was a charnel house, but he kept it secret from me. When I married him all I saw was the beautifully kept façade he presented to the world; I had to live with him and suffer because of him to find out the awful truth, the hideous secrets he was hiding. What I believed was priceless turned out to be a worthless fake.'

'Surely the value we place on things rests on how much we love them?'

'What about the value of being loved?' Claire asked.

'It is because you were not loved, then, that you now reject it?'

The livid smile appeared again. 'I have had a change of heart.' Her voice was dry as dust.

'But surely, is not true love incorruptible?'

'Who is to say what is true? Mine, insofar as I knew anything about love, was one hundred per cent pure, triple-distilled. After Rory you could have smelled its corruption a mile away.'

'What about the possibility of past experience colouring present outlook?'

'Of course. Doesn't it always?'

'So you accept that your present outlook might change?'

'Time – and experience – will tell. I only know that I must never, *never* abandon my self – the *me* that I am – to another man ever again.' She had smiled at him. 'You think I am pure gall, don't you? A perfect example of hell hath no fury.'

'From what you have told me you *were* scorned, but that is not the cause of your bitterness. It is what you see as your failure.'

'It was not I who failed,' Claire said. 'It was love that failed me.'

'You think then, that love depends to a certain extent on being loved?'

'I loved Rory long before I believed he loved me. I was ready to be all he could want, to give all he asked. I thought the sun rose and set on him. I burned for him.'

'The more physical love is, the more precarious its continued existence.'

'You mean that possession is also nine points of the law where love is concerned?' Her voice was sardonic, mocking. 'To Rory, possession meant ownership. He was king and I was subject to his law. My love for him gave him dominion over me, in his eyes.' She got up from her chair, wandered restlessly to the window. 'It is all, if not quite ancient, then past history. It is over. I am free and intend to stay that way.'

'That kind of freedom carries its own chains.'

'I could not even move in the ones he put on me.'

'Have you considered that what you felt for him was never love, but only infatuation? The self-immolation you are describing speaks more of that than love.'

Claire turned on him. 'Whatever it was, I do not intend to be taken in again. I know where I went wrong. Isn't that what I am supposed to do? I have been coming to you, my father confessor, for months now. I have made my penance. Now give me my absolution and let me be on my way.'

'I am not God. And there are still unresolved conflicts in you.'

'There are fifty million people in the British Isles and I'll bet there is not one of them not riddled with unresolved conflicts. Life is a conflict. Something else I have learned. Whatever *you* think, *I* believe I have been scraped clean. You have probed my conscious, my sub-conscious. I've been taken apart and now it is time I put myself together again. In the last analysis, I am the only one who can do it.'

Three days later she returned to the world in order to begin.

Now, she looked at Mollie. 'So, do I give it a whirl?'

'Only if you promise to give it up the moment you start to feel dizzy.'

Claire burst into laughter. 'Mollie,' she said lovingly, 'what would I do without you?'

CHAPTER SEVEN

When he let himself into the Oliver Messel suite at the
Dorchester, Jake Burns was whistling. He had just come
from his first fitting for several pairs of shoes from Lobbs.
He had never dreamed a store would go to so much trouble
to handmake an article that normally he bought at the nearest
branch of Florsheims. At that, the place was like something
out of Charles Dickens. He had been waited on not by one
but by two men; one had measured his foot, length, width,
arch, heel, the whole bit; the other had noted everything
down on a pad. All those details would later be transferred
into a big leather-bound book that had entries going back
more than two hundred years. They had drawn round his
foot too, and a special last would be made from it. It was
on this that his shoes would be constructed. Thereafter, no
matter where he was in the world, all he would have to do
would be to call Lobbs, tell them what he wanted and he
would still get a shoe made to his foot and his foot only.

This country is an education in itself, he thought. You
could lose it in Choctaw County, but they know more ways
to skin a cat than I ever heard of. Judd Bremner had told
him to go to Lobbs.

'Goddamnedest experience I ever had – 'cept for my first
time at Big Nellie's. Whole place is piled with leathers, and
old men like the little statues the British put in their gardens
– gnomes, they call 'em – workin' away at making shoes. I
tell you, it's straight out of Snow White and the Seven
Dwarfs. Fair takes your breath away. So does their bill come
to that, but worth it. And when you get to wear 'em, you
don't know you've got 'em on.' He had also showed Jake a
pair of velvet slippers, hand embroidered with his mono-

gram. 'Cissie bought me these from a shop in Jermyn Street. Ain't they fancy?' So far Jake had not been to New & Lingwood. He never wore slippers. But it was another name on the list he had, every one of them the best in their field. His last social arbiter had scanned it and confirmed most of them as being patronized by the very people he wanted to run with.

As he took off his brand new Burberry – bought only a few days before – Henry came into the foyer. 'You got a visitor.'

Jake raised his eyebrows. 'Who?'

'Says her name is Claire Drummond. She's from that high-class agency.'

'What's this one like?' Jake trusted Henry's judgement.

'Real pretty, nice smile, one of them cut-glass accents. A ma'am.' Which meant, in Henry's parlance, a real lady. 'I put her in the sittin'-room. Gave her coffee and a piece of brownie.'

Once more the blond eyebrows were hoisted. 'That good?'

'I like this one,' Henry said stolidly. 'She didn't turn a hair.'

'You gave her the test, then?'

'Nope. She give it to me.'

'This one I've got to see.'

Jake smoothed his hair, tucked his checked shirt into his Levi's and strode into the sitting-room. The woman seated on the bergere sofa by the windows looked up from the copy of *Forbes* she was leafing through. Henry was right, Jake thought. She was a real looker.

'Hello,' he said heartily. 'Sorry to keep you waiting. I got tied up.' She had risen to her feet; she was tiny; not much more than five feet. Her hair was wine red, she had the fabled English skin: heavy cream and blush rose, and her face was shaped like a heart. Wide brow, slightly pointed chin, pert nose. Her mouth was luscious, short upper lip, full lower one, but it was her eyes that held you. Large, heavily lashed, the colour of wood violets. When she smiled, it was enchanting.

'Mr Burns,' she said. Her voice was as crisp as new money. She handed him a card. He took it, read it.

'Claire Drummond,' he read out loud. Then, 'You Scotch?' he asked.

'A Scot. Scotch is what you call our whisky.'

'I'm a bourbon man, myself,' he drawled. He waited until she had re-seated herself then folded his long length in the matching chair opposite.

'Come to check me out?' he asked. 'I see you are the boss lady.'

'One of them, and yes, I have come to see why it is that we cannot seem to meet your requirements.'

'I told you the score.'

A brief smile. 'Minus three?'

'Not my fault,' he denied virtuously. 'I had Cora Sue give you the exact specification.'

'A combination of Margaret Thatcher, Joan Collins and Margaret, Duchess of Argyll?'

His grin was white. 'A fair assessment, but I was led to believe you could match it.'

'That is why *I* am here. To make sure it's fourth time lucky.'

'Now that's what I call service,' he said appreciatively.

He saw her eyes dance and that full lower lip tremble slightly. 'We aim to please.'

Jake leaned forward. 'Lady, you can please me any time,' he told her earnestly. They held eyes, hers slightly startled, and then her smile appeared. Well howdy-doody, he thought, relieved. This one has a sense of humour. He tried her further. 'Henry looked after you all right?'

'Yes. He gave me an excellent cup of coffee and a piece of the most delicious Brownie.'

'Then you're in. Henry doesn't do that for everyone.'

'I had a feeling that he carries more than his weight around here,' she murmured.

192

He found himself grinning. Sassy too. 'Henry is the third part of the triangle. You've met Cora Sue?'

'Yes.' That one word spoke volumes.

'She's out right now. Sight-seeing. Until I get started there's not a lot she can do.'

'Started on what?'

'Meeting people and influencing them. I want to do business. I have money lying around waiting to be used. I want to find out the best places to put it.'

'I thought that was something you had taken care to establish before you came here.'

Quick, he thought. 'I know all about the City of London being the financial centre of things, what I don't know is *who* runs things. Who has the juice.'

'It depends on the kind of fruit you wish to squeeze.'

She was as cool as a Budweiser. You could squeeze this one, he thought, and all you'd hurt was your hand.

'Your reputation has preceded you, Mr Burns. And your status as a corporate raider.'

His shrug was disarming. 'All I do is buy and sell things.'

'At hundreds of millions of dollars at a time? Why do you need a social arbiter, Mr Burns? And why a woman? This city is full of knowledgeable men who could give you what you need.'

'I hope not,' he said, dead pan, and he saw her laugh again. Then, with brisk purposefulness: 'Once I meet the right people, I'll want to entertain them. I want somebody who will know not only who to invite but who not to. Women are much better at these things than men; much more aware of all the – subtleties – under the surface. I want to meet people socially because in my experience, a lot of good business is done over the dinner table, or afterwards, with brandy and a good cigar. I want somebody presiding at my table that these men will know and feel – reassured, by. I'm quite aware that a lot of you British, invited to dinner by a Texan or somebody from out west would expect to be served a mess of beef and re-fried beans. You think that

America is civilized only on its east and west coasts, and that in between we still tote guns, shoot first, and ask questions later.'

'If what we see on television is a true picture, then you still do.'

'You've never been to America?'

'Alas, no.' She did not tell him that it had not been possible for Rory to take her. She had discovered he had an early drug conviction – possession of marijuana – and had therefore been refused a visa. 'But I have read a great deal about it.' Much more since she had decided to work for this tall, lazy-drawling, archetypal cowboy. He was straight out of a John Ford western. Lean, permanently tanned, short back and sides butter-blond hair, amazing eyes of a grey so light as to be all but colourless, the delta of fine lines at their corners indicative of long periods spent squinting into hard sunlight. He was wearing a red, blue and white checked shirt and a pair of faded if spotlessly clean jeans, but what drew her fascinated gaze were his boots. Cowboy boots of soft, supple leather, the colour of a lion's pelt and tooled by a hot iron into an elaborate pattern of whorls and loops. He noticed the way she was having difficulty keeping her eyes from them.

'Best thing in the world on a horse,' he advised. 'You ride?'

'Not in London.'

'I ride wherever and whenever I can. My first love affair was with a horse.'

'Is that what held you up? Hog-tying steers?'

He met her eyes with startled surprise which changed to laughter followed by a grin once he saw that she was undoubtedly teasing. 'Easy on the spurs,' he advised, still affably, showing that he too had a sense of humour. She also had a fast tongue and he was sure the mind behind that lovely face was equally speedy. 'So?' he asked hopefully. 'Are you still of the opinion that you are the one to give me what I'm looking for?'

'I intend to have a good try. However, I should like you to tell me exactly what that is.'

'I thought Cora Sue had spelled it out for you.'

'In *her* words. I would still prefer yours.' All perfectly polite but making it clear that she was under no illusions as to Cora Sue's deeply ingrained prejudices.

'I want somebody with all the right connections to people who can be useful to me. I want to meet those people. I know this country has changed a great deal in the past thirty-odd years, but in one respect I know it hasn't. Unlike my own country, which regards the making of a great deal of money as proof of worth, you don't go for that over here. You can be living hand to mouth, but if you have the right background, went to the right schools, know the right people, you still get invited to the right places. Who you are is what counts over here just as much as what – if not more. Me, I'm a what. I'm looking for a who. Maybe, if the two are put together I can become a who-what – and you go for double-barrelled names over here, don't you?'

'Why do you think a woman will do a better job than a man?'

Deadpan: 'I need a steady date. Two guys may be the way it's done in San Francisco, but not where I come from. I need a hostess; somebody to look good, sound right and above all *be* right. And I'm willing to pay whatever it takes.'

'What was wrong with our three previous candidates?'

'Nothing. I was the one that flunked.'

'Can you tell me why?'

'I have no idea,' he answered blandly. 'Maybe it was the long hours. Maybe it was the workload. You tell me.'

'We – my partner and I – gained the impression that you wanted total immersion.'

Another grin. He liked the accuracy of her summation. 'I'm no Southern Baptist. My folks were Lutheran, but yes, I want somebody willing to take me into all those private pools of privilege and exclusivity. What I want is someone who will hook me into the British "old boy" network. I have reasons, but for now they are my own.'

Claire thought she could make a good guess as to what they were. He obviously knew that even now, even in the meritocritous eighties, with its new money and its rising yuppie class, almost all the money and 95 per cent of the power in England were still held by some 1 per cent of the population, commonly referred to as 'The Establishment'; that the 'old boy' network dominated the City and the great financial and social institutions. What he wanted to do, she realized, admiring his cheek, was bore from within. What she wanted to do, she also realized, was be there when he did it. Great Britain still had an exceptionally rich and varied tradition of seasonal social events and activities which were, even now, after the social cataclysm which had followed the Second World War, still a force to be reckoned with. There was still a traditional calendar which powerfully influenced the leisure of those members of society who were fortunate enough to possess the time and the money with which to continue a life instituted by their ancestors. Not that these events were as exclusive to the rich or well-connected as once they had been. If they were, Jake Burns would not have a hope in hell of partaking in so much as one of them.

'I want somebody who has the right of entry to that world; not only that, who has the clout to take me with them,' he was saying.

'It is not unusual for Americans to enter it.'

'Sure, but they happen to be named Whitney or Mellon. I don't want to do a Joe Kennedy. Nobody *ever* accepted him over here, which is maybe why he rammed his son down your throats. I want to do it right.'

'Which is why you need the right base to do it from?'

'Right!' They smiled at each other, perfectly in charity.

'Let me lay this on you,' Claire said, her English vowels using the American expression in a way that had his grin splitting like a melon. 'How about if I find you the perfect house. Would you take that as proof of my – capabilities?'

'Damned tootin' I would.'

'Leave it with me, then. I will see what I can come up with.'

'Lady,' Jake Burns said earnestly, 'anything you can come up with is all right by me.' His warm words congealed in the face of her cool.

Claire rose to her feet. He did too. 'You will be hearing from me, then.'

'The sooner the better.' He walked her to the door, which he opened for her. His hand came out again. 'Nice to have met you, Miss Drummond. I've got a good feeling about this meeting.'

Snap! thought Claire, but she shook his hand warmly. 'Then I will do my best to see that I come up with even more goodies.'

A last smile and she walked by him and out of the door. He watched her as she moved away. Nice action, he thought. Good conformation. I'll bet she's got a dandy bloodline.

When he went back Henry was clearing away the coffee tray. 'I think we've finally got ourselves the right key,' Jake told him.

'Pretty, too.'

'And smart as a whip.' Jake looked round, 'Drummond . . .' he said. 'Let's see just exactly who they are . . .'

'By the window,' Henry said, knowing what Jake was looking for. The copies of *Debrett* and *Burke's Landed Gentry* he had ordered from Hatchards.

Henry stood over him while he riffled pages. 'Here we are . . .' He read rapidly, then whistled. 'She's the goods, all right. A member of the Clan Drummond . . . shit! They go back nine hundred years! The Drummonds of Glen Drummond. They've got armorial bearings, a clan badge and their own tartan. And her mother is the daughter of an Earl!' He looked up at Henry and the light eyes glittered like the sun on water. 'And they live in a castle! We've got ourselves a real live aristocrat.'

'That's what you're payin' for, ain't it?' Henry grunted.

Jake cocked an eye. 'And worth every penny, don't you think?'

'Time will tell,' was Henry's opinion.

Three days later Claire took Jake to look over some houses. She had gone straight to her old employers, who were delighted to see her again and only too happy to help. She looked through their listings, picked three; one a penthouse in Eaton Square, the second a three storey pied-à-terre in Wilton Crescent and the third a newly converted mews house tucked away behind Montpelier Square. All were to the highest standard of luxury, all were fully furnished and equipped, all were hideously expensive.

'Now this is more like it . . .' Jake enthused, as he gazed out over Eaton Square to the looming mass of Victoria Station, the gardens of Buckingham Palace and the traffic jam at Hyde Park Corner. 'I've heard of Eaton Square . . . now where was it?'

'Perhaps you are thinking of Eaton Place,' Claire suggested. 'I believe you had a television series of ours – *Upstairs Downstairs*? The Bellamys lived in Eaton Place.'

'Right!' Jake snapped his fingers.

He also liked the elegance of Wilton Crescent, but when he saw the mews house he flipped. It was secluded, painted white, its glossy front door gleaming with highly polished antique door furniture, green bay trees in brass-bound tubs on either side, bright flowers in boxes outside the ground-floor windows. Inside, imaginative use had been made of much more space than was at first realized.

'It was three cottages,' Claire explained. 'They removed the interior walls and made it into a single house.'

A small square hall, its floor a gleaming expanse of beautiful parquet, gave way to a staircase that flowed upwards to six bedrooms each with bathroom en suite; all with separate shower stall. The carpets were of the sixty pounds a square foot variety, and the curtains were all interfaced and interlined with felt, to keep out noise as well as light. There were flowers everywhere, and the furniture was a blend of genuine antique and twentieth-century Italian design at its best. Downstairs, off the hall on one side, was a drawing-room that ran from the front of the house, overlooking the cobbled mews, to the back, where it overlooked a small but enchanting garden with a lawn that was as thick as the carpets, surrounded by a border of flowers chosen so that there would always be a show of colour no matter what the season. The furniture was all antique here; eighteenth century, and the fireplace was real. 'Adam,' Claire explained. 'Purloined from a country house which had fallen into disrepair and scheduled for demolition.' The lighting was from at least half a dozen lamps; carved rock crystal bases surmounted by pure silk, hand-made shades. A chandelier hung from a central point.

The dining-room had a regency table which could be extended to seat twenty, with a set of superb Georgian chairs, including two carvers, and a matching Sheraton sideboard. Portraits hung on the deep warm rose silk of the walls, and the curtains were of heavy silk velvet. The carpet was Chinese; delicate pinks, soft blues and green. A swing door led to a huge kitchen, all stainless steel and every possible mechanical aid. Jake had only one comment. 'Need a bigger refrigerator.'

'I'll have it changed for one of the bank-safe sized kind they sell in Harrods.'

'Bigger the better. Henry likes a nice big refrigerator.'

Behind the dining-room there were two other rooms; one a study, the other a sitting-room. 'This will do for Cora Sue,' Jake decided. 'It will need a desk.' Claire made a note.

Jake peered into cupboards, fingered towels, turned on taps.

'Gas-fired central heating,' Claire said. 'A big enough boiler to provide a constant supply of hot water to all bathrooms. A gardener comes in twice a week.'

'Garage?'

'This way . . .' She opened a door off the kitchen. It was a triple; concrete floor, a stack of shelving, a tap for washing the cars. Underneath the house was a spacious cellar. One wall was all wine-racks.

'This is it,' Jake said with a satisfied sigh. 'Exactly what I was looking for.' He turned to Claire. 'Now hit me with the damage.'

'You can lease – £250,000 a year – or buy. Two million pounds.'

'Lease. I can work tax savings.'

'How long?'

'A year for now. We'll see how it goes.'

'Stores?' he asked next. 'Henry has to know where to buy what he has to cook.'

'Harrods is just around the corner. Their Food Halls supply everything you could possibly want.'

'Good. Open a cheque account.' Once more Claire made a note. 'And I want those empty wine racks filled. I like good wine.'

'Perhaps a visit to Berry & Rudd?'

'Fix it.'

'The house is attended by a cleaning service twice a week, but there is a daily woman.'

'Fine.' She followed him back through the house. 'I see there are plenty of telephones,' he commented. There was an instrument in every room. 'But I'll want a private line for my own use.' Another note was made.

'I'll want a telex machine in the office.'

'I'll contact British Telcom.'

'And a fax, a photocopier and a word-processor. Cora Sue will choose them. I'll also want stationery printed. Cora Sue can do it if you tell her where. I need a good travel agent; one who can set things up in hours rather than days. I often have to leave at a moment's notice. I also want a car; it has to be fast, comfortable and come equipped with a phone. Cora Sue doesn't drive and Henry doubles as chauffeur when

200

necessary, so there'll be room for your own car. That goes with the job so choose one for yourself too. Lease, don't buy. It's – '

' – a tax saving.'

'Right!' confirmed Jake. 'I don't break the law but I bend it every which way to keep the government – any government – from getting rich on my money. I use the London branch of an American bank, but maybe I'd better open an account in a British bank. Set it up, will you? Here . . .' He took a card out of the inside pocket of his jacket. 'Call Bob Raffelson at this number, tell him what you want and he'll do the rest. Tell him a couple of million pounds to start. How's the rent paid?'

'In advance, every quarter.'

'Okay, pay the first quarter now. I'll also want a household account set up for Henry for those small things he doesn't charge. Other things I like and you can't get here I'm having shipped across.'

They were in the china pantry, a square room lined with green baize-covered shelves. Jake picked up a cup: 'This okay?'

'Yes. It's Wedgwood Napoleon Ivy. That is Spode Italian, and that one there is Minton Haddon Hall.' The china occupied one side; breakfast sets, tea sets, dinner sets. The other was crystal. Mostly Waterford with some Baccarat. He also checked on the cutlery and Claire once again confirmed that it was the best. Of silver, in a Georgian fantail pattern. He checked on the table linen, the soap in the bathroom – all baths were jacuzzis – and even checked on the toilet paper.

'Fine,' he said when he had seen everything. 'This is it. How soon can I move in?'

'As soon as you like.'

'Okay. Tomorrow.' He paused. 'You have any preference as to which bedroom you want?'

'I want?'

'Sure. You'll be presiding at my table; you won't be

expected to leave with the guests, so when we entertain you sleep over. The dark-blue one's mine, by the way.'

'I'll take the one with the sleigh-bed.' It was decorated in Wedgwood blue and white – the one Jake had chosen was navy-blue with touches of scarlet – and it had a lovely pictorial wallpaper showing a French seventeenth-century hunting scene. 'I take it, then, that I have passed my entrance examination?'

'With flying colours,' he assured her. 'Tomorrow we start in on the lessons.'

'I see what the others meant,' Claire told Mollie, on reporting back. 'He knows what he wants and when he is not sure he asks. Thinks on his feet and regards wasted time as money lost. But from the way he is prepared to spend that is no object.'

'I hope you know what you're doing,' Mollie said lugubriously.

'I don't intend to make *that* mistake again,' was Claire's crisp retort.

The next day she took him to Jack Barclay, where he came away with a Rolls-Royce Corniche the colour of a new penny. It had two phones, one in the front, one in the back. It had a cocktail cabinet, a tiny television set, and under the arm rest was another screen which could relay the latest stock exchange information. The windows were tinted and the upholstery was of a silky suede which matched the paintwork. It could do a hundred and forty in seconds and cruised at seventy with absolutely no noise except the sound of your own breathing. Claire chose for herself a Volkswagen GTI, in black. There was plenty of room, in the huge garage, for both, though the Rolls dominated the small VW.

When they got inside, Henry was in his kitchen, making coffee.

'Well, Henry?' Claire asked. 'Will it do?'

'I guess.'

It had both gas and electric ovens, as well as a microwave. It had a Cuisenart, a big butcher-block table; it had an electric can opener, a six slice toaster, an ice-breaking machine, and as well as the filter-type coffee maker there was one that produced Italian espresso.

'Your American fridge will be here this afternoon. I ordered the biggest one they had. If you like, I'll take you to Harrods this afternoon and you can see what they have to offer.'

'Suits me.'

Henry, Claire surmised, did not say much, but she was quite certain that he knew everything.

He placed before her a cup of his ambrosial coffee and a freshly made muffin bursting with blueberries. Claire was reduced to picking up crumbs with a damp finger. 'You are a great cook,' she complimented.

'I like to see people appreciate it.'

'How long have you been with Mr Burns?'

'Ten years.'

'And Miss Mennenger?'

'He inherited her from his father. She ran his office back in Tulsa.'

Ah, thought Claire. That's why she is so proprietorial.

Jake came in and behind him trotted Cora Sue. Claire wished her good morning and was rewarded with a sniff and a look that would have felled an ox. Cora Sue did not approve.

'Cora Sue has taken the pink bedroom,' Jake said.

'I thought she might,' Claire said tranquilly. It was very feminine; all ruffles and Austrian blinds.

'And Henry is in the green one.'

'Six bedrooms!' snorted Cora Sue. 'Spending money like it was going out of fashion. And for what?'

Jake ignored her. Claire had a feeling that he had learned to shut down when it suited him. In her turn, Cora Sue ignored Claire and sat herself next to Jake at the counter of the central cooking core of the big kitchen; turning her back she proceeded to tell him that she had carried out the instructions he had left her that morning. 'I called Chicago and they'll telex the information as soon as it comes to hand. Chuck Walters is in Dallas but when I called he wasn't available. I'll try later. The Pointchartrain stock is up two points, and Jerry Curtiz wants to speak to you about that Simmonds merger.'

Jake nodded, saying, 'Fine, fine . . .' but it was obvious that he was giving her only half of his attention because he turned to Claire to say: 'I need some suits. Could you tell me where I should go to have them made?' Casually: 'A friend of mine recommended somebody named Tommy Nutter.'

'Yes, he is a very good English tailor with American pizzaz, if that is what you want.'

His look was quick, recognizing that she did not approve. 'You know best,' he conceded.

'Then Huntsman, I think, have the cutting edge over everybody else.' She did not mention that they were Rory Ballater's tailors, or that he had in one afternoon spent ten thousand pounds on half a dozen classic three-piecers. 'They have beautiful cloths from their own mill in Scotland.'

'Ah, you're prejudiced,' teased Jake.

'So is the rest of the world. They have an unbeatable reputation.'

'Okay. Huntsman it is. Fix it.'

She came to learn that those two words were his way of giving orders.

'You will have to make time for fittings, at least six.'

'Okay. Whatever it takes.' Then: 'Where should I go for shirts?'

'Jermyn Street. It is full of shirtmakers. Turnbull & Asser, I think.' Rory's shirtmakers.

And it was there that her cover was blown. No sooner had she set foot in the shop than a face she recognized from having shopped here with Rory exclaimed pleasurably: 'Lady Ballater! It has been a long time . . . How nice to see you again. I trust Lord Ballater is well?'

I don't, Claire thought, but she only smiled and for the

first time damned her discreet Scots divorce. Obviously the news of it had not percolated southwards yet. 'This is Mr Jake Burns. He would like to have some shirts made.' She was aware that Jake was looking at her and she walked over to where the bolts of cloth were displayed.

He followed her, and they spent some time choosing various colours and patterns. Jake ended up ordering two dozen.

'I thought your name was Drummond,' Jake said, as they left the shop and walked back along Jermyn Street in the direction of Fortnum's, where she wanted to buy some tea. Henry had suggested she do so. 'I ain't familiar with tea,' he'd apologized, 'and seein' as how you British drink it all the time . . .'

'It is,' Claire replied coolly to Jake. 'It was Ballater. I am recently divorced. Drummond is the name I was born with and have returned to.'

He said no more. Her tone of voice warned him off. They bought the tea, and Jake eyed the elegant assistants speculatively.

'Should I have an account here too?' he asked after they had passed an assistant serving a small plump lady who looked as if she had been pulled through a hedge backwards but whom he addressed as 'my lady'.

'If you wish.' He opened one.

Then he wanted cuff-links so she took him along to Garrard's in Regent Street. He asked her advice and she advised him. Plain gold, square cut, heavy, classic. He paid up without a murmur.

When they came out it was twelve forty-five. 'How about some lunch? A good English lunch.'

She took him to Wilton's, back in Jermyn Street, and as luck would have it, once again Claire came up against her past. She was again recognized – Wilton's had been one of Rory's favourite watering holes: a dozen oysters from Wilton's was his idea of good food – but it was as they were studying the menu that a voice said: 'I wasn't sure it was

205

you but there is no mistaking that hair . . . how are you, sweetie?'

She looked up, recognized one of Rory's gambling cronies. 'Hello, Peter.'

'It's been an age . . . not since before you and Rory bolted for all that lovely grass on the other side of the fence. I was *terribly* upset when I heard he'd fallen . . .' A snide giggle. 'I hope it was not flat on his face. It is his fortune, after all . . .' Rory's crony looked at Jake, obviously seething with curiosity.

'Lord Peter Daventry, Mr Jake Burns,' Claire introduced.

'Oh, an *American*,' Peter Daventry cried with delight. 'I've only just come back from New York. My *favourite* city. Don't you just *adore* it?'

'Mr Burns is from Oklahoma,' Claire said gently.

'Really!' Then: 'Where exactly *is* that?'

'Next door to Texas,' Jake said amiably.

'Oh, *Texas*.' A shudder. Peter Daventry turned back to Claire. 'I *feel* for you, darling,' he sympathized. 'Too, too devastating, being divorced. My sister has done it twice and it left her an absolute *wreck* every time. I am *so* glad to see that you have survived the storm.' He blew her a kiss and went back to rejoin his own luncheon companion, a very beautiful young man wearing a brocade waistcoat and an Oscar Wilde cravat.

'Who was *that*?' Jake asked.

'A well-known pederast,' Claire answered shortly. 'Not the kind of man who can do you any good. As it is, everyone he meets will be left in no doubt as to the fact that I am very much the gay divorcee.'

'Do you mind?'

'I do that it should be him. He is a malicious gossip.' Her tone of voice once more closed that avenue of conversation, but Claire opened up another. 'Miss Mennenger told me you had a "whole slew" of letters of introduction.'

'Yes . . . I made a list. Here . . .' He took out his wallet and Claire made a note of the fact that he would need a new one. This one was limp, coming apart at the seams and stuffed far too full. He handed her a typewritten list. Claire studied it.

'I suppose you know all of them,' Jake asked hopefully.

'No, not all, just most of them.'

He watched her studying the names he had been given as being men of power and influence, and thought that from what he had learned this morning, he had found the person who had the necessary clout to see that he met them. The fact that she had once been married to a Lord came as no surprise, but he could not help wondering why that marriage was over. He made up his mind to see if he could find out just who this Lord Rory Ballater was, but if that queer they had just met was a sample of the company he kept he was not someone who belonged on the list. He had used Huntsman, though, for there too, Claire had been greeted as Lady Ballater. So the divorce was very recent. Which no doubt accounted for the arm's-length position. He had been aware of a 'strictly business' attitude from the start. She was prepared to assist him to get what he wanted, but using tongs. Well, he thought, as his smoked salmon was laid before him. We all have things to hide.

Claire was ticking off those names she knew with a pencil. 'James Ramsey went to school with my eldest brother; I went to school with Henry Broadbent's wife; Hugh Fitzwalters is a cousin on my mother's side and Christopher Mortimer is an old friend.'

'Good.' Jake squeezed lemon over his salmon. 'So how do we go about meeting these people and influencing them?'

'I'll give them a ring, let them know I am back in town' (and in circulation, she thought). 'That will start the ball rolling. Over here, people don't like to be taken for granted. Whatever invitations I receive I'll accept and ask if I can take you along. That will get you introduced. You can take it from there.' She paused. 'But if you will take a word of advice. Take it slowly.' Her smile took the sting from her next words. 'I would put you down as a man who likes to do things *now*, rather than later.'

The white grin appeared. 'True . . . patience is not one of my virtues.'

'Then what virtues do you possess?'

'I don't ask of people what I am not willing to do myself; I keep any promises made. I'm kind to animals and I never forget a favour.' Pause. 'On the other hand I don't forget injuries either. I pay my taxes on time, treat my employees well and never forget anniversaries.'

'And you love horses.'

'Right.'

'That will stand you in very good stead in this horse-mad country. Do you like racing?'

'Do I?'

'Good. Our five classic races are also highly social occasions.' Claire paused to let the waiter refill her glass with Chablis. 'Have you ever played polo?'

'Some.'

'It would be a good thing to do. One of the most powerful men in the City has his own team . . . I could introduce you; after that you're on your own.'

'Whatever you say.' Jake was obviously content to put himself in her hands.

'The Season – which is what we call our social calendar – does not begin properly until June. By that time, you should have become well enough known to be invited to join it.'

'Sounds great.'

One thing would have to be accepted, Claire thought. Shepherding this mega-rich American through the minefield of English society would necessitate her own return to it, where she would be forced to mix with people who had known her before; would provide constant reminders of the life she had lived among them as Lady Ballater. There would be gossip, mainly from Rory's friends anyway – snide and barbed remarks to the effect that *she* had driven *him* away;

the poor lamb forced to bide his time on the Continent while his ex-wife was reinforcing Anglo-American relations. Well, you wanted a challenge, she told herself unemotionally.

Over lunch they mapped out a provisional plan of campaign, then, as Jake had work to do with Cora Sue, he went back to the mews while Claire returned to brief Mollie. She would report back at ten the next morning.

When she let herself in all was quiet, but for the faint sound of a typewriter. Following her nose she went through to the kitchen. Henry was busy at his central cooking-cum-eating core and he smiled as he went instantly to the coffee percolator.

'I just now made a batch of cornbread. Want some?'

'I was hoping you'd say that. I only had coffee for breakfast.'

'Set yourself down.'

'Where is everybody?'

'Cora Sue is workin' – she's always at her desk by eight o'clock. Mister Jake is still sleepin'. He had a late night.'

'Entertaining already?'

Henry grunted. 'More like bein' entertained . . .' His dark-brown eyes met Claire's head on. 'She's still sleepin' too.'

Claire knew she had been thrown in the deep end so she let herself float to the top, where she trod water. 'I'm glad he has made a good start,' she murmured.

Henry relaxed. 'Women and Mister Jake is like ham'n eggs,' he confided frankly. 'Don't usually see one without the other.'

Not surprising, Claire thought. In his lean, taut, dried rawhide way, Jake Burns was an attractive man, but his attitude to her had been wholly impersonal. She was business, and she was already quite sure that he kept that quite separate from whatever his pleasures were.

Flyin' colours, Henry approved. No constipated, sneerin', 'Oh, well, *Americans*' look. This one would do. Good eater, too, though she was as delicate as one of those china figurines he had to handle so carefully when he dusted. She had a second wedge of cornbread.

'Henry,' she sighed, as she finished off the last crumb. 'If everything else around here is as good as your cooking I am going to enjoy myself enormously.'

Henry smiled. 'More coffee?'

'Please.' As he poured it: 'Where are you from, Henry? You don't sound like Mister Burns. You are a southerner, aren't you?'

'How'd you know that? Most English folks can't tell one from another.'

'I've seen *Gone with the Wind* several times,' Claire said with a straight face.

Henry's laugh rumbled. 'I'm from Kosciusko, Mississippi.'

'And how do you come to be working for Mr Burns?'

'I was tendin' bar in Tulsa, 'bout ten years ago now. He come in one night. There was some southern gentlemen insistin' on offerin' me some of their famous hospitality. Mister Jake took exception to the way they was offerin' it. We been together ever since.'

'But you haven't always been a cook? Where did you learn, anyway?'

'I was a short-order cook once. I been a lot of things one time or another.'

'Including a boxer?' She was eyeing his broken nose.

'You got sharp eyes.' But he was not displeased.

The swing door swung open and someone came in. Claire turned round. Jake Burns was standing there, bright-eyed and bushy-tailed. He was wearing a tracksuit and running shoes. 'I jog every morning,' he said to her obvious surprise. 'Back in about thirty minutes.'

'Mister Jake, he likes to keep in shape,' Henry explained.

By night *and* by day? Claire thought amusedly.

'Time to wake Sleepin' Beauty,' Henry said, following Jake through the swing doors.

An unconventional household indeed, Claire decided. No wonder Diana got narked. She's Rory's female equivalent.

Jane would not approve while Shuna – what went wrong with Shuna? she wondered. For what he is paying, minding one's own business comes easy.

But while Henry had gone one way, Sleeping Beauty had come downstairs the other. Hearing the swing door Claire turned once more. A blonde stood there, poured into a strapless sky-blue evening gown, a silver fox fur hanging from one scarlet-tipped forefinger. Her body was lush, her face chocolate-box pretty, her hair an artfully arranged tangled mane. Even at this hour she was perfectly made-up. 'Jake?' she asked.

'Gone.'

'Oh.'

Henry materialized behind her. 'Taxi waitin',' he announced.

'Oh,' said the blonde again, obviously put out.

'Outside,' Henry prodded.

The blonde shrugged. 'All right,' she snapped. 'I can take a hint.' She flung the fur around her shoulders and something fell from the pocket in its lining. A folded wad of notes. It was scooped up so swiftly it might have been an illusion. This time it was stuffed down the very low decolletage, then she turned and swept out.

So that was a member of his 'harem'. Very young – no more than twenty – to be a professional. But the fact of her Claire found intriguing. What was a man of Jake Burns's wealth and personality doing with hired bodies? Oh, well, she told herself. That side of his life is nothing to do with you. In fact, it is an added safeguard. It would appear that you have come to work for a man who doesn't want to become emotionally involved either.

While he was out, she went through to his study to make some telephone calls, to let people know that she was back in circulation. The first call she made was to Caroline de Beaumont, now Viscountess Larborough.

'Darling!' she screamed. 'How are you? It's been an absolute age . . .'

'I know. How are things?'

'Never mind me. How are *you*?'

'Getting back into circulation.'

'I heard it was all but cut off.'

'I recovered.'

'We must meet. I am simply dying to see you. Lots to tell and be told. Can you lunch?'

'Not today. But I would like to see you.'

'When and where?'

'Can I ring you?'

'Any time, darling. We are in town for a much needed breath of good old London air. I have to drag Rupert up to the smoke; he simply loathes leaving his muddy acres.'

'While you loathe returning to them?'

'Darling, you know me. Jersey to me means Lily Langtry, not a herd of long-lashed cows. I have to have a fix of Annabel's and lunches at Tante Claire to restore my blood sugar level.'

'You always did have a sweet tooth.'

'What are you doing in town? I thought you had gone to earth with the grouse.'

'Not any more. I'll tell you when I see you.'

'I can't wait. Do make it soon, won't you?'

'As soon as I can.'

Claire made another half a dozen calls, all to people who were delighted to hear from her, dying to see her. And dish the dirt, Claire thought as she put the receiver down on the last one. Well, she thought, you wanted to prove yourself. So prove.

CHAPTER EIGHT

Mollie Hoare-Browne yawned widely, rooted around on the floor for the shoes she had discarded. 'We must go . . .'

'Why?' Claire asked lazily. 'It's Sunday tomorrow.'

'Sunday, Monday, whatever, I still wake at 7 a.m. And we do have to drive home.'

Claire looked down the length of the drawing-room to where Jake and Clive were having what seemed to be an almost conspiratorial conversation. 'You mean Clive does.'

'It's his turn. It's been a lovely evening. God knows how many pounds that dinner is going to cost me. What a cook that Henry is! I must ask him for the recipe for that scrumptious pie – what was it called?'

'Key Lime.'

'Delicious . . .' Mollie patted her ample rump. 'Those two slices I had have gone straight to the wrong place.' She glanced down the room herself. 'What are they talking about? By the look of them it's a world take-over, but then, judging by the high-powered people you had here tonight that wouldn't suprise me. I'll say this for you – when you say you'll do a thing you certainly do it. I thought Michael Beresford was a difficult man to winkle out of his lair.'

'Oh, I've known Michael for years. He's an old friend of my brother Iain, ever since Eton.'

'The playing fields of Eton, how beautifully they stand,' carolled Mollie, paraphrasing Noël Coward. 'And you've somehow managed to get Jake in as a day boy.'

Claire smiled. 'I have done rather well, haven't I?'

'*He* thinks so. In fact, he thinks you're some sort of Open Sesame, but considering the doors you've taken him through these past months it's no wonder. I always knew the English upper classes were inbred, but from what I've seen lately they're positively incestuous! I never knew you had so many cousins and second cousins and I've lost count of your godparents.'

'My mother was one of six children – through my various uncles and aunts I'm connected to umpteen other families.'

'Not to mention all your friends from school.' Mollie paused. 'And talking of friends, do you think it's wise to allow that flighty Caroline Larborough to flaunt her latest conquest?'

'I introduced her to Jake; the rest was all her own idea.'

'Oh, she's got ideas, all right. I can't say the same for her husband. Is he all there?'

'I can assure you he is. He may look half-asleep and sound like it, but that's only his cover.'

'Then he must have seen his wife playing up to your employer.'

'I have no doubt he did.'

Mollie shook her head. 'I'll never get used to the casual way the upper classes commit adultery; like making a phone call.'

'Caroline has done her duty; she has provided the heir – two, in fact.'

'So it's all right to provide the gossip columnists with plenty of fodder?'

'Caro has always been best grist to the gossip mill. It comes of being her mother's daughter.'

Mollie sighed. 'And they say the world has changed . . .'

'Some things *never* change.'

'Not when it comes to hanky panky, that's for sure.'

'You know what they say,' Claire said with a straight face, 'the higher the class, the lower the morals. As long as the heir is genuine – or supposed to be, anyway. But I've seen Caro's twins: they're the image of Rupert.'

'Let's hope the next one doesn't resemble Jake.'

'Caro isn't that stupid.'

Something in Claire's voice made Mollie change the subject.

'How is Jake doing anyway?'

'Very well. He may come on as a hick-from-the-sticks but he's anything but. I found out, for instance – and not from him – that he went to Brown University, one of America's best. His mother's family come from Providence and all her family have gone there for generations. I also found out that he has Scottish ancestry. The name should have told me. Cora Sue said he was English on his father's side but it turns out his great-grandfather was from Paisley.'

Mollie grinned. 'I told you he was sharp.' Thoughtfully: 'Maybe that's why he's taken up with Caroline. Her husband's family own one of the older merchant banks.'

'Which Rupert does not work for. He's much happier as a landowner.'

'But he has more connections than Battersea Power Station, even so.'

Claire shrugged. 'Well, then; you know how Jake is determined to plug into as many as possible. Perhaps, through Caroline, that's what he's doing. I wouldn't put it past him. He is quite ruthless in business.'

There was a pause. 'Speaking of ruthlessness,' Mollie said casually, 'have you heard anything of Rory lately?'

'As a matter of fact I have. I ran into an old flame of his last week at Annabel's.'

She and Jake had been dining there. Claire had been a member with Rory and had sponsored Jake, with Caroline as seconder. It had been a Wednesday night, much less frantic than the over-crowded weekends. Claire had been confident of not running into any of the old crowd, who regarded the club as their second home, but as luck would have it, a party of six had come in on gales of laughter and among them had been a woman she recognized. Her 'damn' had been almost soundless but Jake had heard.

'Friends of yours?'

'No. My ex-husband's.'

Georgina de Torres had been one of Rory's women; one of the bed-hopping, husband-swopping polo crowd. She had left her first husband, a well-known player, for Rafael de Torres, the Argentinian ten-goal player, but before, during and after both marriages she had been one of Rory's mistresses. She was a creamy blonde, voluptuous of body, always superbly dressed and bejewelled, always on the prowl. Her sexual predilections were a by-word. It was rumoured that she had once emulated Messalina; she and a well-known prostitute had taken on as many men as were capable to see who could accommodate the most. Georgina had won. Newly married, Claire in her innocence had not even begun to realize that while she sat by the ropes at Smith's Lawn or Cowdray Park, waiting for Rory to appear for the next chukka, he was behind the tea tent in the long grass engaged in sexual congress with Georgina. Once, he had told her later, when he used to give her blow-by-blow descriptions of his sexual encounters, it had been in the back of somebody's Ferrari; Gina with her legs draped over the front seats, her skirts over her head, Rory's head buried between them.

'Gina is the supreme exponent of the quickie,' Rory had told her with brutal candour. 'She can never have enough. A true nympho . . . one minute squeezing the last drop out of you, the next fixing her lipstick, smoothing her hair and sitting down next to you cool as a Pimms, looking like she'd never seen a man's cock, much less had it – every inch – deep in her throat.' His laugh had been a guffaw. 'Many's the laugh we had over it . . . Gina sitting next to you, sweet as honey, but still dripping my own honey underneath her dress.'

Now, as the bored gaze drifted her way, Claire saw it brighten with malice. 'Claire . . . darling . . .' Gina bent to brush cheeks but Claire moved away from the false greeting. 'It's been an age . . . how long has it been now?'

'Not long enough.'

'Come now . . . you really can't go on playing the injured party you know, not when we all know it was Rory who suffered the grevious bodily harm. Isn't it enough that you've driven the poor man into exile? As a professional virgin, you should know that the last man in the world you should have married is Rory Ballater.' Having injected her venom she turned her attention to Jake. 'Hello,' she said throatily. 'I'm Gina de Torres.' Her golden eyes went over him with the assessing glance of the expert: what she saw obviously pleased her because her smile widened. Ah ha, it said with lascivious anticipation, what have we here? She had a way of looking at a man which registered his wealth, physical attributes and possible performance in bed. Claire wondered fleetingly what it would be like if Gina and Caroline were to enter the ring in competition for the same man. She knew where her money would go.

Jake rose to his feet. 'I've often seen your husband play. I'm Jake Burns.'

'Oh . . .' It was laden with meaning. 'So *you* are Claire's American. I've been hearing about you everywhere I go . . . Shall you be playing next year?'

'I hope so.'

Gina was studying him. 'You do look familiar . . .'

'We did meet once. At Palm Beach – the World Cup? Your husband's team won.'

'Of course . . . you were on the losing side.' Claire looked sharply at Jake. When he had expressed an interest in polo he had not told her he was good enough to play in a world cup. 'Then I must tell Rafe about you. I know he would be delighted to have you play on his side next time.'

'I'd like that.'

'We shall all like it,' Gina purred, leaving him in no doubt as to where her own personal pleasure lay. Her gaze went back to Claire. 'It will be quite like old times, won't it?'

'Not if I can help it.'

Gina smiled. 'We ran into Rory, you know, at the Argentine Open. Poor darling, we all urged him to come back where he belongs as *soon* as he can, and he promised, faithfully promised, that he would. Unfinished business he had to attend to, he said.' Looking at Claire, Jake saw that her face was pale, her eyes dark. 'Enjoy yourselves,' Gina taunted, before flipping a bejewelled hand and drifting away.

'Bitch!' Claire muttered.

'Look, if she's going to mess things up for you I can do the polo on my own. Rafe de Torres is the best introduction I can have.'

'You gave me the impression that polo was something you wanted to try.'

'Over here, sure. I've played back home and in Australia.'

'Then you don't need me.'

'I do. Being with you is very different from being a lone American – but from the way Mrs Torres talked it's obviously best for me to do it that way.'

'I don't need you to fight my battles.' Her voice had the edge of a Sabatier carver.

Jake raised his hands. 'I'm not looking for a fight, believe me. But she is.' And for some reason he could not as yet analyse, his first reaction was to warn and protect. Claire Drummond, he had discovered, was a feisty little thing, but it would be a case of the rabbit and the stoat. This woman, he understood now, had been in the defensive position from the start. She had been clobbered once, and she was damned if anybody would get the chance to do it again. He had always been conscious of a back-to-the-wall wariness, but with enemies like that de Torres woman, that was where he would be standing right now. What lay behind the butter-would-not-melt demeanour, the confident assumption of the position to which her birth and background entitled her, was a rag-bag of emotional, sexual and God knows what other leavings from a marriage that had not so much gone wrong as gone berserk. What the hell kind of a guy was this Rory Ballater? The more Jake learned the more he found it hard to square with the Claire Drummond he was coming to know – scarifyingly honest, crisply competent, quick of tongue and sharp of mind, with a compassionate heart and an understanding tolerance of the foibles and idiosyncrasies of human nature (look how sweet she had been to that cantankerous old dame who was her aunt, who had told her niece that she looked peaky and Jake that he should never wear anything but a plain shirt with a dinner jacket), with the shit that Rory Ballater was turning out to be.

He had asked Caroline one night. 'Tell me about this ex-husband of Claire's. What's he like?'

'A shit. Handsome is – and my God but he's good-looking – but in no way handsome does. A gambler, a liar, a thief and an adulterer on a world-wide scale. He had Claire coming, going and every which way. She couldn't see straight because of him – couldn't see anything except that handsome face and gorgeous body. He married Claire for her money; she married him for love. It never would have worked. He ruined her.' Caroline sighed. 'Claire has got it into her head that it was all her fault but I know who planted the idea.' Caroline had sighed, turned on her back. 'I told her she had a tiger by the tail but she was convinced he was nothing more than a pussy cat at heart. So she got mauled.' Pensively: 'She was too young, too – straight, too innocent. Her family are – well, not exactly stiff-rumped but old-fashioned, I suppose. She was taught to be honourable, truthful, decent and clean. Now she feels that when people look at her, all they see is the shit Rory dragged her through. He was involved with a lot of shady people who dabbled in very dark things.' Pause. 'Like drugs. He was, as you would so graphically put it, buddy buddy with a Brazilian named Bruno de Souza!'

'Shit!' Jake exclaimed. 'He's a big-time operator.'

'Exactly. I don't know all the ins and outs – Claire has never said a word – but other people have. You know how it is; people love to rake over other people's bones.' Caroline had propped herself on one elbow. 'Do I detect something more than an employer-employee relationship here?'

'The hell you do! If I so much as stretched out a hand she'd have it off at the shoulder! She never put it into words, but it was made crystal clear – the line I was never to step over.'

'But you toyed with the idea?'

'Not me. I've got a good thing going here. She's helped me plug into the power lines in this country. That's what I came to England for. Besides, I don't believe in getting involved with women who work with or for me. It leads straight to trouble.'

'Then it's just as well I didn't take the job. I did toy with that idea myself but Rupert wouldn't hear of it. In his world, wives do not – repeat, do not – work. It casts aspersions on their manhood or something.' Her hand drifted down Jake's chest. 'And talking of manhoods, how is yours doing . . .?'

'They told me you supposedly cool English aristocrats were in reality hotter than the Texas panhandle . . .'

'It all comes from our lack of central heating . . . we have to keep warm somehow.' She giggled as Jake swiftly reversed their positions, so that she was lying under him. 'You turned me on the moment I saw you at that first dinner party . . . but I had to make sure I wasn't stepping on Claire's feet.'

'You won't find them moving in my direction.'

'I know. She told me she only worked for you.'

'Did she now?' Jake sounded affronted.

Caroline laughed. 'The old double standard? You will respect her "thank you, but no thank you" attitude but you prefer to think she did it regretfully, is that it?'

'Sharp,' Jake said, then grinned. 'Like your hip bones . . . you could do with a few more pounds.'

'God forbid! I spent a fortune at Shrublands to acquire this body; besides, another pound or two would *ruin* the hang of my clothes.' She ran her tongue around one of his nipples. 'On the other hand, I'm not wearing any right now . . .'

Gazing down the room at Claire, Jake now found himself wondering – as he had more than once in the past months – about the body under the lovely Victor Edelstein dress, an exact match to her glorious eyes. She was tiny but perfectly proportioned; rounded where Caroline was fashionably – almost uncomfortably at times – lean. Maybe she was right, he thought. Maybe I would have availed myself of the opportunity. Well, he thought on a sigh, as they say over here, chance would be a fine thing . . . And it *would* be stupid to mess up a very satisfactory business relationship. Through Claire Drummond he had met the men who ran things, was already involved in structuring a couple of very fine deals. And that, he told himself, is still the object of this particular exercise . . .

Mollie's boisterous laugh rang out. Like her, it was full-throated, unashamed, larger than life. He liked Mollie enormously; she had no pretensions, and he relished her bracing, North-Sea-air attitude to life. He also liked her husband: totally her opposite, soft-spoken, mild-mannered, but awesomely intelligent and a Foreign Office mandarin. Clive Hoare-Browne had been invaluable in his advice, offered in an off-hand yet acutely aware way. He had done the right thing when he chose that agency, he reflected. Not only was he establishing future profitable relations, he was doing it in the nicest possible way. The last three months had been a round of cocktail parties, dinners, first nights, viewings, city banquets – the latter especially valuable because to the City came the top brass of both big money and politics. The Prime Minister of England had been present at one he and Claire had attended (courtesy of one of her Uncles who was Chairman of a mechant bank), the one the Lord Mayor gave for the City power brokers. He had looked round and made a quick summation of the total amount of money present; come up with a rough estimate of £15 billion. And that was not including the glorious Hall and its huge collection of eighteenth-century silver. In a month or so they were due to attend the biggest one of all – the new Lord Mayor's Banquet, at which tiaras would be worn and Margaret Thatcher would speak.

They had 'done' the St Leger – where not only had he backed the winner, but he had been introduced to the legendary Charlie Cochran, who turned out to be an old acquaintance of Claire, and through him Jake had been taken on a tour of Newmarket and its stables. But when Charlie had suggested they go up to Scotland for the Ayr meeting Claire had declined; for some peculiar reason she seemed loath to go back to her own neck of the woods – so he had gone alone. In October they had attended the Horse of the Year Show, but the highlight so far had been the State Opening of Parliament, where, as guest of Claire's Uncle George, who was her mother's eldest brother and Earl of Carnforth, they had watched from the Strangers' Gallery overlooking the Chamber of the House of Lords as the Queen of England, with her husband and her daughter, took her position on the throne, donned a pair of horn-rims and read the speech prepared for her by her government. To Jake she had glittered like a Christmas tree; he had never seen such jewels, or anything like the Crown she wore, though he had seen it through glass when Claire had taken him to the Tower of London. Seeing it in the flesh had really been impressive.

Cora Sue, who had kindly been invited along, had been beside herself with excitement. She had even been cordial to Claire, a rarity in itself, because she was both fiercely jealous and invariably spiteful. He had felt constrained to explain, somewhat lamely he thought now, that Cora Sue was an inheritance from his father. 'He was first a lawyer then a judge and she was with him for more than fifteen years. I guess she kind of took it for granted that when I took his place she'd carry on as before . . . And she is a damned good secretary. Knows as much about everything as I do.'

'I'm quite aware that she is utterly devoted to you,' Claire had murmured, which was a tactful way of saying that Cora Sue was both surrogate mother and office wife.

They had not taken her to his first hunt, where he had worn his new Huntsman coat and white buckskin breeches, along with a hard bowler. He had eschewed a top hat. Claire, to his surprise, had come down wearing a well-cut black habit, her hair coiled neatly under a net, her top hat silky, her face glowing under its veil. When he had hoisted her up she had vaulted into her side-saddle with the expertise of a seasoned rider. He had memorized her clear instructions: as a visitor, he must introduce himself to the Master and pay his cap and field money. He was to remember that the Master was in complete command at all times. *Never* overtake the Field Master and *don't* allow your horse to kick hounds; always turn his head towards them. And at the end of the day, thank the hunt staff – financially as well as verbally. She had also pointed out a regular follower and advised Jake to keep close – 'as long as you don't ride in his pocket. This is an opening meet and that means best country, so you will probably have to ride hard. If you get lost, don't worry . . . everybody for miles around can direct you back to the castle.' His horse had been a big grey, obviously an old hand and raring to go. His ears had pricked and as they moved off, he had pranced and snorted, his breath white in the damp yet crisp November air. Claire was mounted on a horse as black as her habit; only the white of her stock and the vivid pink of her lipstick, allied to the shining violet of her eyes, provided flashes of colour.

They had found very quickly, and obeying orders, Jake had fixed his eyes on the pink coat he had been told he should follow. It being a Friday hunt the field was large; about a hundred and seventy. The big horse leapt into the gallop as though the baying of the hounds had applied a spur; he had the easy action of a well-oiled piston, and he took the fences that appeared before him with almost impatient ease. 'What a jumper you are!' Jake praised him exultantly, and dammit if the horse didn't lengthen its stride. As always, on the back of a good horse – and he must remember to compliment Claire on her excellent judgement – nothing mattered but the combined sensations of thin November sunshine, fresh wind, the smell and feel of horse, the creak of saddle, the power under his knees, the eagerness of the mouth under his hands, the soaring flight as the horse gathered himself, daintily lifted his forelegs, shot out his hind-legs and swanned over a fence-cum-ditch. He found he had lost the particular pink coat he had been following; there were half a dozen of them in front, so that he did not know which was which. No matter, he thought, as he bent low to avoid an overhanging branch, if they're wearing pink they're old hands; anyone will do. Where Claire was he had no idea; everything in him was concentrated on the sheer pleasure of riding hell for leather on a great-hearted horse who was determined to enjoy himself as much as anybody. He only hoped that one of those pink coats was not the Master; if he over-rode him that would place him on this particular Hunt's shit list. He tried to rein in slightly, but the grey was not having any.

Jake, like the hounds baying as they hotly pursued the fleeing fox, had got scent of the joy in the air; the sheer exhilaration of being alive on a morning like this, with the first hint of frost, the last fading traces of mist against which the branches of low leafless trees made a tracery of delicate veins, the thud of hooves, the rasp of his horse's breath, the sense of flying as he and the grey – now one single element – sailed through the air to land sure-footed on the other side of a hedge from which a startled rabbit bolted in terror, and galloped on.

He did get lost; somewhere along the line, amidst the folds and hills of the rolling countryside, he and the rest of the hunt parted company. He could hear them, but he didn't give a damn. Being in at the kill had never held any particular charm. He rode for the sheer pleasure of it, and this morning, he decided happily, was as pleasurable a morning as he had ever had in his life. No; more than pleasurable – joyous. When finally he pulled the grey up, they were on top of a hill, and far away, in the little valley it dominated, he could see the crenellated battlements of the castle to which Claire had brought him for the weekend. The Duke who owned it had been in the same regiment as her father, until suddenly he inherited a title he had never expected to come his way; he was also one of her godfathers. He was a very tall, very thin man with a shy smile who, Claire had told Jake, had won the VC when he single-handedly wiped out a machine-gun nest which had been wreaking havoc among the besieging forces of Monte Cassino during the Italian campaign. He had warmly invited Claire to take her pick of the horses in his ample stables and she had come up with this beauty; this lion-hearted, wickedly intelligent animal who now, the edge of his eagerness having been blunted, happily hacked his way home with unerring accuracy. Jake just sat and let him, acknowledging the greetings of the people he met on the way; tired, sweaty, thigh muscles aching pleasurably, looking forward to a long soak in a hot bath and the hunt ball that would celebrate the opening of the season that night.

His bathroom had a bath that had been put in when Edward the Seventh reigned; it was encased in mahogany and the taps were of shiny brass. The water made more steam than a volcano but there was also a bright fire burning in an old fashioned grate, and the manservant who was looking after him brought him a whisky and soda to sip as he lay soaking.

'This,' Jake opined to him, on a blissful sigh, 'is luxury.'

'Not quite what American visitors are used to,' the manservant acknowledged humorously, 'but we find they usually appreciate the difference.'

There were thirty at dinner, in a room that reminded Jake of Grand Central station, and the ball started proper at ten o'clock.

'How nice you look,' Claire praised him, when he got downstairs. 'White tie suits you no end.'

'You don't look so bad yourself,' he complimented, of her deep-rose duchesse satin dress with enormous puffed sleeves and a neckline that revealed a subtle hint of cleavage.

The ball was an eye-opener, in more ways than one. It began sedately, evolved into a riot, with lots of drunkenness, horn-blowing, roll throwing and disappearing couples. The Duke presided benignly, while his wife, as tall as he was but built like Boadicea, whooped it up on the dance floor with the energy of at least a dozen of the young things who were capering more and more wildly as inhibitions disappeared in a sea of claret-cup. It ended with the Gallop – from which Jake was careful to distance himself – along with his host, and they stood watching while everybody linked arms as the horn blew tally-ho and the guests galloped round the room faster and faster and faster, ending, like Ring-a-Ring-a-Roses, in All Fall Down.

'Now you know,' Claire told him, breathless and panting, 'how the English amuse themselves.'

'I don't know about them, but I've had a whale of a time. Just one thing . . . how the hell will they be fit for tomorrow's meet?'

'Now comes breakfast . . . watch!'

And he did, amazed, while platefuls of bacon, eggs, kidneys, mushrooms, grilled tomatoes and heaps of hot buttered toast were wolfed down, along with copious draughts of tea or coffee.

It was 5 a.m. when Jake got to bed, where he had five hours' sandbagged sleep before he was awoken at ten to prepare himself for the move-off at eleven.

On the Monday morning he slept all the way back to London while Claire drove, having made the Duke an offer Jake thought he would not refuse for the big grey, whose name was also Duke. Which was no doubt why His Grace did refuse, but he invited Jake to return. 'Field Master told me you rode very well indeed. Hard to hounds, eh?'

'That,' Jake had told Claire sincerely, when they got back, 'was the best weekend ever.'

'Then we shall do it again, some time – schedule permitting.' She gave the penultimate word its American pronunciation.

Cora Sue, jealous at being left out, not that she had ever sat a horse in her life, sniffed and said: 'Calls have been piling up while you've been sashaying around. Time you stopped being seduced by all this high life and got down to what we

226

came for. Hunting foxes indeed . . . you can't eat them, so what's the point?'

'The top of your head?' Claire murmured *sotto voce* to Jake, who grinned, and said: 'Oh, come on now, Cora Sue . . . you know I like to ride.'

'You spend far too much time and money on horses, you ask me.'

'Which reminds me,' Claire said thoughtfully, when they were having a cup of Henry's coffee, 'I understand you have a rather remarkable horse at stud back home.'

'Who told you that?'

'The Duke. He says you told him.'

'He knows as much about horses as anybody I've ever met. We had a fascinating conversation.'

'Then I know the very thing to stand you in the most excellent stead with the horsey fraternity over here.'

'So tell me.'

'Let your horse stand at the National Stud for a while – gratis.'

Jake looked at her. 'Now why didn't I think of that?'

'Because I did. I gather your horse is remarkable.'

'That he is.'

'Won the Triple Crown,' Cora Sue put in proudly. 'Only eleven horses have done that for the past hundred years.'

'What's his name?'

'Centennial. I called him that because he was the hundredth foal of a horse called Centurion, but it was his mother which interested me. I bought him at a minor sale in Florida a few years back; he was somewhat small and his breeder reckoned him to be a disappointment. I got him for fifty thousand dollars.'

'And now he's worth five million,' Cora Sue said, even more proudly. 'Won the Eclipse award before Jake retired him to stud.'

'What's that?' Claire asked.

'Oh, a celebrity thing,' Jake said dismissively.

'Best racehorse performance of the year,' Cora Sue

informed Claire. 'Big occasion held at the Fontainebleau Hilton in Miami Beach.'

'You reckon it would do me some good where it matters, if I let the National Stud have him for a while?' Jake asked Claire thoughtfully.

'I most certainly do.'

'How long?'

'Well, quarantine regulations here make six months mandatory; say – a year?'

Jake pursed his lips. That would mean losing a fortune in stud fees. Centennial's cover charge was $200,000. But, as the British say, he thought shrewdly, set a sprat to catch a mackerel. He made his decision, quickly, as always. 'Fix it,' he ordered.

Now, he looked down the room again. Is there anything you can't fix? he thought wonderingly. This woman, he thought, is a combination of Elizabeth Taylor and Henry Kissinger. Tell her to do a thing and she not only does it, she does it damned well. Which made it even more of a puzzle that she should have allowed herself to be dumped on by some son-of-a-bitch whose only saving grace was his good looks.

'Yes, she is remarkable, isn't she?' Clive asked quietly.

'You read my mind,' Jake grinned. 'She's been worth her weight in gold to me. She knows everybody – and I mean *everybody*.'

'Claire is exceptionally well connected.'

'Clever too. You never have to explain things twice. I was just now thinking she'd make a great business manager.'

'Yes,' mused Clive. 'I think that is what her husband resented. Certainly he did his best to cut her down to size.'

'You knew him then?' Jake asked casually.

'Not very well. My wife and I met them in Paris a few years ago.'

'Now that's a partnership!'

Clive smiled. 'Yes, my wife is another remarkable woman.'

'Which you don't mind in the least.'

'Why should I? Women have every right to use and be proud of their capabilities, whatever they are.'

'Right!' Jake agreed approvingly.

'Whatever Claire has done for you, I think you have been very good for her too. She needed badly to be – appreciated – for what she was.'

'Oh, I appreciate her all right,' Jake said fervently. 'I've been wondering how I can hang on to her once I go back home.'

'Ask her, of course.'

'Easier said than done. Her world is one thing; mine is another.'

'I think you will find that Claire can move *anywhere*,' Clive said emphatically. He smiled. 'Even the United States.'

Which gave Jake even more food for thought. The one indigestible fact was Cora Sue. She had been difficult from the start, where Claire was concerned. She complained endlessly about her 'taking over', whereas Jake knew very well that Claire had walked on tiptoe around his secretary. Just as he had sensed the invisible line she had drawn for him, so had she never crossed over into the territory that was ruled over by Cora Sue Mennenger. Cora bullied him, nagged him, but she was loyal to her last breath. He had known her all his life: she had run his father's office with an iron hand; trouble was, she saw no reason to cover it with a velvet glove. If he brought Claire in on a permanent basis – and what the hell as? he wondered – Cora Sue would take umbrage, to say the least. Jesus, she'd take fire! And for the day to day organization, the fly-paper memory, the flair for detail, the hard slog of the boring grind, Cora Sue was invaluable. No; what he had in mind was for Claire to provide the gloss; give class to what was already a smooth running operation. Social secretaries were not unusual back home, from the White House down, but normally only women had them. If a man employed one it was invariably taken as another euphemism for mistress, and that, he thought nervously, was the last thing Claire Drummond would stand for.

He would think about it some more, he decided. He had plenty of time. Another six months at least. He now had more deals cooking than he had room for on his stove; as it was he was juggling, but so far they were all cooking nicely. He would have to go back home for a while come December; Cora Sue had been nagging him about spending Christmas at home. They had not been there for the festive season for several years, but he supposed it had to be faced some time, and lately, he had been coming round to the idea that it might not be so bad after all. If Claire Drummond could get it together after what she had been through – and he still did not know the ins and outs of that, except it had been a skilled job of butchery – then surely he could face his own past. You can't run for ever, he told himself now, following Clive down the room to Claire and Mollie.

The thought crossed his mind that perhaps Claire would like to come too, but in the next second he decided against raising Cora Sue's dudgeon any higher: it was almost through the ceiling as it was. Slow but sure, he counselled himself. You still have plenty of time. And that, he thought, as the Hoare-Brownes prepared to depart, was just about the nicest thing of all.

CHAPTER NINE

When Claire let herself into the house – quietly because it was almost 1.30 a.m. – she was in high spirits. She had dined with Mollie and Clive, a pre-Christmas celebration during which those spirits had been copiously present in kind as well as metaphorically. In less than twenty-four hours she was going home for Christmas. Already her anticipation's edge was keen; she loved the night sleeper to Inverness. The familiar faces on the platform at King's Cross, the ancient tweeds, the lolling tongues of the yellow dogs straining impatiently on leashes. She loved the good night's sleep which always came easily and quickly; brought on by the sound of the wheels on the track, the sudden flurry of lights as they roared through a station, the warning blare of a klaxon as they approached a level crossing, the pleasant good morning of her berth attendant as he woke her with a cup of hot, strong tea, pulling up the blind to see the heart-lifting scenery of the Highlands: snowcapped mountains, the deep vivid blue of a loch, the smell of the damp Scottish air which flooded through the eagerly opened window. There was no feeling quite like that of returning *home*, and this time there was the added sense of returning after a job well done.

It would be a quiet, family Christmas. Since her father's death, her mother seemed to have lost her zest for a houseful of people. Now, she preferred her family about her. 'Just you, Iain, Moira and the children, and your Aunt Isobel, of course,' she had said, the last time she and Claire had talked. 'Although I did wonder – were you perhaps thinking of inviting Mr Burns?'

'He's going back to America for Christmas.'

'Oh, well, he can always come another time. Perhaps at the end of your tenure . . . whenever that is.'

'Another six months at least.'

'You sound as if you are looking forward to them.'

'I am.'

'Good, I'm glad it has turned out so well, darling. It has obviously done you good, not to mention Mr Burns.'

'I think he is satisfied with my efforts on his behalf.'

He had said so when presenting her with a large, gaily wrapped box, 'not to be opened till Christmas'. 'With my thanks,' he had said, making it clear that they were considerable.

He had been dining with Caroline tonight; he might come home, he might not, but he had several things he wanted to discuss before leaving to catch his plane, which was why Claire had come back to the house instead of returning to her flat. Cora Sue had for once been pleasant to Claire, obviously delighted to be spending Christmas back home. 'First time in five years,' she had said. Claire had wondered why; Christmas was the one time in any year when home was the place to be. But then, Jake had never ever talked of 'back home' in anything but general terms. She knew his parents were dead, that he was an only child, in which case there was really no home to go back to.

She decided not to bolt the front door in case he did return. No matter what the hour, he would still be bright-eyed and bushy-tailed come morning; he always was. He had a seemingly inexhaustible supply of energy.

She made for the stairs, but as she set foot on the bottom step the sound of breaking glass had her freezing. It came from the drawing-room. Her first thought was burglars, her second that nobody could break into and enter this house, protected as it was by a photoelectric cell barrier and a plethora of state-of-the-art security systems. Perhaps Henry was still up . . . Like Jake, he too was a night owl. But on opening the drawing-room door she found it was not Henry. It was Jake, black tie hanging loose, shirt undone, hair tousled, face flushed, and very, very drunk. He was sprawled in one of the big chairs, and on the lamp table next to him a broken glass lay dripping what remained of its contents on to the carpet. The bottle he was holding was half empty; the square bottle containing Jack Daniels, his favourite tipple, and he was in the act of raising it to his mouth. As the door opened he looked up, scowled, and at the look on his face Claire found herself taking a step backwards.

'Where the hell have you been?' He was truculent, obviously not a happy drunk.

Taken aback – worse, taken back to the times she had found Rory in just such a condition – Claire's instant reaction was defensive, to answer placatingly: 'You know where I've been. Dining with Mollie and Clive.'

'You're supposed to be here when I want you.'

'I was not aware that I was wanted.'

'You were not aware,' Jake mimicked. 'Hoity-toity . . . did I speak out of turn?'

Claire was dumbfounded. This foul-tempered, sullen drunk was not the Jake Burns she thought she had come to know. He looked ugly, sounded the same way, and she had bitter experience of what such moods could lead to.

'I'm supposed to be the horse-lover, but you're the one with the high horse.'

'You're drunk,' Claire said as calmly as she could. 'I think it would be best if you went to bed.'

'I've been to bed – as if you didn't know.' Claire knew he was referring to Caroline, but that he should refer to her so coarsely was, once again, not like the Jake Burns she knew. His affair with Caroline was his business, and Claire had never, since introducing him to her friend, made it hers.

The best thing she could do was leave him to it. If he had rowed with Caroline she was not prepared to let him take out his bad mood on the first person to hand. She had had enough of that sort of thing to last her for several decades. But as she turned to leave he snarled, in a voice that stopped her in her tracks: 'I didn't tell you to go.'

233

'It's late, and I'm rather tired – '

'Rather tired,' he mimicked prissily. 'Jesus, that ice-princess act of yours is old hat by now. I'm sick and tired of the way you look down at the rest of us poor slobs.'

'As you are at least fourteen inches taller than I am I can't quite see how I manage to do that,' Claire said, striving for lightness, but becoming progessively more dismayed and not a little alarmed.

'You know damned well what I mean.'

Claire turned. 'If you are unhappy – '

'Unhappy! What the hell would you know about un-happy? One lousy marriage and you're convinced you're the world's worst loser! Unhappy! Jesus! You haven't any idea what *that* word means.'

Claire was totally at a loss to account for this sudden and unexpected attack. Why was he getting at her? And what had brought it on in the first place? He had wanted what she represented and she had given it to him. Every single item in his specification had been supplied. If he had wanted more, why had he not stated his requirements, then she would have known whether or not they were within her capabilities. It was no use complaining now. It was the liquor talking, she decided. It always declared an amnesty on imprisoned feelings, and right now, Jake's were bent on burning down the jail.

Humour him, she thought. Don't let him get you upset. 'If you will tell me what I have done – ' she asked politely.

'Done? Why, a great job, of course. I've got a list of top-drawer contacts as long as both arms, I've dined with Dukes, I've even ridden to hounds with one, I've been to the House of Commons *and* the House of Lords, I've been to City banquets and shaken hands with Margaret Thatcher and even seen the Queen of England in the flesh!'

'I thought that was what you wanted.'

'How would you know what I want?'

'I know only what you told me; likewise I did only what you asked.'

'How about something I didn't want, didn't ask for – something *you* thought I'd want, *you* thought I'd like . . .'

Dear God! Claire thought bemusedly, he's not this angry, this drunk, because I didn't ask him home to Scotland for Christmas?

'You have been scrupulous in your attitude, Christ how scrupulous! You have taken me here, taken me there, sat me down at High Tables; done everything to earn the very high fee I paid for such services. You have given me the inside track, but not once – not once – have you ever given me so much as a smidgeon of yourself.'

Claire's astonishment had paralysed her.

'You have taken me up, but by God you have also put me down. You have handled me with tongs, lady.' His laugh was a slap. 'Like a piece of sugar in those fancy silver tongs you use when you dispense tea. You took my money – that was good enough, but I wasn't. You've never once *seen* me; *me*, Jake Burns . . . not the brash American with more money than your national debt, but a human being, not made of greenbacks but flesh and blood.'

Claire's mouth opened, but no sound came. She was horrified. He was talking about her as though she was the worst, the most appalling of snobs, when the reality was that if she had been, she would have flatly refused to act as his paid guide, and soon disabused his idea that money opened all doors.

'That is not true,' she managed at last, and shakily.

'It is so true!'

'I am not going to argue with you – '

'Of course not. *Ladies* never argue, do they?'

Claire rounded on him. 'That is what you were buying and that is what you got! I work for you, Mr Burns. Your money buys my services; it does not buy *me!*' She jerked open the door and ran straight into Henry. 'Oh, thank God,' she said jerkily. 'He's drunk, Henry . . . I've never seen him like this . . .'

235

'I have. You run along. Leave him to me. Go on, I know what to do.'

Claire needed no second bidding. She ducked under Henry's arm and made a run for it, but not upstairs. She was not staying in this house tonight – not any night. The front door slammed behind her, and the last thing she heard was Jake's drunken bellow: 'Come back here – ' But she was hailing a passing taxi, scrambling in and driving away, trembling violently, dazed from the explosion that had just destroyed her rebuilt self-confidence and reduced it to rubble.

Back at the house, Henry advanced on Jake, who had lurched to his feet and was swaying dangerously. 'You shouldn't have let her go – I wasn't finished with her.'

'Maybe not, but I think she's finished with you.' Henry chided. 'I thought we was finished with all this? It don't do no good.'

'What do *you* know about what does me good?'

'A lot more'n you think. Come on now, let's get you up to bed . . . things will all look different in the morning . . .'

To Claire it all looked horrible; in the course of a sleepless night she had gone through shock, horror, disappointment and fright, ending up on the jagged rocks of anger. What is it with Americans? she thought, that they expect you to love them all the time? He issued the specification and there was nothing in it to indicate a man looking for *that*. If there had been I wouldn't have taken the job. What did he expect of me, for God's sake? She thought in past terms, because she had reached a decision: not to go back to the job. Obviously he thought she had failed in certain salient aspects, so let him look elsewhere for somebody who had it all. She simmered as she did her packing, and ignored the ringing of her telephone. She had no desire to speak to Jake Burns right now – not at any time, if his behaviour last night indicated how he really felt. Face it, she told herself, you are still a lousy judge of character. But that affable, pleasant, briskly confi-

236

dent Jake Burns should turn out to be such a sullen, vituper-
ative drunk both shocked and saddened her. What had
brought it on? She determined to find out.

She was lunching with Caroline, who was flying off that
evening with Rupert to the Caribbean, where they had a
house in Barbados; but when she got to Tante Claire she
found her already on her second Martini – Jake had introduced her to the delights of the American variety – and
somewhat less than her ebullient self. Ah, thought Claire
. . . so there *was* a row.

'What's up?' she asked.

'Nothing. It's all down – and out for the count.'

'Rupert?' Claire asked deceptively.

'God no . . . I can handle him. It's Jake.'

'What has he done?'

'It's not what he's done, more what I've done.'

Claire perceived light at the end of her tunnel. 'Like what?'
she asked.

'Would you believe fallen in love?'

'Oh, dear . . .' Claire said, hearing the click as things fell
into place. 'Of the unrequited kind, I take it?'

'I wish you would,' Caroline said mournfully. 'I don't
know what to do with it. I didn't mean to do it. I just
couldn't help it. It was meant to be a bit of fun. I fancied
him, he reciprocated. I never meant to get involved. I never
get involved, you know me.' Caroline's blue eyes filled with
tears.

'Oh, love . . .' Claire reached out a distressed hand. She
had seen Caroline sail blithely through a dozen affairs, some
brief, others fairly lengthy but none of them meant; she had
always reached the marker buoy first. Love, to Caroline, had
been a game, one she was good at. Unlike Claire, she
had never had any illusions about it, regarding it as she
would the bubbles in a glass of her favourite champagne –
Roederer Cristal – insubstantial and equally prone to go flat
if not consumed quickly.

'Did you tell Jake you loved him?' Claire asked.

237

'Of course not! Give me credit for some sense! In any case, I never got the chance. Last night was my *congé*. It's over. Oh, he didn't actually kick me out of bed but I could tell. I've done it too many times not to know when it was being done to me. It was just one of those things, as the song has it. And the thing that did it was this – ' She dropped on to the table a three-inch-wide band of diamonds and sapphires.

'Wow!' breathed Claire.

'Bracelets like that either come at the beginning or the end. This one is my graduation present.'

'You could be wrong – '

'I'm never wrong where men are concerned. It's over. I knew it as soon as he walked in. He was – well, he was there but not with me, if you know what I mean. He was going through the motions, and what I ended up with was the shitty end of the stick.' Her eyes filled again. 'What am I going to do, Claire? What am I going to *do*?' Caroline wiped her eyes on her napkin. 'Now I understand about you and Rory. I never did before, not really. I always thought you mad to fall for a professional teaser, but now I've gone and fallen for a man who doesn't want to know. Oh, he was nice about it – he couldn't have done it better – but he was also quite final. And it's not as though he wasn't honest from the beginning. He told me he wasn't in the market for permanency. Let's just enjoy each other, he said. No strings, no fancy words. What we've got here is a good old fashioned case of lust at first sight.' Caroline buried her face in her napkin again. 'Love *is* blind . . . I read l-u-s-t as l-o-v-e. That's what becomes of being dyslexic.'

'Do you have any idea what brought it on?'

'None. He was fine the last time I saw him, but I took one look at his face last night and I knew . . . I know all the signs. God, I should by now. And when he made love to me his heart wasn't in it. He was being kind. That's the worst, I think. I can't handle kindness. It's not something I'm used to.'

238

'Yes, Jake is a kind man,' Claire said absently, yet truthfully. 'But something must have happened to cause the change.'

'Well I can't find it. He was – sad, somehow, and it had taken him to where I couldn't reach him. The fun had gone out of it . . . I longed to comfort him but I knew that was the one thing I shouldn't do.' Caroline's blue eyes still dribbled tears. 'He was – suffering, Claire, and I still don't know why.'

Neither do I, Claire thought, but it must have been very painful. Had he got drunk because he felt guilty? Because he had known he had hurt someone but had no choice? Her previous anger had evaporated. All she felt now was a kind of wrenching pity. I didn't know him at all, she thought uncomfortably. I *am* a lousy judge of character.

She shook her head at an advancing waiter who, in keeping with the impeccable standards of one of London's greatest French restaurants, immediately sailed by their table as if he had never been on his way to it in the first place.

'I hate love,' Caroline said miserably. 'It comes up behind you and mugs you when you least expect it. You are so right to hold it at arm's length. It's not cloud nine and moon and June and all that greetings card sentimentality. It hurts . . .'

Yes, thought Claire. It does.

'Where have I gone wrong?' wailed Caroline. 'Why couldn't he have fallen in love with me?'

Poor Caroline, Claire thought. For too long she had been the spoiled little girl with a nursery full of every toy she took a fancy to; for the first time in her life she had been told she couldn't have the one she wanted most of all.

'Go on,' she sniffed morosely, 'tell me I had a jolly good run for my money.'

'You did start at an early age,' Claire pointed out frankly.

Caroline smiled through her tears, but she said waspishly: 'Maybe if you had gained a little more experience you wouldn't have been taken by the first handsome face you saw.' Then her face fell again. 'Not that my experience has done me much good.' She sniffed, dried her eyes. 'I shall be like you,' she said decidedly. 'No man comes within six feet of you any more because he knows he'll get his equipment frozen by your first breath.'

Claire stiffened. 'Is that how you see me?'

'It's how you *are*, these days.'

'Oh . . .' Claire said, and it sounded as if she had been hit by a bullet.

'Well you are, honestly. I wouldn't say it if it wasn't true. Your warning lights are flashing at all times and as soon as a man crosses the line your sirens go off too. Just because one man did you wrong is no reason to banish the entire sex to Siberia. You used to be such *fun!* Now you tend to chill the atmosphere. Even Jake said it was a case of frost in May.'

'Jake!'

'Oh, don't look so shocked. He's an American. They aren't like us stuffy English, they take a real interest in people. But he said you made it plain from the start that even that was Not Allowed.' Caroline was well into her feelings-relieving gallop by now. 'You can't spend the rest of your life regarding men through the slit in your visor. If you intend to live a celibate life, why don't you enter a convent?'

'I'm just not ready – '

'You're always ready, but you chill instead of charm.'

'Then why are you sitting here crying into your Martini?' Claire demanded angrily.

'Because I feel like it. That's your whole trouble, don't you see. You've made a vow never to feel anything ever again. You're like an ex-smoker; you can't understand why people don't see the error of their ways and give up the daily weed, except with you it's love not tobacco that you've renounced.'

Claire sat silent, shocked to her core. Caroline had just shown her a picture of Claire Drummond that she found entirely repellent. No wonder Jake had said what he did. Worse, it had all been true . . . Her entire body writhed with shame. Jake had said she looked down on him. But I didn't know I was doing it, she pleaded in self-justification. All I wanted to do was prove that I could do a good job. So? Does it cost to be friendly while you do it? She looked back down the past months, and illuminated in the hard bright light of Caroline's words saw several occasions that made her hot with shame. She had been so single-minded in her haste to reach her goal that she had knocked against many a sensibility and trodden on a good deal of pride. No wonder he was furious with me, she thought. He has every right.

'Oh, for God's sake don't look so tragic,' Caroline said impatiently. 'I'm the one who's in need of consolation.'

'And you are the one who will find it,' countered Claire.

'See!' It was Caroline's turn to look affronted, but soon her unfailing sense of humour elbowed its way impatiently past her much weaker sense of drama, and she giggled. Then she said seriously: 'That's the difference between us you see, sweetie. I get straight back on my horse again. You have yours taken away and shot! Why don't you come with us to Barbados. It's crawling with thoroughbreds at this time of year. We'll find you a nice, steady one, not too fast until you get your nerve back – '

But Claire was shaking her head decisively. 'I couldn't. It's no use, Caro, I'm just not up to it yet. I'm sorry if I've appeared to be a – '

'Zealot?'

'Well, that's a bit far-fetched, but – '

'It's true, darling. Would I lie to you? Haven't I always told it as it is?'

Claire nodded, still having trouble keeping her hands from her ears.

'Then I shall rely on you to tell me who, where Jake is concerned.'

'Really, Caro, that is – '

'None of your business. You should have that printed on your cards. Well it *is* your business; *he* is your business. You took him on and you are not doing your job properly if you abandon him to the first Mayfair mercenary who comes along.'

'It's still a case of "hope springs eternal" then?'

'I am relying on you to keep an eye on him for me.'

'I shan't see him for ten days.'

'Oh, I'm not worried about America. The Jake Burns type is thick on the ground over there; it's over here that they are rarer than hen's teeth, which is why he will be got at unless you look after him.'

'I'm not his mother,' protested Claire irritably.

'Well, I can't very well ask you to act in any other capacity, can I? I mean – would you keep him warm for me?' At Claire's expression: 'I thought not. So mother him instead. I would have thought he'd be going to Scotland with you, but I suppose he has something or someone to spend Christmas with back home.'

Claire forbore to say that the thought of inviting Jake to Scotland for Christmas had never occurred to her. Nothing had been able to get through her determination to prove herself. As what? she thought now. The Iron Lady?

By the time she poured Caroline into a taxi, the wine she had drunk had her taking another in the opposite direction. But Jake had gone. The house was empty. There was no note, no nothing. She fell into the large chair in which Jake had been sitting only hours before. The room was tidy, quiet, only the little ormolu cupid clock ticking. Face it, she told herself bleakly, you've blown it.

Her mother was waiting at Inverness.

'You look fagged,' was her critical greeting. 'Not working too hard?'

'No.'

'Good. You can relax for a couple of weeks now, anyway. Just the family and a nice, quiet, traditional Christmas. The usual glen festivities, of course, but no madding crowd until Hogmanay.'

And it was good to help her mother decorate the tree,

choose the yule logs to burn in the twin fireplaces of the Great Hall, to hear the twins as their voices echoed around the rooms and corridors, admire the new baby, who would be christened over the holidays. Fergus, now doing a stint at Rosyth, would be coming home for the New Year, and Aunt Isobel, her father's only and elder sister, arrived on Christmas Eve in a blizzard, having had to be collected by Iain in the Range Rover once her ancient Daimler got stuck in a drift.

It was a white Christmas; the world was dazzling when Claire awoke. Her ruffled emotions were once more smooth after some intensive preening and though she was fully resolved to do better – her previous determination to tell Jake Burns what to do with his job having undergone an about face – her sense of guilt was compounded when, on opening the box he had given her, she saw a gorgeous, pure cashmere Hermes scarf in their famous horse design. All she had sent him was a Christmas card. Rory, she thought wryly, had left an important gap in his education of her: he had not taught her anything about Americans. What a good thing, she told herself, that I'm a fast learner . . .

Her mother, all her family, were naturally curious about 'her American'.

'Just what exactly is it that he does?' her mother wanted to know.

'Make money.'

'All Americans do that. I mean in what way.'

'Wheeling and dealing. He's an entrepreneur.'

'But he started in oil, didn't he?' her brother Iain asked.

'Yes.'

'Pity you didn't bring him up here for the holidays. I could have asked his advice. I've got an offshore company putting out feelers about that land I bought up in Sutherland; they want to build a new terminal. He'd be the man to ask.'

'Why didn't you bring him?' her mother wanted to know.

'It never occurred to me,' Claire confessed.

'Well, there's plenty of time yet.'

Is there? Claire wondered. She had heard nothing from him since their altercation. No word as to when he was coming back or whether he would want her to be there when he did. It would serve me right, she thought. I must have been insufferable. He was not to know that it had taken all her courage to take him into a world that had brought her nothing but grief. She had been so conscious of herself, so concentrated in her aim to let them see that Rory Ballater had not done for her, as was popularly surmised, that Jake and his aims had gone by the board. She had seen her job from only one angle – her own. No wonder he had been angry. She had thought: you have to remember he is an *American*; even their language is different. The fact that he paid her a salary, did not, in his eyes, mean that being an employee proscribed them being friends. No, it was Rory's pernicious influence which had done that. You will never be your own self as long as you keep looking over your shoulder, she warned. Your emotional wounds will never heal if you let his memory pick away at the scabs. Number One on her list of New Year Resolutions was to Turn Over a New Leaf.

And then, one day, coming back with the twins from a long ramble over the hills, where they had hoped to have a sight of the red deer, as they came out of the trees and on to the lawns, she stopped dead at the sight of the big American car standing on the gravel sweep by the front door.

'Visitors!' whooped the twins, running forward gleefully, the dogs leaping excitedly in pursuit.

He was in her father's chair in front of the big fire, long legs stretched towards it, listening to her mother telling him about Drummond history, but he was on his feet the instant Claire came round the big coromandel screen which kept draughts from the front door from sweeping in to lower the heat.

'There you are!' her mother said comfortably. 'Come and

get warm. These are my grandsons, Mr Burns. Jamie and Hamish. Come and say how do you do, boys.'

They came forward, fire-headed tearaways, and shook hands politely.

'Is that your car?' Jamie asked.

'Yes.'

'It's awfully big. Is it a racing car? It looks like one.'

'No, but it's fast. It's called a Thunderbird.'

'Is that 'cos it flies?'

'I wouldn't be at all surprised.'

'Run along upstairs to the nursery,' their grandmother said, and though it was softly spoken it was an order they obeyed. 'Nanny will have tea ready . . . fresh bannocks.'

The twins needed no second bidding. They raced off up the stairs. Claire had stood silently by. Now Jake turned to her and said politely. 'I had to come up to Aberdeen; there's an offshore oil conference there I thought I'd take in, and being so near I called the Castle. I thought maybe I could drive you back to London.'

'I told him to come over at once,' her mother said.

'How was your Christmas?' Jake asked, still politely.

'Very nice, thank you. How was yours?'

'Fine.' It was too hearty to be true. He looked tired, she thought. There were signs of strain.

'Are you alone? Where are Cora Sue and Henry?'

'Henry's gone back to open up the house. I left Cora Sue back in Oklahoma. She went down with jaundice over the holiday and she's not fit to travel yet.'

'Heavens, you're all damp,' exclaimed Lady Margot. In the bright light of the fire, Claire's red hair was covered in a shimmering mesh of moisture beads; they even clung to the ends of her dark red lashes. 'Go and have a quick soak in a hot bath. You've got time. The scones are still in the oven . . . run along now. I will entertain Mr Burns.'

Claire soaked in hot bubbles for ten minutes, then changed into a pair of well-cut mole-grey velvet trousers and a paler cashmere sweater. She brushed her hair, but left it loose, tying it back with a purple velvet ribbon, and applied the minimum of make-up. She was still on holiday, after all. She smoothed her sweater, turned this way and that in the glass. She felt strangely nervous. He had come. He obviously wished to continue the arrangement, in spite of his hard words, so it was a plus rather than a minus. That was what encouraged her to go back down.

Over tea, Jake met Iain and his wife. Claire's Aunt Isobel never came down for tea; she always rested in the afternoons until it was time for dinner. Jake did full justice to the plump scones, the fresh oatcakes, the home-made shortbread and the dark, shiny Dundee cake.

Afterwards, with her usual intuition, Claire's mother said: 'Why not take Mr Burns on a tour of the castle, Claire? But if you go out, do wear a warm coat. The glass tells me the temperature is dropping.' The dogs got up from the fire and padded after them.

'So this is a real Scottish castle,' Jake said. 'I guess it's pretty old.'

'Sixteenth century.' She showed him the shields and the claymores wielded by long-dead Drummonds; the Raeburns and the Reynolds portraits of men and women who had lived in the castle over the centuries. He showed a keen interest in everything, even tried to lift one of the two-handed claymores, but showed no sign of shame when he found he couldn't; only shrugged and said on an admiring headshake, 'You'd have to be a Goliath to wield that thing in a battle.'

'That was my father's firm belief: that his ancestors were much stronger than we are today.'

'They must have been. You'd need a crane to lift that thing.'

Of her father's portrait he said, head cocked first this way then that: 'You don't look like him except for the colour of your hair.'

'No; I take after my mother's family.' She must have sounded distant, trying as she was to formulate an apology that would not appear either makeshift or fulsome. She could

246

detect no discernible difference in his manner towards her except in one puzzling particular; what she had come to think of as his bright spirit seemed to have been dimmed. He had always been cheerful, even when he was being sarcastic or impatient. He was not the kind to brood or sulk or plunge everyone else into gloom by the weight of his mood, but though he talked as easily as ever, smiled as often, there was a definite dullness to his shine. Something, she thought uneasily, was on his mind. Snap! she thought wryly. Perhaps he has come to put things right. Even as she had the thought he brought it out into the open in the direct, impatient with shilly-shallying manner that was Jake Burns's signature. 'You're mad I came, aren't you?' he asked bluntly.

'No,' Claire said, 'I'm glad. I wanted to apologize for not inviting you for the Christmas holiday. My mother was surprised – and rightly so – at my bad manners.'

'Well, I came because I wanted to explain mine. I was out of line that night. I don't remember exactly what I said – I never do afterwards – but it must have been pretty lousy for you to take off like that. Henry gave me six demerits and said it would serve me right if you made me eat my words.'

'After the tea you've just put away?'

His white grin flashed, dazzling with what Claire realized was relief. 'Now I know I'm forgiven.'

'Can you stay the weekend?'

'Sorry, no. Conference begins tomorrow.' Offhandedly: 'Want to come along? You might find it interesting to see a bit of my world.'

Begin as you mean to go on, Claire told herself. 'Yes, I should like that.'

'Good. Shall we go back? While you get your things I'll have a word with your brother about the oil terminal he mentioned.'

'Would you? He'd really appreciate that.'

'Anything to oblige a friend,' Jake said readily.

*

'Such a *nice* man,' Lady Margot said *sotto voce* as she accompanied them to the car. 'Gracious!' she exclaimed, when she saw it, 'it positively squelches my poor Mini!' Her handshake was warm. 'I am so glad to have met you, Mr Burns. You will come and see us again, won't you, when next you are in Scotland?'

'Thank you, I'll do that.'

As they drove off down the drive he said to Claire: 'Now I know what you'll be like in thirty years.'

The snow had turned to rain but it was cold. Jake turned up the heat and Claire snuggled into the snow-fox collar of her coat. She felt so relaxed now as to be drowsy. She teetered on the edge of sleep, and as she did so her body slid gently towards Jake's, until she was slumped against him. She looked, for once, wholly defenceless and vulnerable, not at all the cool, unflappable, crisply competent woman he had come to like and respect. He wished he could remember what he had said to her to make her take herself off in such high dudgeon, but he had obviously drawn blood, and Henry had made his disapproval plain. 'This ain't no bimbo. It ain't one of your bought blondes, neither. This is a well-born lady and you don't speak to them like they was nothin' more than a lowly gofer. You got fences to mend, and if I was you I'd go get my gloves on.'

Which was why he had made the long journey to Castle Drummond. And what a fairytale place it was. The castle had risen out of acres ancient lawns like something in Disneyland: the perfect Scottish castle, seven storeys high with straight uncluttered walls crowned by a profusion of fairytale turrets, high-pitched roofs and decorated stonework. And the family – her family – were also straight out of a storybook. Close, at ease and affectionate with one another, especially her mother. He'd always believed you got a glimpse of the future by meeting a woman's mother. Claire's marriage had clearly been less a fairytale than a nightmare; so nasty that the whole thing had had to be dispensed with.

He slowed down to take the last corner before the final

leg to Aberdeen, and Claire moved slightly, murmured something indistinct before sighing once and snuggling down again. Her face in the dimness of the car was a pale flower, fragile and delicate, the luscious mouth slightly parted. Very kissable, he thought, and pulled his thoughts firmly back to his driving.

Claire became aware that someone was saying her name, shaking her. Opening blurred eyes she saw Jake grinning down at her.

'Come on, Sleeping Beauty. Time to wake up. We've arrived . . .'

'Where?' she mumbled sleepily.

'Aberdeen.'

'Oh . . .' She shoved herself upright. 'Have I slept all the way?'

'Every mile. And had lovely dreams by the smile on your face.'

He saw her lovely flush colour the creamy skin. 'How on earth did you manage to drive with me slumped against you?'

'It's an automatic.' His eyes, once more mountain-stream clear, were filled with laughter as he added mischievously: 'But I'm not.'

'I know. I've seen the blondes.' The minute she said it she knew she had blundered. The lights went out. She babbled the first thing that came into her head. 'Reservations?'

'Made.'

She gave him her best smile. 'Why keep a dog and bark yourself?'

'To keep the wolves away?' The blackout was lifting.

Now what have I done? she pondered, as Jake registered. He had a suite with two bedrooms. Got you, she smiled to herself. He had planned this, and while she was somewhat surprised by his confidence, she found herself approving of its strength, and of the way he was hailed, hand-wrung, back-slapped by men obviously delighted to see him. The conference was, naturally, predominantly masculine, though there were several women present, mostly in the capacity of assistants or secretaries, though one or two of them had fingernails which had never touched the typewriter.

'Want to come to the bar for a nightcap?' Jake asked, once dinner was over.

'No thanks. I'm for bed. You go and talk to your friends. I'll be bright and smiling come tomorrow.'

'Okay. See you at breakfast.'

Voices woke her. Checking her travel alarm she saw it was 2 a.m. One of the voices was Jake's. She'd know that laugh anywhere. She wondered if there was a blonde in the company, before turning over and going back to sleep.

The first day of conference was fascinating. Lectures, group discussions, seminars, huddles and, she had no doubt, a lot of Jake's favourite game. He introduced her to so many people she could not remember all their names, neither could she drink all that was pressed on her. Come dinner Jake refused all offers and bore her off to a table for two.

'You don't have to desert your friends because of me, you know,' she remonstrated.

'Don't be fooled by all the back-slapping. They have knives in their other hands. Anyway,' the light eyes were glittering, 'I would much rather be with you.'

'That's nice.' She kept it light.

'You're nice.'

Oh no you don't, she thought. I may have lowered the barriers but you still need a visa. Glancing round the crowded room: 'Full house,' she commented, 'but then, oil is the name of the game here, isn't it?'

'It used to be mine, but reserves won't last for ever. That's why, a couple of years back, I decided to diversify, spread my money around and use it to invest in other things. But oil made it possible for me to spread my wings –'

'And you like flying?'

Another grin. 'Right.'

Over their smoked salmon – he had become as addicted

to it as Claire was – he asked casually, 'So what have you got planned for the coming year?'

'Well, winter is quiet. Most people are away skiing or shooting or whatever.'

'I like to shoot.'

'Then I'll see if I can arrange a week's shooting for you,' she said easily. 'Then there's Twickenham.'

'What's that?'

'Where they play the Rugby internationals. I'm sure if I mention my brother Fergus's name I can get us tickets. He plays for a recognized club.'

'Popular?'

'It's England versus France so they'll come from all over the British Isles – about sixty thousand people.'

'Sounds great,' Jake said happily.

'What about golf?' Claire asked next.

'Don't play it.'

'Tennis?'

'Take it or leave it.'

'Well, there will be more polo later on – do you fish?'

'Have done, but it doesn't thrill me.'

No, thought Claire, too slow. Jake Burns liked everything that was fast-moving.

'Then I think a point-to-point,' Claire said decidedly.

'Now you're talking!'

'And there's Cheltenham in March, of course.'

'That I do want to see,' Jake agreed. 'Anything with horses.'

'Right,' Claire said, 'I'll fix it.'

They both laughed, then Jake saw Claire's light-heartedness hit the ground with a thud when a voice drawled, 'My dear, dear Claire. What a – dare I say pleasant – surprise?'

She had gone bone-white, and he saw that her pupils had dilated with terror, that she seemed to have stopped breathing. She did not look up at the man who had stopped by their table, and when at last she spoke her voice was strained when she said, 'No, you may not.'

'Still bearing grudges, I see.'

'You loaded me with them.'

She had still not looked up, was staring blindly and fixedly ahead. She was, Jake thought in shock, scared shitless. He looked up. The man was very tall, incredibly handsome. He had vividly blue eyes and hair the exact colour of a pedigree red Irish setter. Jake instinctively loathed him on sight, just as he instinctively knew who he was.

'I had hoped, by now,' the molasses-rich voice was saying in hurt tones, 'that you would be willing to let bygones be bygones.'

'You are the only thing I wish to be gone.' Her voice was unsteady and Jake saw that she was hanging by a thread.

Christ! he thought, horrified. This is awful. But it explained a hell of a lot. Why she took off if you got too close; why she took so much care to see that you didn't in the first place. Why he had always had the impression that she was always surrounded by a force-field. Because of this bastard. He saw she was clutching the table; her long fingers were white with the strain. The hell with this, he thought, but before he could get to his feet the rich voice went on tauntingly:

'You always were so violent in your passions . . . Aren't you going to introduce me to your friend?' The blue eyes interrogated Jake, from the cut and cost of his tweed jacket, the checked shirt and the faded chinos, to the watch on his wrist, then they dismissed him, but Jake was quite sure he would not be forgotten.

'Why?' Claire was asking, loathing making her voice shake. 'Still having trouble making any of your own?'

Jake saw the blue eyes flash, but Claire was already turned to stone.

'One thing at least hasn't changed. You still have a serrated tongue. You may bear the grudges, Claire, but I bear the scars.' He turned on his heel and sauntered away.

Jake saw Claire close her eyes and seemingly sway. He signalled a passing waiter. 'Brandy – a double on the double.'

He moved along the banquette to put his arm round her. She was as stiff as a board. 'It's all right, he's gone.'

She did not answer. Her face was deathly white and there was perspiration on her brow and lip. The brandy came and Jake put it to her lips. 'Go on – sip it. You need it.'

She managed a sip then shoved the glass away. Putting the glass down he pulled her against him. She went into his arms as if seeking refuge. As always, she smelled of roses. He held her without speaking until he felt the rigidity melt into convulsive trembling, so violent it made the table shake. 'Say the word and I'll go belt that son of a bitch,' he offered hopefully.

'No!' More controlled: 'No. Don't get involved. Not with him. He is a vicious and vindictive man who never forgets a slight. He would get even with you, no matter how long it took, and in as nasty a way as possible.'

'You sound as if you know him well,' Jake said carefully.

Claire's laugh was a choke. 'I ought to. I was married to him once.'

'That's your ex?' And how, Jake thought.

'It's two years since I divorced him. This is the first time I've seen him since.'

'What in God's name did he do to you that you should be so terrified of him?'

'I'd rather not talk about it.' The way she said it made Jake long to go and put his fist in that handsome face. 'I'm sorry . . .' she went on jerkily. 'This has spoiled your dinner . . . It's just . . . I wasn't prepared for him.' Bleakly: 'I don't think I ever will be prepared for him.'

'I'd still like to ruin that profile.'

'No, don't, please. He's dangerous – and he never fights fair.'

'He won't harm you while I'm around, and that's a promise.'

'Where is he?' Claire asked, still not able to look.

Jake glanced round. 'Gone . . .'

'You're sure?'

Jake checked again. 'He's not in the restaurant.'

Claire carefully pulled herself upright, glanced covertly round the large room. Only when she saw no sign of Rory did she heave a shaky sigh.

'He's gone,' Jake repeated. But not forgotten, he thought.

'I'll have that brandy now . . .' She gulped it down.

'Look,' Jake said baldly, 'maybe we should leave right now. If he's hanging around, this is no place for you.'

He could almost hear the sound of tearing choices. On the one hand she would like nothing better than to do a runner, as they said over here. On the other, she was both ashamed and embarrassed. Jesus, he thought. The British and their stiff upper lip. Why is it they regard their emotions as something to be ashamed of? They look upon any display of feeling as 'shocking bad form'. One English lady had said as much after quizzing him at length on the peculiar American habit of seeing a psychiatrist: 'We are taught that one's troubles are one's own affair; they must never be used as an excuse. Actually to *tell* them to a stranger is something beyond one's comprehension.'

'No,' Claire said at last, confirming his suspicions. 'You came here for the conference. I'm only along for the ride.' A glimmer of her smile appeared. 'I can't allow you to be run out of town by the Scottish equivalent of a hired gun.'

'How can I concentrate on business when I know you're concentrating on your stiff upper lip? What's another conference? We can get up from this table right now and leave, with no comebacks. Okay?'

'It would be very wrong of me to impose my troubles on you – '

'Where I come from it would be very wrong not to offer.'

Claire's second smile was just that much stronger. 'It looks like a case of the irresistible force meeting the immovable object.'

'I'm willing to move as soon as you give the word.'

Claire looked longingly in the direction of the hotel foyer. 'I won't deny I would feel better away from here.'

'So we go.'

'Then let's take the train. I can't allow you to drive all night – unless we share the journey.'

'You'll get no argument from me. We'll take turns to drive.'

They were on their way south within thirty minutes, the big car purring effortlessly down the A94, Claire giving directions at Perth where they joined the motorway. She did not talk, neither did Jake. She sat huddled in her corner, staring out at the darkness. Jake was conscious of a despair that shrouded the car like a Scottish mist. Eventually, she drifted off to sleep, and it was as they were coming down through the Northumberland moors that she began to move restlessly, uttering blurred murmurs and the occasional indistinct word until, suddenly, in that crystalline voice she used when she was all *hauteur*, not to say *froideur*, she said clearly: 'No, I will *not* do that!' Then, less certainly. 'No I won't . . .' Then obviously begging: 'Please, Rory, don't make me do that . . .' She caught her breath on a sob before proceeding to plead, in a terrified, imploring voice: 'Please don't hurt me, Rory . . . not again . . . please . . . ah, Rory don't!' Her voice rose, broke off in a shuddering gasp. Jake's foot hit the brake. He bent over her and she must have sensed him because her eyelids fluttered, lifted. In the faint starlight she saw the shape looming over her and at once both arms went up to shield herself.

'Jesus Christ!' The fury in Jake's voice brought her fully back to consciousness, and as she realized where she was, who he was, he saw her pale face flood with bright scarlet embarrassment.

'Claire – '

She scuttled back from him. 'I'm sorry . . . bad dreams,' she babbled, looking anywhere but at him. 'I'm sorry,' she said again dully, hopeless with defeat. 'It was seeing Rory again . . .'

'I've had a few nightmares myself.' Jake sounded as if he knew all about them.

'I haven't had one for so long . . . I thought they had gone for ever.'

'Unexpected shocks like the one you've had can throw you out of gear.'

'He ruined mine,' Claire said bitterly.

'I should have belted him.'

'He would only have belted you back. Rory was a boxing Blue at Oxford – before he got sent down.' Her smile was no more than a movement of the mouth. 'You're very kind. I'm sorry to be such a nuisance.'

'Have I complained?'

'I have no right to inflict my troubles on you – '

'Which is the nicely polite British way of telling me to mind my own business?'

'More a warning not to get involved. What time is it?'

'Twenty after midnight. What do you say we stop for a cup of coffee at the next service station?'

Another smile. 'You won't like it.'

'So I'll know better next time.'

He took one sip and made a face. 'I told you,' Claire said, but she laughed.

'Worth it just for that.'

'Why not let me drive for a while now?' she suggested, as they walked back to the car. 'I'm not tired.'

'Okay.' Probably scared stiff to go to sleep again, he surmised. What the hell had gone on in that marriage? he wondered, as Claire put the car into gear. Rory Ballater was as handsome a man as he'd ever seen, but Caroline had told him it was only window dressing. The man himself was obviously a shit; the kind who used violence. He had never seen anybody so scared. No wonder Claire was so cool, so distant. She'd probably had men up to here and back again. That little scene in the restaurant had explained a lot, but not how a woman like Claire Drummond, with her intelligence and innate taste, had come to marry such a man in the first place. He had been filled with hate, for starters. The blue eyes had been implacable with it: icy yet burning with the light of the obsessive. Claire, he thought, divorced or not, was not yet free of that son-of-a-bitch. That man, he decided, regards his ex-wife as still being his property, and Claire is scared stiff that he might try to claim it back. Not while I'm around, he resolved. I've got a good thing going here and I'm damned if I'll let anybody break it up. He liked Claire; he admired her. She was so got-together, all the more so since she was clearly held together with spit. Time I did some digging into Mr Rory Ballater – no, he's a Lord, isn't he? That means he's got clout. Okay, so I've got money. We'll see what matters most. Having settled the matter in his mind he shut his eyes and went to sleep.

By the time they bypassed Durham he was dead to the world. Claire put her foot down as she moved into the fast lane. The car fled south as if being pursued by demons. Claire found she was weeping silently, tears that in no way melted the hard core of her misery. She wound down the window, hoping the breeze would dry her face, realized she was gripping the steering wheel far too tightly. A glance at the speedometer showed her she was doing ninety. She eased her foot on the accelerator.

Just beyond Doncaster they ran into rain, so she slowed the big car right down, peering through the blurred windscreen. No sense in hurtling this machine across dangerously slippery surfaces. But by Leicester the rain was left behind so she increased speed again. That was when Jake woke briefly to ask: 'Where are we?'

'That's Leicester over there.'

'What happened to York?'

'Way behind us.'

'Want me to take over?'

'No. I'm all right if you are.'

'Sure,' he said, and closed his eyes again.

The miles flew under the wheels, but it was Claire who felt she was being driven. As they left the motorway at Hendon, though it was still dark, she felt relief and a sense of reassurance. Stopping for a red light she glanced in the mirror. She was pale, tense, tear-stained. As she gazed she saw that Jake was awake and looking at her.

'Not far now,' she said, as the lights changed.

'You okay? Not too tired?'

'No, but I'm looking forward to a cup of Henry's coffee.'

'Me too . . .' Jake sat up, yawned, raked his hair with his hands. 'You're a good driver.'

'I've driven to and from Scotland these many years.'

'Well, once we get back you can take it easy.' Casually, he went on: 'I've been thinking. Why don't you move into the house? It's not as though there isn't room, and with Cora Sue not here there might be one or two things I'll need doing . . . you can take dictation, can't you?'

'Yes.'

'Would you mind if I co-opted you into my business as well as my pleasure?'

'Not in the least.' She knew what he was doing and she was so grateful she wanted to weep again.

'Okay. Until Cora Sue comes back you live in.'

Once again their eyes met in the mirror. 'Thank you,' Claire said quietly.

His grin was cheerfully matter-of-fact. 'What are friends for?'

Claire seized her chance. 'I've been meaning to speak to you about that. I'm sorry if I was – well, what Cora Sue calls hoity-toity before. My mother quite rightly took me to task for displaying such bad manners and not inviting you to Scotland for the holidays. I would very much like us to be friends as well as employer and employee.'

'I've never thought of you that way.'

'I know you haven't. That was my mistake. I'm sorry.'

It was simply said but it was no mere platitude. He knew she meant it and he was touched as well as fielding his own embarrassment. What the hell *had* he said to her that night? He had taken so much bourbon on board that all memory was drowned. Whatever, he thought, relieved, it was all okay now. And with a character like Ballater bent and determined on some kind of revenge she would be a lot safer with two men – because he knew that Henry held her in equally high regard – around to offer protection. And that had been a perfect apology: no hedging, straight from the shoulder, objective but not abject. But she had that knack; that quality of being able to handle herself in any situation barring those where her ex was concerned. In that direction she had no control over the ball. Not that it was any surprise to him that Ballater was a sore loser. Claire Drummond was quite a woman. Cultivated without being stuffy, sexually highly charged yet never blatant or vulgar. Since meeting her he had come to understand what the word 'patrician' meant. Now he said: 'That's settled then. You move in right away.'

'Yes.' Her sigh was one of great content. 'It's settled.'

CHAPTER TEN

The summer was over. For the last six weeks, Claire had had the feeling of having drifted through it with no purpose but pleasure, when in fact the real – the only *intended* purpose – had naturally been business.

She had been surprised when Jake had told her casually that he had been invited to join Nico Constantine's party aboard his yacht *Circe*, which would cruise the Caribbean for a month then spend a couple of weeks at Newport, Rhode Island. 'Want to come?' he'd asked. Claire had hesitated. Her last experience of yacht cruising had been her honeymoon. 'Nico's a nice guy. Real catnip to the ladies. Rich too . . . An opportunity to sail away on the *Circe* is one that a lot of them are always prepared to fight for.'

Claire smiled teasingly. 'Do you need me along, then?'

'Not really. I'd just like you along, that's all. Do you mind?'

'No. I'm flattered,' she told him truthfully.

'It's not meant as flattery. You are good company.' Casually he added: 'Better than hanging around London on your own – unless you intend to go up to Scotland.'

'No. I'd made no plans. Mine were contingent on yours, naturally.'

'Then mine are to join the *Circe* in Miami.'

You'd be safe there, were the words unspoken, and with a rill of shock Claire realized that in the past three months she had given not so much as a thought to Rory Ballater. Standing in for Cora Sue, whose jaundice had turned into hepatitis, had been both enlightening and educational as well as highly enjoyable. She had learned much, not in the least how Jake Burns out-thought and out-fought his entrepreneurial rivals. And with no Cora Sue to punctuate every sentence with a disapproving sniff, or conduct herself either in frigidly disapproving silence or carping criticism, it had been even better. Jake might play hard but he worked even harder. In fact, he was a veritable demon. By now he was well known in the City; he appeared regularly in the financial pages. Only the previous Sunday he had been featured under the heading 'Lone Shark Tycoon joins battle for Morgan Mitchelson' under the byline of the City Editor. He was in the throes of a takeover; through a subsidiary owned by a subsidiary he had acquired 39 per cent of the shareholding, driving up the price meanwhile. Morgan Mitchelson was frantically looking for a white knight to ride to the rescue, but Claire suspected that once he was sighted, Jake would unload his shares at a considerable profit. What he was doing was practising a little 'greenmail'. He did not want the company as such, but he was quite ruthlessly using it to make a profit. She had been shocked, the first time she realized what he was doing. It had seemed to her to be unethical.

'No it's not,' he had said, 'the company is undervalued. Sloppy management and lackadaisical day-to-day control. All I'm doing is lighting a little fire under them. These fat cats need to know they can't expect to eat well for nothing. You watch – once people realize the potential there'll be a scramble. Somebody with the necessary wherewithal will finally come along and eat it up but it won't be me. I don't need this company. But I like to apply a little pressure now and then. Keeps my hand in.'

'And your profits high?'

'I don't do it for love, that's for sure.'

Claire was now his Executive Assistant, and had acquired a great deal of knowledge along with her title, as well as an increase in salary. She had learned the meanings of several all important words. Like *arbitrageur*, which meant a market professional who took positions over shares in companies involved in takeovers; *bear hug*, which described a notice to a target's board that a takeover was imminent; *block-purchase*, which meant buying a large number of a company's shares in relatively few transactions, often – especially so in Jake's case – with the identity of the purchaser disguised; and finally – one which tickled her fancy – *crown jewels*, used to describe a company's most valuable assets.

Jake Burns, she had discovered, was a corporate predator. He had formed a consortium – no wonder he had been so keen to meet certain important people – its major funding emanating from Burns Enterprises. Within a week of taking up her new duties she had found herself involved in Jake's pursuit of another independent oil company named North Star. Her instructions were to liaise with his broker – to whom she had introduced him – and as a nominee to buy as many shares as she could at the going price. The market was taken by surprise. North Star was small, unspectacular, but somehow Jake had found out – and he had a positive legion of agents worldwide – that they had discovered a huge new field in an area of exploration long ago pronounced dry. They needed to develop it but the initial venture capacity was beyond their present financial ability.

Claire watched in fascination while Jake ruthlessly acquired shares, so many that North Star finally broke and ran for cover to one of the Seven Sisters, with whom they merged, never to be seen again. It was then announced that North Star had discovered an apparently bottomless source of oil, whereupon the share price soared and Jake unloaded his holding for precisely three times what he had originally paid.

'But surely, wouldn't it have been wiser to have acquired North Star?'

'Nope. The oil is there all right, but it's going to cost to get it out. They'll pay it because at least they won't be in hock to the Arabs, but only one of the giants has the sort of money – and I'm talking billions – to develop it. I'd rather use mine to play a little more poker.'

'How did you know that North Star had made a major find?'

'I make it my business to know these things.'

'I asked how, not why?'

He had grinned. 'Nosy.'

'No, just interested. I find all this quite fascinating.'

'Good. Stick around, that isn't all you'll learn.'

But he never did tell her. Jake Burns played a mean hand at poker – and he played as often as he got the chance – because his sunny countenance gave no indication of the cards he held at any time. He had acquired a controlling interest in a North Sea drilling rig, and one of Claire's jobs was to pay the bills from the helicopter operator who ferried the crews to and fro. It was the tops in its field, with an excellent safety record, used by all the North Sea companies and competitively priced, but Claire had spotted that Jake also used a smaller, independent company, whose prices were that much higher.

He had readily explained why when she had asked him. 'Power balance. If I put all my eggs into one basket, what if one day I can't hire that basket and I badly need to get my eggs to market. They will see I am desperate and hold me to ransom. But if I know of another basket . . .'

Then there was the deal in which he acted as agent. A communist satellite country had suffered a series of bad harvests and was desperate for grain. Politically, the cold war being very chilly at that particular moment in the early eighties, it could not deal direct with the United States. Somebody, somewhere, thought of Jake, and through a firm of commodity brokers – again another introduction of Claire's – he immediately arranged to buy American grain. It was then shipped to Belgium. Once in Antwerp it was transshipped by rail to its destination, where the manifest showed Belgium as the grain's country of origin. Everybody was happy, especially Jake, who made a nice fat commission.

'You realize you were committing a cardinal sin in the eyes of your country?' Claire had asked sardonically.

'No way! We invented the fast deal. You think a business-man will say no to a multimillion-dollar deal because he doesn't like the politics of the buyer?' Jake had laughed. 'Politics is one thing, but as the President of General Motors once said – Big Business is America's business.'

She was soon totally, committedly involved. It did not take her long to discover not only how Jake worked – fast – but how he thought – like lightning. Soon, he was relying on her, trusting her with information that was Eyes Only a great deal of the time. She still presided at his dinners, still went with him as his 'date' to the social occasions he used quite ruthlessly to further his purposes. That he also generously provided little windfalls now and then for certain valuable people did him no harm at all, and when buttonholed by someone who wanted to know if a certain share was to be regarded as worthwhile, he always considered the question seriously and gave a truthful opinion. The blondes once more came and went. Caroline he continued to meet socially but that was all. It seemed he wanted no long-term relationships, even if they were short on emotional content.

'I thought I asked you to keep him warm for me,' Caroline said to Claire reproachfully, one evening at Leighton House. 'He's gone quite cold.'

'Jake is *never* cold.'

'Well, what passes for cold in his case.'

'I thought he was perfectly friendly.'

'Yes – *friendly*.'

Caro's glance was rancorous. 'You and he seem to be awfully chummy these days.'

'That's because we're friends.' She shook her head at her friend's disconsolate face. 'There is *nobody*, Caroline. No Mayfair Mercenary, no greedy-fingered suburban on the make. He's back to the blondes again.'

'*I'm* blonde.'

'But not a transient. They come and they always go. I don't think I have ever seen any of them more than once, and even then it's not a full-time thing. Sometimes I don't see one for weeks, then there will be half a dozen on the trot.'

'Doesn't it make you *wonder?*'

'No,' lied Claire, because she had, and frequently. 'They are a fact of his private life and I don't – repeat don't – have anything to do with that.'

And it was true. Jake had involved her deeply in his business, but even now, while she knew a great deal about the businessman she knew very little about the private man. He had his moods; he had been born without patience. He could be irritable, short-tempered, he could be scathing when crossed, he could be chillingly cold-blooded. But he could also be kind in a way that was like being wrapped in the ultimate in security; he had a decided sense of humour, he turned out to be a serious reader – he had a regular order at Hatchards for books he marked in red on the literary pages of the newspapers – he played a cut-throat game of Scrabble, rarely lost at backgammon, but poker was his favourite. Regularly, once a week, there was a game which went on all night. The players were usually American, but sometimes Claire would hear an English voice. She never intruded on them. Henry saw to the food and the drinks: American sandwiches, pretzels, peanuts and big pitchers of American beer – Coors was Jake's preference. He never ate breakfast, while lunch, unless it had a purpose, like persuading somebody to see things his way, was invariably taken on the run, but he liked a good dinner, and when it came to playing the host his hospitality soon became legend-ary. It had not taken Claire long to realize that behind the easy-going façade was a complex maze of wheels and pulleys, and that the light which shone in the pale eyes was no more than a mirror in which you saw what he intended you to see.

She herself, once it became known that she had his ear, was soon courted and flattered, both of which were, by now, water off a duck's back. Which was one of the reasons Jake had deliberately drawn her deeper into his maze. No risk of some smooth-talking, knife at the ready pirate taking her hostage. There was nothing you could get hold of.

One morning he asked her casually, 'How'd you like to see one of my horses run?'

'Very much.'

'Good. We leave tomorrow.'

At his suggestion she had acquired the necessary visa, so that when they flew off on the 10.30 Concorde the following morning – Sunday – there was no trouble entering the United States. At JFK they changed planes; a private jet belonging to one of Jake's friends, which flew them to Chicago. By one o'clock they were lunching with a group of friends prior to watching the race he had come to see. His horse won. At eight-thirty that evening they boarded a Chicago to London flight which got them into Heathrow at ten, the next morning. Claire went back to the house while Jake went off for a game of squash. That was typical of his schedule.

'How does he do it?' she asked Henry blearily. 'I'm dead. I never can sleep on planes. He was asleep as soon as the Unfasten Seat Belts sign came on.'

'Mister Jake is like a cat. He could sleep on a high wire.'

And frequently does, Claire shuddered. If I took the risks he does I'd dream I was falling and wake to find I was.

'He's got a lot of energy,' Henry explained kindly. 'He has to use it somewhere.'

'He is – highly charged. Doesn't his battery ever run down?'

Henry turned away to reach for the coffee percolator. 'I guess he always has a new one in his pocket.'

Which was why Claire, who had carefully prepared a full summer schedule, now tore it up without a qualm. Jake Burns knew what he was doing at all times, and in spite of the bit about 'fun' she was in no doubt that the real purpose of the cruise as far as Jake was concerned was business. She knew he was involved with Nico Constantine in a deal that was as yet known only to the two of them.

A week before they left, Cora Sue returned, physically recovered from her illness but now seeing everything through eyes that were pure canary. To find that Claire had now crossed the line that had been so threateningly drawn pleased her not at all. Her dislike now changed to open hatred.

'Pay no mind to Cora Sue,' Jake said briefly. 'She's jealous, that's all. I can handle her.'

And he did so in a way that had the yellow turned to sunshine by the time Henry drove them to London airport to catch the morning Concorde.

'What *did* you tell her?' Claire marvelled.

'That she was in charge. That I was relying on her to keep the stove going but make sure nothing got burned. That I knew things were in safe hands. That kind of thing.' He grinned. 'Not that it isn't true. Cora Sue can be a pain in the ass sometimes but I can't fault her loyalty or capability. She'll keep her beady eyes on every last thing, you'll see. Nobody gets one past her unless they blindfold her first.'

'You don't find her rather – possessive?'

'Sometimes, but she had a hand in raising me so I guess it's only natural she should want to mother me. The thing is, that with Cora that means smother.'

'She raised you?'

'My mother died when I was a kid. She'd been my father's right hand for years before that so he more or less turned to her to help out with me.'

'How old is she?' Claire asked curiously.

'I don't know. She admits to forty but that's giving away at least ten years.'

'Hasn't she any family of her own?'

'Not any more. Her father was my father's law partner – he died years ago. Her mother was an invalid – a professional one in my opinion – who ran Cora Sue ragged, but she coped with her until she died about five years ago. I guess I'm all she's got, really.'

Claire marvelled yet again that a man with Jake Burns's lack of patience was willing to suffer an interfering busybody like Cora Sue Mennenger, but it made one thing clear:

he was very loyal to old friends, a trait she approved of wholeheartedly. If ever I was in trouble, she thought, I would want this man on my side.

Nico Constantine's yacht, *Circe*, was a floating palace of some twenty thousand tons; white as the icing on a cake, with polished teak decks and brasswork which had you shading your eyes. He was not on board when they arrived; he had been called to New York on business, but they were welcomed by a woman whom Claire recognized at once, having seen her on the screen many times. In the flesh, her olive-skinned, dark Italian beauty – she was a Neapolitan – was every bit as potent, and the glorious body was exhibited with casual indifference in a body-skimming Azzedine Alaïa dress of matt white crêpe that emphasized her expensively acquired tan. People were known to shrug and say: 'Well, Onassis had his opera singer; Constantine has his movie star. You know how these Greeks are. Deadly rivals in everything.' It was an on-off relationship; their fights were legendary. Once, she had destroyed a whole Limoges dinner service by throwing every single piece at her lover's head. She would flounce off into the arms of some other man – there was always a waiting list – while he would install some other woman, but eventually there would be a reconciliation. Right now, the signals were green.

'Jake . . .' Oriana Falucci purred in her throaty voice. 'How nice to see you again. And this is Miss Drummond?' The cat's eyes did a quick scan, smiled when they realized there was no sexual competition, and a friendly arm was thrust through Claire's. 'Come, let me show you to your quarters . . . you're in your usual place, Jake,' she tossed over her shoulder, as she took Claire away.

'Do you like cruising?' Oriana asked pleasantly.

'I've only done it once.'

'Then you have something to look forward to. Tell me, how do you like working for Jake?'

'Very much.'

'A charming man,' Oriana agreed, 'if something of a

268

mystery.' When Claire did not answer: 'Do you not think so?'

'I have always found him very open,' Claire answered cautiously.

'But of course; that is how he is able to hide so much.'

'I dare say you have known him longer than I have,' Claire said diplomatically. *

'About five years . . .'

Another one, Claire thought. All Jake's friends were recent ones. Only Cora Sue had known him for years. It was as though he had sprung to life from nowhere in 1980, fully formed and raring to go. Where was he before that? Claire found herself wondering yet again. Cora Sue was a clam, and her attitude to questions was to regard them as prying, no matter how casual. Claire was mystified as to why a man so affably open was also so reticent about his past; but as she had her own secrets locked in a cupboard, she told herself she was the last pot to be calling the kettle black.

Her suite was sumptuous; luxuriously appointed sitting-room, a vast bedroom with a bed shaped like a gondola but hung like a hammock, swathed, like the Cristoflé dressing-table, in pure silk chiffon of the palest eau-de-nil. Big picture windows gave a marvellous view, hidden at the touch of a button by heavy felt-lined silk curtains. The adjoining bathroom had a sunken bath tiled in mosaics taken from a Minoan temple and depicting Neptune in his Chariot drawn by dolphins. The taps – also in the shape of dolphins – were gold plated.

Talk about conspicuous consumption! Claire thought, but knew, when Oriana asked, 'Do you like it?' what her answer must be, to be rewarded by a gratified smile. 'I did it myself . . . If I was not an actress I would enjoy being an interior designer.'

Everything was provided; from cosmetics – Estée Lauder – to shampoo, bath foam and matching talc, thick cakes of Guerlain soap – Fleur des Alpes – and perfume: none of them the kind Claire wore. She used only the one: Jean

Patou's 'Joy'. Behind one wall of mirrors were huge closets, and in addition to a selection of swimsuits from Christian Dior there were thick fleecy towelling robes from Ralph Lauren.

'The suits are Lastex – they stretch to fit you perfectly,' Oriana explained negligently. 'I didn't know if you prefer the maillot or the bikini so I have given you both.'

'Thank you,' Claire murmured, eyeing the swirling colours and minimal coverage. She had brought her own: a parma violet maillot with a high, straight-cut front but a deeply scooped back. It was part of her trousseau but it had not been worn since her honeymoon.

'Jake told me you were small,' Oriana said pityingly from her own five feet seven inches, 'so I took that into account. If there is anything you need that I have not thought of, please ask. Nico's instructions are that his guests must want for *nothing*.'

'What more could I possibly want?' Claire asked, gesturing to the surrounding splendours.

On a tinkling laugh: 'You are easily pleased,' Oriana said. Then: 'Jake is at the other end of the deck.'

'That is no concern of mine,' Claire said evenly.

'It's true, then? You actually do only work for him?'

'Absolutely.'

Oriana shrugged. 'Ah, well, you are not blonde, are you?'

'No, and I do not intend to be.'

Oriana surveyed her thoughtfully. 'You could do worse, you know. Much worse.'

I already have, Claire thought drily, but said, 'Jake and I have an excellent business relationship. We are also friends. And that, as he would say, is all she wrote.'

Oriana laughed. 'Well, there will be a first-class selection of very attractive men within easy reach should you feel so inclined.'

That'll be the day, Claire thought, but only smiled and said nothing. She met most of her fellow guests that evening at dinner, where she was glad she had chosen to wear one of her

Paris dresses; the Yves St Laurent of palest, pink slipper satin, cut low, with long tight sleeves, and sashed with purple velvet. Oriana was swathed in one of Mme Gres' classical Greek columns of virginal white, with chunks of rock crystal and gold twined around her throat and wrists. The other women were also of the type who believed their identity lay in the designer labels they wore, and as cocktails were served there was a quick examination of the competition to see who had the edge. The men were of the same calibre; not one of them would see thirty-five again, and some were doing their best to avoid hitting fifty. It was as they were drinking and chatting that Nico Constantine arrived back earlier than expected, and with him was a man on whom the women at once converged.

'Charlie!' Oriana swiftly swept them to one side as she moved in. 'What a delightful suprise.'

Nico came across to Claire. 'Miss Drummond . . . I am sorry I was not here to welcome you to the *Circe*. I hope Oriana saw you settled comfortably.'

'Very comfortably,' Claire replied, shaking hands.

'Now we are all here we can sail at once . . .'

'Not before you introduce me,' a dark-brown voice said, and Claire looked up into a pair of eyes as black as obsidian. 'Miss Drummond, this is Charles Whitman, a very old friend,' Nico said resignedly.

'Charlie to my friends.'

Claire found she felt strangely breathless in the face of something totally unexpected. His large hand enfolded hers. He was very tall, very big; very much in the style of Rory. He had hair as black as his eyes and a skin that indicated blood that came from Southern climes. His voice was the kind that raised hairs and he exuded a sensuality that mesmerized. He fixed his gaze on Claire, held her helpless for a moment then wound on the shutter. Claire felt a sizzle of electricity run from his hand to hers, right up her arm to her brain, where it set off sparks.

'I'm an old friend of Jake's,' Charlie Whitman said. 'We go way back.'

271

'How long would that be?' Claire asked lightly, conscious of nothing but him.

'We are from the same part of Oklahoma.'

'I see.'

'So do I – now. Like what Jake has been keeping to himself all this time.'

'Jake does not keep me anywhere,' Claire said, making her position clear. 'I only work for him.'

'Lucky man.'

'I make my own luck.' Claire turned to see Jake standing by.

'Hello Charlie.'

'I was just telling Claire, we go way back, you and I.'

But you don't like each other, Claire thought, immediately sensing an animosity, especially on Jake's part. She knew that look, that stance. What goes on here? she thought.

'I didn't know you would be along,' Jake was saying.

'I ran into Nico in New York and he told me you would be, so when he asked why didn't I come too I naturally changed my plans.' His smile was lazy but Claire again sensed the undercurrent of hostility. Charlie Whitman was taunting Jake. Why? She glanced at Nico, but he was talking to somebody else, giving no sign that he was aware of the two men bristling at each other.

'I guess I'd better go and get changed for dinner. I hope you've put me next to Claire,' Charlie said to Nico, slapping him on the shoulder.

'No, she is next to me,' Nico said on a parrying smile. 'Your turn will come later . . .'

Once again the obsidian eyes turned Claire's way. 'I can't wait . . .'

As he sauntered away, moving like some big cat, Jake said, 'Yeah, ain't he though?'

Claire found herself flushing. 'He does tend to – '

'Come on? That's par for the course with Charlie.'

'He said you were old friends.'

'We've known each other a long time.'

272

'Is he an entrepreneur too?'

'No. He's a lawyer. One of the high-priced, international kind.'

'But not yours?' Claire knew the name of Jake's American lawyer and it wasn't Charlie Whitman.

'No. Not mine.'

Not your anything, Claire thought, knowing Jake well enough by now to know that he was far from pleased that Charlie Whitman was along for the ride.

He was down the table from Claire at dinner; she sat on Nico's right, while Jake sat at the other end on Oriana's right; Charlie was somewhere in the middle, but he had the two best-looking women on either side. Afterwards, it was Claire he made a beeline for as they sat with their coffee, and her he set out to charm, much to the obvious chagrin of the other women, all of whom were with a man. Even Oriana, who was drifting around with a hostess's eye, managed to whisper *sotto voce*, while Charlie was refilling his brandy glass: 'Beware of Greeks bearing gifts, my dear. Charlie is what Jake would call an Indian-giver.'

That would account for the dark skin, Claire thought. Greek ancestry. Which explained why he was such a friend of Nico's.

'I understand you are a lawyer,' Claire said when he returned to her.

'You understand right.'

'A Clarence Darrow or a Jerry Geisler?'

'The best of both, I hope.' He looked around the room. 'I've seen most of these women through at least one divorce.' His glance was shrewd. 'I'd have acted for you for free.'

Claire stiffened.

'Sorry,' he said at once apologetically. 'Sore point?'

'One divorce has been more than enough for me, thank you,' she replied with chill politeness, wondering who had told him, certain only that it had not been Jake, but still furious to find she was, even at this distance, a target for gossip.

273

He then proceeded to score a bullseye: 'If you are wondering how I know about yours, I was Bruno de Souza's American lawyer.'

'Was?'

'Not any more. I don't do drugs, in or out of court. I recognized you from your picture.'

'Picture!'

'In one of the English magazines your husband still read. An article on Jake . . .'

'Oh.' Claire remembered the one.

'Where was this?' she asked at last.

'Rio.'

'Is he still there?'

'No idea. I haven't seen or heard of Bruno since I told him to find another lawyer.'

'I see.'

'Okay, so you're divorced,' Charlie Whitman said on a shrug. 'So am I. Who isn't, these days?'

For some reason Claire found the name Jake trembling on her lips but she did not utter it.

'From what I saw of the guy you're well rid of him. He was decidedly flaky.'

Oh, yes, thought Claire. More layers than a *mille feuille*.

'So,' Charlie Whitman said, leaning back comfortably, 'how do you like working for Jake?'

'Very much.'

'I haven't seen much of him since he took to travelling the world.'

'Do you live in Oklahoma?' Claire asked politely, her mind still dealing with what he had told her.

'No. New York. But I still have an office in Tulsa.' He sighed. 'I've just come out of a nasty lawsuit in which both parties trashed each other to hell and back so I was glad to take up Nico's invitation. I need a break.'

'Are you his lawyer too?'

'That I am.'

'So you too are combining business with pleasure?'

His grin was amiable but he said approvingly, 'You are every bit as sharp as they told me you were.'

'Who told you?'

'Oh, people who'd been to Europe and knew what Jake was up to. I suppose you've found out already that Jake is an object of everyone's curiosity.'

'No,' Claire disagreed politely, 'I haven't, actually.'

The grin flashed again. 'Oh, very English. I love the way you say that word – actually. English as she is really spoke is a real put-downer. Makes us look like the Colonial hicks we are. I guess that's why we anglicize our names as soon as we can and pay a thousand dollars a time to be in the same room as royalty. Take the present company, on this yacht; Victor Burger, for instance. He was born Vittorio Buorgognoni, and Harry Lester was once Hectore Lasenza. They both came out of the Lower East side and now live in the Upper. Victor's present wife was once cruise director on one of his liners whilst Susie Lester started life as a waitress in one of Harry's hamburger joints. They are both millionaires umpteen times over and at the same time have had themselves made over. But you are the only real lady on board this boat right now. And they know it. That's probably why Nico asked Jake to bring you.'

Claire salted that surprise away with the ones he had already dealt her. 'Jake knew what he was doing when he took you on – but then, Jake is a man who takes good care always to know what he is doing.'

'And you don't?'

'*Touché*,' he said, flashing his grin again. Then: 'You were introduced to me as Claire Drummond. Don't you use your title any more?'

'It was mine only while I was married to its owner.'

'Not all Englishwomen think that way. A client of mine was a former duchess when she married again; when she got divorced she went back to calling herself Duchess.'

'Every woman to her own taste,' Claire said crisply.

'What are yours?'

275

'I am not in the witnessbox, Mr Whitman.'

'Charlie.'

'Not what we call a "right Charlie" I trust?'

His laugh was full throated. 'Nico said you had a sharp tongue.'

'All the better to cut you with,' Claire said sweetly, before getting up and leaving.

She was conscious of Charlie Whitman's eyes on her during the rest of the evening. There was dancing, or a movie, or backgammon, none of which interested Claire, who made a point of slipping away from the salon as soon as she could.

The July night was balmy, the sea calm, the wake of the ship sparking like showers of diamonds. The moon was almost full, and it rode low in the sky, which was cloudless. She found herself a steamer-chair and sat down to think. It disturbed her that a man she had never met before knew so much about her. There had been a knowingness in his eyes. God knows what Rory had told him. *Damn* that magazine article! She had not wanted to be included in the first place, especially under the caption 'The Ultimate Girl Friday?' Jake had laughed, thought it apt, but she had thought it snide. And had Nico Constantine asked Jake to bring her? If so, why? If he had thoughts of replacing Oriana he could damn well think again. She was perfectly content as she was, thank you very much. She liked the freedom that no emotional ties gave her. Not to mention the absolute sense of safety. She was deep in her thoughts when a voice said, 'I would offer you a penny for them but they look as if they are worth a fortune.' Charlie Whitman eased himself into the next chair.

'If you are as persistent in court as you are outside it you must be an awfully good lawyer,' Claire observed tartly.

'Once I know what my case is, I never let up,' he acknowledged gravely.

'I don't need a lawyer.'

'I'm not offering myself in that capacity.'

'I am not open to offers either.'

'You haven't heard mine yet.'

'Nor wish to.' She rose to her feet. 'Don't waste your time on me, Mr Whitman. I am not on the market. Good night.' She swept by him only to find him by her side as she walked swiftly in the direction of her cabin.

'Let's start again,' he offered pragmatically. 'Miss Drummond, I find you very attractive and I would like to spend as much time in your company as you are willing to grant me.'

'Why?' Claire asked baldly. 'I don't "put out", Mr Whitman.'

'That's not surprising since you were so put upon.'

Claire whirled on him. 'Who have you been talking to? Making my business yours without permission! All right, so you know my former husband. That gives you no right to assume that you have the right to know me. Furthermore, no friend of his is a friend of mine.'

'I didn't say he was a friend. I said I had met him, and only the once.'

'When he no doubt gave you his own version of events.'

'He gave me nothing – except the creeps. All right, so when he saw the magazine article he got a bit uptight about it. He seemed to resent your obvious success.' A shrug. 'I'm an American, so I don't resent successful women. They come by the dozen where I come from. I guess they're not so common in Europe – not that you are common in any way. *Au contraire*; on this boat you stand out like a nun in the red light district.'

In spite of herself Claire had to laugh. This man was pure sorbo rubber.

'That's better. You have a lovely laugh.'

'And you have a nerve.'

'When you represent a woman asking for fifty per cent of everything her husband made long before he even met her you need one.'

'Do they really – ask for that much, I mean?'

'Only because it's not likely they'll get the hundred per cent they'd rather have.'

'Mr Whitman, you are a cynic.'

'Nope. I'm a lawyer – and a damned good one.'

'I told you, I don't need a lawyer.'

'And I don't chase ambulances any more.'

Claire was fascinated. 'Did you ever?'

'Of course I did. That's how I got started.' He took her elbow. 'Let me tell you about it . . .'

When she got back to her stateroom it was well after midnight. Charlie Whitman had held her spellbound for more than two hours. He had the cheek of the devil and the charm of a daredevil. He made her laugh, he made her mouth round into an O with descriptions of the cases he had fought. She had been so enthralled that she had neither seen nor heard Jake, who had come looking for her; not realized he stood in the shadows watching for a few moments, an expression she would have recognized on his face, before turning on his heel and striding away. But Charlie Whitman had.

She sat down at the Cristoflé dressing-table to remove her earrings, only to find to her chagrined astonishment that her hands were trembling and in the hollow of her throat was a fluttering that kept perfect time with her heart. Wide-eyed she looked at her reflection in the mirror and saw a face she had not seen in a long time: flushed, radiant, alive. Her eyes sparkled; lit from within as once they used to be. Charlie Whitman, it seemed, had managed to find the well-concealed switch.

How? she thought. Why? Why *him*? He was the sort of glib-tongued, irritatingly over-confident man she had hitherto given a very wide berth. All right, so he was clever and she admired brains (and to be awarded a full scholarship to Harvard at the age of sixteen, to be followed by graduation Magna Cum Laude at the age of nineteen, and a Law Degree at twenty-two was, to say the least, brainy) but he was too full of himself, absolutely confident that he only had to stand and wait for the ripest plums to fall into his basket. How come, then, that the past two hours had seemed no longer than the blink of an eye? As the song said, Why this feeling, why this glow? So unexpected and from what she would have considered, had she been warned, entirely the wrong direction. Hold on there, she told herself. You *were* warned. Oriana told you to beware of Greeks bearing gifts: that he was an Indian-giver, which meant, according to her newly acquired ability to speak and understand American, that what he gave he invariably took back. The question before the jury, she told herself sternly, eyeing her reflection with the cold eye of reason, is do you want it? No – not want. Need. Do you *need* it? No, she answered herself. I don't. Want I can understand, but need – need is something I intend never to take me captive ever again.

That decided, she got ready for bed, only to lie staring up at the darkness, going over it again.

Next day, Charlie Whitman launched an assault that had her on the ropes before she could begin to weave and dodge. She found herself waking each morning with a sense of anticipation as sharp as any of Henry's beautifully kept Sabatier kitchen knives. Charlie was fun to be with; he was light-hearted, he was a witty and amusing conversationalist, he was highly intelligent, and he was a marvellous dancer. Claire loved to dance; it came to her naturally. That was one of the penances of going anywhere with Jake; he had absolutely no sense of rhythm; he couldn't carry a tune either, but Charlie Whitman could whistle like a bird with absolutely perfect pitch. He could also play the piano, and for the first time in years Claire found herself playing duets. He had a smile that drenched you in its sexuality, and he could charm the heart out of your body without you feeling a thing. And he never laid a finger on her. Not until, having made a leisurely perambulation through the Caribbean, they turned north once more, making for Nantucket.

Here, he hired bicycles for them both, and Claire found herself making a round trip of some twenty miles, from Nantucket Town to Surfside then back again to Milestone

Road, all the way to Siasconset – pronounced Sconset, he told her. They dined together at the Woodbox, and he took her to her first clambake. He took her surf-fishing, where he caught a big bluefish which he himself cleaned and cooked over a driftwood fire on the beach that night. They went for sundaes at the Sweet Shop on Main Street, and ate Eggs Benedict at Arno's.

'Oh, this has been marvellous,' Claire sighed, on their last night, as the *Circe* prepared to sail for Newport. 'I've fallen in love with Nantucket.' She turned to Charlie, leaning on the rail beside her. 'Thank you so much.'

'My pleasure, and I mean *pleasure*.' Then he said what had been said about her before. 'You have the knack of turning even the smallest act of kindness into a source of the greatest pleasure. I like that.' He paused. 'I like you.'

She found herself pinned by the shiny black eyes, did not – could not – move when he bent from his great height and put his mouth on hers. Claire felt her stomach plunge. She put out a hand to clutch at his sleeve as her whole body went with it. When she came up for air she found herself trembling and held in an embrace that had her off the deck, looking over Charlie's shoulder and straight into the ice-cold eyes of Jake. Charlie felt her stiffen for he released her, turned. 'Hi, Jake . . .' he said lazily. 'Something we can do for you?'

'Not right now,' Jake answered. 'I was just wondering where Claire was, that's all. I haven't seen much of you lately,' he said to her pointedly.

'I'm sorry.' Claire felt stiff with embarrassment and not a little anger.

'Come on, Jake, this is vacation time. All work and no play makes Jake into a very dull boy.' The mocking quality was there again. Claire was in the middle of that same powerful current of animosity she had felt once before.

'I must go and change for dinner,' she said hurriedly. 'If you will excuse me.'

Walk, don't run, she counselled herself firmly, and managed to throw a smile which encompassed them both before making a quick exit, but not before she heard Jake say, in a voice that strangled on the rage he was boiling: 'You haven't changed, Charlie. You're still the same unscrupulous son-of-a-bitch.' And to her horror, she heard Charlie laugh.

In her stateroom she fell on to her bed and tried to make sense of what had happened, not in the least her own, instant, wholly uncontrollable reaction. She was churning inside from Charlie's kiss. She, who had believed all feeling dead, murdered by Rory and with coldly deliberate malice afore-thought. Charlie had kissed her tonight because somehow he had known Jake was there. Why? What goes on here? Her instincts told her that she had blundered innocently into a situation bristling with unsuspected dangers. For God's sake, she told herself irritably, Rory has made you suspect everything and everybody. Then how come Charlie had such a devastating effect? Because in spite of what you thought, your certainty that Rory had left your feelings for dead, they are very much alive. It was a dismayingly unexpected development, one which brought her face to face with a fact she had studiously walked around ever since Charlie had joined the cruise. The fact that at first glance she had found herself powerfully attracted, even as she knew he was the kind of man she had learned to distrust; the kind who could lead any woman down the garden path, no matter whether it was paved with good intentions, high hopes or sweet dreams. While he had stuck to the main, well-lit path, she had been the one to eye the shadowy cul-de-sacs, the dimly lit turn-offs. Now, she was uncomfortably aware that she had landed up right at the bottom of the garden, in a newly dug section marked 'bedding plants'. She was also confused: Charlie had somehow flourished her at Jake with something like derisory contempt. Why? I don't understand any of this, she thought restlessly. I only know I don't like it. Neither did she like being torn between the eager dictates of her emotions and the coldly experienced logic of her head.

She slept badly; her mind refused to shut down. She kept

wondering what it was that lay between the two men, kept telling herself it was nothing to do with her, that she should refuse to become their particular bone of contention. Cool it, she decided, as she once more pounded pillows preparatory to another try at sleep. Remember your family motto and 'Gang Warily'.

She slept late next morning, awoke to find that the *Circe* had already docked at Goat Island. It was noon by the time she went on deck, to find the boat deserted. When she went to the dining-room for a cup of coffee she found Jake there, reading *Newport This Week*.

'Hi.' He smiled up at her. 'Thought I'd wait for you, take you for a look-see at Newport.'

'That would be nice.' Claire seized at the straw with relief. He did not mention Charlie. Neither did she, but she did ask, 'Where is everybody?'

'Ashore. The women anyway. Buying out the stores. The men have gone fishing.'

'And you don't care for fishing.'

'Right. I'd rather show you Newport.'

'Do you know it well?'

'I've been here a couple of times.'

'Then do you think we could see the Mansions? I've heard so much about them. I'd like to see the so-called "cottages" where the Vanderbilts and the Astors and the other legendary families spent their summers.'

'Sure. Why not?'

So they spent the afternoon with the rest of the tourists, stood in line to see The Breakers, Marble House and Rosecliff, where Claire felt overpowered by the size and ultra-lavish decoration of vast houses built and furnished with one aim in mind – to impress. In the Gold Ballroom at Marble House, she goggled at the carved gilt wall panels, the enormous chandeliers, the giant mythological figures perched – and looking in danger of falling – on the corners of the grey marble fireplace. 'Golly!' she breathed, blinking in the dazzle.

'Of course,' Jake said, straight-faced, 'I don't suppose this comes anywhere near that palace you took me to – the one called after the battle.'

'Blenheim Palace?' Tactfully: 'These are – different,' she murmured.

'And few. You have them by the dozen, besides which, you were born in a castle.'

'Not like this! Do you realize that this cost eleven million dollars *then*. I shudder to think what it's worth now.' She shook her head. 'Castle Drummond is positively *shabby* compared to this.'

'Well, it's several hundred years older.'

'Can't you imagine what it was like when they held a ball? No wonder it was called the Gilded Age. Every last thing *is* gilded. What a pity Henry James never wrote about rich Americans here, instead of them being taken in by calculating, degenerate Europeans.'

They didn't have time to see all the mansions, and as Claire said truthfully, the three they had 'done' had given her decorator's indigestion. 'It was all that gold leaf,' she said later, over a drink at the White Horse Tavern. Later, the stores being open until nine, they prowled Bowen's Wharf, where she bought herself a pair of Topsiders and several T-shirts, as well as one for Caroline and another for Mollie. For her brother Iain she bought an antique duck decoy, and for her mother – for whom she had already bought a Nantucket Lighthouse Keeper's basket – she bought a lovely primitive painting of a small child holding a dog, *circa* 1810. For Fergus she bought a marine painting of an America's Cup winner: Harold S. Vanderbilt's 'Ranger' trouncing the competition. They went back to the yacht laden, Jake hefting a selection of plastic bags and Claire equally burdened.

They found the women already back, having themselves plundered the stores, but mostly for clothes and jewellery. The men trooped in later, having caught a goodly selection of bluefish, swordfish and – caught by Charlie naturally – a white marlin. Dinner was gay, with much laughter, and having stuck to her all day, Jake seemed disinclined to unglue himself from Claire's side. Now and again Claire caught Charlie's quizzical glance; it told her that he knew exactly what Jake was doing.

Next day, they piled into cars and drove to The Inn at Castle Hill for brunch, which they ate out of doors to music played by a good trio of piano, guitar and double bass, and that night they took in the Newport Jazz Festival, where one of Claire's favourite singers was appearing: Mel Tormé, 'the velvet fog'. His set was rapturously received, and Claire applauded till her hands stung.

'What a way to end a holiday,' she sighed, as they drove back to Goat Island. 'And another twelve days to go . . .'

'I'm glad you're enjoying yourself,' Jake said.

'Enjoying! That's the understatement of this or any year.'

'Want to see the rest of the mansions tomorrow?'

'Yes please!'

After Château-sur-Mer, The Elms and Kingscote, Claire refreshed her jaded palate in the Hunter House on Washington Street.

'Ah . . .' she breathed. 'Now this is perfection. This is what we think of when we talk of American houses. I could live in this one. Small but perfect, absolutely perfect. No gold leaf, no gilt, no marble, no ostentation: just good taste. This is a true national historic landmark.' And she was delighted to see, in one of the bedrooms, a George II jug, a replica of which stood in the hall at Castle Drummond. She enthusiastically bought several postcards of both the interior and the exterior to show her mother. 'She would *love* this.'

Then Jake took her to see a game of Jai Alai; as it was a Tuesday night it was also Ladies Night, and Claire received a free reserved seat. Afterwards, she demolished a three-pound lobster which she liberally dipped in melted butter.

Next morning, Jake was called to the phone and when he came back he said casually, 'I've decided to throw a party on our last night – a week Saturday. Would you organize it for me?'

'Of course? Where? Here on the yacht?'

'No. I've hired The Breakers for the evening.'

Claire goggled. 'You've *what!*'

'From The Newport County Preservation Society. They let you rent a mansion for the night. Swells their funds. You have to promise not to break anything and pay if you do, but you did say you would like to have seen what such a house looked like – *en fête* was your expression, as I remember.'

'I was merely speculating! I never expected you to take it as a wish!'

'Why not? You know I like throwing parties, why not the biggest one yet?'

'But The Breakers is huge! We are twenty on the yacht.'

'There'll be a few more than that.'

'How many?' Claire asked suspiciously.

'Oh . . . another hundred or so. I thought people could come across from Nantucket and I've met up with a lot of old friends here in Newport . . .'

Claire looked askance. 'You are a pious fraud,' she scolded roundly. 'I think you've been planning this for some time.'

Sheepishly: 'The thought did cross my mind.'

'Then why leave it until it gives me exactly eleven days to organize it!'

'I wanted you to see them all before making your choice.'

'But – food, flowers, an orchestra – not to mention invitations!'

'Here.' He thrust a name and telephone number at her. 'This is the name of the lady at The Newport County Preservation Society. She said she'd be glad to help. She knows, as you would put it, the drill.'

And she did; she provided Claire with the names of the 'right' people to turn The Breakers into a lantern-hung, flower-filled, champagne-high, glittering setting for a ball that eventually made the columns. But it took most of Claire's time over the next twelve days. If she was not conferring with the florist she was planning the buffet with the caterer, deciding on the various kinds of lanterns, hiring dozens of gilt chairs, arranging for the exquisite Grand Salon, all white and gilt and heavy gold curtains, to be cleared of furniture so that the dancing could take place there, and for the immense dining-room with its vaulted ceiling also to be cleared to allow the long buffet tables to be set up. There were dozens of things to be seen to, and if she was not dashing here she was dashing there, so much so that Charlie complained.

'I never get five minutes with you,' he protested.

'I don't have one, never mind five. I've too much to do.'

'I think Jake knew that when he asked you to arrange it.'

Claire felt a frisson of shock. Why had she not thought of that? But she said composedly, 'Your over-active imagination is working overtime again.'

'Is it? I think old Jake is jealous, so he dreamed up this little extravaganza just to keep you on the hop and out of my reach.'

'You seem to forget, this sort of thing is my job.'

'You mean he's made it so.'

'Charlie, I really haven't time to discuss Jake's motives, whatever they may be. I have to see about the tablecloths and the china and – God, a hundred and one things . . .'

And she had made a quick exit, only to find herself mulling over what had been said. Had Jake entered on this hugely expensive, intricately detailed enterprise for the sole reason of prising her from the pursuing arms of Charlie Whitman? Surely not, she told herself. Jake has not so much as given you a second glance as a woman. Use your much vaunted common sense. It's Charlie who is jealous, not Jake. And she found that that knowledge gave her a glow. On the other hand she was perversely glad that she was so busy. Charlie had been getting entirely too close for comfort. If nothing else, what Jake had done was provide her with breathing space. Such a *kind* man, she thought. He understands my fears. But then, he met Rory . . .

Every invitation was accepted, from as far away as Los

Angeles. But there was one – to her – significant omission: not one of the names on her list came from Oklahoma.

As it was a ball, it called for something splendid in the way of a gown. She decided on the paper taffeta Balmain; a great sweep of a dress inspired by the crinoline worn by Anna Leonowens in the 'Shall we Dance?' scene from *The King and I*, only instead of pink it was of deep, glowing amethyst. With it, she would wear the jewellery her Aunt Isobel had given her last Christmas: a delicate confection of cabochon amethysts and pink sapphires in the shape of violets, with black pearls at their centre. 'I was going to leave it to you in my will,' that redoubtable old lady had said, 'but since that scalliwag you married made off with what jewellery you had, you might as well have it now.' It had been given to her Aunt Isobel when her husband had been Governor of a princely Indian State, and in addition to the necklace there were earrings, at least four inches long, and a matching bracelet. In keeping with the kind of dress it was, she had her hair dressed in the style known as 'cottage loaf' with curling tendrils at brow and nape, and the varnish on her nails was an exact match to the pink of her lipstick.

As she stood with Jake, welcoming the guests as they arrived, she was conscious that her appearance was making quite a stir, which Charlie confirmed when, as he bent over her hand, he murmured, 'Oh, yes, yes indeed.'

In keeping with the kind of ball it was, and the situation in which it was being held, Claire had provided dance cards of thick vellum with tiny gold pencils attached, and she was not surprised when Charlie plucked it from her wrist to scribble his initials all over the place. 'You're not getting away from me *this* time,' he promised.

She was never off the floor; so that it was almost midnight before she found time to take a breather, when she took her glass of champagne up to the first-floor loggia, hung with Japanese lanterns and awash with great marble urns filled with cool green ferns, its vaulted ceiling covered in a mass of tiny mosaics set in a design of the Italian Renaissance.

The breeze was refreshing; not cool but still welcome after the heat of the dance floor; best of all, it was deserted. Leaning her elbows on the marble balustrade she gazed out over the lantern-lit cliff walk and the terrace beneath, where couples were dancing to the music of the orchestra recommended by the lady from the Preservation Society. The moon was full, the sky cloudless. Sighing with pleasure she eased off one high-heeled lilac satin sandal to rub her aching foot up and down her calf before flexing her toes and placing her foot flat on the cold tiles. Ah . . . bliss. It felt so good she eased off her other sandal, at once taking three inches off her height and a load off her mind. It had gone well. Everyone was enjoying themselves, and the food she had carefully chosen had all been devoured; sea-food cocktails of chunky lobster, crab and shrimp; poached and smoked salmon, quails' eggs, fresh asparagus wrapped in smoked salmon and rolled in wafer thin brown bread. Fat raspberries she had got her mother to send over from Scotland, which she had marinated in white wine, piping hot vol-au-vents stuffed with devilled chicken or spicy mushrooms; huge hams, baked then glazed and studded with cloves, and as *pièce de résistance*, two huge haunches of venison she had also asked her mother to send. And crates and crates of champagne. At 8 a.m. she would provide, English fashion, a typical post-ball breakfast; bacon, eggs, kidneys, mushrooms and tomatoes, with lots of coffee. Jake had approved of the latter. 'One of the better English customs,' he had enthused.

He was out on the dance floor somewhere; with his endless energy he always milked these occasions to the last drop. She had had a couple of dances with him, but he had been so busy playing the host that apart from the occasional 'It's all going great' from him, they had hardly seen each other. He had complimented her on her dress, in his own fashion: 'Nice,' was all he had said, but a 'nice' from Jake Burns was worth a dozen more fulsome compliments from anybody else.

Oriana, resplendent in a striking Oscar de la Renta of

scarlet satin, had murmured, 'So very English, my dear,' and the topaz eyes had been somewhat hard, but Nico had been openly admiring. 'Perfect, quite – perfect.' And who is to know that this dress is almost three years old, Claire thought now, smoothing its folds. She had bought it in Paris, but this was only the third time she had worn it.

She sipped her champagne and luxuriously wiggled her toes on the marble floor.

'Hi,' a voice said, and she whirled to see Charlie regarding her smilingly, a glass of champagne in each hand. 'Taking five?'

'Ten if I can manage it.'

'You can. Everybody is too intent on enjoying themselves to notice your absence.' Pause. 'Except me.'

Claire put down her now empty glass and took the one he offered.

'You certainly know how to organize a party,' he complimented.

'Thank you.'

'I expect you've had a lot of experience.'

'Enough.'

'Jake certainly found himself a paragon of all the virtues when he found you. How was that, by the way?'

'He contacted the agency I was helping to run at the time.'

'Are there any more at home like you?'

'Sorry, no. I have three brothers.'

'How come I can never seem to find a Claire Drummond?'

'Come to my agency.'

'Ah, but you won't be there.' He eyed her over his glass. 'But would you be open to a better offer?'

'I am not open to anything,' Claire told him distinctly.

'Why not?'

She set her glass down on the top of the balustrade. 'I don't play your sort of games, Charlie. They're not my style.'

'Well, you do have plenty of that,' he said, eyeing her dress, her jewels. 'Tonight you are apiece with this overly ostentatious mansion; very clever. I congratulate you.'

'Thank you.'

'You know, I always used to wonder what the phrase "butter wouldn't melt in her mouth" meant.' Another pause. 'Now I know.'

Claire took a deep breath and her courage in both hands, but before she could say anything he got there first.

'Why is it,' he asked sorrowfully, 'that I keep getting this feeling that you are not only not with me but quite beyond my reach?'

'What is it you want with me in the first place?' Claire asked bluntly.

'Come, come,' Charlie chided softly. 'No woman who looks like you should find it necessary to ask that.'

'I do because – ' she hesitated, 'because I have a definite feeling that there is more here than you are willing to admit.'

'You mean I have an ulterior motive?' He grinned.

'Not *that* one,' Claire said crossly. 'I mean that – well, that there is some sort of – rivalry – between you and the man I work for, and that I am pig-in-the-middle.'

'So what's new about male rivalry?'

'Nothing, when that is all it is, but ever since you came on board the *Circe* I have had this feeling that you and Jake have – for reasons as yet unknown to me – old scores to settle, and that you've decided to use me as your instrument.'

'What's wrong in showing Jake that he doesn't realize what he has in you?'

'I can assure you that he knows exactly what he has. A damned good Executive Assistant cum Social Secretary. Which, I might add, is all he was ever interested in as far as I'm concerned.'

'More fool him.'

'Which brings me to my point: I am not going to make a fool of myself with you.'

'Which brings you right up against mine – you obviously feel so inclined but for some reason you're afraid to take the risk.'

Claire shivered. She was conscious of a sensation not unknown to her: that of being swung over a bottomless pit, where Rory Ballater had held her suspended once before. Not since him had any man made her feel so unsure, so nervous, so afraid. Rory had dropped her, and quite deliberately, and the fall had shattered her. It had taken time and courage to knit her broken self together again, and even if the present result was not perfect it still managed to fool most people most of the time, who had no idea that she was still not up to handling any kind of emotional involvement, and that any other kind was anathema to her. Every instinct she had was telling her – had kept on telling her since she had first set eyes on him – that Charlie Whitman was capable of inflicting the same kind of emotional damage. Oriana had really not needed to warn her. Something in her had recognized something in Charlie that rang all her alarms. Yet being with him, close to him as she was now, only a breath away, it was very hard to maintain not only her equilibrium but her cool.

'You are a lady who has been badly hurt, I know that,' Charlie said, his voice a caress, 'but hurt is the last thing on my mind.'

He moved in closer. 'You need love, Claire . . . I knew that right off. That distance you maintain is for protection; you're not the Iron Lady they say you are.'

Claire felt a jolt. She had not even known they did say so.

'You are warm and loving and very, very vulnerable . . . you have been hurt, so badly that you feel you daren't risk a second chance. But you would have nothing to regret with me, I promise you that.'

'I don't play those sort of games,' Claire said with an effort.

His smile was reproachful. 'This is playing?'

'Yes,' Claire said clearly, knowing it to be so even as she uttered the word. Charlie was a world-class player at sexual fun and games; in that respect he was another Rory. She stiffened as she felt another *frisson* of shock. Of course! she thought numbly. That is what it is . . . he reminds me so much of Rory . . .

'Now what?' Charlie asked narrowly, his eyes never leaving her face.

'I'm not ready for what you have in mind,' Claire said slowly. 'Perhaps I never will be, I don't know. I only know that my answer is no. Quite definitely – no.'

'I've told you, you will be safe with me. I would never hurt you as you so obviously have been hurt.'

Claire regarded him sadly. 'Oh, but you would, Charlie – if it suited you.'

He moved away from her. She was conscious of anger, yet his shrug was amiable as he said, 'Okay. Maybe it *is* too soon . . . but I can wait. I am always prepared to wait for something worth having.'

'You'll wait a long time for me.'

'Why?' he asked bluntly. 'What did that bastard you were married to do to you that you should be so wary of men?'

Claire said, 'Everything you could think of, and a lot you couldn't.'

He spread his hands. 'Okay, point taken.' Pause. 'For now. But I don't give up easily, and challenges always act as a spur. I'll be in Europe towards the end of the year. We will see then.'

Claire shrugged, so relieved that she felt confident enough to do so, only to find she had been over-confident. She found herself being seized, held and kissed in a way that had her mindless. 'Something to remember me by,' he said, as he put her away from him before taking himself off.

She leaned back against the balustrade, shaking like a leaf. Everything in her had responded to Charlie. She bent to replace her sandals with hands that shook so badly she had to straighten, take deep calming breaths. Her heart was knocking like a labouring engine and under the delirium of aroused feelings she felt the queasy slick of sharp fright. Every instinct was shrilling the news that Charlie Whitman was dangerous, even while her body craved more of the same. Some tiny yet still rational corner of her mind insistently warned her that if she got involved with him she would be sorry. She had the first time, hadn't she?

What is wrong with me that I should find myself unable to resist a certain physical type? she thought despairingly. I should have learned my lesson. Everybody makes mistakes, but only fools repeat them. Underlying the jumbled mass that was her feelings, was a deep pool of unease in which lurked the dread certainty that Charlie Whitman was using her to get at Jake Burns. She could not explain it; she only knew she felt it. What Jake called a gut reaction. Oh, God, she thought, trembling violently and wanting nothing more than to go off to a corner and hide. What have I got myself into here? Am I being stupid? Other people treat this sort of thing as a game, why can't I? It's not meant to be taken seriously, any of it, only as fun. Fun. Something so very American. Everything was 'fun' with them. A restaurant was a 'fun' place; so was a resort, a shop, a designer.

And so was an affair. I can't be like that, she thought. I *can't*. Sex to me is serious, *meant*. It is a giving of myself. I can't do that unless it's serious, and my gut reaction is that serious is not what Charlie Whitman ever is where women are concerned. He's a womanizer; the last thing I need. All I need – and right now – is to be left *alone*.

Five minutes later, the shaking stopped, her sandals back on, she swept downstairs again and threw herself back into the throng. At once, Nico Constantine came up to her. 'At last,' he said. 'This is our dance . . .'

He was light on his feet, even if he tended to hold her rather close. He smelled of Aramis, tobacco and brandy. 'You have given us a wonderful "occasion",' he complimented her warmly. 'No wonder Jake regards you so highly.'

Not you too, Claire thought.

'It has been a great pleasure, having you on the *Circe*.'

'I have enjoyed it very much.'

'Good. Then you must do it again.'

'That depends on how busy Jake is.'

'He does work you pretty hard, doesn't he?' His smile was

an invitation. 'You wouldn't consider changing to something a little less – onerous?'

'No, thank you. I like my job. I like Jake. I'm quite content.'

'A pity. I have a villa on an island in the Aegean which I know you would love. Legend says it is where Odysseus heard the sirens sing.'

'I've heard many a siren song myself,' Claire replied gravely.

He laughed delightedly. 'Jake is indeed a lucky man. Wit as well as beauty. Now, may I get you some more champagne – or is there something else – anything else – you would prefer?'

Claire knew she had only to say and he would get it, even if it meant giving Oriana her marching orders.

'No, thank you. Champagne would be fine.'

He bowed, went to fetch it, not in the least abashed, as though he had expected her to play hard to get. Why is it people always want what they imagine someone else has? she thought wearily.

It was noon by the time she fell into bed. She had stayed on, once everybody had gone, checking that there was no damage, seeing the caterers and the waiters off the premises, all empties crated, all wilting flowers removed, the remains of the breakfast – greatly appreciated – cleared away. She had stood with Jake while the guests departed.

'Swell party, Jake. Next year?'

'Hope so . . .'

'Don't forget now, we'll be in London around Christmas to do some shopping so we'll see you then . . .'

Charlie had taken her hand, lifted it to her lips. 'A great party,' he had complimented. Then to Jake, banteringly: 'You always could pick them, Jake.'

'Still jealous, Charlie?'

For a moment the black eyes had contained a look which made Claire shiver, then it was gone and the lazy big-cat indolence was in place. 'Envious,' the dark voice corrected. 'The younger, prettier sister . . .' Now it was Jake's turn to stiffen but he said nothing, only turned to the next departing guests.

What goes *on* here? Claire asked herself. What lies between these two? All she was sure of was that it was something bad.

When the last car had driven out from under the *porte cochère*, Jake yawned hugely and said sleepily, 'Great party. You did a first-class job, as always. Thanks.' He stretched, muscles cracking. 'I'm bushed . . . thank God there's nothing on tomorrow.' Another yawn. 'You coming?'

'In a while. One or two things to see to. I want to make quite sure that all this is handed back in the condition in which it was handed over.'

'Looks fine to me.' He eyed her. 'So do you, come to that. You had a good time?'

'Wonderful.'

'Well, don't stay too long.'

'I won't.'

He flipped a hand and headed for his car. An odd one, Claire thought affectionately, but a nice one. He had spent countless thousands of dollars on this party yet he had no compunction about borrowing when it suited. When she had asked him why he didn't have his own plane he had been astonished. 'What for? I know a dozen guys only too glad to let me borrow theirs. Puts them in good with me, right?'

It was in keeping with his refusal to buy when he could lease. 'That way it's a tax benefit.' He had none of the trappings of a billionaire (and by now she knew his worth). No big house – the London house was naturally leased – no flashy fleet of cars except the leased Rolls and his own far-from-new Thunderbird. His watch was a ten-dollar digital and his cuff-links, until Claire had taken him to Garrards, had been bought at K-Mart. Yet he spent a fortune on horses and always used the latest technology. And she knew that were she to ask him, he would gladly write her a six-figure cheque without a qualm.

Smiling, she turned to do a last check of the house, and

in doing so came across various items either lost, forgotten or mislaid. Such as a solitary Ferragamo satin evening sandal, size 7AA; a pair of Juel Park pure silk crêpe-de-Chine French panties: a single, diamond solitaire cuff-link, a twenties style pochette of fine silver mesh embellished with leaves made up of diamonds and pearls, and a gold cigarette case bearing the initials WdeDW in diamonds. Opening it, Claire found the cigarettes were of marijuana rather than tobacco. 'How could anyone forget this?' she marvelled to the head waiter, who had stayed behind to help out.

'Considering the amount of champagne that was put away tonight I wouldn't be surprised if he found the body to go with it. Besides, there wasn't anybody here tonight who couldn't afford a dozen replacements. Goes with the house, I guess.'

Claire laughed. 'The former owners called it a cottage.'

'It still isn't my idea of a home, and from what I hear the people who lived in it had their fair share of troubles.'

'True . . .' Claire thought of Consuelo Vanderbilt, locked in her room upstairs by a mother who was determined to marry her to the Duke of Marlborough, and kept there until she agreed. The wretchedly unhappy eighteen-year-old had been forced to keep her veil lowered all through the wedding ceremony because her face was so badly blotched from her hours of solitary weeping.

With me, it was the other way round, Claire thought. I was radiant: it was my mother who wept. Odd, she thought. All evening she had been conscious of Rory's wraith hovering in the background. Probably because he would have adored all this ostentatious vulgarity, as he loved anything that reeked of money . . .

'I guess that's everything.'

She came out of her thoughts to find her helper regarding her hopefully.

'Yes, I think so . . . Let's find the nightwatchman and hand over the keys . . .'

CHAPTER ELEVEN

Six weeks later, Claire stopped her car behind the one she had followed to this industrial suburb of Newark, New Jersey, where Jake had long owned a large parcel of real estate, mostly warehouses no longer used and now about to be demolished to make way for a new housing development.

Before leaving on a trip to Zurich, where he went regularly and always alone, he had told her to give the warehouses the once over: 'Have a look at what's inside. If it's junk then get rid of it, but there might just be something of value.' Like the 1912 Rolls-Royce Silver Ghost he had found in a garage that was part of another of his real estate buys. It had started first go and eventually been sold to a collector – who already had fifteen of them – for $250,000. Looking at the rotting hulks of the three large warehouses she had come to inspect she doubted if he would strike lucky this time.

'They're all full of junk,' the man from Jake's demolition company had told her. 'All sorts of stuff that belonged to people who put it into storage years ago. Only fit for burning now, if you ask me.'

Like the buildings themselves, Claire thought, as she picked her way through rubble towards the rotting, peeling door the demolition man was unlocking for her. Whatever had been stored there was probably stolen ages ago. And sure enough, once inside, it was obvious that thieves had been in because everything was strewn haphazardly and most of the windows were broken.

'See,' the demolition man said to her disgustedly. 'What did I tell you? Nothing but worthless junk.'

Nothing but the truth, Claire thought, wrinkling her nose at the dust which rose in clouds as it was disturbed. Every inch of space was crammed with furniture which, from its style and condition, had been mouldering away for decades. A cloud of moths rose in alarm from a dilapidated velvet sofa.

'Only fit for the fire,' the demolition man said.

'That would seem to be the case.' She sneezed as the dust tickled her nostrils, and exclaimed as she snagged the hem of her Bruce Oldfield suit on a protruding spring.

'I guess somebody bought all this in a firesale and stored it against the day when they'd be able to unload it,' her companion observed. 'Only nobody in their right minds would spend good money on this trash.'

There were cardboard cartons by the hundred containing clothes, such as the platform-soled shoes of the early seventies, leather mini- and maxi-skirts, multi-coloured wigs, racks and racks of the Courrèges plastic-square dresses, so 'in' at the time they were created, so totally 'out' nowadays. There was even a pile of store-window dummies heaped up in a corner. Claire shuddered. 'Nothing here either . . .' but as she spoke her eye lighted on what looked like a portable wardrobe half hidden by the pile of bodies. 'Hang on a minute, though . . .'

Heaving the dummies aside she cleared a path to reveal some half a dozen free-standing plastic travelrobes, coated with dust. Smearing it away from one of them Claire could see what looked like fur. Tugging at the zip which ran right round all four sides, she pulled it down to peel away the flap from the top. It *was* fur! Moreover . . . she reached in a hand to finger it. My God! she thought, her heart skipping a beat. It's sable! She pulled the zip down all the way, lifted the fur out. Inside the thick plastic of the robe it was shrouded again in pale-pink fine cotton from which emanated the faint smell of lavender and mothballs. Removing that, Claire found herself holding a full-length coat of lustrous Russian sable. It was long – fifties style – and untouched by moth or time. Looped over its padded silk hanger was a small silk bag which, when she touched it, gave off the same smell.

Oh my God, she thought, faint with excitement and shock. What have I uncovered here?

'Found anything?' her companion called impatiently.

'Yes . . . six portable plastic wardrobes filled with clothes. I want them carefully, *very* carefully, removed to the BurnsCo storage depot in Queens . . . and as soon as possible.'

'Okay . . . I guess that can be arranged.'

'Remove nothing,' Claire ordered, replacing the coat in its shroud before hanging it back in its plastic sheathing and zipping it up. 'And leave them closed. I don't want any risk of moths scenting a feast.'

'Whatever you say.'

'Do it today. I don't want them left here.'

'What about the rest of the junk?'

'Take it away and burn it. But not these . . . whatever you do, not these. I think I've found buried treasure.'

By three o'clock that afternoon, a detailed examination of the wardrobes and their contents confirmed her suspicion. Every one of them contained furs, coats, dresses, evening gowns, ball gowns, lingerie, gloves, handbags – an entire wardrobe. Her hands were shaking with excitement as she revealed a cache of designer treasure worth a fortune.

The style ranged over some thirty years; from the thirties with their bias-cut dresses, to the forties with their square shoulders and detailed jackets, to the longer length of the late forties, when Christian Dior had set off an explosion that still reverberated around the world of fashion, through to the unmistakable styles of the fifties. Claire stroked the silvery softness of chinchilla, the rich sheen of mink, the thick length of silver fox. The clothes had been made for a tall woman; when Claire tried on the silver fox it enveloped her like a tent.

She turned her attention to the one containing evening gowns; gold lamé tubes, swathes of white silk jersey, floating drifts of chiffon, heavy sweeps of taffeta and velvet. Whoever had owned these clothes had been rich. Even the lingerie was perfection, all of it in natural fibres; pure silk, heavy satin, fragile lace. And there were no tights, only stockings, in nylon and pure silk. These clothes had been in storage a long time; from the late fifties onwards at least, Claire judged. She had a picture of her mother in a suit like the grey flannel one she held up; short, tight-waisted jacket with peplum, huge skirt – and there was the ever-present umbrella that went with such a suit, and the small hat. Yes, definitely at least twenty-five years, Claire thought. Who was she? Why had all this lain forgotten for so long? She searched the handbags, all in real leathers: alligator, crocodile, supple calf. All were empty. She went through pockets. Nothing. Not even a handkerchief.

And then she noticed that the fur coats had initials embroidered in the lining. GK. GK? They rang no bells. Yet to have worn clothes like these she must have been well known. They were – especially the evening gowns – flamboyant, even theatrical. That's it, Claire thought as she lifted down a floor-length skirt and wide-sleeved bolero jacket of mink, the skirt split to reveal a lining embroidered in the most amazing design of butterflies in gold thread and tiny multi-coloured crystal beads. Theatrical. Then it hit her. GK.

'My God!' she breathed out loud. 'Of course . . . Gina Kendall . . . She wore this in *Broadway Lady* . . . I saw it umpteen times.' She could see in her mind's eye the tall Junoesque figure, the fabulous legs, revealed when she spread the skirt to dance. 'Well I'll be damned!' she muttered. 'Gina Kendall . . . No wonder these have been lying here forgotten. She's been dead for years.'

Claire was a movie buff, and quickly her retentive memory provided the salient facts. At the height of her fame, though no longer young, Gina Kendall had abruptly announced her retirement from the screen. For twenty-eight years, 1930 to 1958, she had been a Hollywood legend, still remembered by film buffs as the greatest of all the Glamour Girls, and then out of the blue, after completing her last movie – what was it called now? Something about heaven . . . *Stairway to*

Heaven, that was it — she had left Hollywood and disappeared. Not until her death, ten years later, was it revealed that she had spent those years in a Swiss clinic, a helpless sufferer from Alzheimer's Disease. At only fifty-eight, she had died in a state of advanced senility . . . Claire shuddered to think of all that vital, radiant beauty reduced to a mindless – thing. No wonder she had disappeared. She had lived for her beauty; had not been able to stand the thought of people seeing it destroyed.

She must have hoped for a cure. Why else store her fabulous wardrobe; all these glorious dresses she had worn in her movies which always, once a picture was finished, had become her property. It had been written into her contract, Claire recalled. For years she had been the silver screen's Best Dressed Star; the great designers had vied to design for her: Adrian, Travilla, Irene, Edith Head, Travis Banton, Walter Plunkett . . .

My God! she thought half-hysterically. I've discovered Aladdin's cave! Then, soberly, she told herself: Now think. You're a movie buff so use that memory of yours . . . Gina Kendall had four husbands but they are all dead, like the old Hollywood. She had no children and the only people who turned up at her funeral were those she had worked with. There was no sign of any family. Besides, when Jake bought this warehouse I'm sure he had clear title. Better check that. And her will . . . there was something about her will . . . yes, I remember. She had nothing to leave. All she had, she had already given to the Clinic to fund research into the disease which killed her. So . . . there is probably nobody alive to question Jake's absolute title to all these clothes. They have been stored here since she left Hollywood – and thank God she protected them so lovingly. Lifting one of the small satin bags hung around each hanger, she sniffed it, rubbing it with her fingers. The friction released the still strong smell of lavender and mothballs . . . Shut away in darkness, shrouded in their linen bags and sealed in protective plastic, they had been preserved like a fly in amber. And every item of the highest quality. These will sell for top dollar, that's for sure . . .'

First things first, she cautioned herself. You can't sell a thing until you've made absolutely sure that they're Jake's to sell. See the lawyers then decide how to dispose of them . . .

Two days later she walked into the reception area of Despard's New York, presented her card at the reception desk – it read 'Claire Drummond, Burns Enterprises' – and asked to see Kate Despard. As she expected, it opened all doors.

'Miss Drummond.' A tall, stunning redhead came to meet Claire as she was shown into a large, spacious office. 'I'm Kate Despard. How can I help you?' She was open, friendly; no sign of the power Claire knew she wielded except in the confidence of her manner.

'I think I have something worth while selling at one of your auctions.'

'Oh? And what might that be?'

'This is a sample.' Claire opened the briefcase she was carrying, lifted out a knife-pleated dress of pure silk so fine it had folded to nothing. When she held it up on its hanger the pleats fell effortlessly into place, perpendicular in the full skirt, horizontal on the low-cut bodice which was suspended from rhinestone straps.

'Oh, lovely . . . French? Balmain? Early Dior? *Circa* 1949 I should think.'

'Hollywood 1947. It belonged to Gina Kendall.'

'The sex symbol? Oh, yes, I remember . . . She had a reputation for elegance, didn't she? Gorgeous looking, and talk about sexy . . . But she's been dead for years.' Kate Despard's golden eyes were keen. 'You mentioned it was a sample . . . ?'

'I've got six wardrobes full of what were once her clothes. All the dresses she wore in her movies.'

Kate Despard's mobile face lit. 'Really! Do tell . . .' Claire told how she had come across them. 'And you want us to auction them for you, is that it?'

'If you think they would sell.'

'Sell! My dear Miss Drummond, they will be fought over! But why Despard's?'

'I was in New York last spring when you auctioned the effects of a contemporary of Gina Kendall's. I saw the kind of publicity that sale attracted, the nostalgia – and the incredible prices.'

'I think you must be referring to Jack Reilly. That sale proved once and for all that people are prepared to pay anything in order to possess something that once belonged to a star. Would you believe that a woman paid five thousand dollars for the top hat he wore in *Dance, Everybody* and another paid a thousand for the coverall he wore in make-up? My experienced nose tells me blood will flow in the battle to own a Gina Kendall dress. Where are they, by the way? Somewhere safe, I hope – and in perfect condition?'

'Yes, they are – safe and in perfect condition. I checked.'

'Good.' Then Kate Despard leaned forward. 'Tell me, what is he like, Jake Burns? One hears such stories . . . My husband says he is out of his time and belongs to the era of the robber barons. He says he wouldn't be surprised if he had the nerve to try and take over ChanCorp one day!' Her eyes sparkled. 'Now that would be a battle!'

'He's a man with a god-given talent for making money,' Claire replied honestly. 'But nice with it. Don't believe everything you hear.'

'Spoken like a loyal employee.'

Claire's smile was wry. 'That remains to be seen. He doesn't know about any of this yet. I'm doing it off my own bat.'

Kate laughed. 'How nice to hear English spoken as we both know and love it!'

'That's also why I came to you. We Brits have to stick together in a foreign land.'

'Good for you – and for Despard's, of course. I've already

got some ideas floating around on the best way to handle this sale.'

'I leave all that to you,' Claire said hastily. 'You're the expert. All I want is to be able to forestall any comebacks by the size of the cheque I hand him.'

'I can promise you it will be sizeable. Now then, I've got an expert on the staff who is a dab hand at the nostalgia market. She was the one did the Jack Reilly sale. She knows to the dollar what this sort of thing will bring. Let's have her in and find out . . . then we will need to take a look at the clothes.'

Joyce Marshall's verdict was that they would come from far and wide for a chance to acquire clothes once worn by the legendary Gina Kendall. Claire stood by, fascinated, listening to her and Kate planning the best way to do it.

'. . . blow-ups of all her Hurrell stills around the walls,' Kate was saying. 'And models to wear the dresses – looking as much like Gina as possible. If they aren't blondes then they can wear wigs. And I think invitations to those designers who are still alive to come and receive homage.'

'And those stars who were her contemporaries,' suggested Joyce. 'There are still a few around . . . Bette Davis, Barbara Stanwyck, Claudette Colbert, Ruby Keeler, Ginger Rogers . . .'

Claire gulped. She had not envisaged anything like this; a star-studded occasion in the full blaze of as much publicity as could be arranged. In her innocence, she had thought of a quick sale and a fast profit, without such things as a superb, full-colour catalogue, models to display the clothes, champagne and the TV cameras out in force. On the other hand, such a sale would undoubtedly bring very high prices, and wasn't the object of this particular exercise to demonstrate her expertise in Jake's field? Well, the small, easily handled part of it.

She came out of her troubled thoughts to realize that Kate Despard was talking to her. 'Sorry, I was miles away . . .'

'I was asking if you – or rather Mr Burns – has clear title to what will be sold. No danger of anyone coming forward to dispute his absolute right to sell?'

'None. I cleared everything with the lawyers. Gina Kendall left no family; the studio is defunct. Also, it was in her contract that once a film was finished the costumes she wore in it became her personal property. On top of that, when Jake bought the warehouses and the land they stand on, it was with clear title to buildings and contents.'

'Excellent. No chance then of any legal disputes, which in this litigious country are the last thing we want.'

You're telling me, Claire thought on a quiver.

'So, we will announce the sale as Property of a Gentleman, I think,' Kate continued, after a quick glance at Claire's worried face. 'No names, no pack drill.'

'Can that be done?' Relief blazed.

'Easily. We do it all the time, mostly for people who don't want to alert the tax man.'

'When?'

'Well . . . catalogues have to be printed, announcements made, advertising placed, people invited . . . three months minimum.'

Claire mentally reviewed Jake's diary. He was due to pay a visit to the Middle East in a week; they would then go to Ireland where he had a horse at stud; from there they would fly to Sydney, where they were scheduled to spend ten days; from Sydney to Honolulu, where Jake had an interest in a ranch – a week was pencilled in there. Then there were three clear weeks in London followed by another of his mysterious, solitary visits to Zurich. As far ahead as she could see, they ought to be in London when the sale took place. Thank God. A paragraph in an English paper about an auction of clothes belonging to a deceased Hollywood star would raise neither interest nor eyebrows. Jake read the headlines, the financial pages and the sports reports.

'Fine,' she said. 'That will suit very well.'

They shook hands on the deal. All that remained was for

contracts to be drawn up. Claire, in her capacity as Jake's Personal Assistant, always had the power to sign in his absence. It was a measure of his trust and her power.

'Are you in New York for a while longer?' Kate asked, as she walked Claire to the door.

'Only a couple of days.'

'But you will be back for the auction?'

'Well . . . that depends,' Claire evaded. On where Jake is, she thought.

'Aren't you interested in buying anything?'

'Nothing would fit me. Gina Kendall was tall, like you.'

'Thank God, because there's a white jersey sheath would go a treat with the emerald necklace my husband bought me when our son was born . . .'

'Lucky you,' Claire said, sincere with envy.

'I know. Sometimes I can't quite believe it all . . .'

I know what you mean, Claire thought, as she hailed a passing cab. I often have to do a doubletake myself.

She kept a close eye on the saleroom columns during the following weeks, but it was in the American Diary of the *Daily Express* that she saw the first mention of the sale, reported as attracting enormous interest within the Hollywood community. Claire held her breath but Jake either did not read it or did not care. And when her copy of the catalogue came, Claire abstracted it from the rest of the mail and took it upstairs where she sat and gloated over it.

Gina Kendall was on the cover; one of her Hurrell stills, and wearing the white dress Kate Despard coveted, only with diamonds instead of emeralds, her long blonde hair falling seductively over one eye, her sultry mouth gleaming, her sexuality giving off smoke. Hard to imagine all that glorious beauty as a drooling, mindless old woman, Claire thought on a shiver. We none of us know what lies in store . . .

Which was why she was thrown into a minor panic when Jake announced, three days before the event was due to take place, a sudden, unscheduled visit to Lake Tahoe. Claire showed none of the dismay she felt. There was bound to be much more publicity in America; Jake could hardly fail to become aware of the auction. Damnation! she thought, as she went ahead and made travel arrangements.

They flew to San Francisco, where they changed their jet for a smaller, private plane which took them to a large, walled estate on the edge of the lake. There they were met by some men Claire felt sure were Mafia hoods. Beautifully dressed, impeccably barbered and groomed, yet deadly. It was probably her imagination, she told herself, but she couldn't help thinking that the men who constantly surrounded their chiefs were carrying guns.

Sensing her unease, Jake whispered, 'Don't worry,' as the welcoming committee came towards them. 'I'm not about to be made an offer I can't refuse . . .' Which reminded her of the offers that would be made the day after tomorrow.

'What *do* they want?' she whispered back.

'Something I've got. I'm here to see how badly they want it.' And from Jake's jauntiness, when later on he strolled into the sitting-room which was part of the two-bedroom suite they occupied, she knew they had wanted it badly.

'So – what was it they wanted?' she urged.

'Speedbird.'

'Your horse!'

'The same.'

'But I thought you were going to breed from him.'

'Changed my mind. I like to ride 'em but I don't have the time or the patience to wait till they grow up. They were willing to pay my price so . . .'

'Don't tell me they're setting up a stud? I thought fixing horse-races was more their style.'

'Keep your voice down,' Jake warned.

'You would do business with the devil if it would make you a profit,' Claire hissed.

'Of course. Why not?' He went to the window, stood looking out over the lake, jingling the coins in his trouser pocket. 'I'm going to be tied up for the next couple of days, so if you want to take off somewhere – go back to San Francisco and raid the stores or whatever – feel free. Just be back for Friday night, because that's when we fly back to London.'

Showing none of her sudden excitement: 'I take it that means you're going to spend the next forty-eight hours playing poker?'

'You bet I am.'

Good, thought Claire. 'Then, if you don't mind, I will go and do some shopping . . . but in Los Angeles.'

'Wherever . . .' His mind anticipating his favourite pas-time bar one, Jake hardly heard her.

'See you Friday afternoon, then.'

'Sure . . . fine.'

Claire arrived in LA on the afternoon of the auction and called Kate Despard.

'I'm so glad you could make it,' she said happily. 'This is going to be a night to remember. The interest generated has been tremendous . . . let's hope the prices will be the same.'

'I just want to sit in a corner unnoticed. I'm supposed to be on a shopping trip.'

'Then you shall play Little Jack Horner, but come early for a preview. The auction starts at eight – come for seven. It's black tie, naturally.'

Promptly at seven o'clock, a cab dropped Claire off at the entrance to the Beverly Hills Hotel. She was wearing a plain black dress, one of Jean Muir's simple little masterpieces, under the short wild mink jacket she had treated herself to last Christmas.

'Nervous?' Kate Despard smiled, as she tucked her arm in Claire's before leading her to the bedlam behind the scenes in the huge room where the auction would be held.

'Terrified. Jake is practically round the corner at Lake Tahoe . . . I thought the auction would happen safely in New York.'

'Not for Gina Kendall! It has to be pure Hollywood. Whatever, I'm sure you will approve what has been done.'

'Approve!' Claire gazed wide-eyed at the huge blow-ups of publicity and film stills taken of Gina Kendall in her heyday, all cunningly spotlit. Everywhere were huge arrangements of white roses – the flower associated with her. Behind the scenes it was controlled mayhem. Model girls, all blondes, all tall, were dressing, having last-minute touches put to their hair and make-up, giving themselves the final once-over in the many mirrors.

'I thought you could discreetly watch from behind the scenes,' Kate Despard said. 'That way you've got a good view of the audience and their reactions as the girls go down the runway.' This was covered in deep-blue carpeting and sliced right through the serried ranks of brittle gilt chairs.

And there, her hands tightly clasped with nervous excitement, Claire sat and watched the famous faces arrive; men and women she had sat and gazed at on the silver screen. Naturally, as she was older, so were they older now, but they were the same glamorous people of which the stuff of her young dreams had been made. The handsome dark-haired men who had been Gina Kendall's leading men were white-haired now, one or two completely bald, others wearing skilful toupées.

It was an emotional reunion for many of the women, as they met, often for the first time in many years, the men who had designed not only Gina's dresses but their own.

'My God!' she heard one former dancing star exclaim tearfully. 'You made the dresses for the first movie I ever made . . .' The conversation was full of 'remember whens' and 'do you recalls'. As the press coverage would have it the next morning: 'No, they don't make 'em like this any more . . .'

It was a sell-out from the start. Rapturous applause greeted the first dress, along with an emotional buzz of recognition, and the bidding was greedy, even frantic. Claire was aghast at the prices reached. She had taken out her notebook and pad so as to keep a running total, but as, one by one, the outfits the models paraded, always to music from the film in which a particular dress had been worn, went for five and sometimes, like the embroidered mink skirt, six figures, her hands shook so that she could hardly hold her pencil. Never had she expected anything like this. It was obvious that the final total would be in seven fantastic figures.

'Well?' Kate quizzed, as the chairs were whisked away and the buffet and champagne were served.

Claire spread her hands helplessly. 'Words fail me.'

'If he's not pleased by the size of the cheque you hand him – even minus Despard's commission – then he's even tougher than they say. He still has no idea?'

'Not so much as an inkling.'

'Clever girl.'

'Just so long as he thinks so.'

'Now, come and have a glass of champagne.'

'No, I won't, if you don't mind. I'd rather slip away quietly. There are so many photographers around.'

'As you wish. Where shall I send the cheque?'

'To the London address.' She shook Kate's hand fervently. 'Thank you. All this has been so much more than I expected.'

'Thank *you*. And remember Despard's if you come across any more finds like this.'

'Oh, I will . . . I will.'

In the cab going back to the Century Plaza Claire sat and stared at the grand total; added the column again – and again – to make absolutely sure. There was no mistake. She had made Jake a net profit of one million, three hundred and seventy-five thousand dollars. I'm an entrepreneur! she thought, dazed. I've pulled off a deal all on my own! I was the one who spotted the potential and decided on an auction. Sold any other way those dresses would not have realized even half as much. Jake will be pleased, she told herself. With him, the bottom line is always the profit margin, and this one is wide enough to drive a truck through!

When she got back he asked absently, 'Spent all your money, then?' obviously still counting his own.

'No.' She had hastily bought a few things as proof that she had indeed been shopping. 'How about you?'

His laugh was gleeful. 'No way! I came out well ahead.'

Within the hour they were on their way back to London.

The cheque arrived, addressed to Claire as arranged, ten days later. She smoothed it rapturously. The proof of her first – profitable – deal. The first, she hoped, of many.

She picked her moment to present it to him, telling herself roundly that she was a fool to be scared. This was not Rory; this was Jake, a different man, a different outlook. On life, women – everything. Rory would have been furious at her having, as he would have put it in his paranoid way, 'gone behind his back'; daring to do something – anything – without his say-so. Jake was different. He expected her to think for herself, act for herself; more – for him, if it became necessary. And she *had* made him a profit. That was all he would care about, and he would be glad. Rory would have been even more furious because it meant she was as capable as he was and, worse, had demonstrated it publicly.

So she laid the cheque in front of Jake without explanation.

'What's this?' He read it, raised his eyebrows. 'Nice . . . but I don't know who Despard's are and why they're paying me more than a million dollars.' He raised his eyes to hers. They were full of curiosity well leavened with surprise. 'What have you been up to?'

Claire told him. He did not interrupt, go red with anger as Rory would have done. He merely listened, and with great interest. '. . . it was incredible,' Claire finished. 'They almost came to blows over some of the items. Every single thing went, even the garter belts!' Jake still said nothing, and for a split second Claire wondered if she had misjudged him after all. He was the man who could turn into a drunken stranger without warning.

Then he sighed: 'Gina Kendall . . .' he said dreamily. 'I

remember her. They used to show her old movies on the *Late Late Show*.' Another sigh. 'I used to fantasize about her in my teens.'

Ah, Claire thought. So that's why he only goes for blondes . . . Well, she thought on an inner shrug, Rory taught you all about male fantasies.

Then Jake picked up the cheque again. 'Well I'll be damned . . .' He chuckled, which became a full-throated yelp of glee. 'I'll be double-damned!'

Even having expected a good reaction, Claire still felt enormously relieved.

'You've been hiding your light under a bushel, girl,' he said to her. 'I always knew you were smart, but this is straight A stuff! Tell it all to me again . . .'

This time she added all the little touches she had omitted in her haste to get the story over and done with. He nodded approvingly as she explained how she had been careful to obtain clear title. 'Good, good . . . and Despard's? Why did you go to them?'

'Well, Kate Despard is English, which was a point in her favour, and she is also a woman running a huge, highly successful auction house. I was sure she would understand.'

'I see – a case of all girls together?'

'Why not?'

'I'm not complaining . . . far from it.' He picked up the cheque again. 'If this is a sample of what you can do, feel free to do it again as often as you get the chance.'

'You mean it? I can do a deal on my own?'

'Provided it's on my behalf . . . or do you intend to go into business on your own?'

'I don't know enough yet to do that – but I'm learning.'

'Okay, I don't mind that. And you can, as you once said, earn while you learn . . . let me see . . . ten per cent of this is one hundred and thirty-seven and a half thousand.'

Claire felt faint. 'Ten per cent?' she croaked.

'Your cut – commission – whatever you want to call it.' Claire swallowed. 'You acted as my agent, right? You sold something I owned at a clear profit to me, so you get your ten per cent.'

Claire cleared her clogged throat. 'But – you already pay me . . .'

'That's salary. This was a deal.'

'But –'

'You want it or not?'

'I want it!'

'So don't argue yourself out of it, then. You won't get far as an entrepreneur if you don't value yourself as high as any deal you do. Always charge what the traffic will bear but be sure not to get run over.'

As she closed his door: Yes, Claire thought. That last lingering doubt as to my own self-worth. That is what I have to shed. Jake has just made it clear that he values me. So stop hanging back, being so politely self-effacing. You have both his permission and his encouragement. Use them both.

A month or so later she got her chance. Jake came to her one morning and asked her diffidently if she would do him a favour.

'Of course.'

'An old friend is in town and he wants somebody to take his wife shopping. She's never been to London before – never been outside her own country before – and doesn't know her way around. Would you take her?'

'Where and when?'

'Today. She's at Claridge's. Just ask for Princess Khalima.'

'An Arab! Does she speak English or French?'

'French. That's why I thought of you. Let her buy what she wants but see she doesn't get ripped off. All she knows is Marks and Spencer's but take her to Harrods and Harvey Nichols and all those upmarket stores in Knightsbridge and Bond Street. Money is no object.'

Sensing Claire's doubt: 'She's a nice kid. Newly married. Young. Her husband wants somebody English because he was educated here and he likes this country. You met him a while back – tall, thin, wears a patch over his right eye.' Claire remembered him. Very handsome, very proud. Enormously rich. 'He asked for you, as a matter of fact. He knows you can provide the kind of help – not to say guidance – his wife needs.'

'I'm flattered.'

'Why? It's the truth.'

'I'll be glad to help.'

'Good. I'll tell them to send the car round right away.'

It was a black Mercedes not quite as long as a London bus, with darkened windows, and the chauffeur was a middle-aged Englishman with a South London accent.

'Never done this before, Miss?' he asked shrewdly, as he guided the car into the traffic.

'No.'

'Nothing to it. I've been driving them for years now. You've never seen such wads of money as they've got, and eager to spend it on anything as takes their fancy. Some is not as kosher – if you'll pardon the word seein' as we're talking about Arabs – as others, but the Prince is from the top. They want the very best, his kind.' He was eyeing her in the mirror. 'You know what I mean,' he went on, 'the real thing.' He paused. 'A lady.'

'Thank you,' Claire answered gravely, hiding her smile.

'There'll be a bodyguard along, by the way. Always is when they're as important as the Prince. He'll carry the money – as to what else he's carryin' it's best to turn a blind eye. We need their money and their oil so it's my belief the police turn their own blind eye to whatever else they might have about them, if you get my drift.'

'All advice gratefully received,' Claire answered truthfully.

At Claridge's, the mention of Princess Khalima had them bowing and scraping like a violin section. Claire was escorted up to the large suite and there she met a small, veiled figure who murmured a greeting in French. It was difficult to see her face through the black chador, only large, liquidly black

314

eyes, very lovely and painfully shy, but obviously eagerly impatient to be gone. More flunkeys bowed and scraped them down to the car, where the bodyguard, a tall lean Arab wearing black, wraparound sunglasses, got into the front with the chauffeur. In the back, Claire gently asked the Princess what it was she wished to buy.

'Whatever I like,' was the soft answer. 'I have heard of Marks and Spencer's. May we go there?'

'Of course.' Pressing the button on the arm of her seat which had been shown to her: 'Marks and Spencer's at Marble Arch please, George,' Claire ordered, marvelling at the casuistry which permitted Arabs to spend fortunes at a store owned by a well-known Zionist. There, the Princess pored over the underwear, buying a set of pure silk teddies in every colour and dozens of bras, size 36C.

The bodyguard toted two baskets which were soon piled high. Claire had a word with an assistant and the baskets were taken away to await payment and collection while they picked up two more and proceeded to fill them. The Princess bought scarves by the dozen, tights of every colour and pattern seemingly by the gross; she bought nightdresses, blouses, always one of every colour, cashmere sweaters (for the desert? Claire wondered) also of every colour, and, of all things, leather blouson jackets; one in black, one in wine and one in chestnut brown.

The bodyguard paid; wads of fifty-pound notes came out of the briefcase he carried, after Claire had scrutinized the bill and told him the amount. She noticed that he did not bother about the receipt; as long as a party streamer.

'Oh, that is a wonderful shop!' exclaimed the Princess with childish, unself-conscious delight. 'Can we go into that one now?' She pointed to Selfridges on the opposite corner.

'Of course.'

They plundered Selfridges of costume jewellery, always gold with lots of glittering stones. They acquired more underwear, more nightgowns and negligees of satin and lace and chiffon. They bought shoes – the Princess had tiny feet and took size three – of every colour and design, they bought handbags. But it was in Harrods that the Princess went wild. When she said she wished to see evening gowns, they were shown into a small private room where models paraded them and not only two women but a man attended to them. Not surprising, Claire thought drily, as the bodyguard settled a bill that ran into many thousands. Afterwards they went down to the pink marble perfume hall, where the Princess bought boxed sets of exclusive French perfumes, talcs, body lotions, creams, lotions and lipsticks. There was an orgy of sniffing, and, on being asked her own favourite perfume and saying it was 'Joy', the Princess insisted on buying Claire the largest bottle available as a gift.

'Oh, this has been so wonderful!' the Princess said when they arrived back at Claridge's three hours later and a bevy of pages unloaded the Mercedes of its plunder.

'I'm glad you enjoyed it,' Claire smiled. 'I did too.' Even when Rory was flush and in an indulgent mood, Claire had never been able to go out and spend what she estimated was around £50,000.

She was invited to stay to lunch, and tactfully agreed. Anything to help Jake, she thought, as she tucked into crisp-skinned, perfectly roasted lamb. They were having coffee – black and thick and almost edible, which the Princess herself had made: a signal honour, Claire was to learn later – when the Prince returned. The Princess jumped up excitedly and insisted on showing him everything. She had unveiled herself once back in the penthouse, to reveal a delicate, oval, olive-skinned face which sparkled with delight as she pulled out the boxes and displayed her booty.

'As long as you enjoyed it,' he said with fond indulgence. Turning to Claire: 'My thanks to you, Miss Drummond. My wife has enjoyed it all enormously,' he said with faultless courtesy.

'So did I,' Claire answered truthfully.

The car drove her back to Chelsea. 'Are they all like that?' she asked George, still shell-shocked from the experience.

'Most of 'em. Money has no meaning to them, they have so much of it.'

'And do they all take a companion?'

'No. I've gone along with them myself more than once. But the Prince is a stickler for the proprieties – the most important ones always are. Some of the women go into the first ladies' room we can get to and change – the young ones anyway – take off those blacksack things and come out in jeans and T-shirts. Then they shroud themselves again before going home. But the ones like the Princess, they're kept on a tight rein. If you hadn't been along she'd have never been allowed on this morning's little spending spree.'

Little! thought Claire.

But it was on getting out of the car that George, holding the door open for her, said, 'You're forgetting this.' It was a plain white envelope with her name written on it. Opening it, she found ten, crisply new fifty-pound notes inside.

'What on earth . . . !'

'Your tip,' George told her kindly. 'You did them a favour, see? This is their way of saying thank you.'

'Five hundred pounds' worth!'

'Fifty pence in their eyes. Don't feel insulted, they're only showing gratitude.' He hesitated then said, 'Look, I drive for these people all the time and you're just the sort of lady they feel safe letting their own ladies go about with. If you like, I'll steer them your way when they want to go shopping. That way we both do ourselves a bit of good. I get a tip for my own services, see?'

'I already have a full-time job, but . . .' An idea was forming. 'I do have friends, every bit as ladylike as I am, and with a title to boot. Give me a ring next time you need someone; I'm sure I can provide the perfect companion.'

'You're on!'

Claire had more than a dozen school friends to call on, beginning with Caroline, who accepted with alacrity when she heard how much money she could make and then helped Claire compile a list of those school friends who would be willing to join a Companion Ladies agency. The first one Claire tried, Sooty Shelburne, a distant cousin, was married to a man whose father had had the bad luck to die before the family trust he had set up could take effect, thus more than halving the family fortune. John Shelburne was struggling to retain his hold on the family seat – Shelburne Mount, a listed building of historic importance but now sadly depleted of its art treasures. His wife had a small art gallery while he farmed the acres he still owned, but money was tight; two sons down for Eton and a daughter whose nanny had to be paid for, as well as the au pair and John's subscriptions to his clubs, and the horses, of course . . .

'So you would be interested in making some pin money?' Claire asked when they met for lunch at the Ritz.

'Would I? Darling, you've no idea how I tug at both ends to make them meet. We are down to two hunters and John's had to buy some enormous shire horses because we just can't afford a new tractor and – '

'I know how you can do it.'

'Oh, but I couldn't possibly do a full-time job like you. I've heard how high-powered you are these days, working for your American tycoon. I was wondering what happened to you after all that horrible mess when you shed Rory. I warned you he was a shit, didn't I? I would have told you at the time but well, we were friends and how do you tell a good friend that she's making the most ghastly mistake – '

'This isn't a full-time job. It entails hours, not days.'

'Doing what? A bit of art cataloguing maybe . . . I mean I did get my credentials at the Courtauld – '

'Nothing to do with art,' Claire interrupted. Sooty had always tended to run off at the mouth, but she was top drawer, her husband was a Viscount and she knew and was known where it mattered to rich Arabs.

'Well, what then? I'm not really fit for much, you know . . . I wasn't educated to be anything but the wife of the right man.'

'Maybe, but you're connected to half *Debrett* and you're known and accepted where it counts.'

'To whom?'

'Rich Arabs.'

Sooty's blonde eyebrows rose to meet the alice band holding back her simple, ostensibly self-made hairstyle, in reality a bit of Michaeljohn cunning.

'Arabs! I don't think John would approve . . . do you know they've bought the Heriot place next to us . . . they even had the temerity to approach John himself. They just don't seem to understand about heritage. They think money can buy anything.'

'They pay for time very handsomely.'

'Darling! You've not gone into the call girl business!' Sooty leaned forward to hiss. 'They say they will pay a thousand pounds for an assignation.'

'I wouldn't know about that. What I'm talking about is taking their wives about London – to the right shops or perhaps – if the Arab is liberated enough – to the right restaurant. They don't pay you as such, but they tip very well.' Claire told Sooty about her own tip.

'*How* much?' Sooty's rosebud mouth made an awed O. 'For toting some veiled lady round Harrods? Darling, lead me to her . . . Our own account is rather behind hand . . .'

So Lady Shelburne was recruited, and Caroline Courtney, and Victoria Markham-Smith and Pamela Gordon-Leigh and Charlotte Illingham; all aristocrats and all impoverished. All agreed with alacrity to accompany the wife of a rich Arab on discreet shopping expeditions, to introduce them to the 'right' shops, hairdressers, jewellers and so on. Claire would receive ten per cent of whatever they made.

When she cleared it with Jake he was dumbfounded for a minute then said slowly, 'Why didn't I think of that?'

'Because I did.'

He eyed her, shaking his head in slow admiration. 'No doubt about it. You've got an eye for an opportunity.'

'It won't interfere with my work. George contacts me and

I contact one of my Ladies. All very discreet and performing a service on both sides.' She paused. 'The Princess, by the way, has asked for me again . . . this coming Thursday. She wants to look at furniture. Evidently a new house is now being built in Riyadh.'

'I know,' Jake said. 'I've seen it. Okay. It so happens Thursday I'm going to a point-to-point. She's all yours . . .'

This time, after acquiring a treasure from just about every antique shop in Mayfair, Claire once again came away with a hefty tip; this time amounting to one thousand pounds, again in crisp new fifty-pound notes. Evidently, the size of the tip was commensurate with the amount spent.

The agency was an instant success. Claire's selectiveness paid off. Her Ladies were much appreciated, and in no time she had other friends begging to be taken on as Companions. George, too, appreciated his own increased income no end.

'I've got more work than I can handle nowadays,' he told Claire happily. 'Had to buy a second car and take on my brother-in-law. Keep up the good work, Miss Drummond. It was a happy day when the Prince asked for you.'

'So how does it feel to be an entrepreneuse?' Jake quizzed her, when she had just arranged for Lady Shelburne to accompany the wife of a Prince of the Royal House of Saudi Arabia on a trip to Harrods to buy china.

'I like it,' Claire sparkled.

'I've had complimentary reports filtering back. Arabs like people who are discreet and that's what your Ladies are, all right. Rich Arabs have been played like sucker fish by too many sharks not to appreciate the real thing when they find it.' Casually: 'How are the bookings looking?'

'I've got to the state where I shall have to recruit more help.'

'How lucky to have so many old school friends,' Jake commented drily.

'It was an all girls school . . . still is, for that matter. And its motto happens to be Honour Above All . . .'

He laughed. 'Okay, go for it. It's your pigeon. You pluck

it . . . I'm doing all right where the Prince is concerned and that's got a lot to do with you, so I'm not complaining.'

How different from Rory, Claire thought. He would have muscled in, jacked up the commission to 25 per cent and kept it for himself – as well as all the credit, of course.

But Jake left her alone to handle things; his only contribution was to introduce even more Arabs of his acquaintance, eager to put their wives into the safe, reliable and trustworthy hands of Miss Drummond and her friends. Business boomed. Only Cora Sue – as usual – carped.

'Fancy goings on,' she sneered. 'Ayrabs now, is it? You're leading Mister Jake down some mighty strange alleys.'

'It was he who led me,' Claire corrected. 'I started out by doing him a favour.'

Cora Sue sniffed. 'Not to mention the one you're doing yourself.'

Claire blandly regarded the sour-with-jealousy face. 'Would you like me to put you on my books, Miss Mennenger?'

Cora Sue bridled. 'I would not!'

'Then why don't you continue to do what Mr Burns asks of you and I will continue doing what he asks of me.'

Cora Sue's highly-coloured face empurpled alarmingly. 'Don't you take that high and mighty tone with me. You don't fool me for one minute. All ladylike on the outside but stainless steel inside. I can see behind the prim and proper face you show to the world; always so cool and dignified. But you've been feathering your own nest ever since you fooled Jake into taking you on. All the while you seem to be doing what he wants, it's what you want that matters. You think I haven't seen through that decorum you use to wrap up your sex-appeal?'

Claire was dumbfounded. She had not realized that Cora Sue's jealousy ran so deep or so virulently, or that the impression she was so careful to give – that of a woman who was always there but never available – had been taken as a come on. She said, icy with anger, 'I think this discussion had better be terminated before it gets out of hand.'

'It's what you aim to get your hands on I'm talking about.'

'And what is that?'

'You know damned fine what it is – or rather who it is.'

'*Who?*' Claire demanded in a fury.

Cora Sue did not heed the sudden drop in temperature because she was too heated to feel anything but her own rage. She had resented this flawlessly polite woman tinged with more than a touch of *hauteur*, with her indefinable yet instantly recognized aura of breeding, from the moment Jake had introduced them. One look into the long-lashed pansy-purple eyes and Cora Sue had been gripped by a terrible fear that had not left her for one moment since. That she was being riven by jealousy never occurred to her; she only knew she feared – and therefore hated – this wine-haired, well-born, cultivated yet understated woman with the lovely voice, flawless accent and sweet smile. 'Got our-selves the real McCoy,' Jake had gloated to her proudly. 'She's exactly what I had in mind. The real thing, Cora. She'll get me where and what I want, you'll see. Worth every penny – and more.'

'You think so,' Cora Sue had sniffed.

'I know so! You saw her, talked to her – '

'She's a snob,' Cora Sue snapped.

Jake looked astonished. 'But that's just what she's not. The real ones never are.'

'Real what?'

'Ladies. The ones with the kind of class you find in a really great horse.'

'You're the one who's letting his imagination run away with him. What I don't understand is why you need such a woman in the first place.'

'I've *told* you. I need to meet certain people and to have them accept me. The only way I can do it is by having one of them introduce me.'

'And you think this is the one.'

'You bet.'

'You'd lose.'

But he hadn't. Claire Drummond had fitted into the space Jake had created as though she had been specially made for it. And that fact had continued to rankle with Cora Sue. So did the fact that Claire was always the perfect lady; walked well, spoke beautifully, unfailingly said the right thing, was never rude or bad-mannered, even when Cora Sue was downright rude to her. She was afraid that Jake was dazzled by all that cool elegance, the self-command, the absolute control that operated at all times. When he had taken up with *that woman's* friend, Cora had been mightily relieved; she was different. A lady but a much more approachable one, a much more *human* one. She'd been sorry to see her go, even though she had known it wouldn't last. Nobody ever did. Not since . . . She adroitly switched points to avoid that dead end. What worried her was that Jake kept putting off his final return home. He had to go sooner or later. He couldn't run or hide for ever. Things had to be faced, and the longer he stayed over here living this fancy life and spending far too much money, the more Cora Sue feared for him. Even more she feared for herself.

Now, she glared impotently into the lovely face and hissed, 'Who? You know damned well who.'

'Please do not put your thoughts into my mind, Miss Mennenger.'

'Miss Mennenger,' Cora Sue mimicked. 'Can't even call me by my given name.'

'One calls only those one thinks of as friends by their first names. You made it plain from the very first day that you had no wish to be any friend of mine.'

'Because I saw through that act of yours. I know ambition when I see it and you're eaten up by it. The nerve of it – to go and do a deal on your own! I've been with the Burnses, father and son, for more than twenty-five years and I'm not given that sort of licence. Now you've got this escort agency going. You latched on to Jake the minute you set eyes on him and don't think I don't know why!'

'Then perhaps you would enlighten me.'

'You're after a second husband – only this time one with money.'

Claire laughed, and Cora Sue was nonplussed at its genuine amusement. 'That is the furthest thing from my mind, I assure you. I have no interest in Mr Burns except as a good employer.'

'Then how come it's you he totes along everywhere he goes?'

'Because he asks me to go.'

'Once you've persuaded him not to take me.'

'You over-estimate my influence.'

'I don't underestimate you at all! I can see right through that iceberg act of yours.'

'Allow me to dispel your ridiculous fears. I am not in pursuit of Mr Burns. Nor is he in pursuit of me. We have a purely business relationship but I also regard him as a friend – a good friend. And that, Miss Mennenger, is all there is to it.'

'You mean you would like me to think so!'

'What you think, Miss Mennenger, is the product of an over-heated imagination, but if you're not prepared to take my word for it, then go to the fountainhead himself. Ask Mr Burns.' Claire levelled a look that demolished. 'If you dare.' The door closed behind her.

But it was Jake who asked Cora Sue. Even he noticed the atmosphere between the two women and it was strong enough to make him confront Cora Sue and ask: 'What gives with you and Claire? Why can't you get along with her?'

'Why don't you ask her?'

'Because I'm asking you. Because Claire gets along with everybody. You are the one exception, which tells me it's your fault.'

'*My* fault!'

'I'm aware you took a dislike to her from the start.'

'I've got no use for that kind of woman.'

'What kind would that be?'

'All flash and filigree.'

'I'll grant you the filigree but never the flash. Far from it.'

'She doesn't fool me. I've no time for these European society women. And for the life of me I can't understand how come you have.'

'I'm sorry you feel that way,' Jake said, 'because I intend to have a lot more time for Claire. If you find it so difficult then I suggest you go back home – where you constantly keep trying to drag me.'

Cora Sue knew an instant, serious fright. Jake's voice was calm but it held that inflexibility which meant something would have to give – and it would not be him. 'How would you get along without me?' she blustered. 'All I'm doing is watching out for you.'

'I'm old enough to do that for myself. I've got a smooth-running operation here, Cora Sue. Don't mess it up. If you stay here you take off those spurs. Understand?'

Oh, I understand all right, Cora Sue thought. And I'm not going anywhere. But she saw that she would have to tread softly from now on. That bitch had her hooks in deep. Well, let her think she's won for now, she thought. But I'll be watching – and waiting my chance . . .

'All right,' she said humbly. 'Whatever you say, Jake.'

'Look,' Jake said to Claire later, 'I know Cora Sue's been giving you a hard time, but that's because she's jealous.'

'I know. What I don't understand is why.'

Jake fiddled with the pencil he was holding. 'She's used to being closer to me than anybody – businesswise, I mean. She resents the fact that you can do things for me that she can't.'

'I've tried not to interfere with what I know to be her side of things, but it seems she resents my being here at all. Perhaps you should take her with you on your future trips abroad. I know how important she is to you in many ways;

she knows so much more about your business than I do – '

'And I allow her pretty much a free hand. But there are places she just wouldn't fit in the way you do.' He ran a hand through his hair. 'That sounds awful snobbish but it's a fact. What the hell would she have done on the *Circe*? And I sent you to Newark because you've got an eye for things she wouldn't see if they were shoved under her nose. Cora Sue is a first-class workhorse for the day-to-day grind, but she would never be accepted for the Kentucky Derby.' Pause. 'You would.' His hair was all ruffled by now so Claire put him out of his misery.

'I know what you mean,' she said gently, 'but – well, perhaps if you included her occasionally . . .'

Jake looked glum at the prospect, but he saw the merit of Claire's suggestion. 'Okay,' he agreed reluctantly. 'I'll see what I can do.'

But it was to Claire he said, one morning in early November: 'It's Thanksgiving in a couple of weeks. I thought I'd give a small dinner followed by a party.'

'Turkey and cranberry sauce and pumpkin pie?'

'Real pilgrim stuff. Henry can see to all that. Will you organize the rest? Not too many – about twenty to dinner and another couple of dozen people afterwards.'

'It will be a pleasure.'

She and Henry conferred, and once he knew how many would be coming – and every invitation was accepted – he cooked up a storm. Three thirty-pound American turkeys, a huge ham, bowls of corn, juicy pumpkin and pecan pies, fat Idaho baked potatoes, an enormous chocolate cake, plates of Brownies, bowls of salad – he had all three ovens going all day. Claire saw to the liquor, and had the drawing-room cleared for dancing, making sure there were plenty of the latest tapes to provide the music.

Twenty finally sat down to dinner at eight o'clock, and by ten-thirty the rest of the guests began to arrive. They were all Americans.

'Old Home Week?' joked Claire, as she greeted them.

Until the party really took off she was kept busy circulating, she doing the room one way while Cora Sue, determined not to be left out, did it the other. She made sure nobody had an empty glass, and that Henry was not being given tennis elbow by his use of the carving knife. The music was lively and the dancing under way when, as she floated here and there, a hand caught her arm: 'Hold on there, Lady Claire . . .' It was Charlie Whitman.

'Gate-crashing, Charlie?' Claire asked, feeling her heart turn over.

'Just because you didn't send me an invitation is no reason not to attend any party organized by you. I remember the last one . . .'

'I didn't even know you were in London.'

'I did tell you I'd be coming. Anyway, stay a while; everything is fine and dandy.'

'Just Jake,' chuckled the round-faced, plump, ever-smiling man standing next to Charlie, whom Claire remembered Jake greeting as an old friend long not seen. 'Always is around Jake. That's how he got his name.'

'Jake?' Claire's interest was spiked.

'Sure . . . that's what he'd always say when you asked him how he was doin'. "Just Jake", he'd say, and the name stuck.'

'Are you saying that Jake isn't his real name?'

'It's David,' Charlie said, watching her, 'David Winfield Burns.'

'Good heavens,' Claire said, faint with surprise.

Just then, a gorgeous blonde came up and dragged Charlie on to the dance floor.

'Jake suits him best,' the plump man said comfortably. He eyed Claire pleasurably. 'So you are Jake's left and right hand.'

'I help out.'

'Some help, if what I hear is the truth of it.'

'You're an old friend of his, aren't you?'

'Known him all his life. His pa was my oldest friend.'

'Are you an entrepreneur too?'

'No. I'm a judge.'

'Did you work with Jake's father in his law practice?'

'I did. Me and Marty Mennenger both.'

'Ah . . . So you're an old friend of Cora Sue's too.'

'Cora Sue and me go way back.'

'Like Jake and Charlie?'

'Sure . . . they went to school together.' Did they now, thought Claire. 'Even went with the same girl, till Jake snaffled her – right from under Charlie's nose.' The judge sighed. 'That was a real sad thing.'

'Was?'

'Stella dyin' like that; so young, so pretty . . . Jake was hurt real bad. It's good to see him lookin' so happy. I haven't seen him so chipper in a coon's age.'

'How long?' Claire asked, when she could.

'Well . . . it must be five years now . . . yes, five years.'

'What was she like?' Claire asked.

'Small, like you, but dark. She was part Cherokee; her Indian name was Star-that-Shines but everybody called her Stella.'

'Star-that-Shines,' Claire repeated, for some inexplicable reason feeling her throat clog. 'What a beautiful name.'

'Just like her. She was beautiful.'

'How did she die?' Claire asked.

The judge stared into his glass. 'It was an accident,' he said. 'A tragic accident.'

Something in his voice told Claire not to ask any more questions. Not that she didn't have enough to mull over.

The judge looked up to smile at her. 'But I can see you've been good for him. You live up to your reputation.'

'I didn't know I had one.'

The judge chuckled again. 'Everybody back home has heard about Jake's English Lady.'

While nobody here so much as suspects that Jake is a widower, Claire thought. So that was the reason for the blondes. His wife had been a brunette. How hurt he must have been, she thought on a pang. How desolately, unhealably hurt. She looked round for him. He was on the dance floor with another blonde, whose dress appeared to have been sprayed on, displaying a bottom that had the men eyeing her lustfully. He was laughing, light eyes glittering. Why had it never occurred to her that Jake might have been married? He was thirty-six, most men either were or had been married by that age. She was at a loss to account for the quality of her surprise. For some reason as yet unclear, she felt stunned. And yet it made so much else plain. The blondes, for instance. Always transient, because Jake was still, after five years, grieving for a wife he had lost. An accident, the judge had said. What sort of an accident? A car crash? A plane crash? Whatever it had been, it had left Jake unable, even now, to make a permanent commitment to any other woman. And he had never said a word. Well, she thought, you tried to keep your own murdered marriage to yourself, didn't you? So what's the difference. But suddenly the noise jarred, she felt the need for a little peace and quiet, to go somewhere and think. She turned to the judge: 'I must circulate, play the hostess.'

'You go ahead. I'll talk to you later.'

She made for the buffet table, where Henry was presiding, only to see him disappear into the kitchen for fresh supplies. Following him, she found him in the act of bringing out the third turkey.

'How we doin'?' he asked.

'Fine. Everybody is floating.'

'The amount of liquor as is laid on it ain't surprisin'.' He eyed her over the vast turkey. 'You okay? It ain't catchin' up on you?'

'I thought perhaps a restful five minutes with you . . . you *are* very restful, Henry.'

'I could say the same about you. You ain't no fusser. I don't go a bundle on women as fusses and Cora Sue can fuss somethin' terrible.' From his private store he placed before her a tall, well-iced, deeply pink glassful. 'Compliments of the house.'

'Why are you so good to me?' Claire asked, touched.

'Ain't you been good to us?'

'And have been well paid for it.'

'You done more than any money could buy. You been real good for Mister Jake.'

'He has been good for me.'

'It was a happy day when you decided to come see for yourself, and that's the truth.'

But only part of it, thought Claire. Truth to tell, Henry, I don't know even the half . . .

She sipped her Campari.

'I see Charlie Whitman brung himself along,' Henry observed darkly.

'Yes . . . you know we met him on the *Circe*?'

'So Mister Jake told me.'

'He told me he and Jake are old friends.'

Henry grunted. 'They've known each other a long time, but they ain't friends. Rivals, more like. Charlie Whitman has always been jealous of Mister Jake, and always will be.'

'Why?'

Henry shrugged. 'The Burns had money. Charlie's father run off when Charlie was too young to remember and his ma had to bring him and his brothers up by herself.'

'She did very well. He's a very successful lawyer.'

'Oh, he's clever, all right. But don't be fooled by him. He's great at foolin' people, is Charlie. It don't do to believe all he says.'

'He hasn't said anything,' Claire said truthfully.

'He will. If he's around it's because he's still burnin' with that jealousy of his. I wouldn't trust him no further than I could throw a steer.'

Rivals? wondered Claire. The rich, successful lawyer still jealous of the school friend who had never had to struggle? Rivals, perhaps, for Stella? She longed to ask, but repressed the question that trembled on her lips: if Stella had been, as the judge had said, part of the reason for Charlie's jealousy.

Her sigh was unconscious, and Henry eyed her dubiously.

She looked uptight about somethin'. He only hoped it wasn't because Charlie Whitman was back to make a play for her again. Mister Jake had told him about the yacht. It was always the same with Charlie. Whatever Jake had, Charlie felt the need to take it away from him . . .

Claire looked up, met his gaze and he saw what he always thought of as 'the plastic bubble' wreath itself around her again; the one she always wore when she seemed to withdraw from everything; to go inside herself and look out at you from a place where she couldn't be got at.

'I must go and do some more hostessing. Thank you for the drink and the restful conversation, Henry.'

As she went back into the party, she ran right into Charlie.

'Where have you been hiding?' he asked accusingly. 'They're playing our song . . .' Before she could resist he had her in his arms and on the dance-floor, totally unprepared for him. Aware now where her fatal weakness lay, she knew that if he started focusing on her again he would blind her with his dazzle. Even as she thought it he drew her close, murmured: 'Oh, how I have missed this . . . and you.'

'You should have told me,' she countered coolly.

'I thought I did.'

'Not what I wanted to hear.'

'Tell me and I'll say it. Whatever, wherever.'

'You're flirting again, Charlie.'

'I know. Ain't it fun?'

'While it lasts.'

'Is that regret or anticipation?' He held her eyes. 'I'm game if you are.'

'I told you, remember? I don't play those kind of games.'

They made a spectacular couple; Charlie's dark good looks set off Claire's cameo fragility, her wine-dark hair glowing above a dress that was a smoky drift of delphinium blue. They moved together like a dream, through one dance and into another.

'Charlie up to his old tricks?' the judge asked Jake with a disapproving frown.

'Claire is not easily fooled,' Jake answered shortly.

'Looks like Charlie's doin' his best to prove you wrong. What's the matter? Lost your touch? That's a fine lookin' woman. Smart, too.'

Jake did not answer. He was watching them steadily. Claire's face was cool, distant, Charlie's intent. He was saying something in a low voice, and as Jake watched, he danced Claire down the room until they were right opposite the door leading to Jake's study, and in a trice, he had the door open before whisking her inside and shutting the door behind them. The judge turned to Jake as if to say, What did I tell you? but the look on Jake's face stilled his tongue.

Claire had been so intent on her own feelings that she was not prepared for Charlie's sudden assault. She found herself being held tightly and kissed passionately in a darkened room; the object of the kind of assault that conjured memories she had hoped were buried for ever. It was all too familiar; a ferocious strength and purpose that evoked only terror. She struggled violently to free herself.

'For God's sake . . .' She kneed him instinctively and as he recoiled, she wrenched herself away and retreated until Jake's desk jabbed into her back. She was panting, he was furious.

'What the hell do you think you're doing?' he snarled. 'I know you play hard to get but this is ridiculous.'

'I told you — I don't play your kind of games.'

'Games!'

'Sexual games. Casual, mindless, emotionless games. I have had enough of them.'

'I'm not playing with you.'

'Oh, yes you are. And I know why. It has to do with Jake. You see me as a means to some peculiar end of yours and I will not go along with it. It would probably be the end of me.'

'Is this an example of that famous Celtic precognition?'

'No. Just bad experience allied to feminine instinct.'

'You make your ex sound like a combination of Casanova and Jack the Ripper.'

'A perfect description. You remind me of him so much!'

'Ah . . . I see . . .' It was a breath of realization. 'That is why you won't trust me.'

'That, and the fact that my instinct tells me that you are not a trustworthy person.'

'You mean Jake Burns has been doing a hatchet job on me!'

'He has never said *anything* to me about you.'

She could tell by the sound of his voice, the dim stance of his body, that he was very angry, but his voice was softly persuasive when he said, 'You are throwing us away, Claire. We could have been good together.'

'At what?'

'You name it, we could have had it.'

'No hearts and flowers, if you please. Hail to the Chief is more in your line.'

He sighed. 'What do I have to do to win you then?'

'I'm no man's prize.'

He considered her. 'You're scared,' he said finally. 'That kook you were married to really did a job on you.'

'Yes, he did. I told you – you remind me of him so much.'

'I'm not like any other man,' he said roughly. 'Charlie Whitman is an original.'

'Original what? Womanizer?'

'You're an emotional coward!' It was a flat accusation.

'I don't risk myself, if that's what you mean.'

'This is life, baby. Everything is a risk – if you really live it.' He paused. 'That's your trouble. You don't have the courage.'

'Not when it comes to involving myself with a man like you.'

'Jake *has* been talking to you!'

'You flatter yourself. I don't need to be told what you are, Charlie. I was married to you under another name!'

333

'Now you flatter *me*! Your ex has a reputation that far exceeds mine. And for things I have *never* done.'

'You're the same type, from the same mould.' Candidly: 'I suppose that was what attracted me to you in the first place. But I know now what I didn't know then, and that's why my answer is no. If you suspect that Jake has been telling me about you then it only proves that there are things to tell, but I assure you, I have no wish to know them. I do know one thing though. Your "pursuit" of me has to do with whatever lies between you and Jake. By having me you can somehow get at him – though God knows what for – and I have no intention of allowing you to use me in that way!'

'What you lack in courage you make up for in imagination.'

'Wrong. It's that same Celtic precognition.'

Charlie considered her thoughtfully. 'Why so protective of Jake? He can handle himself – and I should know.'

'Jake Burns has been kind to me, he has – helped – me, given me back things I had thought gone for ever. For that alone I shall always be grateful.'

'Jesus, now *you* are playing Hearts and Flowers!' His laugh was harsh. 'I could tell you things about Jake Burns – '

Claire waited tensely but he only shrugged, laughed. 'The hell with it. Why should I? Better you find out for yourself . . . You're so goddamned clever.' He moved towards the door. 'Okay, we'll let it go for now. But I'm not letting it go for good.' She saw the white teeth flash in a wolfish grin. 'I always did think the chase was more fun than the kill, and you do lead a guy a hell of a run. I only hope you're worth it.'

'You'll never know,' Claire said contemptuously.

He laughed. It was the voice of confidence; the voice of one who knew he had only to wait. Claire shivered. She had heard that same voice so many times before.

'We're not finished yet.' More familiar words. 'I knew the moment I set eyes on you that I had to have you – and I will. I'm a patient man when it comes to something

334

I really want. Think on that.' The door closed behind him.

Claire felt her way to the nearest chair and fell into it. Her legs felt jellied, her insides were churning. She knew she had done the right thing yet his accusation of emotional cowardice stung like a blow. Well, haven't I every right? she asked herself. Oh, God, Rory . . . you did do a perfect job on me. Even now, I'm not rid of you.

She was sitting there when the door opened, letting in a stream of light which exposed her whilst only silhouetting Jake. 'Some people are leaving,' he said, in the clipped, colourless voice she knew meant Technicolor feelings. Her own rose to meet it, satisfyingly drowning the humiliation she felt at his being perfectly aware of what had been going on. Without a word, she rose and stalked past him.

For the rest of the evening she never went near Charlie, though she was conscious of him down to her nerve ends. Catching sight of herself in a mirror she happened to meet his eyes. He smiled. She flushed and looked away. What *am* I going to do? she thought wretchedly. He knows damn well the effect he has on me; that's why he's so sure. That same, compulsive attraction had succeeded in shattering the comfortable, untroubled relationship she had formed with Jake. That easy, shared companionship which she had wrapped around herself like armour. Jake would not be around for protection where Charlie Whitman was concerned. Somehow she knew that. Jake did not like Charlie. Disapproval had cloaked him in ice. You're on your own, she told herself bleakly. So she tilted her chin, pasted a smile on her face and proceeded to give a star performance as a woman having the time of her life.

It was well after three by the time the last guest had gone tipsily through the front door, leaving behind the skeletons of the turkeys, a shining ham bone, a litter of dirty plates and glasses, overflowing ashtrays and a layer of smoke that hung like smog. Claire went round opening all the windows so that a cross-draught would clear the air, and it was as she was opening those in the drawing-room that she heard from the dining-room next door the sound of Jake's furious voice.

'What the hell do you think you're playing at, Charlie?' Rage made his voice thick. Shock held Claire frozen. She had thought Charlie long gone.

'What game did you have in mind?' Charlie was smooth as a purring tiger.

'You know damn well what I mean – and who I mean! The name of this particular game is Claire Drummond.' Claire shrank back against the curtains.

'None of your business,' Charlie tossed with indifferent spite.

'The hell it is! Claire works for me and I want her to go on doing so. Don't mess it – or her – up, Charlie.'

'Or you'll do what!' Charlie's voice wielded the whip of contempt. When Jake did not reply, Charlie went on tauntingly, 'Claire is old enough to know what she's doing.'

'Not when you pull out all the stops! I *know* you! I've seen you operate too many times before. You get them so close to the edge the only place they can go is over!'

'Ah, but Claire is such a well-balanced girl.' Claire cringed at the smug purr in the dark voice.

'Not right now she's not. She's as vulnerable as hell and I won't stand by and watch you walk over the pieces. I saw you disappearing with her tonight.'

'I know you did.' Charlie didn't give a damn; in fact, he was gloating.

'I'm warning you, Charlie. Not this one too. Lay off.' Too? Claire thought.

'Why not this one? Claire is a real challenge, and haven't I been meeting and beating them all my life?'

'Claire is no – no fool. She'll see straight through you.'

'You mean through those holes you've been hacking in my character?' Charlie laughed softly. 'So you can peddle your own wares? I don't tell you how to handle your blondes,' Charlie went on, sounding bored.

'I don't give them a snow job. They know what I want and it stops there.'

Charlie's voice was like silk when he said, 'And we both know why, don't we?'

In the sudden, crackling silence, Claire squeezed her eyes tight shut. Belt him, Jake, she pleaded silently. Oh, please, belt him . . . But all she heard was rapid footsteps along the parquet flooring then the sound of a slammed door. Jake, of course. He always slammed doors. Claire held her breath. She heard Charlie laugh, triumphantly, then his own soft footfall and this time, the quiet opening and closing of the door. Claire waited until she heard the front door shut and then she was off and running, up the stairs and into her room, where she shut and bolted the door before throwing herself on her bed in a storm of tears. To be fought over, like a juicy bone, was the last straw. How *dare* they? She was not staying in this bloody job a moment longer. She was getting away from Jake Burns and Charlie Whitman both. There was something very wrong here, not in the least the fact that Jake – *Jake* – was afraid of Charlie Whitman. Why? *Why?* What was it that lay between them, like some bottomless pit, its sides bristling with sharpened stakes? It had something to do with Jake's blondes. What had Charlie said? 'And we both know why, don't we?' Know what?

Oh, God, she thought, helpless with nerves. What have I got myself into here? Questions and speculations buzzed inside her brain like angry bees. And it was a bitter consolation to have her instincts about Charlie confirmed. He was pursuing her to achieve some hidden purpose which had to do with Jake. Which had to do with Stella. Star-that-Shines. The judge had said that the two men had been rivals, that Jake had won the prize. Was that it? Was Charlie still jealous? She must have been a remarkable woman, Claire thought on such a pang that it made her eyes well once more. Jake still grieved and Charlie still rankled. And why had Charlie said that about Jake peddling his own wares? Not once, in all the time she had been with Jake, had he shown the

337

slightest sign of interest other than that of – at first – a considerate employer to a valued employee, and later, a trusted friend. It had always been a friendship thing; there had never been anything sexual. Yet Charlie had obviously spotted something. What?

Tossing and turning, she thought, It's all so complicated . . . The more I think the less I understand. I only know – feel – that there is a situation here; a nasty triangle with very sharp edges. Cut yourself and you could bleed to death. She felt so taut with frustration that she knew she would never sleep. Her run-in with Charlie had left her emotionally overwound and overhearing the argument had tightened her spring even further. She had the feeling that unless she could loosen it she would snap.

She got up from the bed and began to undress. Perhaps a hot shower. It didn't work. She sat down to brush her hair; that always soothed her. This time it didn't. And then, the tantalizing thought of the Niagara of liquor downstairs entered her mind. Candy is dandy but liquor is quicker, she thought. She was not much of a drinker. Campari usually, and then always well diluted with soda. Strong spirits were what she needed. Like a double slug of Jake's favourite anodyne: Jack Daniel's. That would put her out. She began to perceive why it was that Jake – not often but still often enough – got drunk. He was trying to drown something. Since that first time, Henry had always tipped her the wink, and she had been careful to give Jake a wide berth.

'It's his way of unwindin',' Henry had told her briefly. 'He don't go on the toot often and then only when it's the only way.' But he had never said why. She had been at a loss to find a reason. Jake seemed to have everything under control. Only now did she see the reason staring her in the face. Stella. Star-that-Shines, still shedding her light in Jake's heart and illuminating it in such a way as to expose, every now and then, the emptiness at its centre.

Claire felt her heart ache. She had been so full of her own misery that she had not spared a thought for Jake's. A man

338

who turned to drink, as he did, obviously seeking oblivion, was a man who was deeply unhappy. Yet beyond a cursory curiosity – tinged with moralizing disapproval – she had given it no thought. Apart from anything else, Rory has made you selfish, she told herself bitterly. Charlie was so right. You *are* an emotional coward. Other people have bad marriages yet still they marry a second time. You, on the other hand, have been parading your self-pity around on a sandwich board.

What a party this had been! It had turned into a wake. She stared into her dressing-table mirror. Go on, take a good look, she ordered herself. If you want to put your marriage behind you, why in God's name do you persist in laying flowers on the grave? Dispose of the remains. Preferably by cremation. Then, maybe, you can really start again.

If it's that easy, then why can't Jake? her reflection asked her bluntly. Because he is grieving for something that was obviously very, very good; something he still misses terribly. You don't miss yours so why are you still in mourning?

'Oh, all right!' she spat at her wild-eyed reflection in the mirror. 'If needs must then needs be.' She donned her negligee, opened her door stealthily. All was dark and quiet. Everyone had gone to bed. Soundlessly, she padded down the dark stairs in her bare feet. The dining-room was lit only by the light of the street lamp coming in through the windows from which she herself had drawn back the curtains and gave her enough light to see the long table, still littered with bottles. She went straight to the Wild Turkey, a liqueur bourbon Henry said was 'liquid lightnin', poured herself a jiggerful and tossed it back. She felt it hit her like a live coal. Coughing and spluttering, she wiped her eyes before pouring another. She would take that one to her room. If she drank it here she might not make it back.

Holding the brimming glass carefully she turned to retrace her steps – and found Jake standing at the end of the table watching her. He had taken off his jacket, loosened his tie and shirt and was obviously in the middle of a bender. Her heart lurched as he raised his own glass in an ironic salute. 'Welcome to the club.'

'I couldn't sleep,' Claire said defensively. 'I thought perhaps a drink.'

'A drink? That's your second belt you're carrying.'

Guilty anger flaring: 'Take it out of my salary!' She made to stalk past him, but he reached out a lazy hand to grasp her arm and swing her round. The bourbon slopped, splashing her hand.

'Ooops! Sorry. I know how important every last drop is. Here, let me give you a refill.'

Still holding her arm like a vice he pulled her after him back to the bottle of Wild Turkey. Picking it up, he filled a six-ounce tumbler to the brim, and handing it to her said: 'There . . . that ought to do it. If you are that desperate it takes much more than you think.' He exchanged it for the jigger. The mockery in his voice, savage and taunting, flicked her raw.

'I am *not* that desperate!'

'Liar,' he said lazily, contemptuous with unshakeable knowledge.

'It's far too much and you know it!'

He shook his head gravely. 'It's never enough, I know *that*.'

'Yes – you ought to!'

She saw his face darken. 'By God, Ballater was right about you. You do have a serrated tongue!'

'If you will kindly let go my arm you need suffer it no longer.'

'Oh, I suffer from lots of things. What do you suffer from – apart from a case of the hots?'

Claire gasped, but she rallied gamely. 'Insomnia!'

He laughed. 'Liar,' he said again. Then: 'It's Charlie, isn't it?'

'None of your business!' But Claire felt the hollow inside her fill with dismay.

'With Charlie shoving it down my throat!' The clear eyes

were a-glitter with fire. They burned her, made her skin crawl with humiliation, which led her to spit: 'Then choke on it!'

With a wrench she freed her arm, but it was the one which held the glass, and the violent movement spilled its contents all over her, drenching her throat and breasts, running in rivulets down into the vee-neck of her robe.

'Now look what you've done! Of all the . . .' Her wrathful voice faded as she saw his eyes; fixedly following the liquid as it ran down her throat to soak into the lace of her robe, causing it to cling damply, outlining the firm thrust of her breasts, chilling the nipples into stiffness. She heard his breath jolt, saw the clarity of his eyes darken into smoke. The look in them made her turn in panic to flee. But he still had her arm fast and she could not move. In dreamlike fashion he reached out to pluck the all-but-empty glass from her hand and set it down on the table, but his attention was wholly on her and it dropped short and fell to the carpeted floor, unseen, unheard. Their attention was welded to each other in an awareness that screamed. Again Claire tried to break free but his hand was a vice, fastening on her arm with a grip which drew her to him helplessly. She twisted her head away and moaned softly, half in terror, half in excitement.

Time had thickened, congealed, to render everything into slow-motion. The only thing that raced was their hearts. Claire could feel the grip of every finger, holding her fast. Slowly, oh so agonizingly slowly, he brought her right up against him before bending his blond head to put his mouth and tongue to the damp skin of the flesh between her breasts, where the robe fell open, murmuring in a thick, languid voice: 'What a waste of good bourbon . . .'

Claire arched convulsively as she felt his mouth; hot and greedy and arousing. She tried to lean backwards to escape it but there was no getting away from the deadly progress of the lips and tongue which travelled across her breasts, the tongue flicking the hardened nipples, making her buck and gasp. One of his hands left her arms to pull at the shoe-string

341

straps which tied her robe at the neck, and he used his mouth to push it away from her shoulders so that she was left in only her nightdress; a high-waisted fall of rose-red silk with a bodice – now damply clinging – of blond, filigree lace.

'You're all wet . . .' he murmured dreamily, still in that thick, drugged voice, his mouth hot and burning. Claire was trembling uncontrollably, and not only from fear. It was that mouth; insidious, weakening her will. Too much was happening too fast. This was Jake! This was all wrong . . . Yet though her mind knew it, her will was fogged by her feelings and unable to receive any instructions. She kept telling herself it was the wrong man, the wrong time, the wrong situation, but Charlie had tampered with her emotional brakes to such an extent that she was no longer capable of stopping. All she could feel, try to fight against, feel sunderingly, was the progress of that hot, senses-shattering mouth as it travelled tantalizingly across her damp and heated flesh. Its effect had her trembling uncontrollably, and as it neared her mouth, coming up her throat, she heard herself, with terrifying shock, moaning with anticipation. Horrified, she struggled, and he raised his head to look down into her eyes. His own were hot and fierce. The only sound was their harsh, rapid breathing. Somewhere, she stood outside herself, watching a film in slow-motion, but that self was incapable of penetrating the thick, intense silence of the dream.

Time came to a stop as they gazed into each other's eyes; he seemed enormous, as close as this. The mountain-stream eyes glittered like water in sunlight, but they did not chill; they melted. She could feel the intensity of his gaze opening her up like a flower. Slowly, unable to bear it, her eyelids fluttered then closed.

When she felt his tongue, for a wild moment she stiffened and she pushed against him with her arms: it was like trying to overturn a tank. He was not a big man, but he was a strong one. His mouth devoured her, his tongue exploring leisurely, savouringly. She could feel herself slipping, losing control. The kiss deepened and he shifted his hold to bring her more fully into his arms, never lifting his mouth from hers.

Once again she could hear moaning; realized again that it was her. The last thing of which she was clearly aware was her own arms going up and around Jake's neck as she opened her mouth fully under his, returning his kiss passionately, grinding her hips against the hot, hard centre of his body as the long-smouldering fuse of frustration and self-denial which Charlie had lit went off in a searing flare of eroticism that took her up and away; over the edge.

Her nightgown slithered to the floor while her hands greedily shoved away his jacket, unbuttoned his shirt, her blood roaring in her ears, her body on fire for him, all self-restraint in shreds, every last remnant of cool self-protection reduced to ashes. Everything she had learned from Rory came thundering back like an express. It had been a long, long time. She covered his face with kisses, felt the tide of her blood crash and meld with his. When at last, naked together, he lifted her from her feet, her eyes opened to meet his once more, felt them deeply search her own. Again, as though she could not bear to look into them, she closed her eyes, hid her face in the hollow of his shoulder. Then he carried her to the stairs.

CHAPTER TWELVE

Claire lay on her back, staring up at the ceiling of Jake's bedroom. Beside her, he lay on his stomach, the long length of him fitted to her like a piece in a jigsaw puzzle, face buried in the curve of her throat, breath fanning her naked flesh; deeply and tranquilly asleep.

She was wide awake and in a state of disbelief. What were you thinking of? she demanded of her inner self, only to hear that self retort: Thinking! *Thinking!* You were far beyond thinking, my girl. Which is why you've gone and ruined everything. He was drunk and you were handy. In your oh-so-scrupulous avoidance of being used by Charlie, you went and let yourself be used by Jake. *He didn't even know who you were!* Her eyes welled at the recall: Jake's voice, vibrant with love and joy, hoarse with passion, saying, 'Stella, oh, Stella, Stella . . .'

You had a good thing going here, she accused herself bitterly, so what do you go and do? You get the hots for one man and end up in bed with another. Serves you damned well right. You and your damned whisky. Except we both know it wasn't whisky which caused your little bout of *delirium tremens*, don't we? It was Jake Burns.

Claire had been instructed in the pleasures of the flesh by the man who had done all the original research, and, until Jake, she had only that one man to use as a comparison. Now, after Jake, in spite of what he had said, she saw, finally exposed in the light of what Rory had done, that what she had believed to be a true union, the two-now-one ideal, had in reality been nothing more than a series of benefit performances, with the proceeds and the acclaim going to

Rory every time. It had taken Jake Burns, of all people, to show her that with Rory, sex had been his starring vehicle; that after every 'performance' he expected nothing less than a standing ovation and at least a dozen curtain calls.

Jake, on the other hand, had given of himself in such a way as to make her aware that her pleasure was his pleasure, her fulfilment his own, inflating her ego to the point where it had exploded like a Roman candle – only to sear her pride by calling her by another woman's name. Rory had taken all the private boxes of self labelled pride, integrity, honour, decency, turned them upside down to empty their contents then stamped those contents to smithereens. Charlie, she had been warned, was an Indian-giver. Never would she have expected Jake, of all men, to give her everything then take it all back again, down to her very identity, reducing her to the status of just another of his thousand and one fly-by-nights.

That's what you get for pulling a fast one, her inner self said. For God's sake, aren't you capable of learning *any* lesson?

I thought I had, she told herself, mortified. I thought that even if all else was gone, I had the memory of how it used to be between Rory and me. Now, even that has been exposed for a fake . . . Anguished tears welled as she gazed back at the infatuation she had mistaken for true love, saw how she had created Rory out of her own illusions then, when the rot set in, blamed herself for being inadequate, never him. Now she had gone and made another horrendous error; given herself to a man who had not even known who she was.

How could you *do* it? her inner self asked reproachfully.

Because I was starved! she flung back. He only had to lay a finger on me and I went off like a rocket. That's why!

Haven't you forgotten something? Like the fact that you knew – you deep down, damn well *knew* – that after the run-in with Charlie, Jake was more than likely to be up and about the business of getting drunk. Your 'need' of a drink was only an excuse; what you really needed was somebody to put out the fire Charlie had lit; only after Jake had slaked his thirst he crumpled the paper cup and threw it away . . .

How's that for a laugh? she asked herself with bitter irony. Except the last thing she felt like doing was laughing. What she had wanted and what she had received had never been so much as introduced to each other. Half hysterically she thought that she literally had not been able to see the stud for the tease . . .

You've ruined it all, of course. You realize that. You cannot possibly stay on after this. Your safe, purely-business relationship has been vaporized – and not by the heat you and Jake generated either. You have gone and done what you swore you would never do. Casual sex was something she had always abhorred. She had been brought up to think of it as a betrayal of self-respect. A woman's body was not something to be handed around like a dish of after-dinner mints. It was a gift she gave to the man she loved. She had been a virgin when she married; her own innate distaste for illicit sex, allied to an upbringing which taught that such behaviour cheapened your worth, had prevented her from playing the games that others – Caroline, for instance – played with such careless disregard for consequences. She had given herself to Rory because she had truly believed she loved him. She did not love Jake Burns. She liked him enormously, she trusted him, admired him, regarded him as a valued friend, but love – love was something else again, something she had learned was a con man of the calibre of Rory Ballater himself. She had determined never to be fooled again; to be very sure that the next time she gave herself to a man he was worthy of her. And what had she done? Given herself for no other reason than she did not have the self-control to say no.

Rationalize it all you like, she told herself contemptuously. Go on, parade your excuses, give them all twenty-eight days' detention. Black is still black and that is the colour of your anything-but-true love's hair. You got straight on your high-horse when Charlie propositioned you, but where Jake was concerned you asked him for a lift! How *could* you? How in God's name *could* you? How can you ever look him in the face again and not feel humiliated? He didn't even know who you *were*!

The ache at her centre was a hot hard stone; a true case of heartburn. It caused fresh, hot tears to erupt from her eyes and trickle silently down her cheeks, to drop from her chin on to Jake's own closed eyes, waking him.

He blinked, and though every vestige of alcohol had been burned away, for a brief moment he was not sure where he was. Until he inhaled the familiar fragrance of roses. At once, memory connected and flashed a series of lantern slides across his brain, illuminating the sequence of events that had begun with spilled whisky and gone on to damply clinging red silk and —

'Claire,' he murmured gladly, moving closer to the warmth and fragrance. It had not been another fantasy after all . . .

'No!' The violence of her voice was matched by the way she flung his arm away, but before she could quit the bed he had his arm back across her, pinning her down.

'Wait a minute . . .' Bewilderment gave way to anger. 'What brought this on? Why the injured party act?'

'How would you know where I hurt?'

His mind picked out the relevant word and held it out for inspection. 'I hurt you?' He was cautious if unbelieving.

'Not where it shows.'

He frowned, a mixture of doubt and interrogation in his eyes. 'What did I *do*, for God's sake? You weren't complaining a while back . . . far from it.'

'How would you know what I was doing — you didn't even know who I was!'

A heartbeat went by before he said, 'Of course I did.'

'Then why did you call me Stella?'

He did not move, but suddenly he was no longer with her. She could tell, by the sudden difference in the weight of his arm, the tension which crackled like distant lightning.

Then, just as suddenly he did remove himself, lifting his arm and rolling away, right over to the other side of the bed where he lay on his back with his hands behind his head.

'Why should that bother you?' he asked with brutal frankness. 'Do you think I didn't know you were pretending I was Charlie? We were both fielding substitutes!'

Her hand cracked across his cheek, all her fury and humiliation behind it. His eyes blurred and his ears rang.

'You bastard!' She was incandescent with anger. 'That is not true and you know it! It may have started out that way but I didn't carry it through. I knew who *you* were *all* the time!'

'I was still a substitute!' His own anger rose to meet hers. 'Charlie Whitman has had you teetering ever since you met him; tonight he pushed you, but because he wasn't around to catch you, you fell into my arms. Thank you for nothing!'

'Which is how you've made *me* feel!'

'Good. Now maybe you'll understand what you've done to me.'

Claire had been fumbling with her nightdress. Now she stopped, glared at him, tears still dribbling. 'I've met every single item in your specification. What you wanted I saw you got.'

'Oh, you met the specification all right. You were as efficient and capable and well-connected as I could wish, but you did it all with about as much warmth as a New England winter. You've handled me with tongs, lady, and you never so much as looked at me – I mean really *looked* at me – while you did it.'

'That's not true! I – ' She stopped, eyes wide, recalling Jake's slurred voice saying those very same words the night she had found him drunk, when he had accused her of being the Fair Miss Frigidaire. Caroline had told her the same thing.

'You knew my situation,' she flared defensively.

'And understood it, but did you ever understand mine?'

'I wasn't aware – ' Claire began.

'You're damned right you weren't, especially of me.'

'I would have thought tonight had more than made up for *that*!'

Suddenly the heat seemed to go out of Jake. His voice was quieter when he said, 'It did. It confirmed what I had long thought. That underneath the ice-cap was a volcano that was far from extinct.' His sigh was heavy. 'You think you have gone and made another mistake, don't you? Gone and let the side down, as you would put it. I can see you getting ready to do the right thing – tidy the remains, give them a state funeral then erect a monument before consigning them to history.'

'It *was* a mistake! One I never thought to make. I am not in the habit of sleeping with my employer!'

'See! You're at it again. It was *me*' – he stabbed his naked chest with his fingers – 'me, Jake Burns, you slept with, not Burns Enterprises!' He was getting angry again.

'Whoever, whatever, it was still wrong.'

'Why?'

'Because it ruins everything.'

'How?'

Claire gaped. '*How?* It changes everything – '

'If it's for the better I'm not complaining.' He paused. 'If it's for the worse, kindly tell me how.'

'I *work* for you – '

'So?'

Claire's exasperation got the better of her. 'If you don't know then I would be wasting my time explaining it to you. We have different standards, obviously.'

'I don't think so. But yours are impossibly lofty – like your attitude sometimes.'

'Now look here – '

'No, you look. What's at issue here is not that we slept together: what gets you is that I called you Stella.'

'How would you have liked it if I had called you Charlie?' Her voice was raw.

'I wouldn't, I guess.'

'I had enough of that with Rory. All he ever thought of was himself, his own gratification – '

'Is that what you're accusing me of?'

'What else am I to think?'

'I think that it's very strange you haven't asked me who Stella is.'

Claire dropped her nightdress over her head; it made her feel infinitely more secure. 'I know who she is. Your friend the judge told me you had been married and that your wife was dead.'

'Did he now.' Jake's voice was thin.

'That is *all* he said.'

'But more than enough, obviously.'

'The least you could have done was known whose body it was.'

'I did know.' Jake paused. 'If I called you Stella it was because being with you was like it used to be with her. It was no insult, believe me. It was a compliment.'

Claire stared at him, nonplussed. That had never occurred to her.

'I wasn't taking anything away from you by confusing you with her, and considering the fire we lit . . .' Jake shrugged. 'It's been a long time since – ' He stopped abruptly.

Claire stared hard at the image his words drew. 'Is that why – I mean – the blondes?'

'*Now* you ask me.'

'I didn't know I was supposed to!'

'And you still wouldn't. You British lean over backwards to avoid prying into other people's affairs.'

'Where I come from it is regarded as bad manners.'

'Where I come from it is regarded as genuine interest.' He considered her. 'You never asked me if I was – or had been – married.'

'Your private life was none of my business.'

'But you must have been curious.'

Claire moved her shoulders uneasily. 'Curiosity killed the

cat.' Then, awkwardly, making the gesture: 'It did come as a surprise to learn that you are a widower.'

'For almost five years.'

'How long were you married?'

'A little over four.'

'Not much longer than me.'

Jake regarded her sardonically. 'Walking wounded, the both of us. And if we hadn't run into your ex in Aberdeen I wouldn't have known the reason for your shell-shock.'

'Which is why it hurt when you called me by another woman's name.'

'Stella was not just any woman, but if that hurt it was not meant to. I would never willingly hurt *you*.'

Now Claire felt guilty. She knew Jake well enough by now to know that he never lied. 'It was too close to home, I suppose,' she allowed. 'I had more than enough of that with Rory.'

'I'm no Rory Ballater.' His voice was hard.

'I'm aware of that.'

'Are you also aware that Charlie *is*?'

Claire froze. 'I know what Charlie is.'

'Is that why you cut him off at the knees?'

Claire could not help her smile.

'What's so funny?'

'Your marvellously explicit American.' Then, dismissively: 'Let's not talk about Charlie Whitman, if you please.'

'We have to, because he's part of what happened to-night, just as Stella is. She is the reason he moved in on you.'

Claire frowned. 'What do you mean?'

'Stella was Charlie's girl. I took her away from him.'

'So? What has that to do with me?'

'Ever since she died he has been taking women away from me.'

Claire stared at him. 'But – why should he think I *could* be "taken away"?'

'Because he found out I was – interested – in you.'

Claire sank down on the side of the bed. 'You kept it very well hidden,' she said at last.

'I had no choice. You went around with your ten-foot pole at the ready. I didn't dare risk making it plain because I knew it would get back to him.'

Too late, Claire now saw that the iceberg, of which she had glimpsed only the tip, was every bit as big as the one which sank the Titanic.

'I told you Charlie and I go way back, didn't I?'

'Yes.'

'We come from the same small town; Cimarron, Oklahoma, population at the last count, 22,683. I was born there. Burns Oil is the major employer, but Charlie was five when his parents brought him. His father had got himself a job with the company. It didn't last, though; he ran off one night and that was the last his wife and sons ever saw of him. My mother was already ill by that time; she had never been strong and then when I was born they discovered she had a rare blood disease. She died when I was eight, but my memories of her are always connected with a sickroom. That's why, after Charlie's father ran off, my father offered his mother the job of running our house and looking after me. My mother had nurses and we had a cook and a maid and a gardener, but they needed somebody to light a fire under them sometimes and my father hadn't the time. Mrs Whitman had gone to him to explain why her husband hadn't turned up for work and to ask if there was a job for her instead, so she came to work for us. She and Charlie and his younger brother Pete lived with us, and I guess Mrs Whitman was as much a mother to me as my own.

'Charlie and I were the same age so we became friends. But always, with Charlie, there was rivalry. He had to win over me at everything. All through school it was endless competition. He made the football team, I beat him at track. He took the English prize, I took the math. I was to go to Brown, where my mother's family had always gone – she was from Providence – so Charlie had to go one better and get an open scholarship – at sixteen – to Harvard. He came out top in the entrance examinations. Charlie was – is – very smart. So we didn't see much of each other except during vacations, and I wasn't always home then. My father encouraged me to see the world before I settled down; he'd done it and he said travel broadened not only the mind but the outlook, so I spent my summers mostly with my mother's family back east. After we both graduated, he went on to Harvard Law while I went to Harvard Business School. We'd see each other now and again but that was all. Charlie was ambitious; he was going to be a rich, successful lawyer, and after he got his degree he went to join a prestigious law firm in Tulsa. That was where we met up again. At a big party given by one of his firm's clients who happened to do business with us. He had Stella with him. She was the loveliest thing . . . but not the type he usually went for. He'd always had a string of them, always the same: elegant, sophisticated, experienced. Stella was quite the opposite. I vaguely remembered her from school – she was that much younger than us; shy, much more serious than was usual with Charlie's girls, and she was a widow. She'd married young, her childhood sweetheart, just before he was sent to Vietnam in the last year of the war, and he was killed only three months after getting there. So at nineteen she was a widow. When I met her she was twenty-four, three years younger than me, and she was a legal secretary with Charlie's firm. Like men do, I asked him if he was serious about Stella and to my surprise he said he was; that she was – "different". "There's a quality of innocence about her," I remember him saying, "that is very refreshing. She has old-fashioned, small-town America ideas even after five years in Tulsa." Which meant she wouldn't sleep with him. That would intrigue Charlie, all right. I could see he was working on her and that it would only be a matter of time, because I'd never known any woman say no to Charlie for long – if at all. But as I got to know her – I was involved with a woman at that time and we used to make a foursome regularly – I began to think that maybe Charlie had met his match.

'Stella *was* different. She was shy, but she was very determined. She'd been raised the old way, and she believed in those ways passionately. I liked that. I liked her more and more as time went on, and the wonder of it was that she liked me too. It got so that when we all went out together it was to see each other. Then I had to go abroad again and before I went I thought – the hell with it. I love Stella and I think she feels the same way, so I told her.' Jake smiled; it made Claire's heart wrench. '"I've been waiting for you to tell me," was all she said. When she told Charlie he was anything but pleased. Here he'd been, biding his time, playing his cards carefully, and I had come along and stolen her from under his very nose. He accused me of doing it deliberately, because I knew she was important to him; that I always had to have what he had. When I said I was going to marry her he said he had decided that was what he wanted, but Stella was firm. She regarded him as her friend, but she loved me and that was that. He did everything he could to get her to change her mind but she wouldn't budge. And when she invited him to the wedding he knew he'd lost.

'Stella was a Catholic – that had a lot to do with her inner strength; her religion was important to her, and the only way she would marry me was in a Catholic church, with me promising that the children would be brought up as Catholics. I'd have married Stella under water if that was what she wanted and religion wasn't an important thing to me. My father had been of the opinion that it was responsible for at least half the world's ills and he had brought me up to think for myself about everything, including religion. "Never trust any organization that tells you not to ask questions," he used to tell me. "Blind faith is just that – blind." But it was what Stella wanted and by that time whatever she wanted was all right with me. So we got married in a Catholic church and the children, when they came, would be Catholics too. I built us a big new house in

Cimarron and gave Stella a free hand to furnish it, and when we came back from Hawaii, where she wanted to spend our honeymoon, we moved in and everything was perfect.

'Stella got pregnant right away and she was on cloud nine. She loved children, wanted a whole slew of them. But she lost the baby at nine weeks. It hit her hard. But the doctors said these things happened and there was no reason why she shouldn't have others. Only she lost the second one at twelve weeks. She was really depressed after that; she took to spending a lot of time in church. I had her see a top gynaecologist and he said a minor operation would put things right. So she had it and as soon as they gave the all clear we tried again. Stella never had any trouble conceiving; it was carrying that was the difficulty, so when she became pregnant the third time she took to her bed. She was bent and determined that nothing – absolutely nothing – would go wrong this time, and I could see she was very uptight about the whole thing so I went along with it, even though she wouldn't let me touch her all that time. That caused our first arguments; I couldn't see why I should have to take cold showers but she was adamant: she was not going to take even the slightest risk. So I put all my energy into work.

'My father had run Burns Oil but I had ideas for expansion. We'd always serviced our own rigs and I put together a division of the company that specialized in nothing else. Soon I was getting enquiries from all over Oklahoma and Texas, from Louisiana and even up in Wyoming. Then I had an idea for a leasing company. I'd acquired a lot of equipment as payment of bills some wildcatters couldn't pay. I bought new stuff and soon the leasing company was as successful as the servicing one. I was making money hand over fist. Stella got past the danger period and everything was going well. I furnished a nursery with every damned thing a baby could need, and when Stella went into labour I was there, with her, when Christopher was born. He was perfect; six pounds, with her black hair and blue eyes. Stella was ecstatic. I'd never seen her so happy . . . Then, when he was almost four months old she found him dead in his cot one morning. No reason; he'd been fine when she put him down. It was what they call a cot death. Stella went to pieces. Couldn't handle it. She sank into a depression as deep as the Pacific trench. She used to spend all her time in the nursery, sitting in the rocker I'd bought so she could nurse him. If she wasn't there she was in church. It got to the stage where we had become strangers; and at night she would cry. Christ, how she would cry . . .'

Jake's voice thickened. 'She felt she'd failed – me, our marriage and most of all herself. The whole purpose of marriage, in her eyes, was to produce children. She'd hoped to get pregnant from the start, but every time something went wrong. Now she had lost three babies and how could it be anybody's fault but hers? Nothing worked. She was obsessed. All her warmth and loving kindness darkened into a hopelessness that was killing her spirit. She was the prettiest thing – blue black hair like perfumed silk, big blue eyes – now she never bothered with herself, for days on end she never took off her nightgown and wrapper. I suggested we adopt but she went wild, raged at me, screamed that she wanted her own children, our children, not those of some other woman. And she prayed; hours and hours she spent on her knees. She'd got it into her head that it was because she had rejected Charlie; that in causing pain it was her punishment to receive it. I got angry, told her that she was fooling herself if she thought Charlie would ever have married her; he was not the marrying type. What she had represented to him was a challenge; all he wanted was to get her into his bed. Once he'd done it he'd have dropped her, like he did all the others. We argued about that. She accused me of being jealous of him, of being fed up with her, of regarding her as a burden, a barren wife who had failed in her duty to her husband. I told her it didn't matter; that as long as I had her I was happy. She turned that into my not caring how she felt, not seeing how important it was to hear that she fulfil her destiny as a true wife. It got so bad that I took to working longer and longer hours, staying out of the house because by that time there was nothing to go home to. I began to make regular trips abroad – by this time I had Arab clients. And after I returned home after one trip she threw herself at me, said she was sorry, begged me to forgive her and to try again.'

Jake laughed. It was strained. 'Try again! She wouldn't leave me alone. I would come home dead tired but she would expect me to be ready for nothing else than to try and impregnate her. If I told her I was tired she'd accuse me of neglecting her. She took her temperature every single day; she ringed her calendar, she never left me alone. I got angry because it seemed to me that all she saw me as was a stud. The arguments became rows and they became more and more frequent. She accused me of seeing other women; that was why I had nothing left for her. Other women! I hadn't so much as looked at one. In spite of everything I loved Stella, because I knew the kind of woman she really was; that this thing of the baby was twisting her every which way. I'm a one woman kind of man; I'd had women, sure, but all the time I was looking for a Stella. What I couldn't handle was that I was losing her. She'd been interested in my work, proud of my achievements; she'd presided at my table like she'd been born to it; everyone said I was a lucky man. It was this damned obsession of hers about not being a real woman until she had a healthy living child I couldn't under-stand, because it crowded everything else – including me, except in my capacity as a stud – out of her life. We had each other; if that was enough for me why couldn't it be enough for her? She said that if I couldn't understand then I wasn't the man she'd thought I was, and so on – and on – and on . . . The night before I had to leave on a trip to the Gulf we made love but – it just wasn't the same any more. Stella wasn't giving of herself like she used to; she wasn't loving *me*, she was milking me, using me – '

'I know how that feels,' Claire murmured desolately.

'What had been so much more than sex had become just

357

that; nothing more than the mechanics of reproduction. I told her she had better shape up or else I was shipping out. I couldn't take any more. Then I left. It was a long trip; six weeks, but after a month I got a letter – anonymous of course – telling me that my wife was running around with Charlie Whitman.' Jake put his head in his hands. 'If only I had sat down to think – but instead I got mad. She had accused me of seeing other women, but now she was playing around with the one man she knew would cut me up. I took the first plane home.'

There was a long silence. When Jake continued his voice was harsh with control. 'I suppose it was inevitable I should find them together. Oh, not in bed – nothing so easy. They were having dinner, of all things, Stella all gussied up and looking like she used to. I went crazy. I threw a punch at Charlie, he blocked it, and the next thing I knew we were hitting each other all over the dining-room, Stella screaming at us and begging us to stop; that Charlie was a friend, that she had asked him to come and see her so she could ask him to forgive her . . . But the thought of her telling him our private troubles only made me madder. Neither of us paid any attention to her; we were too busy settling the old grudge, the old bitter rivalry. We weren't fighting over Stella; we were fighting to prove who was the best. It had been a long time coming but once it had we let loose with everything we had.

'I don't know when Stella left us; I only know that when I staggered back from the front door after throwing Charlie out, dazed and bleeding from a cut over the eye, she was nowhere to be seen. I stormed upstairs, hammered on her bedroom door. It was locked and she screamed at me to go away, back to my other women, back to my precious companies which meant so much more to me than she did. I accused her of cheating – we had a hell of a row, her on one side of the door, me on the other. I couldn't break it down; when she'd done up the house she'd bought all the doors from an old church. It was six inches thick. So I went back downstairs, still mad, and I poured myself a drink . . . The next thing I remember is waking up, sprawled all over the dining-room table, with somebody screaming from upstairs. I had a head like a steam-hammer but I ran upstairs and found Encarnación, our Mexican maid, in Stella's bedroom, making a hell of a racket. Stella was on the bed; she was in a brand-new nightgown, I can see it now – deep sapphire-blue silk with blue ribbons tied at the shoulders. She had her hands folded on her breast like some medieval saint and she was cold. She'd been dead for hours.'

'Oh, my God . . .' It was scarcely a breath.

'She'd taken what Encarnación said was almost a full bottle of Valium. She'd found her when she took up her breakfast tray. The door had not been locked then.'

Jake raised his head from his hands; his eyes were dry but burning. 'I don't think she meant to kill herself; the unlocked door proves that. It was a cry for help; a last-ditch attempt to make me understand how desperately unhappy she was; how helpless, how afraid.' His voice broke. 'She must have hoped that I would make another attempt, find her and – and put things right, but I was downstairs, so drunk I had passed out, and she died.'

Deeply distressed, Claire moved instinctively towards him. 'Oh, Jake . . . Jake . . . I'm so sorry . . .' She put her arms around him, conscious of a need to assuage and soothe.

'It's my fault she's dead. If I had only thought for one minute . . . Stella would never have been unfaithful. She was a Catholic; she took her marriage vows seriously. She was what Charlie had described to me as "small-town moral". And if she had felt the need, she would never have picked Charlie; Stella was not a cruel woman, far from it. I didn't believe Charlie when he said he and Stella had been lovers for months; that every time I went away he came to her.'

'He *told* you that?'

'Yes, but I knew Stella better than he did. What was – to him – normal, everyday adultery would have been a mortal sin to Stella. He just wanted to hurt me, get back at me for taking Stella from him in the first place. Even now, I'm convinced that it's what rankles with him; not that Stella is dead but that he lost her long before, and to me, of all people.

'But do you know what the final irony is? The autopsy revealed that Stella was newly pregnant . . . She must have conceived the night before I left on my trip. I don't believe she knew . . . her calendar was ringed in red and if she had waited only another forty-eight hours . . . or if that damned letter had not brought me back . . .'

'You don't know who sent it?'

'No. I put a private investigator on to it but he found nothing except it had been mailed in Tulsa. One thing I know, though, is that the writer lived in Cimarron; how else would they know Charlie was visiting Stella? It was their vicious mind that twisted everything . . . made them write to me the way they did. I think Stella was desperate; that somehow she wanted to ask Charlie to forgive her for ditching him for me. Then maybe God would let her have the child she craved. Charlie's version is that the child was his; that he and Stella had been getting together every time I went away; that he knew it was because she was desperate to conceive again and if I couldn't manage it then he could, would and did, thus proving, once and for all, that he was the better man.'

His pale eyes opaque, Jake said heavily, 'Most of the time I know he's lying; that it's his way of making me pay for having taken something he wanted. But now and then . . .'

'You get drunk.'

'Yes. The way I did the night Stella died – and did after she was dead. So drunk that I became a hopeless alcoholic until I had the sense to seek help and take the drying-out cure.'

'I had wondered,' Claire said delicately. 'I mean – you don't drink at other times . . .'

'No. I daren't. Except at those times when it's the only way I can sleep . . .'

'Oh, Jake, Jake . . .' Claire put her arms about him again. His went around her like a vice. 'Forgive me, please . . . I had no idea . . .'

'How could you? It's not something I go around advertising. Jake Burns, the man who got self-pityingly drunk and let his wife kill herself.' His voice was muffled against her body. 'Sometimes I think maybe it's God's punishment; that maybe I should never have come between Stella and Charlie; that maybe she would have been happier with him, had a whole pack of the children she needed so badly.'

'It wasn't your fault that Stella miscarried twice, or that your son died.'

'Maybe, maybe not. I did leave her alone a lot. We did row – Christ, how we rowed. There were times when I wished I had left things alone; when I hated her – especially for seeing me as nothing more than a means of getting her pregnant, not loving me, Jake Burns, the man I am, but only her own, private sperm bank.'

'But she saw herself as a failure as a woman. To her way of thinking – her beliefs – marriage meant children. Why else marry in the first place? Perhaps she thought you wouldn't want her any more because she couldn't have them.'

'I *told* her it didn't matter; that if I had her it was enough.'

'But not for her; for what she had been brought up to believe. The Drummonds are Catholics, you know, except for my branch of the clan. My great-grandfather was also married to a woman who couldn't have children – or so they thought. It took them fifteen years to have their first child, after which they had another five on the trot, but during those first years, when it seemed as if they would never have any, the priest came to them and made it plain that because of this, they would of course henceforth live as brother and sister. My grandfather threw him out and never set foot in his church again. He said that how he and his wife lived was nobody's business but theirs. That's why the Drummonds of Strathdrummond are now Presbyterians.'

'Stella's religion was important to her, maybe more

important than I was, because after the second miscarriage – it had been difficult for her – the doctors said she shouldn't conceive for at least six months to give her body time to recover. So she turned me out of her bed. There was only one reason for sex, she said – procreation.' Broodingly: 'My father was right. Religion *is* responsible for a hell of a lot of misery and suffering. Stella had a passionate nature – like you. She loved making love; it was only when she grew desperate that it became a deadly serious, unemotional, *driven* desire to conceive.'

Claire was silent, reflecting with bitter hindsight on what she had done when she was pregnant. You're wrong, she thought, I'm not like Stella at all.

'But that still doesn't excuse the fact that it's my fault she's dead – a suicide. Her mother cursed me for that. Told me she hoped I would never have another moment's happiness, and Charlie has been doing his damnedest to make it come true ever since. Afterwards, a long time afterwards, when I tried to put it behind me he wouldn't let me. Twice he moved in to take from me a woman I had hopes for; someone to spend the rest of my life with.' Pause. 'The third time was you.'

'I didn't know . . .' she said helplessly.

'I know you didn't. But he did. Somebody must have told him about you – about me. So he turned up to ruin it again, only you were different. You saw him for what he was.'

'Only because I recognized Rory in him.'

'I'm glad. Not because you had a bad marriage which left you determined never to be hurt again, but because it meant I had a chance.'

Uneasily: 'Jake, I – '

'I know. You like me enormously.' His eyes bored into hers. 'But it was more than liking tonight, you know it was.'

'It had been a long time – '

'Even so. Time had nothing to do with it. It was you – and me.'

Claire was silent in the face of the truth in his eyes, the

conviction in his voice. 'It was – unexpected,' she admitted.

'It was glorious. I loved it. I – '

Claire laid her fingers across his mouth. 'Don't, Jake. I'm not ready for that yet. I don't know if I ever will be ready for that again.'

'But you are, don't you see? If you hadn't it wouldn't have been the way it was. You let yourself go – really let yourself go. There was so much longing in you too . . . You need love, Claire. Let me give it to you. Never mind that you can't give it back – not yet, anyway. I'm willing to wait. Just don't – walk away from it, from me. Please. I don't think I could stand that.'

Claire shook her head, withdrawing from him physically and mentally. 'Don't ask that of me, Jake. I've had enough guilt to last me a lifetime. I can't – take and not give.'

'But you *did* give; you were more than ready to give. You are the kind of woman who *needs* to give.'

He took her hands again. 'Give it to me. I need it. And this time I'll take the greatest care of it, believe me.'

'I can't give you absolution,' Claire said quietly.

'That's not entirely what I see in you, though I won't deny that the chance to prove I can do right what I once did wrong is part of it. I'm still as selfish as the next man; I have this good old-fashioned urge to possess and keep. I accept that you don't feel as I do right now; all I'm asking is that you let me try to make you. You do have some feelings for me; they broke loose tonight – '

'I was starved.'

'So was I; that's why I can't let you go. I need what you are and in spite of what you think, you need what I am.' He moved closer. 'So you made a mistake. It's not an unforgivable one, and it wasn't your fault anyway. My mistake *was* my fault. We are both human. You are scared because you are vulnerable – all your efforts have been devoted to restoring the ego your ex-husband shattered, and I have helped there, haven't I?'

'Very much.'

'Then let me complete the process. All I'm asking for is the chance.'

'But it wouldn't be fair . . .' Claire could not help but see the way the scales were weighted; he doing all the giving, she doing all the taking. With her strong sense of honesty in all dealings, that would make her feel as guilty as he was.

Jake could see her struggling with herself as she tried to exercise her judgement over her sexuality. She was not the kind of woman to take a lover without giving great thought to the consequences. In some ways she was out of her time; Strathdrummond was a quiet backwater, and the Drummonds were an old-fashioned family who still held many of the old Victorian values – and virtues. Claire was the kind who had been taught, as the Bible said, to value her virtue above rubies. To take a lover she would have to care for him very, very much. She had a mind that was straight and true and an unshakeable sense of responsibility. All part of why it was so important that she come to him. She was still struggling to come to terms with what had happened to her before; to put the rubble of that ivory tower together again. Even then, there was still the question of whether or not to go back inside and lock the door or leave it behind her for ever. He had the impression that she was weighing his every word, scrutinizing them for flaws and errors and omissions.

But what Claire was thinking of was what her mother had told her, when they had talked, late into the night on the eve of her wedding. 'The compromise is all. The tree that stands is the one that bends with the wind. Absolutes have a high mortality rate, and you do tend to be somewhat – exacting – in your expectations. Nobody in this world is perfect, darling, not even Rory. That is why I want you to remember the magic word: compromise. Don't insist on everything measuring up to your standards or else you will be left with nothing but short ends.'

Which is exactly what I was left with, Claire thought now. Who I thought Rory was and who he turned out to be were two entirely different people. I *know* Jake. I know his strengths and now I know his weaknesses. He has been honest with me, painfully so. And he has given me back to myself. What is wrong in allowing him to share it? She looked at him. He was watching her with intensity. The light eyes were dark with it. You can trust this man, she told herself. You know you can. And you owe him. Drummonds never hold any outstanding bills. And it's because of him that you have the emotional wherewithal to pay this one . . .

Her smile had his face softening with relief. 'You're the risk taker,' she told him, 'while I'm the one who likes to play it safe. Maybe a little of what we are will rub off on each other.'

His own smile was quick with delight. 'Back to the birds and the bees again?'

As always, he saw the swift comprehension that was so much part of her flood her eyes. It had him drawing her to him. He was further encouraged when she did not resist, nor when he put his face to where the lace bodice cradled her surprisingly full breasts. 'You still smell of bourbon and roses . . . whenever I smell them I shall always think of you.'

That particular combination had the effect of clearing out the cobwebs from certain dark corners of his life, leaving every one sparkling. That and the pure bright flame of her which had burned away all the crud that had seemed ineradicable. The smouldering hope, almost out, which he had been blowing on desperately by the time he got to Europe, had been fanned by her into a great big roaring blaze out of which he had come re-formed; able to talk about what happened to Stella for the first time to someone other than a therapist. Claire, he thought, was therapeutic in a way they could never hope to achieve. He had told her because he had known she would understand; that was what made her so different from other women. When he looked into those great big pansy-purple eyes he had known he could tell her – wanted to tell her. Not to heap it on her but to avail himself of that understanding, brought about by hard experience of her own. He had been right in thinking

that the ice was no arctic tundra; not the real Claire Drummond. And now that he had proved it he found the thought
of losing her again had him on the edge of panic.

'You are very special to me,' he told her simply. 'I want
very much to be the only one with you; I want you to be
the only one with me.' She nodded, as though his feelings
were clogging her voice. 'Let me prove how special you are
... please ...'

He felt her hands tighten on his bare flesh. A little pulse
vibrated in the hollow of her throat, and when he put his
mouth there she quivered, buried her face against the side
of his neck as though to hide it. But she made no move
to stop him when he once more removed the rose-silk
nightgown, and when he lay down beside her she put her
arms around him, holding him close to her silky warmth.

'Let me love you,' he whispered, 'let me show how I love
you ...'

She still did not speak, only pulled him closer.

The butterfly wings that were his mouth, and the moths
that were his hands, aroused her in such a way that she
opened fully to him.

'I want to prove to myself that it wasn't just another
dream; one of the fantasies I've had about you for so long
... you are here and I so much want and need to love
you ...'

'I need love too,' she whispered.

'I know you do. Let me give it to you ...'

This time, it was her name he said.

CHAPTER THIRTEEN

It was seven-thirty when she left his bed, deeming it politic to return to her own room before Henry came to wake him. But when she went downstairs for her robe it was nowhere to be found; it had been cleared away with the party debris. Henry was no mean housekeeper. Always up by six, he had everything tidied away and the place back to normal by the time she got down.

The negligee appeared on her bed, exquisitely laundered, that same night. Not a word was said, but Claire was aware that Henry's attitude to her had undergone a change. He had always recorded her respect: now she was aware of both approval and affection.

Not so Cora Sue. Her sixth sense was always set to high around Jake, but she would have had to be blind as well as deaf and dumb not to pick up the signals which hummed between him and Claire; not to have noticed the thousand and one excuses he made just to touch her, not to have read his face and voice when he spoke to her, the way he whistled around the place – and the disappearance of the blondes. Jake was happy.

So was Claire. So much so that when she met Mollie a few days later, at their weekly working lunch to discuss the progress of Crème de la Crème, that forthright lady took one look then asked bluntly: 'What – or who – has turned your lights on?' Claire found herself flushing. 'I always knew it was only a matter of time,' Mollie went on practically.

'That's more than I did.'

'Well, you didn't want to know, did you?' Mollie reached across to pat Claire's hand. 'Me, I am only too happy to see that the ghosts have been well and truly laid.'

Claire burst out laughing.

But Mollie's comment had been perceptive. It was not just the sex, good as that was; after a long period of abstinence, more than her body had been brought to life, and as she and Jake reconnoitred each other's lives, explored each other's pasts, traced the paths by which each had reached their present position, so did she come to realize that the Jake she had thought she knew was only one part of a complex personality.

Unlike Charlie, he and Claire shared no common interests. He was not the man for concerts and art galleries and museums or the theatre; he had no ear for music and his tastes ran to Tammy Wynette singing 'Stand By Your Man'. His interests lay out-doors; he loved his horses and rode as much as he could, he was sports mad, would bet on anything, even the famous two raindrops trickling down a window, and he could not abide wasted effort; soon lost interest in anything that was obviously not going to gell. He also liked to win, and though he was not what he would call a sore loser, he regarded losses as failures; the kind he did not intend to repeat. Yet this same man, who could stake thousands of dollars on the turn of a card, and with a coolness that chilled, was the same man who woke, sweating and shaking, from a recurrent nightmare whose terrors Claire now understood. The man who constantly sought her support and reassurance was the same man who was ready and willing to sell his considerable skills to the highest bidder.

Rory had had his deeps, but Jake was bottomless. He could – and did – demonstrate a tenderness which rendered her down to a melted puddle, but he could also display a ruthlessness that repelled. When he knew what he was doing he was a steamroller at full pressure. But when it came to his sense of guilt and what he saw as his worst failure he was held together with Band-Aids. As she peeled back the many layers of his personality she saw just how much damage Charlie had done, though what had really completed the destruction, she surmised shrewdly, was his discovery that he was not as invulnerable as he had once believed. But he gave her what she needed at this particular time, and as her long-dormant sexuality stirred and came back to vibrant, passionate life, she was happy to give to him all that he wanted. A receptive ear, a ready understanding, a willing, giving body and an emotional blanket which he took and wrapped around him, grateful for the warmth and comfort.

He lavished gifts on her; the first was an exquisite pin in the shape of a rose, its stem of baguette emeralds, its leaves of carved solitaires embellished with diamond dewdrops, the flower made up rose diamond petals. Claire gaped when she saw it.

'Oh, Jake . . . it's gorgeous!'

'It's the colour that suits you best, and you always smell like one . . .'

'"Joy",' she told him truthfully, 'sheer, unadulterated joy . . .'

That was followed by a crocodile handbag from Asprey's, one of Hermes' best, with solid gold fittings and clasp, and one evening, as they were just about to leave for a City dinner, an evening bag made of shimmering silvermesh set with pearls.

Claire looked at him helplessly. 'What am I going to do with you?' she asked in mock-despair.

'Don't tell me now – surprise me later . . .'

He was a man who liked giving things; his pleasure was in her own delight. And she recognized in his lavishness a gratitude that gave her a pang. He had been crucifyingly lonely; in spite of the blondes he was really a one-woman man. He was not trying to buy her affection; he was merely showing how grateful he was for it.

And there was no denying that she felt safe with him, as she had never felt safe with Rory except for the first fresh, unsullied months of their marriage. Jake was careful with her, solicitous of her well-being, ever sensitive of her former hard-usage, and she put her trust wholly in him because she knew he was the last man in the world to betray it.

*

369

'And now, if you please, we've got her mother coming to stay with us!' Cora Sue said wrathfully. 'Talk about giving an inch and taking ten miles!'

Her companion murmured wordlessly, her mouth being full of toasted beef and tomato sandwich. Emmylou Steadman made Cora Sue a very satisfying companion because she was content to listen. They had met up at a Fourth of July reception at the American Embassy, where Emmylou was secretary to one of the Vice Consuls, new to the job and also getting to know London. Together, mostly at weekends, they had done the sights: Westminster Abbey, St Paul's, Buckingham Palace – where Claire had, through her contacts, got them *inside* the gates to watch the Changing of the Guard – Windsor, Hampton Court, the Houses of Parliament – where again, thanks to Claire, they had been shown a great deal more than the average tourist ever got to see. This afternoon, they were going to do the Tower of London, but all Cora Sue had done, since they had met up at their usual spot, the American Express office at the bottom of the Haymarket, before going for a quick lunch, was fulminate against 'that woman'. Really, thought Emmylou, she was beside herself with jealousy. Even so, it was better doing the sights with Cora Sue than on her own.

'I warned Jake from the start, but did he listen? I knew what she was after the minute I set eyes on her, sweet as sugar and so ladylike, but she didn't fool me, not for one minute! Now she's got him so that he doesn't know if it's Christmas, New Year or Washington's birthday!'

Emmylou murmured again as she poured herself a second cup of tea. One of the good things about this otherwise backward country was that no matter where you went you got a good cup of tea. The coffee was unspeakable.

'We should have been long gone by now; we've already been over here more than a year and he only came for six months! I keep telling him there's things waiting, and he was always one for seeing for himself, but no – he runs up a fortune in transatlantic telephone calls and leaves other people in charge, which isn't like him either! I declare, I don't know what's got into him!'

'She's a beautiful woman,' Emmylou said, in the unenvious, matter-of-fact voice of one who knows she is not and never will be.

'He's had a bushel of them,' Cora Sue snorted. 'Good American girls, and there's not an Englishwoman can hold a candle to any of *them*!'

'Well, perhaps it's because she's – different,' Emmylou said.

'You mean because she's a "lady",' sneered Cora Sue. 'Well, the higher the class the lower the morals, as they say over here. She's still his mistress, a kept woman – and I don't mean the ridiculous salary he pays her. He's spent a fortune on her already and it's only been a couple of weeks!'

'It will burn itself out,' Emmylou soothed.

'That's what I keep hoping – just so long as she doesn't burn him out.'

It's you who's being burned, Emmylou thought. Jealousy has got you smoking. 'It's coming up for two o'clock and we have a bus to catch,' she reminded. They always travelled by bus, on the upper deck; that way they got to see more of London. Claire had suggested to Cora Sue that a bus-pass would save them money in the long run, and Emmylou for one was grateful.

Cora Sue grumbled at the crowds of tourists standing in line for tickets, but as Claire had been helpful once more in suggesting they avail themselves of a jumbo ticket which gave them automatic entry into all the major tourist attractions, they were able to go right in. By the time they reached the Jewel House, Cora Sue was complaining about aching feet, but the Crown Jewels were the highspot of the tour and Emmylou was not going to miss them, if they had to stand in line an hour for the privilege, and once they got down into the huge, air-conditioned vault, she blinked at the brilliance of the dazzle radiating from the great central glass vitrine.

'My, oh my . . .' she breathed, awestricken at the accumulated radiance of egg-sized diamonds, great rubies, flawless emeralds and glowing sapphires, not to mention the lustrous pearls, all set in gold and glittering against purple velvet and black-spotted ermine. 'All this must be worth several fortunes.'

'Then they should sell it instead of relying on hand-outs from us,' Cora Sue snapped sourly, but impressed nevertheless.

'All this is history, Cora,' Emmylou remonstrated. 'They were crowning kings over here when we still belonged to the Indians.'

'History for me begins in 1776,' Cora Sue retorted loftily.

Slowly, they inched round the awesome collection, Emmylou reading from the guidebook she had bought. When they came to the salts, Cora Sue barked: 'Salt? What's a salt? That great gold thing is where they keep salt? Why, it must hold pounds of the stuff!'

'They are ceremonial,' Emmylou informed her knowledgeably. 'That's where the saying comes from: "Above and below the salt".'

'Whatever that means.'

'Perhaps you would like me to explain?'

They both turned to see a tall Englishman smiling diffidently down at them. My, oh my . . . Emmylou thought, stunned.

'That would be appreciated,' she said shyly.

He had a lovely voice, she thought, as she listened to him explain, not only about the salt, but about the regalia; the orb, the sceptre, the amulets, the oil, and the part they played at the coronations of English kings and queens. Even Cora Sue was held silent as they listened. It was like being stroked with fur mittens, Emmylou thought dreamily.

'You certainly know your history,' she complimented, as they went back up the stairs to daylight.

'It's a hobby of mine,' he said, almost apologetically.

He was equally helpful when they went to see where the block had stood; where Anne Boleyn and Katherine Howard had been beheaded on the orders of their husband, King

Henry VIII. And he showed them where skeletons had been found, buried under the floor of the little church of St Peter ad Vincula, just behind where the block had stood, and explained how one of them had six fingers on one hand. 'As did Queen Anne Boleyn.'

'I saw that lovely movie about her,' Emmylou sighed. 'The one with Richard Burton as the King . . . it gives me goosebumps to see the actual spot where it all took place.'

And when he courteously invited them to have a cup of tea with him, they were only too happy.

Surprisingly enough, it was Cora Sue who made all the running, shamelessly angling the conversation round to the point where she landed an invitation to be shown around Runnymede, where the Magna Carta had been signed, and where a memorial to the late John F. Kennedy had been unveiled by his widow twenty years before.

'But we don't *know* him,' Emmylou said doubtfully, as they rode back to Knightsbridge.

'I spotted him for the real thing right off,' Cora Sue said dismissively. 'He's got the right accent and he was dressed right too. Upper-class Englishmen stand out, and I've met enough of them since I've been over here to know the real thing when I see it.'

'But he's younger than us,' Emmylou pointed out.

Cora Sue sniffed. 'He's no boy. I doubt if there's more than eight years between us.' (You mean eighteen, thought Emmylou.) ''Sides, he's driving us there. Means we don't have to. I just can't get used to driving on the wrong side of the road.'

Well, I can't get used to your driving, period, Emmylou thought. Cora Sue at the wheel was a menace, which was why she had persuaded her, after their first couple of outings, to use the bus instead. She herself had failed her test on account of her poor sight; back home that was a problem, but it didn't matter at all over here where there was so much public transport. At that, she thought, warmed by Cora Sue's decided confidence, he was a gentleman, no doubt about that. Such lovely manners; pulling out their chairs, and seeing them to their bus stop and taking off his hat when he shook hands. And he had been undeniably elegant. Englishmen wore clothes so well, she thought wistfully. And she could have combed her hair in the shine on his lovely brown shoes.

Even though, she noted, they were far from new. He was, she thought romantically, a man who had seen better days. Not down on his luck, exactly, but no longer able to afford such custom-made suits, such hand-made shoes. What the English call a gentleman of reduced means, she decided. Yet he had insisted on paying for their tea, been so diffident about asking them if they would like to see Runnymede. She was sure Cora Sue hadn't spotted the tell-tale signs; she never saw anything but what first presented itself. But Emmylou knew what it was like to be in reduced circumstances. Her mother had come from a good family who had cut her out when she had married a man who turned out to be a shiftless no-good, and had been reduced to running a boarding-house for what she called 'ladies in exigent circumstances'; in other words, the shabby genteel, eking out a life on a pittance, mending their own shoes and doing their own laundry. Something about Robert James had brought those ladies to mind. He was also, she was sure, clinging desperately to appearances. Well, when we go to Runnymede it will be our treat, she decided, never mind Cora Sue and her counting every penny. We can both afford it. And I shall wear my blue foulard, she decided. May as well get some use out of it . . .

'Cora Sue has found herself a man, I'm sure,' Claire said to Mollie when they met for their weekly lunch.

'Now I know love is blind,' Mollie exclaimed.

'Oh, but I'm grateful to him, whoever he is. He has sweetened her disposition no end. She goes out on her days off now all dressed up like a dog's dinner, and she is suddenly very coy and secretive.'

'I thought she went everywhere with that faded spinster from Baltimore.'

'Emmylou is a nice quiet lady,' Claire disagreed. 'The last person I would have chosen as a friend for Cora Sue. She just needs drawing out, that's all.'

'Well, I'm glad to see you've come out of that shell of yours. These past weeks you've positively blossomed. Jake is obviously what you needed.'

'I do feel – more . . . complete,' Claire admitted.

And it was true. Never had she felt so safe as with Jake. She had the utmost confidence in him, but what woman would not have confidence in a man who made it plain that your happiness and well-being were top priorities with him. Because of his own harsh experience with Stella, Jake was tender with her in a way Rory had never even begun to understand. If he ever had been tender, it had been for his own sake; Jake did it for hers. Except for the first naïve months of her marriage she had never been able to trust Rory. Jake she trusted absolutely. Over the past months he had managed to find every single one of her knots, tugged gently and they had fallen away. Rory had liberated her sexuality, but it was to Jake she gave all that it made her. And with enormous pleasure because he appreciated it so much.

'. . . your mother coming?' Mollie was asking.

'Next weekend.'

'And what will you do then, little girl?'

Claire smiled. 'Nothing,' she said confidently. 'There is no generation gap between my mother and me. Besides, she approves of Jake.' As he approved of her, only too happy to be able to repay the hospitality she had shown him.

She arrived, looking enchanting in a wide-brimmed mink hat and matching coat, bearing a couple of brace of grouse and a Spey salmon which had Henry's eyes gleaming. 'From the deep freeze,' she apologized, 'but none the less good for that. I always freeze them myself within minutes of them being landed.'

Henry poached the salmon for dinner that night, so deliciously that she begged him earnestly for his recipe, even while reprimanding him for being a menace to a middle-aged lady trying to hang on to what remained of her figure. In the next breath she beseeched him to show her exactly how he made his ambrosial coffee.

'Now I see that you must *all* come to Scotland for Christmas. We shall not be a big party; my eldest son, his wife and their children, Moira's parents and my husband's sister –'

'Mother, not Aunt Isobel,' protested Claire. 'You can't inflict her on Jake sight unseen.'

'My daughter exaggerates,' Margot Drummond said imperturbably. 'My sister-in-law is a daughter of the Raj. Her husband was for many years Governor of a large part of India and she has never seen fit to adapt herself to any other kind of life. She tends to be a little – autocratic, that is all.'

'Autocratic!' Claire raised her eyes to heaven.

'But she has a weakness for attractive men so you will do famously.' Lady Margot over-rode confidently.

'Sounds great,' Jake said.

'She is also very fond of food, so you, Henry, will have no trouble.'

'Well, she will have to do without me,' Cora Sue said. 'I've already made other arrangements.' She looked at once arrogant yet slightly uncomfortable, and she eyed Jake with something like uncertainty.

'Whatever you want,' Jake said amiably, feeling relieved.

'Emmylou has invited me to spend Christmas with her.'

And who else? Claire wondered. When she and Jake were alone later she said, 'I think Cora Sue has got herself a beau.'

Jake stared. 'You're having me on.'

'No . . . she's been going out on her sightseeing tours all done up to the nines, and it has nothing to do with Emmylou. It's something new.'

'Well I'll be damned,' Jake said blankly. Then, on a frown: 'I'd hate to lose Cora Sue . . .'

'I said a beau, and even then I'm only guessing because of the coy way she's been acting lately.'

'Cora Sue and men – a man – is not something I've any experience of. They usually run a mile.'

'Well, whoever he is I'm grateful to him. I don't think I could have done with her glowering at us all over Christmas, though I admit it would have been educational to see how she coped with Aunt Isobel.'

'Is she that much of a *grande dame*?'

'Have you ever seen pictures of the late Queen Mary? The one with all the jewels and the pompadour.'

'Sure.'

'Well, that is Aunt Isobel.'

But when Jake was introduced to the tall, upright figure of the Dowager Marchioness of Balquidder he had met enough of the breed to be able to handle her basilisk stare – through the lorgnette she wore – and the catechism she put him through as to his background and antecedents.

'Is she on the breadline?' he asked Claire later, pity in his voice.

'Aunt Isobel!' Claire hooted with laughter. 'She's got more money than we have! She's just careful with it, that's all. Take no notice of the darned stockings or the threadbare tweeds, or the ancient black dress she will wear over Christmas; one she has been wearing for the last twenty years or more.' She did not add that it would be embellished with a diamond bow of sensational proportions, or a triple row of pearls that would have settled the national debt of a couple of third world countries.

'She's an old fraud,' Jake chuckled later. 'She's been giving me a sob story about being in what she calls straitened circumstances and pumping me for information as to the best place to put her small annuity.'

'Small my foot! She lives in one small corner of Balquidder Castle – which by rights she should have vacated long ago because it now belongs to her eldest son – because she's too tight to heat the rest. She spends not one tenth of the quarter of a million she gets from her capital, and she's so mean she has quarrelled with every one of her three sons – who all go in fear and trembling.'

'I think she's a great old girl.'

'That's because you have even more money than she has. Aunt Isobel adores money.'

Just as Jake adored Christmas at Castle Drummond, from the decorations in the Great Hall to the huge Christmas tree standing under the minstrels' gallery at the far end. He warmed his behind in front of either one of the two fires which burned day and night, and enjoyed himself hugely at the Christmas Eve party – held in the afternoon – for the children of Glen Drummond, where Iain, padded, 'though not so much these days', his wife observed tartly, got himself up as Father Christmas and distributed presents from a bulging sack.

'Your young man likes children, I see,' the Dowager observed, eyeing Jake as he helped a three-year-old to ride a new tricycle.

'He isn't my young man, Aunt Isobel,' Claire lied lightly.

'I may be eighty years old but I still retain all my faculties,' her aunt retorted witheringly, 'and it is obvious that Mr Burns has a decided *tendresse* for you.' A brisk nod. 'At that, you could do far worse, even if he is an American. He has given me some invaluable advice concerning the Stock Market.'

'If he recommends anything then it's definitely worthwhile,' Claire said truthfully. 'He's a whizz at that sort of thing.'

'I am glad to hear it. You should never have married that spendthrift Ballater. I gave that as my opinion at the time but you chose to disregard it. Had you been my daughter I should not have allowed it, but my brother always had a soft spot for his only daughter.' Her nod at Jake was wholly approving. 'This time, I would advise you not to hang around, and to make a second marriage that is eminently more suitable.'

'I like your family,' Jake said to Claire later, surveying the throng.

'They like you.'

He looked down at her, eyes aglow. 'I like you.'

At church next morning he sang the hymns lustily, and then, after breakfast, joined in the opening of the presents.

The twins were speechless with delight when he presented them with a BMX bike apiece.

'Mr Burns, you are too generous,' Moira protested faintly.

'I told you, Jake to my friends . . .'

'Jake then, it really is a super present.'

'I remember when all I wanted was a bike.'

Lady Margot was presented with a gleaming crocodile weekend case, and Moira a piece of the Lowestoft china she collected, while the Dowager's eyes shone when her box revealed a two-pound box of *marrons glacés* – of which she was greedily fond – and an exquisite Chinese jar filled with her favourite Lapsang Suchong. 'You have excellent taste, Mister Burns,' she complimented him. Jake and Claire exchanged a smile. It was at her suggestion that he had bought them.

Iain had the latest state-of-the-art car cell-phone – 'Just the thing for the old Range Rover; catch me anywhere on the estate with this' – and Sir George and Lady Menzies, Moira's parents, received respectively a box of cigars – Romeo & Giulietta – and perfume – Floris Lilac. Claire was watched with intent concentration as Jake handed her a box, deep and square, which when opened, revealed a Rolex Ladies Oyster Perpetual Datejust, the dial set with diamonds and a gold crown, the bezel set with rubies and diamonds. There was a collective intake of breath.

'I figured that as I rely on Claire to keep me on track, a watch would be a great help,' Jake said innocently.

'Some help,' Iain muttered *sotto voce* to his wife. 'There's eight thousand quid there give or take a couple of hundred.'

'I told you he was sweet on her,' his wife whispered back, and that, she thought enviously, is a whole bowlful of sugar.

When it was Claire's turn to hand Jake his present there was the same well-bred curiosity. It was a new briefcase; softest, shiniest calfskin, complete with combination lock and his initials in gold.

'Most appropriate,' the Dowager commented approvingly.

'And most welcome,' Jake said. 'Thanks, Claire.' Catch you later, his eyes said.

Christmas lunch was always cold: avocado mousse, then a freshly baked sugared ham, followed by a classic English trifle, thick with fruit and cream; and it was always timed so that they drank their coffee whilst watching the Queen's Christmas message.

Then the senior members of the houseparty retired to their rooms for a post prandial nap; Iain disposed himself in the big chair by the fire with the copy of the new Dick Francis; Moira went off to the nursery to see to her infant daughter; and Jake and Claire went out for a walk. 'Work off some of that rich food,' he said, patting his flat stomach.

'There's more to come,' Claire warned. 'Tea at four-thirty and then dinner at eight – the goose, its attendant trimmings *and* the Christmas pudding!'

'Oh my God . . .' Then: 'Goose! What happened to the turkey?'

'Goose is the tradition around here, my lad. The turkey is an American import since the war. Our goose is hand-reared throughout the year before making the supreme sacrifice.'

Jake sighed, enfolding her hand in his, as he surveyed the estate from the top of the hill to which they had walked. 'This is no sacrifice,' he said. 'Christmas here is the kind I used to read about when I was a kid. Dickens is alive and well and living in Glen Drummond.'

'I'm glad you're enjoying it.'

'Enjoy, she says!' Another sigh. 'It's like somebody stopped the world and we all got off for a while.'

'Our way of enjoying a little R&R.'

'And speaking of that very thing . . .'

Claire met his eyes, read and received the message. 'I know the very place . . .' she murmured.

It was a small room atop one of the towers, entered through a barred and studded door at its foot and climbed to by means of a stone spiral staircase. It had a big chair, a thick sheepskin rug on the floor and a portable gas fire, which Claire at once lit to take away the freezing cold. Jake shivered under his own heavy sheepskin. 'Reminds me of

Alaska.' He peered at the line of books on the shelf below the narrow window. 'Yours?'

'Yes . . . I used to come here as a child. It was my – hideaway. Once that fire gets going it will soon be warm.'

'*Alice in Wonderland, The Wind in the Willows, Robinson Crusoe, Gulliver's Travels, Little Women* . . . Childhood favourites?'

'Yes, read and re-read and re-read . . .'

'*Ivanhoe* . . . *Red Gauntlet, Treasure Island, Kidnapped* – how I envied David Balfour when I was a kid – I've read all of these. But I don't see *Tom Sawyer* or *Huckleberry Finn* . . .'

'My brothers have them. I used to long to float a raft down the Mississippi.'

'I'll take you on a steamboat one day.'

'You mean *Show Boat*?' Her sparkling eyes were too much for him. He pulled her against him and proceeded to kiss the life out of her. In no time, the concentrated heat of the small but powerful fire had them shedding first their coats then their clothes until they were naked on the sheepskin rug in the warmth of the fire, the room dark but for its red glow.

'You are like satin . . .' Jake murmured, running his hand down the flowing curves of her.

Claire's eyes were huge as she shifted in his arms, presenting herself to him fully and openly. She heard his catch of breath as he bent his mouth to her breasts, and her body arched in response; she felt his body pressed to hers and then its smooth, thrusting entry into her own, causing sensations so intense that she cried out before she felt herself enveloped in what, with Jake, was always a white-hot flame which seared every nerve ending with an almost unendurable pleasure. Her body spasmed then stiffened, arching like a bow as she felt his final thrust and then his seed flooding into her. The whiteness turned to a blackness into which she fell before emerging from it in the lovely glow that was fulfilment, to feel herself cleansed and purified by the fire of their mutual passion and find Jake lying spent, chest heaving, body slippery with sweat, heart pounding, eyes closed. She kissed him gently, with brimming gratitude. 'Thank you,' she said softly, still feeling them one.

Silently, softly, he kissed her back, as moved as she was, and their silence declared a new and deeper stage in their understanding and involvement. He pulled her close to him, stroking the bright hair, and in her state of utter peace and tranquillity she fell asleep.

When she awoke he was already dressed. Outside it was quite dark. 'Mmmmm . . .' she stretched gloriously, her body tingling.

'I think we should get back,' he said gently.

'What time is it by my brand-new Rolex Datejust?'

'Just gone four-thirty.'

'Time for tea . . .' But as she looked at him her smile faded and she knew he wanted her again. Just the look in his eyes had her body flooding with instant response. She held out her arms. This time he went into her with a ferocity of passion that at first made her recoil until her own instincts took over and her own greed rose to meet his. Nothing existed but their two, merged selves, becoming one in glory, body and soul, for she knew he had taken that too. He had opened up its darkness and mended the broken pieces of her that she had hidden there and by his passion, welded them together into a singing, unified whole. It was then that she knew she loved him, and she was bemusedly sorting out her words to tell him so when he said:

'I want to be with you, Claire, every minute of every day for the rest of my life, but now I have to leave you for a while.'

Her body stilled.

'That call I had this morning?' It had come just as they were about to leave for church. 'It was from Gus Erlich, the man who runs my oil rigs off the Texas coast; one of them is spilling crude oil into the Gulf. I've got the Coastal Zone Management people, the OCS, a whole slew of shrimp fishermen and the mayors of several coastal towns howling for my blood. I have to get over there and straighten things out.'

'I'll come with you.'

'No. Women on a rig don't mix with crew who spend two weeks at a time without so much as the sight of one, and besides that, I won't have time for anything but the job in hand – a clean-up in every sense of the word. I don't want you hanging round some hotel room waiting for the odd minute I might have to spare for you. I need all my time and energy to deal with this mess. I am facing some pretty heavy lawsuits. The spill is a bad one, and how in the hell it happened in the first place is a mystery to me. The maintenance of my rigs is a thing I'm proud of, and I've met every requirement laid down by the Department of the Interior about storm chokes but something has gone wrong that I have to put right as quickly as possible.'

'With Cora Sue's help?'

'She knows about these things. It's her territory.'

'But not mine.'

'No. Not yours.'

'I see.' But she didn't. Nor could she understand. Not after what had happened between them this afternoon.

'How long will you be away?'

'Can't say. But some time, I guess.'

She turned away to pick up her clothes. 'Well, if you must go, then you must,' she said with a calm she did not feel.

'You know I wouldn't go unless I absolutely had to.' His voice was troubled but built on foundations of absolute finality. 'It's just our bad luck that I should have to go now.'

'I know how important your business is to you.'

'Not just mine,' he said, his own voice meeting the sharpness in hers. 'This is other people's livelihoods.'

'And your own reputation.' She could hear her voice, caustic, angry, but she could not help it. Never had love been so right, so perfect. And no wonder, she told herself derisively. It was all part of his set-up. Oh, you are clever all right, she thought bitterly. You have known all day but kept it to yourself until you judged the time was right – that I was right.

'I have never lied to you about that.'

'No,' she agreed distantly. 'That's true.' But all the rest is lies, she thought. After all you've said, all you've done, how can you leave me now? How can you do without me? How can I do without you?

She fastened her coat. 'We must go,' she said. 'Tea will be over by now and they will be wondering where we are. And you must pack . . . Will you fly from Aberdeen?'

'Yes. I arranged it this morning. A car is coming for me at ten.'

'I see.' She brushed past him. 'Come along then,' she said coolly. 'You haven't got much time.'

'What a pity,' Lady Margot said regretfully, as Jake's bag was stowed in the car, 'but I suppose an oil spill is serious.'

'Very,' Jake said.

'Then do let us know how you go on, won't you? I take it Claire can stay until the New Year?'

'Sure, no problem. I'll be in touch anyway.'

Lady Margot held up her face. 'More snow . . . you had better be on your way. It would not do to be snowed up at this stage.' She held out a hand. '*Au revoir*, Jake. We will be seeing each other again in the not too distant future, I hope.'

'I intend to,' Jake said. 'And thanks for a wonderful – if somewhat short – Christmas.' He turned to Claire. This isn't real, she thought. He can't be going, leaving me . . . obeying the call of something against which no woman can compete. It destroyed Stella. Now I understand how she felt. Burns Oil was a jealous mistress. Why does *he* have to go? He employs people to look after such things . . . There is the telephone, the fax, the telex . . . why does he have to go himself? But she said imperturbably, 'Have a good flight, and I hope things are not as bad as they seem when you get to them.'

Her brother shook his head. 'Oil spills are as bad as anything that can happen . . . they're killers.'

Yes, thought Claire. It's killing me . . . But she would not plead. She had done enough of that with Rory; destroyed her self-respect, her pride. Never again. She would see him in hell before she grovelled. Suddenly she hated him, it rose in her throat like bile. She hated the hand held out to her and which she took and quickly dropped; one of those same hands which had dallied so devastatingly with her only hours before; those hands which could caress her into moaning, willing subjugation. She felt shame burn her cheeks. Every caress had been laden with hypocrisy, shaping her into the right state of mind before he shoved in his knife. He had shone a light on her world; made it again one worth living in; made her see things in that light – *his* light. Oh, yes, he would resolve his problems. What was it a fellow American had said to her once? 'Jake has a way with people; he can defuse any situation.' Yes, and he can light fuses too. And then walk away and leave them to sputter uselessly . . . Now, as he looked at her, she felt a tightness in her chest, yet as she met his eyes, no longer light and clear but dark, she knew he was equally angry, at a loss to understand why *she* found it so hard to understand; his face was stiff as if he was in pain, and she took perverse pleasure in it, even though it in no way eased her own. She felt strangely remote and outside herself; observing clinically through her suffering.

'Jake is clever,' someone else had said to her. 'Under the easy-going cowboy there's another guy, and that one can have you hog-tied before you see the rope in his hands.' Claire looked down at her own, as if to see the rope tied there.   .

Jake threw her one last look but she would not ease up on the pressure. Then he got into the car. Winding down the window: 'I'll call you,' he said.

'I'm sure you will,' Claire returned, with an empty smile.

She stood with her mother while Henry bent down to the car window and he and Jake exchanged some low-voiced words, then Henry stepped back and the car moved forward. The last Claire saw of Jake was his face looking back at her through the rear window.

CHAPTER FOURTEEN

'My dear Claire,' Lady Margot remonstrated, 'it is the New Year we are about to celebrate, not a wake, and this is roast venison we are eating, not funeral baked meats. If you wish me to offer condolences then I ought at least to know the name of the deceased.'

'Ha ha!' Claire snapped.

'Come now, that unrelieved pall of gloom you have been wearing since Jake's departure is a sign of loss if ever I saw one.'

'One has to have something before one can lose it.'

Margot Drummond eyed the mask which passed for her daughter's face these days. 'I think the truth of the matter is that you are stuck with something you cannot give back.'

Claire said nothing. They were lunching *à deux*. Iain and Moira had taken the twins down to Edinburgh for the day and the Dowager was lunching with friends. The Menzies had departed to spend the New Year with their younger daughter who lived in Perthshire, so they were alone for once.

'Don't do a Rory, Claire. You, of all people, should know that tightly bottled feelings ferment and then explode. I can see that something is wrong – has been ever since Jake's departure. What was it, a lovers' quarrel?' She laid down her napkin. 'Tell you what, why don't we go and sit by the fire and have a cosy heart-to-heart. I am a great believer in post-mortems. How else is one to find out the cause of death?'

'A pathologist too?' Claire observed testily.

'In the thirty-seven years I was married to your father I had my share of them.' She led the way into the library where Logie was just setting down the coffee tray. 'Some brandy too, I think, Logie. We feel the need of a restorative.'

Lady Margot sat herself down in her favourite chair before the bright fire and sighed beatifically before pouring coffee and two hefty measures of Courvoisier. 'That will oil all your gears,' she said, holding one out.

'What is it, Mother? True Confession time?'

'Not from you. Baring your soul never was part of your character. You brood and that is bad. No; I merely thought that it would help if you unburdened yourself. The old cliché is true, as, of course, they all are, no matter how the – what is it Jake calls them, smart-asses? – sneer at them. A trouble shared *is* a trouble halved. I think that what you are suffering from is an emotional hangover and I prescribe a dose of catharsis.'

'I am beginning to think *my* disease is terminal.'

'Self-diagnosis can be dangerous.'

'Oh, I've had this a long time. I suffer from a surfeit of illusions.'

'Ah . . . somebody has burst yet another of your pretty balloons, that somebody being Jake, of course. What has he done?'

'The American phrase is dumped on me.'

'Such a graphic language,' murmured her mother appreciatively, 'but I'm not sure I understand it in this context. Do explain.'

Claire stared into the fire. 'It's a long story.'

'We have the whole afternoon. Come tomorrow and New Year's Eve I shall not have a minute so let us avail ourselves of the opportunity. Begin where it begins to matter . . .'

Claire thought. 'Well, it all started with the party Jake held for Thanksgiving . . .'

By the time she had reached Jake's departure, her mother had the missing pieces of the puzzle. She already had those supplied by Henry, after a most enlightening conversation.

'A pretty tangle,' she mused. 'Like all people suffering from inflamed emotions you are unable to think for the pain.

You are quite determined not to continue working for Jake?'

'How can I? What I thought our relationship was – the most important thing of all to us both – and what it is – a temporary convenience – are two different things. It's like Stella all over again. What matters to Jake most of all is Burns Enterprises and all its glory.'

'But he had a serious oil spill. Moreover – a deliberately arranged one.'

Claire turned her gaze from the fire. 'Deliberate? Who told you that?'

'Henry. It seems that there are things called storm chokes on oil rigs, designed to cope with threatened spills. Those on Jake's rig were found to have been tampered with.'

'He never told me!'

'Did you ask him?' Claire flushed. 'It was obvious that Henry was worried so I did have a quiet word with him.'

Claire knew her mother's 'words'. They invariably led to a full confession. Had she not just now made her own?

'Why would somebody want to do a thing like that?' she asked.

'Industrial sabotage, according to Henry, is as profitable a business as any other kind, and in the oil business is widespread.'

'Then why didn't Jake tell me?'

'Perhaps he didn't want to worry you more than he had to.'

Claire looked askance. 'The only thing he worries about is Burns Enterprises. He hasn't changed. He did it to Stella and he's doing it to me. Making it clear that in the last analysis, what comes first, last and always is business.'

'Come now, Claire. What has happened is serious. Jake has got to clean up the ocean, placate the people who live in the coastal towns and make amends to the conservationists. Henry tells me havoc has been caused to the local marine and bird life. The area is famous for its shrimp beds and they have been devastated. The man has a disaster on his plate!'

'Then why didn't he tell me all this? I would have understood!' Claire's voice was aggrieved, but her mother also detected a defensive note. 'It was the way he did it I didn't like. Softening me up first then throwing a rabbit punch.'

'What on earth is that?'

'Ask Henry – he'll tell you,' Claire snapped. 'He seems to have told you everything else.'

'He tells me that when he approached you, all he got for his pains was a flea in his ear.'

Claire squirmed. Henry had come to her but she had forestalled the explanation he was obviously intent on making. 'No, Henry, I will not be placated by you of all people. Jake has laid the last straw on me!' And she had stalked off.

Reading her daughter's expressive face: 'I think that Jake's behaviour indicated a man who hated having to leave you.'

'He didn't have to leave me in the first place.'

'And what would you have done had he taken you along? Hung around in some hotel room waiting? It was very sensible of him to leave you here, where you would not be alone. His rig was *sabotaged*! What if whoever did it is waiting around to do even more damage? How would Jake feel about having you – who matter so much to him – alone and unprotected?'

Claire's eyes came up. 'You talked to him!' she accused, hot with outrage.

'Yes,' admitted her mother. 'He came to me after his phone call . . . this is not the first trouble he has had. Some time ago he had some in Oklahoma. Somebody had been rustling oil from his storage tanks.'

'Rustling oil! It's cattle that are rustled, Mother!'

'That was the exact phrase he used. Somebody had been siphoning thousands of gallons into those great tankers one sees on the roads – and not just one or two. Dozens of them . . . Somebody, somewhere, is obviously intent on getting at Jake. He told me that there has been a whole series of incidents over the past six months.'

Claire's mind was leafing through its files. 'There was that business about Gamescan.'

'What's that?'

'A company Jake owns. It makes video games. He bought it about a year ago, and with it a twenty-one-year-old genius who invents the games. Somebody had been planting stories in the financial columns that gave the impression that there was something fishy about them; that they had been stolen from another company, which was not true. Peter Bristow invented every single one of them. But it depressed the stock and all of a sudden people began to rescind orders because they were afraid of a copyright battle and losing money.'

'There you are, then! Jake has an enemy somewhere, one who is intent on causing him as much trouble as possible. He is a rich and powerful man, of course, and they always have the resentful and the jealous to contend with. I think it's your own jealousy which is the root cause of your present unhappiness.'

'Jealousy!'

'What else? What you told me about his wife leads me to think that she felt the same way, but I think that was a different case. From what I have learned about Stella, she was what we would call a very provincial girl – small-town, as Jake would say; out of her depth in the new world he dominated so effortlessly. She was never at home there; she resented its hold on him, and coupled with her sad failure to give him children she just could not cope. You, on the other hand, are at home in that world because you were born into it. Jake both admires and respects the way you deal with what Stella found so impossible to handle. And it is because of Stella, don't you see, that he wants to protect you from whoever it is who wants to do him so much damage. He was worried, I could see that. If whoever it is is ruthless enough not to care about other people's livelihoods, you would present them with a heaven-sent opportunity. It is because you matter to him that he has left you behind, where he knows you are safe.' Margot Drummond could see that she was presenting facts which Claire had not been able to see because the mountain of hurt and resentment she had built had blocked her view.

'Then why didn't he explain?' she demanded.

'He thought least said soonest mended,' her mother said regretfully, 'but I told him you were the kind of person who liked to know exactly where you stood – à propos of Rory – but he was quite adamant that you should not be involved. "I don't want Claire put in the spotlight," he told me. "And if I take her with me she will be. Somebody is keeping tabs on me," was what he said. "I wouldn't have a moment's peace if I knew Claire was in their line of fire. Over here she is safer and I feel better, but I'm leaving Henry behind just to make sure. I've got a funny feeling that whoever they are they know exactly what my situation is at all times."'

'He should have *told* me,' Claire wailed in dismay.

'Probably, but he didn't, with the result that you have got yourself into an emotional corner. That is why I decided it was time I did.' Margot Drummond sighed drolly. 'Love will do it every time . . .' At her daughter's suddenly changed face: 'It *is* love, isn't it?' Claire did not answer. 'Don't be afraid to take a second chance,' her mother counselled. 'That, in my opinion, is what drew you and Jake together. You both carry emotional scars and see in each other someone who will handle with care. People love each other for a great variety of reasons, but it is my belief that self-recognition plays a large part; the perception in another of things one already possesses. Human beings are basically selfish and self-preservation always looms large. Jake has done the wrong thing but for the right reasons. He cares for you deeply, as obviously you care for him. It's not like it was with Rory, is it?'

'Oh, no!' Claire shook her head. 'That was something I couldn't help. Jake has – grown on me. I didn't realize what was happening until he said he was going away without me. Then I knew I never wanted to be without him ever. I feel so safe with him, secure as I never was with Rory. That was why all this came as such a shock . . .'

Her mother sighed again. 'Yes, he should have explained things to you, but love warps one's judgement so. And you have to remember that he knew you were afraid to commit yourself a second time. Rory had a profound effect on you, far deeper than you ever realized. You have put yourself back together again but it takes more than glue. And it's Jake who has given you back your self-confidence, restored your spirit and given you the courage to trust once more.'

'I trusted him from the start.'

'Exactly. He touched your mind and your spirit too, as Rory never did. *He* only excited you sexually. Why else didn't you drag this Charlie Whitman to the nearest bed? Sex is important, but love is loving someone sex or no. The trouble is, people have been brainwashed into thinking that the one cannot be had without the other. Nonsense! Everyone is supposed to be so liberated yet they cannot hear the clanking of the chains that bind them to an endless search for sexual fulfilment! Which brings me to another salient fact: not for one moment will I accept that Jake Burns is not a very sexy man.'

Claire blushed. Her mother smiled.

'How do you know so much?' Claire asked wonderingly.

'Experience in the making of my own mistakes. I also have eyes, ears and an excellent memory. The young invariably overlook the fact that the old were once that way too. I know what it is to love: the ecstasy, the doubt, the bewilderment, the torment and the fears. Love should be labelled FRAGILE – HANDLE WITH CARE – yet how do we treat it? Clumsily and carelessly. What is supposed to confirm our humanity invariably shows us at our most inhuman.' Lady Margot sat back, having delivered her judgement. 'You see! Post-mortems reveal so much, not least whether it is in fact death or just suspended animation. In your case I diagnose concussion, which is why you have been wandering around in a daze. Tell him, Claire. Don't sit and brood about it. *Do* something! Seize that second chance!'

Claire left her chair to go on her knees in front of her

mother. 'Oh, but you *are* a girl's best friend!' she said humbly.

'Giving advice is dangerous, and the mortality rate is high, with a comparable ratio of blame. But in your case, my girl, I realize that in your present state of mind, allowances are called for. Where I draw the line is allowing you to let this chance slip by.' She got to her feet, drew Claire up with her. 'Now, having laid down Drummond's Law I propose to lay myself down for an hour or two. Tomorrow is Hogmanay and every moment will be spoken for. Call Jake – have a word with Henry as to the best time. Put things right between you by getting them straight. And after you have given him your love, give him mine.'

Claire hugged her mother fiercely. 'Thank you,' she said fervently. 'I've been such a childish fool.'

'Who isn't when in love?'

Henry was in the kitchen, where he had established himself as a hard worker and been accepted by Mrs McKinnon, who had been cook at Castle Drummond for the past thirty years. She was at work instructing him how to make haggis.

'Can you spare him for five minutes, Mrs Mac?' Claire wheedled.

'I suppose so. But he'll be wanting to see how the haggis is stuffed so don't be too long.'

'I won't, promise.'

'What's up?' Henry asked, as she dragged him into the china pantry.

'I want to call Jake – when would be the best time?'

'Well, I reckon this evening, say about ten o'clock our time. Something up?'

'Yes, my courage. I have to apologize.'

'What for?'

'Acting like a spoiled brat – to you too, Henry. I'm very sorry.'

'He don't see you that way, me neither.'

'I know that – now. What I also want to know is what's

393

been going on these past months; this series of incidents obviously aimed at causing Jake as much trouble as possible. Just what exactly went wrong on the rig?'

'They thought it was a faulty valve, but when they went down to take a looksee they found the storm chokes had been interfered with. And this ain't the first rig as has given trouble. There was an explosion on another one not two hundred miles away; killed two men but fortunately the leak was capped before it could do any damage. And somebody has been rustlin' oil from his storage tanks. Then some real poisonous pesticide got into some preventative spray and destroyed a whole citrus crop on his Florida farm, not to mention trouble at his refinery. He had a new computerized security system installed but somebody got into it and re-versed all the codes and sent everything haywire. Then somebody reported that one of his ships waiting to unload some urgently needed equipment had a case of yellow fever and the port authorities wouldn't give permission for it to dock until they'd investigated; one of his helicopters crashed and they found out the electrical system had been tampered with – it's been one damned thing after another.'

Claire was appalled. 'I had no idea . . .'

Practically: 'You don't have nothin' to do with what goes on back home so why would you?'

'I knew he was worried about something . . .'

'He'd be even more worried if he thought you was in any danger of bein' got at. That's why he left you here and me to keep an eye on you. These days, he don't trust *nobody*.'

'I *have* to talk to him,' Claire said urgently.

'He's here, there and everywhere. I think the best thing is for you to wait till he calls me – he's due to do that some time tonight – and I'll tell him then.'

Apprehensively: 'How is he?' Claire asked.

'He ain't exactly Mr Happy right now, but talkin' to you will lift his load some.'

'I'm sorry, Henry,' Claire apologized again, full of guilty

remorse. 'I got all uptight and snotty and for no good reason except I didn't know what was really going on.'

'He didn't want to spoil your Christmas.'

'Well he did! Not knowing is far worse than knowing.' Indignantly: 'And I shall tell him so.'

But when she did get through to him that night, and it was late, almost midnight, at the sound of his voice all her resolutions folded their tents and silently slipped away, and she found herself saying, 'Oh, Jake, I'm so sorry.'

'What for?'

'Acting like a spoiled brat. You could have explained things to me, you know. I'm not made of sugar.'

'Who told you?' he asked after a moment.

'Mother and Henry between them. I wanted to know, Jake. I needed to. I wouldn't have been so miserable if I had.'

'Yeah . . .' she heard him sigh. 'I've been thinking that myself. I miss you like hell.'

'Likewise,' Claire said, feeling her heart lift. 'Henry said you didn't want to spoil my Christmas but you did. However, I think New Year will be a different matter.'

'Include me when you drink your toast to absent friends.'

'Friends?' Claire asked. 'I thought we'd gone beyond that stage.'

His voice was very careful when he said, 'Are you telling me you've had a change of heart?'

'No . . . you took that with you when you left.'

There was another silence then she heard him ask unsteadily, 'Say again? This line is cloudy.'

'It's perfectly clear and you know it. You sound like you were right beside me.'

'I wish I was.'

'Oh, so do I . . . so do I. I miss you, Jake, and I love you . . . that's what I wanted to tell you. With all my heart and soul I love you – the more so for wanting to protect me, even if it's not me who's in danger. Are you all right?'

'Now I am,' he said, his voice radiating his feelings.

'I couldn't understand why, after what had happened between us, how you could go off so calmly . . .'

'The hell I was! It took all I had not to drag you into the car with me.'

'I wish you had!'

'Hang on a minute – ' She heard his voice, fainter as he covered the mouthpiece with his hand. 'Look, you guys – can you give me a few minutes? This is a personal call . . .' Then: 'That's better,' he said. 'Now, where were we?'

'In love, I hope.'

'I've loved you for a long time now . . . but you made it clear from the start that you weren't prepared to commit yourself so I played it your way. All I could do was demonstrate – '

'That was what did for me, but it took you leaving me before I understood.'

'What a lot of time we've wasted,' he said regretfully.

'Then let me make up for it right now. I love you, I love you, I love you . . . I'd got myself into an emotional corner because I blindly refused to see. Can I plead temporary insanity?'

'In that case,' Jake said, his voice strong and vibrant, 'you had better be put away for the public good – not to mention that of Jake Burns. A life sentence – and in his custody.'

'Oh, yes, Your Honour, thank you, Your Honour . . .'

'I was going to call you,' Jake said after a short, vibrating silence. 'I just couldn't leave it lying any more. I decided I'd have it out with you even if you flayed every inch of skin with that scalpel tongue of yours. You mean too much to me to let you get away. I've loved you so much for so long now; felt I had a future with you, and I couldn't let go of it because I had nothing else. Now that I have you it changes everything . . . you are so very much you, Claire. I'd know you anywhere; deaf, dumb and blindfolded . . .'

Claire blinked away tears. 'And I you . . . I had to think I had lost you to make me realize.'

'Why did you think you'd lost me?'

'Because you didn't take me with you.'

'I couldn't – '

'I know that now. Why didn't you explain, you idiot?'

'I didn't want you worrying.'

'Worrying!' Claire's voice broke. 'I worried far more because you didn't tell me. I thought that when it came down to the bottom line I came second to Burns Oil.'

'No way!' Jake denied hotly.

'How are things?'

'We're making headway . . . but it's going to be a long job.'

'That doesn't matter so much now. I can wait.'

'Maybe when I don't have to spend so much time with other people you can fly over and we can be together.'

'I'd love that. Whenever you say, Jake, and wherever and whatever. I just wanted to tell you . . .'

'Thank God you did. You've been on my mind constantly. Tonight I'll be able to sleep.'

'Oh, darling, forgive me,' Claire said remorsefully. 'All I was thinking about was myself.'

'I've been feeling pretty sorry for myself too.'

'Not as much as I did. The simple truth is that I was an emotional coward.'

'You had every right to be.'

'No I didn't. You can't retire into a corner and sulk for the rest of your life just because somebody burst your balloon, yet that's what I was doing. Forgive me for hurting you.'

'Who was it said – "To know all is to forgive all"?'

'I can't remember but I hope he was right.'

'He was.'

'Then I'll wait for you no matter how long it takes. Just to know you'll be coming back to me is more than I deserve. Know that I love you as I know that I am loved.'

There was another short yet plangent silence and his voice was ragged when he said, 'I do . . .' She heard him take a deep breath. 'Now I've got more reason than ever to get this mess cleared away and get back to you.'

'Or me come to you. Whatever, wherever, whenever . . .'

'How long will you be in Scotland?'

'Till the end of the week.'

'I'll call you tomorrow night, as near as I can to midnight your time.'

'Oh, that would be lovely.'

'It's going to be a great New Year, sweetheart. I feel it in my bones.'

'It won't be for want of trying.'

He laughed. 'I doubt there'll be many people able to come tomorrow night. I wish I could be there.'

'So do I . . . but we will be able to wish each other a Happy New Year thanks to International Direct Dialling.' His laugh was exultant. 'A very happy New Year, my darling. Take care and we'll talk again tomorrow. I love you.'

'This is the first time somebody ever said to me "Have a nice day" and I actually did,' Jake said in a voice which conveyed the grin on his face.

'I intend to see they are all nice from now on. Now here's Henry. Good night, my love.' She made kissing sounds into the receiver and then called out to Henry. 'Your turn now.'

When she put her head round her mother's door she found her reading, but at the sight of Claire's changed face she said, 'All squared away?'

'Yes.' Claire's smile was a nova. 'No more sharp edges.'

'I'm so glad.'

'How do you think I feel?'

'From the look of you, absolutely marvellous.'

'Thanks to you.' Claire bent down to hug her mother fiercely. 'Jake sends his love too.' She yawned. 'Oh, I shall sleep tonight . . .'

'Good. I'm relying on you to carry some of the burden tomorrow night.'

'My strength shall be as the strength of ten because I know I am loved,' Claire paraphrased happily.

And she showed it the following night. Hogmanay at Castle Drummond was the major celebration of the old year. The great hall was cleared for dancing, and the men appeared in their kilts and velvet jackets, lace sparkling at their throats and a *skean dhu* thrust into the tops of their stockings. The band was local, a traditional accordion band, and there was enough whisky to fill the loch. Claire and her mother were both resplendent in full evening dress and jewels, the Drummond tartan sashed over the left shoulder. Claire had pinned hers with Jake's diamond rose, which glittered against the scarlet, yellow and dark green of the tartan, and her face was flushed with pleasure and anticipation of her midnight rendezvous, even if it was with a telephone. She was never off the floor, and as the New Year approached, the reels grew more boisterous and the whoops of the men more unrestrained. It was in the middle of one hectic strathspey that Claire suddenly stumbled and clutched at her partner, the son of a neighbour. Her ears rang and the room blurred; for a moment she felt faint.

'I say, are you all right?'

'A little dizzy. Some fresh air, I think, and perhaps a sit-down.'

'Shall I get your mother?'

'No, please . . . it's just the heat and being whirled around.'

'Sorry if I got carried away . . .' He carefully assisted her up the long length of the hall to the front door, which he was careful to open only slightly, so as to let in no more than a brief blast of cold air. 'I'm afraid that it's snowing even harder,' he said, shivering. Claire was breathing deeply, but two or three breaths soon cleared her head and she felt her flesh chilling rapidly.

'Better now?' Hugh Sutherland asked solicitously, shutting the door.

'Much. I think a short respite is called for, though – and perhaps a glass of something cold but alcohol free.'

He saw her to a chair by the wall and then went to fetch her an iced lemonade. Soft drinks were always plentiful and copiously drunk owing to the exertion of the dance. Claire drained her glass and felt better.

'You okay?' Henry materialized in front of her in his seemingly slow-moving but always alert way.

'I just felt a little dizzy, that's all. Young Hugh Sutherland doesn't know his own strength. He whirled me round like a dervish.'

'If this is how you Scots enjoy yourselves I'd hate to see you when you're not,' Henry said dubiously. 'I ain't seen so much whisky put away since Prohibition.'

'It's the Water of Life to us Scots,' Claire said wickedly. 'That's what it means – the word whisky – *uisge beatha* is the Gaelic phrase. Any self-respecting Scot drinks it the same way.'

'It's where we're gonna put them that worries me.'

'Don't worry. They will all walk away on their own two feet.'

'You okay on yours? It's only four minutes to midnight. I switched the phone through to the library.'

Claire got to her feet and swayed a little. He put out a steadying arm. 'Do you know, I think I have had one dram too many myself!' she giggled.

'Lean on me, then.' He took her away to the library, where she sank down in the big chair by the fire, the telephone to hand on the sofa table nearby. 'You are an angel, Henry,' she told him lovingly. 'What would I do without you?'

'From the way things is goin' I don't see any need to worry 'bout that,' he grinned. 'If he can put his mind to other things you might ask him if he has anything to tell me, okay?'

'He will want to wish you a Happy New Year if nothing else.'

'It's somethin' else that's on his mind right now.'

He closed the door quietly behind him. Claire closed her eyes again. She still felt light-headed. I can't be drunk, she thought. I haven't over-indulged by any means. However . . .' She got up and went across to the cupboard where her father had always kept the decanters and poured herself a half-inch of whisky. 'That won't do any more damage,' she said as she held it up to the light. 'But I have to drink Jake's health . . .'

Just then the phone rang.

She slept late next day. It was noon before she surfaced, and the first thing she did when she sat up was put a hand to her mouth then leap from her bed and run to the bathroom. She was still there, leaning over the bowl, when there was a knock and Henry came in with her tray.

'Mornin',' he called.

'Morning,' Claire called back, in a voice that belied her face and feelings. Quickly she splashed water on her face, patted it dry, ran a comb through her hair. When she went back he was gone but he had left her ice-cold orange juice, coffee and two freshly made bran muffins. She shuddered and placed the tray on a chair near the door. Climbing back into bed she lay back against the pillows. She could hear her heart thudding. It can't be, she thought.

Oh, yes it can, her mind retorted.

But – so soon?

Five weeks?

And one missed period. You're like clockwork, you *never* miss. You almost fainted last night and this morning you've heaved your guts out. If, come January 10th, you miss again then there is absolutely no doubt, but we both know that you will miss again. Face it, Claire. You're pregnant.

She got out of bed again, went to the pier glass and, pulling the slither of bias-cut ice-blue satin that was her nightgown tight to her body, she examined her stomach. Still its usual, gently rounded self. But she knew with every fibre of her being, as she placed her hand there, that she was

carrying Jake's child. She knew it in every bone and sinew.
I'm pregnant, she crowed to herself ecstatically, doing a little
dance around the room. Oh, Jake, I hope you're as happy
as I am about it. And I'll take care, oh, I will take such care
. . . Sedately, she got back into bed again, hugging the
knowledge to her like a comfort blanket. A son, she thought.
Tall, like Jake, blue-eyed, like Jake, but probably with red
gold hair, the perfect mixture of us both . . . Oh, please
God, she prayed, let it be true. Let me be pregnant. I want
this child so much, all the more so because Jake is a three-time
loser. This isn't like it was before. I love him, I love the idea
of having his child. I couldn't stand the thought of having
Rory's. This child was conceived in love – even if I didn't
know it at the time. Let it be born the same way. Please . . .

Ten days later, as she had hoped, her period did not appear,
and her pregnancy was confirmed by a visit to the Brook
Advisory Clinic in London, where she was told she was
approximately seven weeks along and asked tactfully if she
was happy about it.

'Oh, yes . . . I am absolutely delighted!'

The woman on the other side of the desk smiled. 'I'm so
glad. Most of the women who come to us are not – which
is why they come to us in the first place.'

'I'm not one of them,' Claire said. 'I came here because –
well, I want to keep it a secret for a while longer and you
are impersonal in a way my family doctor could never be.'
She paid her fee and left in a haze of joy. Wait until I tell
Jake, she thought. And not over the phone; face to face so
that I can see the look on his . . . Oh, what a reunion that
is going to be.

Part Three

RORY

For the error bred in the bone, is to ask
to be loved alone

CHAPTER FIFTEEN

Jake stood at the window of his Galveston office, high above the Gulf, which, in the deep purple light of the fading day, looked solid.

' . . . it's obvious that somebody is gunning for you. Too many coincidences, too much happening in too short a time to be anything other than deliberate, but I'm damned if there's anything to be found out. I've had my best investigators out there and all they've come up with is a big fat zero.'

'Just give me a rundown on those costs again, will you?' Jake asked absently.

'Whichever way I tell you the total is going to come out the same. Far too much.' But the foxy-faced, carrot-haired man, as thin as a cadaver and as pale as the moon, turned to the sheaf of papers in front of him. 'The clean-up is a minimum of ten million – the goddamn wind had the slick halfway to Mexico before it changed on us. The compensation to the shrimp fishermen – and this figure is by no means final because I'm positive a couple of them are kiting their losses; there's always some smart-ass out to make a fast buck – is another ten at least. I figure it's best to be generous otherwise we face several multi-million-dollar lawsuits. Then there's the beaches – thank God it was nowhere near any of the big resorts otherwise we'd really be in trouble, but they are still screaming about their sea-oats grass and morning glories – so that's another couple of million. What we can never recoup is the bad publicity, and that's the work of the same son-of-a-bitch who's responsible for everything else.' The foxy-faced man picked up a newspaper and shook it frustratedly. ' "Criminal negligence, sloppy maintenance" –

that's a crock and they know it. Burns Oil has a reputation for running a very tight ship.' He flung the paper down in disgust. 'Of course,' he said to Jake's back, 'we know the reason why, don't we?' Jake did not answer.

'It has to be your bid to take over Texoil. The stock is now trading at forty-five dollars twenty-five and that's down ten points since the papers started calling you Buccaneer Burns. I think those boys back in Houston are playing dirty.'

'That's because they're running scared.' Jake turned to face Burns Enterprises' Comptroller, Carl Wynant, known as 'Foxy' Wynant on account of his looks. 'But I know John Vaughn, and this is not his style.'

'He called you a hit and run artist.'

'That's just rhetoric. John Vaughn is a cautious man: he doesn't like taking risks – that's why Texoil is in such bad shape. He didn't get off his ass and put money into developing new reserves, then he got himself stuck with that dumb lawsuit which cost him five billion dollars. When I started buying the shareprice stood at twenty-eight dollars, whereas I know its asset value is at least seventy. That's why I want to get my hands on it, turn it around, make it pay its way.'

'Well, somebody else is just as determined not to let you get your – and I quote – "greedy" hands on it. And all that's happened over the past few months I lay squarely at their stinking door.' With bitter gloom: 'And wouldn't I like to know just who they are.'

'Maybe we'll know more when we know if they're willing to accept my twelve and a half billion offer. The Board is due to give its decision when it meets next week.'

'Well, I think they see it as pressure on your part to make them buy you out; the real clincher will be if we can swing those seats on the board. Then we can light a fire under all their asses.' Foxy paused. 'If we don't do it we sell our sixteen per cent share – that'll cut the price right from under their feet.' He frowned. 'What I don't like is the rumour that Britoil is ready to offer seventy dollars a share.' Then his face cleared: 'Whatever happens, though, we'll come out ahead and I can replenish the contingency fund.'

'Money,' Jake growled, 'is the least of my worries. Burns Enterprises has always been – always will be – cash rich. Nobody will ever catch me going with my begging bowl to anybody's bank.'

'Oh, we're solvent – Jesus, any other company should be so solvent, but rumours and speculation wreak havoc in any market, and there have been far too many about you and Burns Enterprises lately.'

'Well, pay what we have to pay. I don't want this dragging on for the next couple of years; I want it squared away, left clean and tidy so that I can get back to Europe.'

'What for?' Foxy asked. 'I thought you would have had a long enough sabbatical by now. You did a few deals – nice ones too – and came out ahead on all of them, but this is where the real action is.'

'I trust you to handle things.'

'I know you do, but it looks bad you living it up over there while all hell is let loose over here.'

'I came back, didn't I?'

'You had no choice,' retorted Foxy. He hesitated; he had known Jake a long time, worked for him for the past eight years, and they were friends, but there were still areas of Jake's life where he did not have right of entry. 'I guess you want to get back to your English lady,' he said lightly.

'Yes,' Jake said, 'I do, and she's a Scot. Saying she's English is like calling a Southerner a Yank.'

'You'll have a hard time convincing Cora Sue, no matter what she is.' Jake's grey eyes moved from the window to Foxy's face and Foxy reddened.

'You know how Cora Sue is,' he said hastily.

'I ought to. But Cora Sue runs my office, not my life.'

Not for want of trying, Foxy thought. He'd seen pictures of this woman with whom Jake was involved and she was a looker, all right, but the most obvious clue to Jake's feelings about her was Cora Sue's attitude. Which means, Foxy thought, that it's serious; the reason why Jake's original year was now well into its second.

'You're not thinking of seceding yourself back to the British, are you?' he joked.

'No, I'm not. Whatever I do decide, you'll know in due course. You always do, don't you?'

'Sure, fine, only asking,' Foxy said hastily. He saw Jake check his watch, knew it was about time for his nightly call to Claire Drummond. He shuddered at the thought of this month's phone bill. A nothing if not thorough comptroller, he had instituted a system which logged not only the destination but the duration of all phone calls from Burns Tower; local, long distance and overseas. Jake's had been running to marathon lengths. What's wrong with a 38 cent stamp? he wondered. Nobody writes letters any more . . .

Jake was jingling the coins in his pocket, as he always did when thinking. 'So we are just about all squared away, then?' he asked.

'Provided nobody reneges on the agreements we've come to.'

'Fine. You've been a tower of strength, Foxy. You fight a mean fight for a man who's hooked on figures.'

'I do my best,' Foxy agreed, pleased.

'Right, if that's all, then.' Foxy took the hint, began shoving his papers into his briefcase. 'See you tomorrow.'

'Yeah, sure . . .' Foxy was just reaching for the door handle when Jake's phone rang.

'Now what?' Jake snatched the receiver. 'I want this line clear . . . Jake Burns here,' he barked. 'Oh . . . hello . . .' His voice changed, softened with warmth. 'To what do I owe the pleasure . . .'

Foxy quietly closed the door behind him.

'I'm sorry to bother you, Jake, but – ' The normally calm, controlled voice broke as if under enormous pressure.

'What's wrong?' Jake asked, quickly, knowing beyond doubt that something was. He had never seen Claire's mother in anything other than complete control; now, in

408

the obviously shaken voice, he heard the ominous rumble of Gibraltar crumbling.

'Claire has gone missing.'

Jake felt his stomach contract. 'Missing?' he repeated stupidly.

'For almost eleven hours. She left to drive into Inverness this morning at about eleven o'clock to do some errands for me, but we now think she never got there because none of the shops she would have visited saw anything of her. I rang them and they told me so. Then I thought perhaps – an accident, but the local hospital has no knowledge of her either. I've rung round all the neighbours, and the only information I could get was that one of them passed Claire's car on the road – they were coming back from Inverness as Claire was driving in at around eleven-thirty. Since then – nothing.'

'Have you called the police?' Jake asked.

'Yes. The Chief Constable is an old friend.'

Carefully: 'No – messages – from anybody?'

'No. I've been within reach of the telephone all day. I'm dreadfully worried, Jake. This is not like Claire . . .' Or anything I have ever had to deal with, her now open anguish said clearly. 'Henry said I should call you.'

'He did right. I'll leave at once.' Checking his watch Jake saw it was 4.30 p.m. If he was airborne within the hour he could be at Dalcross – five hours behind – by six-thirty Greenwich Mean Time.

'Let me know your time of arrival and I'll meet you,' Lady Margot said gratefully, in such a way as to have Jake saying roughly: 'Don't you worry. This is my responsibility. I had a feeling . . . We'll find her, you hear? And that's a promise.'

But his hand was trembling as he pressed the cut-off button, then punched out another two digits. 'Foxy? Come back a minute, will you? Something's come up . . .'

'I still think I ought to be with you,' Cora Sue harped on, as the car sped them towards the plane she had chartered.

'This is not business, Cora, this is personal. I need you back here to help Foxy tie up any loose ends.' Jake's voice hardened. 'And since when have you been so keen to help where Claire is concerned?'

Cora Sue's high colour deepened. 'All right, so I don't like her – but that was only because I was looking out for you.'

'Then do it over here.'

At the note in his voice she subsided, but sulkily. Missing indeed! she thought. Probably mad as hell because he left her behind and using this little ploy to pay him back. Who would want to snatch that little madam? If anyone can look after themselves it's that butter-wouldn't-melt gold-digger. Well, all the more reason to tie off those ends in double-quick time and then join him to make sure he doesn't get taken to the cleaners.

The plane was ready and waiting; a Lear jet that would have Jake in Scotland in seven hours. 'You know where you can reach me,' Jake said, as he prepared to board, 'but don't unless you absolutely have to. I'll have enough on my mind.'

At the look on his face, the sound of his voice, Cora Sue felt a shiver of apprehension. She was as aware as anybody that there was someone out there doing their damnedest to cause Jake the maximum amount of trouble, but she had never expected it to move in Claire Drummond's direction. We should never have gone to Europe in the first place, she thought, as she watched the plane taxi in the direction of the runway. Worst day's work we ever did . . .

Thanks to a tailwind it was just on 6 a.m. when Jake walked into the arrivals lounge at Dalcross Airport to find Lady Margot and her eldest son waiting for him. Without conscious volition, Lady Margot went straight up to him and embraced him. He could feel her trembling.

'Thank you, Jake,' she said humbly. She looked pale, and there were signs of strain around the eyes and taut line of her mouth, but her courage was up. Iain wrung Jake's hand.

'Feels better already to have you here,' he said gratefully.

'Any developments?' Jake asked.

'No. Claire has just – vanished.' Iain looked hard at Jake. 'We don't quite understand why,' he said bluntly.

'Me,' Jake answered flatly. 'Somebody has been playing dirty games over the past few months; damaging equipment, putting me in a bad light, meddling in my affairs. I think that they are the people who have meddled with Claire.'

'A kidnap?' Iain's voice was incredulous.

'Could be. What have you told the police?'

'Just that Claire is missing. James Dalziel – he's our Chief Constable – is doing all the routine things, searching the dark corners, asking questions – '

'Without result?'

'So far.'

'Then we have to take it further. Where's Henry?'

'Standing by the telephone.'

'Then let's get to him.'

'So what's the story?' Jake asked Henry over a cup of coffee.

'She took her car – a VW Golf GTI – to drive into Inverness, that's about twenty miles. There's only the one major road – the A9 – but to get to that you take two minor roads, first the A940 then the A938. You hit the main route at a place called Carrbridge. It runs through some pretty bare country – a hell of a place to get lost in. The mountains ain't what we're used to but they're awful bleak and we've had a lot of snowfalls lately. If she's been snatched then we have a lot of territory to cover.'

'First off we have to find out who might have taken her.'

Henry shrugged. 'Pick a card – there's no clue that I can see.'

'Her car is missing too?'

'Yep.'

Jake thought. 'How has Claire been?'

'Fine . . . we had a high old time come New Year and then we came back north for her ma's birthday. Had us a real nice party.'

'What about Rory Ballater?'

'First name as come to my mind too. He ain't been seen in these parts in months. His house is closed and the caretaker says His Lordship is abroad.'

'That can be checked. Lady Margot has a lot of high-level contacts.'

Jake sipped his coffee. 'And no – strange calls?'

'Not a thing. Miss Claire went off sayin' she'd be back in time for lunch – which as you know is always at one o'clock. Come nine o'clock that night and her ma was beginning to fray at the edges. She's one strong lady but this is something she's never had to handle. She's called everybody she could think of who might know somethin' but so far nobody has come up with any answers. So she called her friend the Chief Constable and he got right down to it. Tracker dogs, house to house enquiries, search parties up in the hills.' Jake brooded and Henry refilled his coffee cup. 'Kidnappin' ain't something that happens up here,' he consoled. 'And Miss Claire is pretty well known in these parts. Inverness ain't that big neither.'

'Whoever has snatched her has probably got her somewhere well hidden.' In the voice of someone who has made a decision: 'I want Ray Beale on this,' Jake said. 'We've used him before and he's good. He's got a nose for the unsuspected. Call him and get him over here as soon as possible.'

'Okay.'

'Now I'm going to see this Chief Constable, find out just what he's doing.'

He was doing all he could to help an old friend. He had policemen and tracker dogs searching the vicinity of the roads Claire had used, looking for the slightest clue. The dogs had been provided with one of Claire's sweaters, and the men were also checking the roads for tyre tracks and footprints.

'But if they're off the roads, then it becomes much more difficult. However, I've got a first-class man; the best animal tracker in the Highlands. He can spot a broken twig and tell you who stepped on it.'

'I've got a man of my own coming over,' Jake said. 'If that's all right with you. He's part Cherokee and likewise a damned good tracker.'

'Provided he is willing to work alongside us, then of course, he will be welcome, Mr Burns.'

When Jake went back, he found Iain poring over an Ordnance Survey map of the region. 'It's the lack of roads, you see,' he explained worriedly. 'Once you get up into the mountains it is either on a horse or your feet. There are some rough tracks but they are no use to anything except a Land Rover.'

'What about houses?' Jake asked.

'Few and far between, and the police have been to every one of them. No luck. If Claire has been taken – and I think we must accept now, after twenty-four hours, that she has, then she could be anywhere. But if it is off the beaten track then whoever has her must know his way around, which narrows it down a bit. The police are sifting through the known offenders; men who have a record of abduction.'

'I understand Lord Ballater is abroad,' Jake said neutrally.

Iain's glance was sharp. 'He was our first choice too; it's just the sort of a crackbrained thing he would do, but Ballater House is shut up and Rory – so I'm told – is in South America. I've asked around but nobody has set eyes on him for months.' He paused. 'Have you any idea who might want to abduct Claire?'

'I'm working on it. I'm involved in an unfriendly takeover right now but the man I'm fighting doesn't strike me as the type to do a thing like this. This is the work of somebody who hates my guts, and while my opponent and I aren't exactly buddies, I don't believe he would go this far.'

'Perhaps an old enemy, then? I'm sure you must have trod on a toe or two . . .'

'It's possible.'

'Well, I'm going to take a ride up into the hills; there are a couple of abandoned bothies that should be looked over.'

'You do that. I'm going to retrace Claire's route, so that I know what I'm dealing with.'

'We'll have another confab at tea. Trouble is, this is the worst possible time of year for this sort of thing; it gets dark by three-thirty and God help anybody out on the mountains at night in this weather.' He could have bitten off his tongue at the look on Jake's face. Claire never stops telling me I'm tactless, he thought guiltily. Adopting a heartier tone he said: 'Claire is a resourceful girl and she knows the country. I'm inclined to feel sorry for whoever has taken her; she's probably had their guts for garters by now.'

But Claire was not able to talk; she was lying on a camp bed in a stone-walled, windowless room, deeply unconscious.

She had set off for Inverness with a light heart. It was a cold but bright day. She had about another six miles to go when it started to snow, and within minutes she was in the midst of a blizzard, her windscreen wipers working overtime to afford some visibility. She had been forced to slow down to a crawl, and concentrating as she was on peering ahead, she had not at first noticed the big car – a Land Rover she saw when she glanced at it – uncomfortably close to her, so close she had to move dangerously near to the edge of the road, but she felt no alarm, only annoyance, until she realized that it was still crowding her. Opening her window she waved a gloved hand, indicating to it to move away. She could not distinguish the driver; the snow was too thick, but she felt a stab of fear as she felt the big car nudge her own, forcing her to hang on to the steering wheel. Even as she did she felt her own car tilt as its nearside wheels left the road to bump along rough unpaved earth.

'Idiot!' she shouted wrathfully. 'What on earth do you think you're doing?' She cut the engine, stopped the car. The last thing she wanted was a puncture. Honestly, she thought furiously, some people would not be safe on a bike! She saw the Land Rover had stopped too, and she was about to open the door and give them a blast of anger when it was opened for her and a big shape loomed out of the snow. 'If you have come to apologize – ' she began and then her face was suddenly smothered in something that felt thick and smelled sickly-sweet. 'What on earth . . .' but her words were muffled; a big hand was forcing the cloth against her mouth and nose, making it hard to breathe, and when she did she inhaled more of the sick sweetness which made her head swim. Her hands came up but they were caught in a firm grip by another pair of hands. There are two of them! she thought muzzily, frantically trying to wrench her face aside. But another hand caught the back of her head in a firm grip, holding it immovable so that she had no choice but to take in more of whatever the cloth was impregnated with. It was not until she began to lose consciousness that she realized what it was. Chloroform! She struggled again, but could feel herself going, her movements becoming feebler and fewer. She could hear a strange ringing noise in her ears, lights seemed to flash behind eyes she fought to keep open, then the noise and the lights faded, dwindling to a pinpoint. She felt herself drop into a free-fall which ended in darkness.

Jake drove slowly the route Claire would have taken, his eyes scanning the countryside, all of it under at least a foot of snow. It had been snowing when Claire had left Castle Drummond, but not enough to prevent her from setting out. It was only later that a blizzard had set in. 'But we never let that put us off,' Lady Margot had told him. 'If we did we should have to hibernate all winter.' Now, the mountains looked like mounds of the steamed puddings they ate over here, covered with a thick white sauce that had trickled down their sides. This part of the Highlands was fairly well populated, because Inverness – the Hub, as it was known – was the capital of the region with some 35,000 people. The glens around were also full of small villages and quite a few big estates, but further up the mountains there was nothing but the sheep who tenanted the moors. He closed his mind to the picture of Claire somewhere up there; in a small shepherd's hut – a bothy as they called them – at the mercy of some flake with rape on his mind . . . She'll not give him an easy time, he told himself. She's got guts and spirit and a tongue like an asp. He'd missed it like hell over the past three weeks; he'd missed her company, her smile, the lilt of her voice, the warmth of her as they lay fitted to each other in bed, like two spoons. He'd found himself looking up, expecting to see her there and feel the now customary joy. Where are you, Claire? he worried. Who has got you – and why? Who is it knows about us – and who the hell has told them? He felt the hair on his neck lift at the thought of somebody, perhaps for months now, watching and waiting. And I had to go and leave her alone . . . Christ, why didn't I take her with me! I thought I was protecting her but a seeing eye dog does a better job than me.

It started to snow again on the way back; thick flakes driven by a rising wind. The temperature took a nose dive, and by the time he got back to Castle Drummond it was, according to the thermometer on the wall of the outer lobby, already below zero.

There were visitors grouped around the tea-table in front of the roaring fire in the Great Hall. Kitty Melhuish and her husband, who lived at the other end of the Glen. It had been Kitty who had passed Claire, coming back from Inverness, on the morning she had disappeared. Both shook Jake's hand warmly, expressed their concern and assured him that anything they could do . . .

'I mean, one just doesn't expect this sort of thing in this part of the world,' Kitty said, bewildered. 'And Claire, of all people! It just does not make sense. I was only saying to Alexander – '

'When you passed her on the road,' Jake interrupted, 'did she seem okay to you? I mean – was she driving normally?'

'Well, it was snowing so one couldn't drive very fast, but I know Claire's car; it's the only one around here that colour . . .'

'What colour is that?'

'Bright red with a white roof.'

'The VW convertible?'

'We call it a Cabriolet, but yes, that's the one. I had to slow down because the idiot in front of me did a U-turn just as Claire passed me. I tooted the horn and waved and I'm sure she waved back but she didn't stop, of course.'

'What time was this?'

'About half-past eleven. I'd had to go into Inverness early because my youngest had us up all night with toothache and I managed to get a ten-thirty appointment. Mr Innes had to take it out – '

'What was the car in front – the one that did the illegal U-turn?'

'A Range Rover, why?'

'You didn't see who was driving?'

'Two men were in the front, I think.' Kitty frowned. 'I'm afraid I tooted my horn at them too. They could have caused an accident on that slippery surface. One of them had the insufferable cheek to put his finger up at me.' Kitty's pretty face went pink with affront.

'Where was this?' Jake asked. 'And did you tell the police?'

'Yes. I told them everything.'

Jake brought the map over to Kitty, spread it on the floor by her chair. 'Show me where,' he requested.

Kitty laid her finger on the map. 'Right by the pony-trekking centre,' she said.

'Did you notice the number of the Range Rover?'

'I'm afraid not. But I'm sure it was two men.'

'Did you get a good look at them?'

'Not really, just an impression. They were both bundled up in heavy coats; it was a bitterly cold day.'

'What are you getting at, Jake?' Iain Drummond asked.

'Why a car should do an illegal U-turn at the point where it passed Claire.'

'You mean – they recognized her too?'

'Maybe. With nothing else to go on we need all the facts we can get.'

'And a Range Rover can negotiate rough country where any other car would be useless . . .'

'Exactly.' Jake turned back to Kitty Melhuish. 'Did you notice anything else, Lady Melhuish?'

'I'm afraid not. It was all over in seconds . . . and I was concentrating on getting Kirsty back home as quickly as possible. She was rather miserable . . .'

'Even so, you've been a great help. Thank you.' His smile made Kitty Melhuish blink. Really, she thought, no wonder everyone is talking about Claire Drummond's American.

'Are you perhaps thinking that someone has been hanging around, waiting for the right opportunity?' Lady Margot asked bluntly of Jake.

'It's a possibility.'

'But how would they have done it?'

'Maybe forced Claire's car off the road then somehow bundled her into the Range Rover which one man would then drive off followed by the other in Claire's car. It was snowing; visibility was blurred. If people saw two cars stopped, they would probably think one was in trouble and being helped by the other.'

'I wish someone had stopped and helped me when I had a flat tyre coming back from Aberdeen one appallingly wet Sunday,' Kitty Melhuish said. 'I actually had to flag someone down before they stopped, but he was a very nice lorry driver – '

'Exactly. People don't usually stop for a stationary car, not these days – even in the hospitably friendly Highlands of Scotland,' he added gallantly. 'What we have to do is appeal for anybody who did see it – and at the time Claire would have been on the road – to come forward.'

'They do that on the television all the time,' Kitty Melhuish said helpfully. 'Especially after a bad accident; there is always an appeal for witnesses to come forward.'

'Then I think I had better have another word with James Dalziel,' Lady Margot said, rising to her feet.

The appeal appeared on the local television news, after the national programme at nine o'clock, asking for anyone who had seen two cars, a red VW Golf GTI white-roofed Cabriolet and a Range Rover, stopped on the A9 headed towards Inverness, on Thursday 23rd January, between eleven-thirty and twelve noon. They were given a telephone number and asked to call.

Within thirty minutes, the Chief Constable called. Three motorists had answered the appeal; all had seen two cars stationary at the side of the road just where it forked by Loch Moy, all three said it had been at about 11.45 a.m. Two had said that one of the cars was bright red with a white canvas roof.

'James says to compliment you on your quick thinking, Jake,' Lady Margot told him.

'Young Lochinvar from out of the Far West,' Iain said affectionately, clapping him on the shoulder. 'Now we know where they took her and when. What we now have to find out is who and why. Maybe, now that they've heard the appeal, we will hear from them.'

'You mean a ransom demand?' Moira, who had been sitting silently by, asked in alarm.

'Whatever it costs,' Jake said, 'Claire is worth it to me. No – ' he raised a hand as the Drummonds opened their mouths to protest. 'Let's not kid ourselves here. It's me they're getting at; nobody has any reason to kidnap Claire except to lean on me. Either for money or to do something they want me to. What worries me is how they've found out about Claire and me; who could have told them just how important she is in my life.'

'We have not discussed it with *anyone*, my dear Jake,' Lady Margot said quietly.

'We had no idea until Christmas,' Moira added earnestly.

'I suspected, of course, but – ' She subsided under her husband's dark look.

'I didn't for a minute think you had,' Jake said, equally quiet. 'I think the leak lies back in London, and if we don't hear anything in the next day or two then I have to start looking in that direction.'

'Business rivalries?' Iain enquired. He shook his head. 'I had heard of the cut and thrust of American big business but I hadn't realized you fought with real swords.'

'You don't know the half of it,' Jake told him laconically. But I'll find out the whole, he thought, if I have to use every weapon I have. Which was why, before we went to bed that night, he called Cora Sue in Galveston.

When he told Lady Margot next morning, and somewhat diffidently, that Cora Sue would be joining him, she said, 'Of course. I know what a help she is to you.'

'That's why I've asked her to come. And someone else . . .' She looked at him enquiringly. 'An old friend of mine; his name is Ray Beale. He's a private investigator and I've used him a few times in the past. He has a nose for sniffing out clues.'

'A private investigator!' Lady Margot's eyes sparkled. 'Heavens, this becomes progressively more exciting.'

'I'm glad you feel that way.'

'I do, because I have every confidence that you will find Claire, wherever she is.'

'Well, it's almost forty-eight hours now and nothing, which is what worries me. Why haven't they contacted us?'

'Turning the screw?' As their eyes met hers darkened. 'Oh,' she said in a frail voice, 'I see what you mean . . . if they are prepared to do this to you, what will they do to Claire, is that it?'

'No, they won't do anything to her,' Jake lied as strongly as he could. 'She's their insurance. It's me they want to light the fire under. I'm only sorry that the flames are touching you too. All this is my fault. I should never have let her out of my sight. It's – well, I thought that this was the safest place for her. I should have realized that when somebody is as determined as these people are, no place is safe.'

'Kidnapping was a common occurrence during the clan wars,' Lady Margot said, 'and in my own family, back in the early nineteenth century, an ancestor kidnapped his bride and transported her to Gretna Green, where one could marry without any legal paraphernalia, still could until not too many years ago. But in the Nineteen eighties it does come as something of a shock – and in Glen Drummond too!'

'Now you know how I feel,' Jake said wryly. Margot Drummond examined the taut face, the lines that seemed to have been re-etched on his face, the evidence, in the bleak eyes, of nights without sleep, and worst of all, the mountain of guilt he was carrying.

'Jake . . . Jake . . .' she said, shaking him slightly with the affectionate familiarity of an old friend. 'I will not have you blaming yourself for other people's shortcomings! You're as bad as Claire. She blamed herself for Rory and look what that did. It would have been the same had you taken her back to America with you. When someone is bent and determined to do something there is a limit to the precautions one can take. I don't blame you, and I know that's the last thing Claire will be thinking. The fault lies with whoever has this grudge against you, and in this life, who goes through it without incurring someone's envy or jealousy or hatred – and for no good reason except the fact that one exists?'

Jake's smile lightened his face. 'I guess this is what Claire calls "one of your quiet words"?'

'I started it during the war; I was a VAD, filled with thoughts of Florence Nightingale and ministering angels, but they discovered that I had a calming effect on men who were in pain or some kind of trauma, and the only nursing I got to do was by way of sitting by their beds and talking to them. I think that right now you are in need of a hand to hold.'

She squeezed his and in a courtly gesture he carried it to

his lips. 'You really are some lady,' he said simply, 'and I don't mean with a capital L.'

'Now you go off and meet your friends and we'll have a council of war later.'

She saw him off with a smile on her face which only faded as Logie shut the front door on her.

'A trying time, m'lady,' he said, with all the feeling of one who was part of the family.

'Indeed it is, Logie.'

'But Miss Claire is a resourceful girl. Do you remember the time she got lost on the hills when the mist came down; she was only about ten years old, but instead of wandering around and becoming even more lost she stayed where she was and whistled. Miss Claire could always outwhistle her brothers; two fingers in her mouth and you could hear her for miles.'

Lady Margot smiled. 'Yes, I remember that . . .'

'I'm quite sure that wherever she is, her spirits will be as high now as they were then.'

'I hope so, Logie, oh I do hope so . . .'

But Claire was in a state of blank shock. She had awoken with a splitting headache and a sickly taste in her mouth to find herself in pitch darkness. Feeling around, her fingers encountered the hard cold stone of walls and floor, and when she got to the door she found it to be barred and studded. It was cold and damp and smelled of age, and she had absolutely no idea where she was.

She did a complete circuit of the cell – for that was what it was, she was sure; it was like the ones they had back at Castle Drummond: deep underground some of them, where prisoners had been kept hundreds of years ago. The walls were thick, and when she raised her voice to shout the sound was compressed.

Now don't panic, she told herself, as she once more reached her bed and sat down. Think. She did. Down to her last memory of being lifted from her car and flung into another one, where she had been held down forcibly, the cloth still pressed to her face. Between that last memory and waking up here there was nothing but a blank. Obviously she had been chloroformed before being brought here – wherever here was. Dear God, she thought hysterically, I've been kidnapped . . .

She was still fully dressed, fortunately. She turned up the sheepskin collar of her coat, thrust her hands deep into her pockets. Her gloves had gone. But her feet in her boots, though they were also lined, felt cold. God knows what the temperature is in here, she thought, but it must be around freezing. She curled up into a ball, knees against chest, hands under her armpits. They have to come and check on me soon, she thought. She had no idea what time it was; her watch was still on her wrist but she could not see it. There was absolutely no light. The blackness was so intense it was like being blindfolded. The silence was equally as dense. She held her breath and listened. Nothing. She swallowed hard, quelled the panick screams that threatened to erupt from her throat.

Who has done this? she thought. And in God's name why? And then it clicked. This was what Jake had been afraid of; why he had left her here – safe, he had thought. Oh, Jake, darling, she thought helplessly, you must be out of your mind with worry. But under the calm she was imposing on herself the oily slick of fear was spreading. If they were prepared to go this far, what kind of people were they? Did they intend to hold her for ransom? Force him to back away from the takeover Henry had told her about? 'There ain't no holds barred when it comes to the amount of money that's at stake here,' he'd told her ominously. 'We're talkin' billions of dollars.' Which means they think I'm worth that much to him, she thought. Well, he won't let them get away with it. Not Jake. He hates to lose, and if he thinks he's lost me he'll come out of his corner ready to kill. But she still felt fluttery with apprehension, found she was trembling, and it was not from the cold.

Why don't they *come?* she thought. If I know who they are and what they want then I'll know where I am and what I must do. But the shroud of silence did not lift and eventually she drifted off into a light doze. The sound of the door opening brought her bolt upright to see a figure in the doorway; big, tall and carrying a portable lamp. She blinked, her eyes unaccustomed to the light.

'What is the meaning of this?' she asked as icily as she could, but aware that her voice was not steady. 'How dare you abduct me? Where am I and what do you want with me?'

The man laughed at her imperiousness. 'You never did lack for courage,' he complimented.

Claire's mouth dropped. 'Rory!'

He held the electric lamp higher so that it caught the burnished red of his hair and the Adonis face – looking so much *older*, Claire thought through her shock. There were new lines, and the flesh seemed to have been welded to his face. He was no longer an impossibly handsome man: he was the wreck of one. The eyes were sunken and their glitter was such that she shrank from them. 'Surprise, surprise . . .' he announced.

'I might have known,' Claire said, cursing herself for not realizing at once. Who else but Rory Ballater would do such a stupidly dangerous thing?

'I took good care to see that mine was not the first name that came to mind,' he told her smugly.

Claire's quick brain put two and two together and arrived at the only answer. 'You are involved in what has been happening to Jake's company lately?'

'Only in a modest way.'

'It's nothing to do with Jake, is it?' Claire asked slowly. 'It's me and only me.'

'Oh, he has to be punished too. You know I never forgive transgressions. It's against my principles.'

'Really,' marvelled Claire acidly. 'I never knew you had any. You didn't when we were married.'

His hand swung swiftly, caught her face so brutally it flung her back on the bed. 'Mind your manners,' he chided.

'You'll never get away with it,' Claire mumbled, hand nursing her cheek. 'I'm not unprotected now, Rory. Jake will have your guts for garters for this.'

'You think so? Money doesn't buy everything, as you so boringly kept reminding me.'

'And you made great efforts to disprove.' She remembered with whom she was dealing, controlled her voice. 'Don't be a fool, Rory. Kidnapping is a serious offence.'

'I have merely re-appropriated my property.'

'I do not belong to you, Rory. I have the divorce papers to prove it.'

'Stage-managed by that bitch your mother. She and that powerful little cabal she calls her friends saw me off. *I* did not want it. I stand by *my* promises.'

'Take a good look,' Claire flung at him. 'It's a big pile and every one of them broken!'

She saw his eyes flare and knew another blow was on the way so she scuttled off the bed. 'You're mad!' she stuttered. 'You have finally gone right round that bend you were approaching from the day we were married. What can you possibly hope to achieve?'

'The payment of a debt. I owe you so much. For making me look a fool, for assassinating my character, traducing me to my friends, causing me untold trouble and more than a year's exile. You must be punished for that.'

Claire's stomach churned. He smiled at the look on her face. 'Yes, you remember how I punish, don't you? To begin with, I think a mild one. You have been insolent so must therefore do without your supper. Take it away, Wilkie,' he called, making Claire dart a look towards the door where, in the shadows, she now saw another figure lurking. 'Lady Ballater does not deserve it.' He turned to go. 'Perhaps a little further time to reflect on your situation is called for,' he said.

'At least tell me where I am?' Claire begged frantically.

Rory chuckled. 'Where else but Ballater House?'

'But – the house is closed.'

'I know. We are in the ice house . . . you remember the ice house, don't you? The one in the middle of the lake? The perfect place. Disused for years, falling to rack and ruin. Wilkie and I have prepared it for a long stay. We have food and warmth and a radio – no television, alas, but one cannot have everything. Nobody knows we are here. Wilkie and I came back secretly, at night, after disposing of the cars. No lights are visible – we are underground as you no doubt recall. We used to play here as children, remember? I once locked you in . . . Well, once again you are my prisoner. Did you really think I would let you get away with what you did to me?' He tut-tutted. 'I have had you in my sights for months, now, biding my time, waiting my chance, preparing the ground. When your American paramour went off post-haste to Texas and left you behind I knew my chance to punish you both had come. You for your adultery – and effrontery, come to that; he for his arrogance in assuming he could appropriate my wife.'

'I am not your wife!' Claire shouted it.

'No piece of legal paper can erase a bond that was created in the sight of God.'

Claire gaped at him. 'You *are* mad . . . Since when did you ever believe in anything except money and yourself, in that order?'

This time his hand was so hard it banged her head against the wall. She saw stars and slid to the floor. 'You still have the ability to try my patience,' he barked. 'That will be changed. By the time your American gets you back he will not know you – nor want to, when I am done. However, I intend to see that he pays well for the privilege.'

'You are the one who will pay,' Claire said with ringing ears. 'Jake is a very rich man, which means, as you should know, that he is also a very powerful one. You should not have taken him on, Rory. You don't know him as I do.'

His smile made her realize, with sinking heart, that once again she was wrong. He turned to go.

'At least leave me some light,' Claire begged involuntarily.

'Why? There is nothing to see.'

Which prompted her to glance at her watch. The time was ten-past eight and the date was the 24th. She had been here a day! Rory saw her, and turned to come towards her again. She retreated, but he only bent down to pick up her wrist. 'You will not need this,' he said, setting down the lamp out of reach before proceeding to unfasten the Rolex Jake had given her. 'Mmm . . . what an ostentatious piece it is, to be sure. The Cartier I bought you – the plain gold one with the crocodile strap – was in much better taste. I will take care of this for you.' He slipped it into his pocket, picked up the lamp once more. 'I will let you know the time – if it suits me, of course. From now on, my dear Claire, everything will be as suits me, do you understand?' He went to the door. 'Pleasant dreams,' he said. The door shut behind him and the light went with it, leaving her once more in total darkness.

'You're mad,' she screamed after him. 'Stark staring mad!' Her voice was swallowed by the thick darkness. She subsided hopelessly on the bed again. Only a nutter could have conceived this mad act. He must know that once she was free she would tell everyone who had taken her. If, her inner self said to her, you ever are freed . . . A sob erupted. 'Oh, God . . .' she despaired. 'I'm in the hands of a man who has lost what sanity he ever had . . .' She smeared tears away with the backs of her hands. Punishment, he had said. For getting away. For besting him. In that he was like Jake, who did not like to be beaten either, but Jake was not insane: Jake was not a man to brood on a wrong and let a wish become an obsession. He'll turn over every stone, she told herself, reassuringly. You know he won't rest until he's found you. It's only a matter of time . . . Yes, but how much? her inner self asked. It must not be too long otherwise Rory is going to find out something that I can't afford to have him know.

Oh, my God . . . she wrapped her arms around her stomach. The baby. She had forgotten about the baby! If Rory ever got to find out she was pregnant by Jake she was done for; Rory would not let Jake's child live; not when in his eyes she had murdered his own. She was so terrified she felt sick; her heart was fluttering and her breath coming in gasps. Calm yourself! she commanded. Think of the baby. You have to think of the baby. Rory must not find out. You must not antagonize him. Bridle your tongue. Play the terrified fool he takes you for. You've already lost your supper – not that I could eat, she thought. But what if I'm sick – oh, God, what shall I do? She found she was wringing her hands. Try and reason with him, she told herself. Plead, beg, whatever he wants. But don't let him find out. Whatever you do, *don't let him find out*. Oh, Jake, find me, she prayed. I know you will be looking – but this is the last place anyone would look. You don't even know it exists . . . No, but Iain does. Perhaps it might occur to him. Surely they will connect Rory with my disappearance. Nobody else has any reason to kidnap me . . . and then she remembered the events of Christmas; Jake leaving her behind because he had thought the danger lay in the United States. Which brought her up against what Rory had hinted about being involved . . . How? He had never been to America; he couldn't get a visa.

Well, all right, but Americans come over here in their droves. Probably one of them sought him out – yes, that's it. They went to him and it fitted in with his plans. They caused Jake all the trouble he's had to deal with recently while Rory made his plans for me. Yes, but what would Rory get out of it? He's not the type to do something for nothing . . . I can't work it all out, she thought, I only know that somehow he's involved in the whole picture. If he was keeping an eye on me he must also have known what Jake was doing and where. Perhaps he passed the information on . . . They would pay him for that. That must be what he meant. Well, what I have got to do is say nothing, give no indication that I have the remotest idea, and above all, not let him find out I'm pregnant. But she knew, with a sinking heart, that it would be difficult. If Rory meant to punish her she knew what that meant. Pain, both physical and mental, and how could she protect her baby against that? God, please help me, she prayed. Give me strength, and let Jake find me soon . . . please, God. Let Jake find me soon . . .

The tears she had been fighting burst through her defences; she huddled in a ball on the hard little bed and wept herself into a nightmare-filled sleep.

CHAPTER SIXTEEN

Cora Sue and Ray Beale arrived on the same plane, having travelled together. They knew each other not because Ray was from Oklahoma City, which was where Cora Sue hailed from, but because Ray had worked for Jake in the past, whenever Jake wanted an investigation made of a company or a person. He was a veteran of the Special Forces in Vietnam, where he had been trained in counter-espionage and had become an expert in covert operations. It was only after being trapped behind enemy lines deep in Cambodia, where he had been captured and tortured by the Khmer Rouge, that he had left the army after a long period in hospital, and set up on his own as a private investigator. He said little, heard all, and charged a thousand dollars a day plus expenses, but he was worth every cent. His mother had been Cherokee, his father a wild Irishman, and he had inherited the obsidian black hair and copper skin of the one and the capacity for liquor of the other. He was the only man Jake knew who could not only hold his liquor but could carry it and still tread a narrow line. He was just above middle height and spare, and he was always neatly and inconspicuously dressed. He also spoke quietly; Jake had never heard him raise his voice, and he moved like a breath of wind.

Jake wrung his hand warmly. 'Thanks a heap, Ray. This is a real emergency and it needs your expertise.' He turned to Cora. 'Hi,' he said.

'I thought you'd be needing me sooner or later,' she said confidently. 'What's the situation?'

'I'll tell you as we drive back.'

As always, Ray listened and said nothing. It was Cora who asked the questions.

'So she really has been snatched?' she said, showing her surprise.

'What made you think she hadn't?' Jake asked.

'Well, this is Britain and they're always telling us that we're the crime-ridden society. I just thought maybe she was paying you back for leaving her behind and all.' Jake looked at her and she squirmed. 'Okay, so I was wrong.'

'Yes, you were,' Jake said, with such coldness that she subsided into her corner.

Jake turned back to Ray. 'So far there's not a single lead. Any tyre tracks were covered by the snow and nobody has seen anything untoward. This is the third day and it's like she just melted into thin air. I want you to nose around; find out if there's anybody over here who shouldn't be – you know who I mean – and if there isn't, then find out who has the expertise and know-how to carry out a snatch over here.'

'I filled Ray in on the background to the takeover,' Cora Sue offered helpfully. 'He's got names and situations and possibilities.'

'Good,' Jake said briefly.

He's mad at me, Cora Sue thought. I shouldn't have said that about her playing games . . . But I'll bring him round. And he knows he needs me otherwise he wouldn't have sent for me.

But when they arrived at Castle Drummond – and in spite of herself – Cora Sue was at once impressed and intimidated. Their hostess saw them to their rooms to unpack, and when Cora Sue came down again she found Jake and Ray huddled together over a map of the area.

'Come in, Cora Sue,' Jake said, folding the map. 'I want to talk to you.'

'I thought you might,' Cora Sue said complacently.

'I'll just go and take a look over the place,' Ray said vaguely. He nodded and slipped out.

'So?' Cora Sue asked. 'What is it you want me to do?'

'Tell me who you told about me and Claire.'

431

'Why should I tell anybody?' Cora Sue bridled instantly.

'Because you don't like Claire and you've made it plain you don't approve of our – association.'

'I don't, but that doesn't mean I go around complaining of it to everybody.'

'Did you tell Emmylou?'

'Only that you and – ' Cora Sue swallowed before saying the hated name, ' – Claire were a twosome, that's all.'

'What about your boyfriend?'

'What boyfriend?' But her colour had risen.

'Whoever you've been dolling yourself up for lately. Claire told me you'd been going out all gussied up on your days off.'

'Just because me and Emmylou have been going to some high-toned restaurants is no reason to think I've got a boyfriend,' Cora Sue laughed, but to Jake, who knew her every mood, it rang false.

'Would Emmylou tell anyone?'

'Well, she does tend to run off at the mouth sometimes . . . and she's a real gossip. But if she has, then she'll get a piece of my mind,' Cora Sue said virtuously. 'Let me talk to her,' she added quickly. 'I'll soon find out.'

'No,' Jake said, 'I'll do it.'

'It would come better from me.' Cora Sue's laugh was another counterfeit. 'She's more than a bit scared of you.'

'Me! Why?'

'Well, big tycoon and all that. Let me see if she's been gossiping about you. I'll soon get it out of her.'

Or tell her to keep her mouth shut, Jake thought, but to throw her off the scent he said, 'Okay, you do that.'

And when, as he knew she would, she reported that Emmylou swore she had not said a word, he decided to find out for himself.

All of a fluster, Emmylou denied indignantly that she had gossiped about Jake to anyone. 'You forget, Mr Burns,' she told him primly, 'I work for our Embassy here. We are made well aware of the consequences of idle gossip.'

'What about this man you've both been seeing – did he know?'

'What man?' Emmylou floundered, obviously having been warned off the subject.

'The one Cora Sue has been dolling herself up for.'

'Oh, you noticed,' Emmylou said, subdued. 'I told her you would, but she said you never noticed what she wore.'

I don't, Jake thought. It was Claire.

'Look, Emmylou – I'm in a real bind here. You know what's happened – I'm sure Cora Sue told you.'

'Yes, she did,' Emmylou said with genuine concern, 'and I think it is perfectly dreadful, but I'm sure Mr James has absolutely nothing to do with it. He's a perfect gentleman and so – well – English, and you know how polite they are.'

'Mr James?'

'Robert James. He picked – we met him at the Tower of London and he was so helpful. He knew all the historical background to everything and made it all so much more interesting. So when he offered to take us round, well, we jumped at the chance.'

'And you always went as a threesome?'

There was a short silence then Emmylou said weakly, 'Well . . . no. A couple of times when I had to work he and Cora went on their own – but I am sure he's the gentleman he seems to be. He's very quiet really. He told us he had been ill and I think it's because his family lost all their money. I know about these things, Mr Burns. I don't think he has much of a job – '

'Where?'

'In the City, with a firm of commodity brokers, I think he said, but I don't think he's used to working for a living, that's why I insisted we treat him to lunch and buy his entrance ticket. Quite honestly, I don't think he would be able to afford it otherwise. And since he gives us the pleasure of his company . . .'

433

'Old, young, single, married?' Jake asked.

'Well . . . about forty, I should say, and his wife died a couple of years ago.' Emmylou's romantic soul had her saying wistfully: 'I think he's a very lonely man, Mr Burns. He enjoys our outings so . . . I really don't think he's any more than he seems to be: a nice Englishman who took pity on two American tourists who were a bit out of their depth.' He heard the embarrassment in her voice when she begged: 'You won't tell Cora Sue I've told you all this, will you? She said you would only tease her about it and you know how she is.'

'Yes,' Jake said gravely, 'I do.'

Emboldened by his understanding: 'You see,' Emmylou went on, 'I rather think Cora Sue is sweet on him. He had to cancel out one time and she sulked the whole day – but I'm sure it's not reciprocated,' she tacked on hastily. 'He's never anything but scrupulously formal.'

'Thank you, Emmylou,' Jake said warmly. 'You've been a great help. And I won't say a word to Cora Sue. In return, can I ask you to keep all this to yourself? We – that is Miss Drummond's family and myself – want as little publicity about this as possible.'

'My lips are sealed,' Emmylou answered dramatically.

Damn! Jake swore. Another dead-end. I'm getting nowhere fast. I can only hope that Ray comes up with something because I'm damned if I know where to turn next.

They had another visitor that afternoon. The Dowager arrived without warning.

'Now then, what's all this about Claire having disappeared?' was her opening offensive, her stick rapping the floor. 'I had to hear it from that archgossip Alice Muncrieffe. Why was I not informed of what is, I now understand, a police matter?'

'We thought to keep away any unwelcome publicity,' Lady Margot explained with commendable self-restraint.

434

'I can assure you that Edinburgh is seething with it.' She turned on Jake. 'I can only assume that it has to do with you, young man, for such things are a rarity over here.'

'We don't know anything, Isobel,' Lady Margot intervened.

'But who on earth would wish to abduct Claire? And why? The first name that came into my mind was that rascal Rory Ballater, but I'm told he is abroad.'

'Yes, and Ballater House is shut up.'

'Then one must assume that it is to do with the work Claire does for Mr Burns. America is full of gangsters, is it not?'

'Not any more, Aunt Isobel,' Iain said patiently.

'It was the last time I was there!'

'All of sixty years ago,' Iain murmured *sotto voce* to Jake.

'The police are doing everything they can,' Lady Margot assured the old lady.

'Have you spoken to James Dalziel?'

'Yes. We have done everything that can be done. Now come and have some tea . . .'

At that very moment Claire was also gratefully gulping the hot tea Wilkie had brought in to her, along with a freshly cooked bannock. It was her first food since she had been abducted, and she was ravenous. She had been left alone for what seemed hours and hours, and had spent the time dozing intermittently, and when she was awake, pacing the cell to keep warm. She had been sick once, after she had awoken, so had deduced it was morning by her body clock. She had been careful to do so over in the far corner, and not having eaten it had been mostly liquid, but afterwards, she had taken her spray of *Vent Vert* from her handbag – which they had left with her – and perfumed the air. And later on, she had been awoken by a rustling and a squeaking and had known at once that there were rats, attracted by what they could smell. She did not put her feet on the floor for a long time after that.

When Rory, followed by Wilkie, had come in again, she had been suitably chastened in manner, pleaded with him not to leave her here with the rats and he had been gracious enough to indicate to Wilkie that he could leave the tray.

'What time is it?' she asked in a suitably pleading voice. Time had ceased to have any meaning.

'Just after five o'clock in the evening and today is the 26th.'

Three whole days! Claire was shocked. Dear God, Jake must be going crazy, not to mention her mother . . .

'Drink your tea and eat your bannock – you know how good Wilkie's bannocks are – then we shall have a little talk, you and I.'

Claire's stomach lurched. She knew what that meant. But she gratefully drank the tea and ate every crumb; she would need all the nourishment she could get. Tread warily, she told herself. You know his mood swings; one wrong word and the pendulum goes the other way.

She was sitting there, legs drawn up, sick with nervous tension, when at last the door opened and Rory stood there again.

'Come along then,' he commanded affably. 'I have no intention of joining you in this miserable hole.'

She needed no second bidding; she slipped past him and into the short passage which led into the much bigger room, bright with the light from a big Tilley lamp and warm from the heat of a portable Calor gas fire. There was a wooden table, two upright chairs, a camp bed with pillows and a duvet, a portable radio and a portable gas stove of the kind campers used, with two burners and a small oven.

'All the comforts of home,' Rory said with an expansive gesture. 'And stocked for as long a stay as necessary.' There was a pile of cardboard boxes against one wall filled with tins, boxes and packets. But no sign of Wilkie. 'He has gone out to take the lie of the land,' Rory informed her blandly. 'You remember how skilful a poacher he is . . . If you're lucky, there'll be fresh trout or perhaps rabbit for supper.'

'This is all quite ridiculous, you know,' Claire said, with a calm she was far from feeling. 'They will be scouring the district for me, and the first name that will come to mind concerning my disappearance will be yours. Or is it some sort of joke? Just to frighten me? You know Jake will make it a police matter?'

'He can make of it what he likes,' Rory answered airily, 'and so long as it makes him unhappy I do not care.'

Claire was eyeing the passage she knew led to the stairs, but there was the trapdoor at the top, she remembered. And that was surely shut. He would have her before she had a chance to get halfway up the stairs . . . 'Is it a ransom you are after?' she went on. 'Are you in your usual desperate need of money?'

Rory laughed. 'For once you're wrong. No, I'm not short of money, though any that happens to come my way will not be turned down.' He sounded good humoured, though that in itself could be a deceptive sign, but watching him she saw that he was in a glittering, febrile mood which meant only one thing. Rory was high. Her heart sank, and when he said somewhat impatiently, 'Come along, then, take off your clothes,' she stared at him disbelievingly. 'It's quite warm in here, and Wilkie will not come back until he's supposed to.' He giggled. 'He knows better than to interrupt me at my pleasures . . .'

Claire did not move. She was frozen with terror. Deep down she had known what would happen the moment she discovered who had abducted her, but to hear the words still came as a bitter blow.

'Don't be a fool, Rory,' she said, trying to sound reasonable, though her voice was all but uncontrollable. 'Abduction and rape will mean a much longer sentence.'

'Rape? Of my own wife? A man cannot rape his own wife, my dear Claire.'

'I am not your wife!' Claire said, as distinctly and loudly as she could.

'We were married in the sight of God,' he said solemnly, 'and you know how it goes . . . "What God has joined, let no man put asunder." '

Oh, my God! Claire wanted to laugh. Rory quoting the scriptures! He really has gone round the bend, she thought. Oh, dear God, help me.

'I am entitled to my conjugal rights,' Rory was saying, 'and I intend to have them.' He eyed her curiously. 'Tell me, is your American lover as good as I am?'

You name it and he is better at it than you are, Claire thought, but did not say it. Humour him, she thought. Play along with him. Don't argue and don't fight; that only makes him worse. You have to think of the baby. She sank her teeth into her lower lip. Oh, God, the baby . . .

'I'm waiting,' Rory said, his voice hardening.

Slowly, Claire lifted the heavy sweater above her head, and as she painstakingly folded it, laid it over a chair, Rory rose and came forward. 'Hmmmm . . . you've gained a little weight, I think.' His hands thrust down the thin straps of her lace and satin teddy. 'Yes . . . definitely a little heavier . . .' His fingers lifted, weighed, and Claire made herself stand without flinching. Her breasts were larger; blue-veined, no longer fondant-pink tipped but darker, rosier. She prayed he would not notice that.

'You always had beautiful breasts,' he was saying, in a voice that had become a croon. 'I always liked your breasts . . .' He tweaked a nipple so hard it brought tears to her eyes. 'Are you still as hungry for it as you were? You were such a willing pupil, quite the best I ever had. I made you over from a prim little virgin into a woman who could never get enough of me.' He unzipped her cords, thrust them down impatiently over her hips. 'Yes . . . you have definitely gained a little weight,' he said critically, 'but you are still an exquisite odalisque . . . just what I need to while away a tedious hour or two. One gets so bored hanging around here with nothing to do and I never was a reader . . .' The teddy followed the cords and as she stepped out of them she bent to pick them up. 'Leave them!' Rory commanded harshly. 'I want to look at you.'

Claire stood still while he examined her, first with his eyes then with his hands. 'Like a statue of Aphrodite,' he crooned. 'How naughty of you to allow another man to possess it. I shall have to punish you for that, won't I? You belong to me, you know that, don't you? To me and only to me. I cannot have you allowing any Tom, Dick or Harry the use of what is my property. Do you hear me? Mine.' His voice rose slightly.

Don't argue, Claire told herself. Don't antagonize him. He is spoiling for a fight in spite of the apparent cool. He wants you to provoke him. He is high on cocaine and he is in the grip of an obsession that has left the rails. Remember the baby. If you acquiesce then maybe he won't hurt you.

'I thought you had lost interest in me,' she said.

'Lost interest in *you*? Never. Just because you got away from me doesn't mean that it was a case of out of sight, out of mind. I have never lost interest in you, my dear Claire, or what you were doing. In fact, I have taken a keen interest in you ever since your dragon of a mother filched you from me back in Nice. I have watched and I have waited and I have planned. And now, here you are, here I am and it is going to be like old times.' He smiled. 'You remember them, don't you?' His eyes gleamed. 'I do . . .'

'I remember everything about you, Rory,' Claire said steadily, hoping he would take it the wrong way.

But she knew, with the certainty of hopelessness, that her hope was forlorn when he said, in a voice that vibrated with a curiously thready sound: 'Now . . . undress me . . .'

There were only Jake, Ray and Cora Sue at the breakfast table. Iain had been down earlier and had already left the house, Moira was up in the nursery with her baby, Lady Margot and the Dowager breakfasted in bed.

'I thought I'd take a drive around this morning,' Ray said. 'See how the land lies. Oh – and a picture of the missing lady would be helpful; so that I know what I'm looking for.'

'I don't have one,' Jake said, 'but I'll ask her mother.'

'There are pictures in silver frames all over the place,' Cora Sue sniffed. 'Some people seem to think they impress other people.'

'The Drummonds don't need to impress,' Jake said shortly. 'They are already impressive enough.'

But Cora Sue, feeling both overpowered and overlooked and liking neither, coupled with the fact that in spite of everything she had lost Jake to 'that woman', was unable to keep her tongue on a tight rein. 'They certainly don't lack for friends in high places,' she said cuttingly. 'What is a Chief Constable anyway?'

'What we call Chief of Police,' Ray said amiably, aware of Jake's tight face.

Cora Sue sniffed. 'They don't even carry guns,' she said scathingly.

'Only when they have to,' Ray corrected. 'They aren't needed in this situation – yet,' he added cautiously.

'The British have tight gun laws,' Jake warned. 'You can't buy them through the mail like we can.'

'How come there's a room here full of them then?' Cora Sue sneered.

'They are shotguns and every one of them is licensed,' Jake snapped.

'What about that security guard they shot the other week when that bank was robbed – they used a sawn-off shotgun!'

'Illegally obtained,' Jake said irritably. 'If you're a crook you can get your hands on a gun easily enough.' He looked across at Ray, solidly eating his way through a pair of Arbroath smokies. He was always armed. If he got his gun through customs, he thought. He would ask him later, when they were alone. He didn't want to be breaking any British laws at this stage of the game.

He did not see Lady Margot until lunchtime, because he took Ray over Claire's route ending up in Inverness.

'You think maybe she's being held in a house in town?'
Jake asked.

'I shouldn't think so. I think, with all this remote countryside, she is somewhere where there are no nosy neighbours.
I'll take a look around the – what do they call it – the Glen?
– this afternoon.'

At lunch, Jake asked Lady Margot if she could spare a
photograph of Claire.

'Of course! I have dozens, take your choice . . . I'll get the
albums out.'

True to her word, she brought Jake a pile of them, all
leather bound. 'Let me see now . . . these are the most
recent.' Laying the others aside she handed Jake one that
was full of snapshots. 'There's a nice one taken at Flora's
christening . . . that one. She's holding the baby – she was
a godmother – but it is full face and in colour . . .'

'May I take it?'

'Of course.'

Jake took it out of the album, looked at it a moment
longer and then handed it to Ray. 'That's exactly how she
looks,' he said. It showed Claire sitting on a chair in the
drawing-room, her brother's new baby, in the Drummond
christening robe of Honiton lace and silk, cradled in her
arms. She was wearing an expression that wrenched at Jake's
heart.

Logie came in to say that there was a telephone call for
Lady Margot and excusing herself she went out.

Cora Sue had picked up one of the albums and was flicking
through the pages.

'There is a lovely photograph of my niece that was taken
on her engagement,' the Dowager said. 'Hand me that blue
book, if you please . . .'

Cora Sue held it out. The Dowager found what she
wanted and then handed it over to Jake. 'That one,' she
said.

It was a portrait. Claire was pictured against the painting
of her father in the full dress of a Highland chieftain; she

was wearing a dress of gold tissue, and a string of pearls. There was a dreamy smile on her face, and a glow in her eyes. She looked very young, very vulnerable, very much in love.

'She looks radiant,' Jake said, remembering who had been its cause.

'She was. But it did not last, alas.' Her glance was keen. 'But no doubt you know about all *that*.'

'Can I have a look?' Cora Sue asked. Silently, Jake handed it over. She examined the portrait without comment and then began to turn the pages. Jake picked up one of the other albums, found they contained snapshots of Claire as a child and was soon thoroughly absorbed. It was a sound that Cora made which had him lifting his head to look at her. She was staring down at the album on her lap; her face was doughy and her mouth was working.

Jake rose to his feet. 'What's the matter?' His voice shook because even before she told him, he knew. Snatching up the book from Cora's lap he saw what she had been staring at with such disbelieving shock. It was a picture of Claire and her husband leaving the church after their wedding, Claire gazing up at her husband adoringly, he giving all his attention to the camera.

'Jesus Christ!' Cora Sue shrank back in her chair at the note in his voice 'This is the man you've been seeing, isn't it? Isn't it? This is your Mr Robert James!' In his anger he unwittingly gave away to Cora Sue the fact that Emmylou had blabbed all.

Cora's mouth opened, shut again. It was the Dowager who leaned across to peer at what Jake was holding. 'They are indeed two of his names: Robert James Alexander Rory Ballater.' Her eyes raked Cora Sue. 'In that, at least, he was not lying,' she allowed judiciously.

'This is the man who picked you up, isn't it? The man who took you round all the tourist places and to whom you told every last goddamn thing about me and Claire, isn't it?' Jake was white with fury.

'He told me his name was Robert James,' Cora whined, 'and I had no reason to disbelieve him, did I?'

'Miss Mennenger is right, Jake,' Lady Margot said quietly, having returned from the telephone in time to hear the raised voices and hard words. 'To her, Rory was indeed a total stranger.'

'That's right,' Cora Sue said, sensing sympathy and grabbing it. 'I didn't know anything about Claire's husband, did I? All I knew was that she was divorced from him. You were the one who knew everything . . .' And didn't tell me, was her unspoken accusation.

'I think, Miss Mennenger, that you had better tell us exactly what you told Lord Ballater,' the Dowager said crisply.

'Every last goddamn word,' Jake rasped.

Cora Sue decided to play for more sympathy. 'How was I to know? I had no idea what he really wanted . . . I thought he was interested in me . . .'

'In what you could tell him, you mean,' Jake taunted cruelly. Lady Margot laid a hand on his arm and he subsided, but under her fingers the arm was rigid.

'You see, Miss Mennenger, it means that we now know who has taken my daughter, and why, and I am afraid it is the worst possible thing that could have happened. Lord Ballater is – well, let us be charitable and say that he is obsessed by what he believes my daughter did to him – '

'When it was what he did to her that mattered,' Jake interrupted. 'He's as flaky as they come and then some.'

'Like all the Ballaters,' the Dowager nodded.

'But he lied to me . . .' Cora Sue protested virtuously. '*I* didn't know anything about Claire's ex-husband being certifiable, did I? Nobody told *me* anything.'

'It still didn't stop you from telling him everything he wanted to know, did it?' Jake shouted at her.

'I think you had better tell us all about it,' Lady Margot said calmly. 'Iain, a dram for Miss Mennenger. She has had a nasty shock . . . Perhaps we should all have one.'

Cora Sue sipped her whisky, then, in an aggrieved, self-righteous voice, she told them how 'Robert James' had picked her and Emmylou up at the Tower of London and how it had gone on from there. 'He was such a nice man, and he seemed so kind and friendly – men don't normally take any notice of me,' she said tragically, 'and he is so good-looking and so charming. Even Emmylou was bowled over. He took us places and explained things and gave us tea – it was so nice to have a man around for a change instead of just the two of us . . .' She slid a glance at Jake. His face was a mask and the light eyes were pieces of ice. 'I mean, well . . . he is not the kind of man I'd ever had anything to do with.'

Lady Margot was looking the most sympathetic; the Dowager had the appearance of one with a bad smell under her nose, while Iain was staring into his glass. 'He was always so complimentary about my appearance, said I should wear brighter colours.' She let her voice break. 'I had no reason to doubt him,' she maintained piteously. 'He was a total stranger to me, and a nice one – '

'Who opened you up and shook you out,' Jake said in a voice that lacerated.

'So he knew all about the London set-up?' Ray, who had been sitting quietly by, asked.

Cora Sue threw him a scowl but nodded.

'And when Jake went back to America – he knew why?'

Cora Sue squirmed. 'I called to tell him I was leaving – we had a date . . .'

Jake said, 'And you spent Christmas with him, didn't you? It wasn't Emmylou at all. He was why you didn't want to come to Scotland with me.'

Cora Sue went gobbler red. She took her handkerchief from her pocket and dabbed at dry eyes that were burning, but with anger, not with shame. That two-timing, double-crossing bastard! She was seething. He didn't give a damn about me. It was his bloody ex-wife; always that bloody Claire Drummond . . .

'If you had warned me,' she chided Jake. 'But you and Claire never saw anything but your own selves . . . If you had brought me in on things then it might have been different – '

Jake stared in disbelief as he realized she was already justifying what she had done. He stared at the doughy face as though seeing it for the first time. He would have sworn he knew Cora Sue inside out; now he realized that he had never known her, never bothered to try. She was just Cora Sue, who had been around for years. But even she had her secrets.

Ray had been silent, his mind sorting through facts. Now, turning to his hostess he asked, 'You know this man better than we do. If you were he, where would you think of going to ground?'

'Somewhere familiar,' Lady Margot answered unhesitatingly. 'And somewhere which would give him some kind of a thrill – I mean somewhere right under everyone's noses. He would love that. Rory always liked to fool people.' This with an apologetic glance at Cora Sue.

'His house is empty.'

'As far as we know. That is what old Urquhart, the caretaker at Ballater, told the police. He has the keys and keeps an eye on things when the family isn't in residence. But it's a huge place. I'm sure it would be possible to hide there . . .'

'Could we get in to take a look-see?'

'I could arrange that,' the Dowager said unexpectedly. 'I know Calum Urquhart. He has been at Ballater for years – since James Ballater's time, and I was a good friend of Jamie Ballater. It was in his house that I met my husband, thank God, because at one time I thought I might marry Jamie . . . If I tell Calum to let you look over the house he will let you. But I would advise you to go prepared. If that scoundrel Rory is hiding there, he will not let Claire go without a fight. Like all the Ballaters he has a hot temper.'

Cora Sue rose to her feet. 'I think I will go and lie down,' she said weakly. 'All this has been quite a shock . . .'

'Of course,' Lady Margot soothed. 'Would you like a sedative?'

'No, thank you. I'll be all right.' Head down, Cora Sue scuttled from the room like a crab.

When she had gone there was a silence as everyone considered the enormity of the damage Cora Sue had caused. Then the Dowager said, 'Do not be too hard on that foolish woman, Mr Burns. She is not the kind of woman men make a fool of themselves over, but Rory Ballater is the kind of man who can – and has done – make a fool of any woman. I have no doubt he charmed her into telling him whatever he wanted to know.'

'It just makes me so damned mad!' Jake exploded. 'Cora Sue, of all people!'

'But that is exactly why he chose her,' the Dowager pointed out practically.

'After no doubt stalking her for some time,' Iain put in.

'Exactly. I think we must accept that this is no spur of the moment abduction. It has been planned, and carefully, if I know anything about Rory Ballater.'

Lady Margot shuddered. 'It gives me the creeps to think about him watching and waiting in the shadows all this time.'

'And laying a false trail,' Iain reminded. 'That story about him being abroad.'

'Then what we have to do now is try and find out where he is likely to have taken her,' Ray said in his soft voice. 'Only then can we do something about getting her back.'

'The sooner the better,' Iain agreed, adding in his usual tactless way, 'because if he's gone as far as this he must be completely insane.' His mother looked at him and he subsided, red-faced.

'We must consider where he would be likely to go to ground,' Lady Margot said briskly. 'I do not think it can be far away. Rory knows this part of the world.'

'Then first off we take a look at Ballater House,' Ray said.

'We've got to get her back,' Jake said, and for the first time there was fear as well as rage in his voice. 'God knows what he's doing to her right now . . .'

But it had been done. Claire had once more been returned to her cell, feeling as if she had been run over by a herd of horses. Her breasts were sore, there was a dull ache between her legs and it hurt to move. She had not been able to dress herself once Rory had carried her back and dropped her on to her bed. She merely huddled in a ball and pulled her coat over her, shivering, too shocked to cry. She had not fought, she had offered no resistance, had done her best to see that he would not turn from a man with no more than sex on his mind into the bored, looking-for-thrills maniac who got his pleasure from her pain. He had used her sexually in the most humiliating of ways; he had teased and tormented her, made her do things that took her back to the charnel house that had been her marriage. She had tried to close off her mind, had thought of Jake, contrasting his tenderness, his loving care of her, with the self-absorbed concentration of the man who had her spreadeagled, wrists and ankles tied while he worked on her body. She had thought of the baby, tried to protect it as best she could, especially when he had turned her over on her stomach and proceeded to sodomize her.

It had gone on for so long that she was almost unconscious when at last he had had enough and she sensed he was coming down from his high. He had left the bed, but she had watched through half-closed lids as he went over to the table, where he emptied some white powder from a box before proceeding to rearrange it in matchstick lines which he then snorted up his nose through a straw. She had registered the deep breaths he took, the expansive sigh of pleasure as the drug once more wound his spring tight. She did not open her eyes as he came back to stand over her.

She heard him tut-tut. 'No stamina, – ' he reproached. 'But we have plenty of time, have we not?'

He dumped her on her bed and left her there.

'Tell me about this Rory Ballater?' Ray requested later, when he and Jake were alone.

'He's a psychopath. Put Claire through hell while she was married to him. He likes to inflict pain. He is also an addict. He's got this obsession about Claire because she actually got away from him. He likes to be the one to do that; Claire is unfinished business for him. What scares me is that right now he's finishing her off.'

'The fact that we know he's the one who's got her is a bonus,' Ray pointed out practically. 'Now we have to find out where. Usually, kidnappers go to ground in a place they know; it makes them feel safer. Does he have just the one house around here?'

'As far as I know, yes. But Lady Margot will know – or better still, the old lady. Her main interest in life is what other people are doing. She's got chapter and verse on every family in the Glen – and beyond it.' He frowned. 'I'd rather she wasn't along when we take a look-see at Ballater House.'

'No, it's a help. I've picked up enough to know that she's a lady from the very top drawer with a great many powerful friends. He would probably think twice about doing any-thing stupid with her around – if he's there, of course.'

'The Drummonds are not without that same sort of power and influence yet he has taken Claire.'

'She's a different matter. She's personal.'

'Well, let's take Henry too. He's always handy at times like these.'

'Okay. If Ballater is watching his house it will show him we mean business.'

'What about the police?'

'What about them?'

'This is Scotland,' Jake told him. 'They do things differ-ently here.'

'We're just going to look over the house of a man who was once a part of this family, with the permission of the caretaker, if we can believe the old lady – and I do.' Ray smiled. 'That's one tough old bird.'

'She was born a Drummond,' Jake said simply. 'They have a tough history.'

The Dowager was having the time of her life. She had not had so much excitement, she told them pleasurably, as they drove over to Ballater House, since she was involved in the riots during the partition of India back in 1947, when she and her husband had been trapped in Government House while Muslims and Hindus slaughtered each other outside. The caretaker was waiting by the big gates as they drove up, having been alerted by a telephone call. He took off his cap as he clambered into the back of her ancient Daimler.

'Well, Calum Urquhart,' the Dowager cackled. 'It has been a long time since I set foot in this house.'

'Aye, it is that, your Ladyship,' the old man agreed. 'Many's the high old jinks that went on here before the rot set in.' He was small and spry, and had a face like a walnut, as well as an accent that had a lilt like a song.

'I thought you would have been back on Lewis by now,' the Dowager remarked.

'Oh, I intend to end my days there.'

'Then you had better look sharp,' the Dowager advised affably, 'since you can't have many of them left.'

'Your Ladyship knows I am no older than she is,' he observed with crafty indignation.

The Dowager hurrumphed and drew her ancient sables about her shoulders. 'This is Mr Burns,' she said, nodding to Jake. 'He has a fancy to buy a house in the neighbourhood and I thought Ballater would be worth a look.'

'I've not heard anything about his Lordship selling up,' the old man said dubiously, 'but he tells me nothing any more. Comes and goes, and that not very often. I've not set eyes on him since last summer. I'd hoped he would open up the house for the shooting season, like we used to when he was married to Miss Claire, but he didn't. She was the one who did it all anyway. Aye, Ballater House was a grand place when she had the running of it.'

'You've not seen her either, then?' the Dowager asked casually.

'She did come across to see me at Christmas to invite me to the Castle, and that was the last time. But I heard she was living in London now.'

'And what do you hear of Lord Ballater?'

'Nothing. Only that he's abroad somewhere. I send on any letters – and there aren't many of them – to his bank in London.' Turning to Jake: 'The house is shut up,' he explained, 'but I can let you have a look round.'

'I'd appreciate that,' Jake told him.

'It looks like the Houses of Parliament,' Henry said, as the enormous mass of the house, a Gothic fantasia, loomed up as they rounded a bend in the drive.

'His Lordship's great-grandfather was once invited to Balmoral,' Calum chuckled, 'and so his had to be bigger and better.'

'How big?' Jake asked.

'There're over two hundred rooms.'

'Jesus!'

The windows were shuttered, the islands of furniture shrouded so that they looked like miniature mountains. There was dust everywhere and their feet echoed. The huge hall rose three storeys, its walls hung with paintings and the heads of several twelve-pointers that had been shot over the years.

'Good eating,' Ray observed, of the glassy-eyed deerheads.

'In the old days they'd roast the beast in that fireplace there,' Calum said, pointing to the cavern that yawned on one wall.

'I shall await you here,' the Dowager said, seating herself in the big chair he had uncovered for her.

'Can I offer you a dram?' he asked her. 'There's nothing in

450

the house but I brought a bottle from my cottage. Ballater's Best . . .'

'I accept with pleasure,' the Dowager nodded greedily. 'Off you go, then,' she said, waving the three men away. 'Calum and I will have a chat while you are gone.'

They explored every single room, from cellars to attic. All were empty, furniture draped in dust-sheets. They opened wardrobes, tapped panelled walls for concealed rooms, peered up chimneys, under beds. Nothing. It was obvious that the house had not been occupied for some time. It had the smell of disuse.

It was when they were up on the top floor, in the small cell-like rooms, now used for storage but once the servants' bedrooms, that Ray opened a window to lean out and gaze at the view, which from the top of the house was magnificent. Rolling parklands, stands of timber, acres of lawns, and, in the distance, against the majestic mountains, the gleam of water. He had brought along a pair of binoculars, now raised them to see that the water was a small loch, not much more than fifty yards across, he reckoned, and with a tiny island in the middle. There was what looked like the ruins of a summerhouse at its centre. He swept the island carefully. Nothing.

'There ain't nothin' and nobody,' Henry pronounced, coming in to join them. 'This house is as empty as a drunk's pockets after pay-day.'

When they got downstairs again, they found the Dowager and old Urquhart imbibing a second dram and enjoying a comfortable chat, which seemed to be about a past they both saw through rose-coloured glasses.

'What's that lake behind the woods?' Ray asked the old man.

'That will be the upland loch. They used to hold picnics there; the loch is full of trout. There's an old summerhouse, but it's not been used these many years, and we have no use for the old icehouse any more.'

'Icehouse?'

'Underneath the summerhouse; it was a natural cave but the old Lord had it made into an icehouse before he had refrigerators; the loch used to freeze and they'd cut the ice into blocks and store it there.'

Jake and Ray looked at each other, then Jake turned to Calum. 'Thank you very much,' he said, 'this is a great house but I guess it's too big for me.'

'Aye, it's a rare size, is Ballater House. A dinosaur, His Lordship calls it.' He turned to help the Dowager out of her chair, and as he saw them to the car and locked the big door behind him, Jake slipped him a ten-pound note, which was accepted with the dignity of one who knows he has done a service.

'Well?' the Dowager enquired as they started off down the drive. 'Was your visit of any use?'

'Claire is not there, and probably never has been,' Jake said. 'The dust has not been disturbed.'

'Well, according to Calum, Rory Ballater is. A man of moods, these days, and no telling which one it will be. The last time he was here he brought a couple of women with him who were, according to my informant, no better than they should be, and what went on was nobody's business. Except that part of it was violent, because Calum said that when the women left – and it was in haste – one of them looked as if she had been badly beaten. And Wilkie – he is Rory's thoroughly unpleasant manservant – more or less told Calum that if he did not keep his mouth shut he would be out of a job.' With relish: 'The present Lord Ballater, it would seem, is following in the footsteps of his grandfather, who ended his days locked away in one of the upper rooms with an ex-Sutherland Highlander as his keeper. Bad blood,' she announced with the conviction of one who knows. 'On both sides; James Ballater married a Rothes and they were a queer lot. She was a great horsewoman, but when she took to riding around stark-naked they had her put away.'

The three men looked at each other, all thinking the same

thing. When they got back to the house Lady Margot met them, Iain with her.

'Any luck?' she asked.

'It depends,' Ray answered, 'on what you can tell us about the old icehouse on the island in the middle of the loch.'

But it was Iain who answered: 'Good God, I'd forgotten all about that. We used to play there as children – Rory and my brothers and I. Claire followed us once, I remember, and Rory shut her in. She screamed bloody murder till we let her out.'

'What's it like?'

'A huge cave, but made into rooms; they used to store ice and carcases there. It gets well below freezing in winter because it's under the surface – and very damp.' His face changed. 'Oh, my God! You don't think – '

'It's a possibility,' Ray answered. 'It's a place Ballater knows, it's deserted, it's probably the last place anyone would think of. I only saw it from an upper window.'

'Yes, the woods have encroached on it; they used to be kept well back years ago.'

'Is there a road to it – the lake, I mean?'

'There used to be; probably overgrown by now.'

'Could we get to it without being seen?'

Iain grinned. 'We used to. We weren't supposed to play there.'

'Will you show me?'

'With pleasure! When?'

'Tonight? Better in darkness.'

Lady Margot moved uneasily. 'Do you think that's wise? Shouldn't we tell the police?'

'Tell them what? That we suspect Lord Ballater is keeping his ex-wife a prisoner there? Let us find out for sure, first.'

'How? It's underground.'

'I have my ways,' was all Ray would say.

Lady Margot raised her hands helplessly. 'I don't believe *any* of this,' she said fretfully. 'It becomes progressively more nightmarish.'

'Don't worry, Ma,' Iain soothed. 'Mr Beale is an expert in these things.'

Once it was dark, and it was very dark because there was no moon visible, Iain took Ray, and Jake, who insisted on coming along, to the far side of the Ballater estate, where he led them through a dense patch of undergrowth thick with brambles, which came out at the foot of a wall. 'Once over this the lake is only about a hundred yards away.'

Ray went first, climbing on Iain's broad shoulders, Jake next. Iain remained behind, – 'In case this is the way they go in and out and somebody comes,' Ray said.

Iain nodded. 'There used to be a boat kept tied up by a boathouse, but that was years ago. They're probably using some kind of boat, though. Can you row?'

'I can,' Jake said.

'Then muffle the oars and rowblocks; if Wilkie is with Rory he has ears like a cat. He used to be a poacher – notorious around here. And he is nobody I would care to encounter on a dark night so be careful.' All this was said in whispers, then the two men dropped from sight. And the best of British luck, Iain thought, wrapping the collar of his heavy Barbour around his neck, and shoving his gloved hands in his pockets.

Ray led the way, stepping lightly and carefully, Jake, equally silent, right behind him. The ornamental shrubs had gone mutant and were enormous hybrids, reaching out to snag arms and catch trouser legs, but they soon reached the lake, gleaming only faintly in the starlight. All was silent, but for a faint rustle in the undergrowth as nocturnal animals hunted for food, and the distant mournful hoot of an owl. The island, small and bare but for the ruined summerhouse, was a dark bulk in the distance.

'I don't see any boat,' Jake whispered. 'Do you?'

'At the far end – see, by that flight of steps.'

Jake did not have Ray's Indian eyesight but eventually he could make it out.

'Somebody is there, all right,' Ray murmured. 'But I had best make quite sure . . .'

'You'll freeze to death if you try and swim over there,' Jake hissed. 'The water is already icing over.'

'I thought of that. I've come prepared.' And when Ray took off his cord trousers and heavy sweater, Jake saw he was wearing an undersuit of thick fleecy material. 'They call it a "woolly bear",' Ray grinned, as he rapidly drew on a one-piece neoprene drysuit with an integral hood and boots, which he then inflated from a small cylinder. 'Just the thing for icy water,' he said, as he stepped to the edge of the rotting wooden jetty. 'This shouldn't take long, but I'll make it as quick as I can.' With only a silently spreading ripple he lowered himself into the water before disappearing beneath it.

Jake shivered. It was bitterly cold; his breath hung on the thin air but it was fear for Claire which had his skin crisping. Christ! he thought. What a God-awful place. Trust that crazy to pick somewhere like this.

It did not take Ray long to swim the short distance to the island, where he was careful not to cause the pebbles underfoot to chink. Soundlessly he crept towards the mound atop which the summerhouse stood. Suddenly he stopped, sniffed the air. Food, he thought. He went up the crumbling steps and stepped into the circular building. There was the remains of a bench running along the inside, and in the middle was a trapdoor. He put an ear to it. He could hear nothing, but the smell of food was stronger here; somebody had been using the frying pan. He curled his fingers round the heavy iron handle of the trapdoor and pulled slightly. It gave easily: obviously it had been oiled. The smell of food and warmth rushed out at him; there was a flight of stone stairs and a faint glow of light. He listened, but could hear no sound. And then, suddenly, he heard a woman's voice, rising in a pain-filled shriek that died in a sobbing whimper. Then he heard a man's voice raised in anger, another's answering. Then there was a heavy sound, as if of something falling, and then a rumble as though it had caused a landslide. Quickly he let the trapdoor down again and melted silently away into the shadows. There, he waited, but there was nothing more. Only the silence, the sough of the light wind and the rustle of the trees. Like a wraith he eventually flitted back down to the loch.

When his face appeared out of the water Jake said, 'Jesus, I've been counting the minutes.'

'They're there. I heard them and I smelled their food.' He said nothing about the scream. Cool heads were needed here.

'How difficult is it going to be?'

'There's only the one entrance. I couldn't find any other opening. There's a trapdoor and a flight of steps. I think there's a tunnel leading from that to the icehouse.'

Ray took off his drysuit, and accepting his clothes from Jake he rapidly got dressed, then they made their way back to the wall. 'No, we can't take them now,' Ray said when Jake wanted to go in there and then. 'We aren't prepared. Let's not go off half-cocked, okay? Ballater is a flake and his sidekick is a heavy.'

'I'm mad enough to kill them both right now.'

'That would defeat the object. We have to be able to meet anything they can throw at us.'

Iain agreed with Ray. 'They aren't going anywhere,' he argued. 'And Ray is right; we have to be able to meet them on their terms.'

'Then let's go back and get whatever we need. I want Claire out of there *now*!'

Down in the icehouse, Wilkie heaved the unconscious body of Rory Ballater onto his bed. 'Bloody fool,' he growled in his thick Glaswegian accent. 'What use is she to us if you kill her? Who is going to pay ransom for a dead woman? Except it wasn't ransom you had in mind when you did this, was it? You never intended to get anything out of this but your own satisfaction. Well, I've not done this because of any stupid, useless woman. I did it because there was money in it, and the way you've been using that dust you sniff we need every penny we can get our hands on.' But he bent to peer anxiously into Rory's face, smoothed the tangled red hair back from the lax but still sweating face, tenderly drew a quilt over the naked body, no longer as splendid as it had been but showing the signs of years of careless, unthinking self-abuse. 'Ach, you'll have nothing worse than a sore head. It was for your own good. Haven't I always looked after you since you were a wee'un? It suited me to lose myself in the Highlands and let the Glasgow police chase shadows, and God knows you needed somebody to love you.' He bent down, tenderly kissed the half-open mouth.

When he went back to Claire his manner was different. 'All this is your fault,' he accused her savagely. 'Women are the root cause of all the troubles in this world. You should never have married my boy: no woman should. Not after what that bitch his mother did to him. Is it any wonder he feels the need to pay her back?' His anger grew as he surveyed the ruined face: the livid bruising, the weals, the cuts; but not at the man who had inflicted them. It was all her own fault for getting Rory in such a state. 'And if it was not for the money you'll bring he could do what he likes with you,' he muttered as he sponged away the blood. He tried to force some brandy down her but it only dribbled out of her mouth. She was deeply unconscious, her breathing shallow. 'The sooner we get rid of you the better,' he told her. 'You're no use to us dead.' He covered her with a quilt he had brought and when he went out he left the door open in case she should cry out.

Going back into the main room he tidied up the boxes that had fallen when he had heaved Rory on to the bed, replaced the tins that had been spilled.

Then he sat down by the gas fire and poured himself a hefty dram. 'We shall have to have a little talk,' he told the unconscious Rory. 'God knows I've never begrudged you your little games – wasn't I the one who taught them to

457

you? But I'll be damned if I'll let you throw away our last chance to make enough money to get us away to where I've planned we'd go these many years; where nobody will ever catch up with us. I didn't spend five years in Barlinnie to let you kill the one golden goose that has ever come my way. We need all the money we can get because with you spending £500 a time on that stuff you use it doesna last long. Where would you be without me to think and plan for you, eh? Where are all your so-called "friends"? You've betrayed every single one of them – aye, and me too, but I've not turned *my* back. Who was it you turned to when they threw you out of the army? When they expelled you from school? When they sacked you for embezzling clients' money? Who was it looked after you when your mother did a bunk and your father turned to the bottle? Me, good old Wilkie.'

He drained his glass, refilled it. 'Now we've got a chance to make enough money to last us years and what do you do? Insist on having your little fun. Bloody fool!' he swore again, but he got up to put an anxious hand on Rory's forehead. He'd had to hit him a good'un with one of the iron pans. The bump was a big one but raising an eyelid he saw that there was no concussion. 'You'll have a nasty headache, but maybe it'll make you think on,' he growled with rough tenderness. He covered the body he loved with the quilt. 'Aye, sleep,' he said tenderly. 'Wilkie will be here when you wake up. Wilkie will always be here . . .'

CHAPTER SEVENTEEN

Cora Sue was in her room, sprawled on her bed, availing herself of liberal helpings from the bottle of whisky guests always found placed by their beds at Castle Drummond. After the initial, shattering shock, her self-assertion was being pumped back to its normal stone-crusher proportions, its engine well primed by grievance and twelve-year-old single malt. At first she had felt herself diminished; no more than a speck of annoying dust to be brushed from a coatsleeve. But self-justification soon had her convinced that she had been deliberately duped, that's all. It took a smart operator to fool Cora Sue Mennenger and Rory Ballater was obviously king of the con-men. Those long, dextrous fingers had prized her open before he sucked her dry, but nothing he had said, nothing he had done – and she resolutely stumped away from that road – had been meant. Humiliation about that had at first sent her pacing up and down her room; her face, neck and ample bosom brick-red with fury, and the anger soon obliterated any shame.

How was she supposed to know that Robert James was in reality that woman's ex-husband? Nobody had told her anything about him, so what was she supposed to be – psychic? It was all Jake's fault for getting mixed up with her in the first place. She was at the bottom of this whole, stinking mess. And hadn't he been warned? I told him and I told him, Cora Sue thought self-righteously, but had he listened? Had he hell. She had always prided herself on the fact that Jake Burns listened to her, but this time that woman had him coming and going every which way and the only person he listened to was her. Well, serve him right, she thought triumphantly. That's what you get for not listening to those who really have your welfare at heart.

She poured herself another hefty slug and swallowed it down. Its smoky taste was really quite pleasant once you got used to it, and it was amazing how it helped her to see things straight. But the whisky combined with her rage to course through her veins like a high-octane racing engine accelerating out of control and coming up to a dangerous bend, and as she took it on two wheels she seemed to see the competition miles ahead and dwindling to blurs in the distance. All of a sudden she seemed to be driving past the heaps of arid waste her life had become. I've never had anything, she thought. It was all so goddam unfair. Why hadn't she been given a pretty face instead of one that looked like a mound of freshly risen dough; why did she have to be cursed with a forty-inch bosom and forty-two-inch hips? She remembered how they used to tease her when she was young; how they had called her 'elephant ass'. Claire Drummond had been given it all. A lovely face, a slender yet voluptuous body – and the only two men Cora Sue had ever wanted. Where did I go wrong? she wondered drunkenly. I've led a good life, I've been honest, decent, truthful, clean . . . yet all people have ever done is take from me. Nobody has ever given me a thing. It wasn't me that bastard wanted; it was information. He *used* me. All because he wanted *her*. Jake wants her too. Why? Why couldn't he love me? I'm not that old . . . there's only a few years between us. I know him, I understand him. I got him free of that mealy-mouthed whiner he married. I was the one sent him that anonymous letter about her seeing Charlie Whitman. But did he turn to me? No; he went looking for *her*. Now he can't stand the sight of me. I saw the way he looked at me. She shivered at the remembered revulsion that had been in his eyes, and then afterwards his looking anywhere but at her, as though he could not stand the sight. What have I done to deserve this? she howled at the ceiling. She's got everything and I've got nothing . . . nothing at all . . . ' She poured herself another drink.

Jake too, was pacing, waiting. He could not rest. All he saw as soon as he closed his eyes was Claire at the mercy of the sadist who was Rory Ballater. Inside he was churning, restless, febrile, straining at the leash. He checked his watch again. Eleven-thirty. Another thirty minutes to go. He stopped in his pacing when he heard what must be Cora Sue's voice, raised in what sounded like a howl, but when he listened there was nothing. The house was silent. Everyone in their rooms. Serve her damned right, he raged. Whatever she is suffering she brought on herself for believing that a man like Rory Ballater could be interested in her. Yet on a deeper level he was aware of a feeling of shame. He had always known that Cora Sue had feelings for him, always treated them as invisible, because to be quite honest, he did not know how else to treat them. She was too valuable to fire so he had ignored everything but her capabilities. Now, he understood that Cora Sue had felt shut out; the rejected one with her nose pressed against the window, watching everybody inside having a hell of a good time. She had been ripe to the point of perfection, ready to fall into Rory Ballater's waiting hands. But he could not get anything past the anger he felt, because behind that was the ever-present, gnawing fear about Claire. Which Cora Sue had known. 'You are really off the wall about her, aren't you?' she had asked him acridly. Her smile had been like a scar. 'Serves you right.' It was as if she got some measure of relief from her own pain at the sight of his.

He checked his watch again and looked longingly at the whisky on his bedside table. No, he thought. You went down that road before and it's a dead end. Besides, Ray said no alcohol. You'll need a clear head for tonight's doings.

They had discussed the situation; Jake, Ray, Henry and Iain. The women knew nothing. They thought that the right thing was being done, that the police had been informed and that a rescue operation was being mounted. Which it was, except the police had nothing to do with it. Only the four men would set out at midnight to prize Claire loose from Rory Ballater's grip.

Iain would drive them in the Range Rover. They would use the entrance at the far side of the estate, not far from where they had climbed the wall on their first-night reconnaissance. It was kept shut by means of a length of chain which was padlocked, but Ray was expert at picking locks. They would then drive to within fifty yards of the lake, and Iain would stay with the car once it had been parked in the deep shadow of a clump of rhododendron bushes which had gone wild and grown to over ten feet tall. There he would wait, but in touch with the raiding party by means of the walkie-talkies he and Ray carried. He would alert them should old Urquhart be roused, though Iain was confident he would not hear them since his cottage was over by the main entrance, at least a mile away. Jake, Ray and Henry would then take down the already inflated rubber dinghy carried on the Range Rover's roof, which would be used to row over to the island. Then, Ray leading, they would approach the little pavilion and enter the icehouse through the trap door. Ray would at once tackle Rory, while Henry, immediately behind, would go for Wilkie, leaving Jake to find Claire and isolate her from the ensuing conflict. As soon as the kidnappers were overpowered, they would be tied up, and Ray would stay with them while Jake and Henry got Claire away. From the Range Rover, Iain would use his car telephone – 'never thought it would come in handy so soon' – to call the police and tell them where they would find the men they had been looking for.

'It sounds easy,' Henry had grunted, 'which means it ain't goin' to be.'

'Ballater's a big man,' Jake had warned Ray, 'he can give you six inches and sixty pounds, and from what I know of him through Claire, he'll fight dirty.'

'They taught me how to do that in the Army,' Ray said

dismissively, 'but one tap with this and he'll be out of the picture.' He held up a short black stubby object, shaped like a beaver's tail. It was an American police sap, its thick end weighted with lead powder. 'It's what they call an offensive weapon over here,' he'd grinned, 'but as nobody knows I've brought it into the country, I figure I can take it out the same way.' He had looked at Jake. 'You're sure Ballater won't be armed?'

'Pretty sure. They don't use guns like we do. Their laws are much more restrictive. Even so, I don't want anybody carrying a gun. It could lead to real trouble, and our only aim is to get Claire away. Besides,' he'd added vengefully, 'the way I feel right now these could be classified as lethal weapons.' He'd held up his balled fists.

Now, as he checked his watch yet again, Jake became aware that his fists were once again balled in preparation. He went to his window, pulled aside the curtains a chink and peered out. The sky had cleared somewhat, but the moon, which was coming up to full, emerged only fitfully through heavy cloud. It had stopped snowing, and under the moonlight it was a white, ghostly world. As Jake stared out, he saw a dog fox come carefully out from the trees that bordered the drive, pause for a minute and then trot purposefully towards the rear of the house. Also on the hunt, Jake thought. You and me both. He picked up the whisky, hefted it, then put it down again. He longed for a belt, but the way he felt right now it would explode in his veins. When the soft tap sounded on his door he was across to it in an instant, opening it soundlessly. Ray asked, 'You ready? Time to go.'

'More than ready,' Jake told him, and something in his stance, the hot yet icy flare of his eyes, reminded Ray of a cornered beast eyeing the ready-held net and calculating just where and how to spring.

He had asked Henry to try and persuade Jake not to accompany them. But Henry had refused. 'There ain't no way you can leave him behind. He feels all this is his doin'' and to his way of thinkin' – and mine – Mister Jake has to deal with it hisself.'

'Well, he's paying, so I guess all I can do is play the tune he wants.' Ray had shrugged. Now, he looked at Jake and thought: The sooner this is over the better, otherwise he is going to crack. 'Come on, then,' he said.

Jake closed his bedroom door quietly, followed him down the corridor to the stairs. A light was always left burning in the Great Hall, and in its light, Jake could see Henry waiting. Like them, he was in black chinos and a heavy sweater, and wearing topsiders. Now, as they joined him, he led the way through a green baize door and into the passage that led to the kitchens and the rear entrance. The Range Rover was parked out of sight and sound of the house, a good way down the drive. Iain was at the wheel. Ray checked the fastenings on the dinghy, and then climbed in beside him. Jake and Henry got into the back.

'Ready for the off, then?' Iain enquired.

'Let's get the show on the road,' Ray said, and Iain started the engine. With foresight, he had driven the car on to the six-foot-wide stretch of lawn that bordered the gravel of the drive, so that the soft growl of the engine was the only noise, and then in low gear. Not until they were out of the gates and on to the private road did he open up and turn the car in the direction of Ballater House.

When Wilkie heard the whimpering and pleading yet again he moved restlessly in his chair and turned up the volume on the radio, to which he listened with earphones, but even as he was putting them on, a rising sound of hoarse, despairing anguish had him tearing them from his ears and making for the small room where Rory was alone with Claire. 'God, oh God . . .' Claire cried, her voice high and thin with agony.

'Enough,' snarled Wilkie, barrelling into the room where Rory, naked, was bending over the bed. Claire was sprawled on her stomach, and there was blood on the rounded cheeks of her behind. Wilkie's quick glance registered that Rory's still erect member was also covered in blood, while his face wore a look of gloating joy when he said, 'She has to pay for what she did to me, doesn't she? You agreed with me that she had to pay . . .'

'Not with her life, you bloody fool! What good will that do? We'll not get a penny. We've let them sweat, three whole days. Now we can make our demands, get the money and leave this damned hole in the ground.' Roughly he shoved Rory away from the bed, caught his breath in a hiss when he saw the pool of blood in which Claire was lying. 'Christ! You've buggered her good and proper . . . probably ruptured her inside.' He rounded on Rory. 'You and your fun and games? Just a little sexual orientation, you said. Gross humiliation, you mean! That bloody mother of yours has a lot to answer for.'

'You will not mention my mother.' Rory's voice was a warning.

'I'll mention what I like. I'm not one of your frightened women to be mauled and defiled. Get out of my sight!' He shoved Rory violently away from the bed. 'I must do what I can to repair the fucking damage you've done – if I can!'

But Rory followed him into the main room, stood by the table while Wilkie poured warm water from the kettle into a tin basin, picked up a cloth. 'Take back what you said about my mother,' he said with menace.

'Nothing I could ever say would tell the truth of it! She's a whore, who dropped you and then abandoned you – ' His voice choked as Rory lunged forward to press both hands around his throat. Wilkie clawed at them, but Rory's crazed eyes betrayed the strength in the long fingers which squeezed relentlessly, especially his thumbs, centred on Wilkie's somewhat prominent Adam's apple.

'Nobody says such things about my mother,' Rory told him, in the unnaturally calm voice of the truly mad. 'Only I have that right . . . just as I have the right to punish all her sex; that's all I have been doing, punishing Claire. She had to be punished. She humiliated me once too often.' Wilkie was squirming, struggling, fingers clawing at Rory's vice-like grip. He tried to bring his knee up into Rory's groin, but in doing so he caught the table instead and as Rory arched away the table rose from the floor, tilted and then fell over. Wilkie was by this time sinking to his knees, his face darkening, mouth wide, tongue protruding, eyes popping like eggs from a shell. He was wheezing, trying to enunciate words, managing nothing more than a strained whine of effort. Rory's fingers were insanely powerful.

'Apologize,' Rory told him, still in the same, calm, reasonable voice. 'I allow you a lot of licence, Wilkie, but I will not allow you to be foul-mouthed about my mother. Say you're sorry and I will let you go . . . go on, say you're sorry . . .' He shook Wilkie slightly. The hands that were clawing at his were now doing so feebly, no longer drawing blood with nails that had gouged flesh. 'Say you're sorry,' Rory repeated, but Wilkie's hands had now fallen away and he hung in Rory's grasp, a dead weight.

Rory shook him again, impatiently. 'Will you say you're sorry!' He might have been a nanny talking to a recalcitrant child. 'Wilkie!' He shook him again. 'Wilkie!' Rory frowned, relaxed his grip then removed his hands. Wilkie fell to the floor. Rory looked down at him then nudged him with a foot. 'Come on, now, I've had enough. Come on, get up . . .' Then his eyes took in the table, legs in the air, contents scattered. He let out a howl that bounced off the walls. 'Now look what you've done!' He went on his hands and knees, scrabbling in the dampness of the floor for the white powder that had spilled from its plastic bag. It had been half full; now it contained no more than dust. Frantically Rory searched for a spoon and began to scoop it up, but the floor was damp; he began to sob frantically as he saw his precious cocaine turning into wet slime. All he had, by the time he had scooped up all that was possible, was no more than a couple of teaspoons. 'Oh, my God,' he moaned, on the verge of tears. 'Look what you've done you, clumsy fool!' But Wilkie's

466

eyes were not looking at anything; they were bulging from their sockets in a purple, bloated face which bore the empty stare of death.

'Wilkie?' Rory's voice was suddenly high with fury. 'Wilkie!' He got on his knees beside the dead man, took him by the shoulders, shook him violently. 'Come on, Wilkie . . . enough is enough . . . I need you to go back to the house for the cocaine I hid there . . . Wilkie! Will you stop fooling about!' He sat back on his haunches. 'I don't want to play this game,' he said sulkily. 'And if you don't get up this instant I won't play any more games with you, do you hear? I won't let you love me ever again . . .' He got to his feet, turned to the table. 'I shall count to three,' he said loftily, 'and if you're not on your feet by the time I've counted then I shan't speak to you for the rest of the night.' He righted the table, but did not bother to pick up what had been spilled from it. The teapot had been full, and was lying with its spout and lid broken in the spreading pool of tea that had helped to ruin the cocaine. The whisky bottle was also broken, and the two mugs. 'One . . . two . . . I mean it now . . . three . . .' Rory turned to find Wilkie lying exactly as he had left him.

'Wilkie . . .' For the first time fear instead of anger coloured Rory's voice. 'Wilkie?' He dropped to his knees again. 'Wilkie!' It was a wail. He put a hand to Wilkie's neck, feeling for a pulse. There was none. He laid his ear to the dead man's chest, but there was no reassuring heartbeat. Rory sat back on his heels. 'Why are you dead?' he asked sulkily. 'I didn't hurt you. I only wanted you to apologize. Now what am I going to do?' His face and voice held all the petulance of a child whose game had been spoiled. He shivered. The fire was dying. It needed another cylinder of gas and Wilkie took care of that, as he did all the chores. He was the servant, after all. 'Now look what you've gone and done,' Rory accused again. 'How am I going to manage without you? I can't cook, you know I can't.' He let out a cross breath. 'Really, this is most inconsiderate of you.'

He sat for a few minutes, sunk in thought, then he sighed and got back to his feet. In an almost abstracted manner he poured what was left of the cocaine on to the shiny oilcloth top of the table and scrupulously and carefully knifed it into four matchstick lines. Picking up the straw from the floor he wiped it fastidiously clean on the teatowel that was hung on the small clothes-horse near the fire, then snorted up each line. Closing his eyes he felt the drug wreath through his head and then explode into a white light which illuminated what he had to do. Turning to the body: 'Well,' he said, 'if you are dead you are dead and of no further use to me. You will just have to go into the loch.' He giggled. 'God knows it's deep enough . . .'

He bent to lift the body up by its arms, then he let it fall again as something occurred to him. Carefully and thoroughly he went through the jacket and trouser pockets, abstracted a bunch of keys and what money there was, along with a shabby leather wallet. Opening it he counted the sheaf of notes it contained. 'Why you sly thing,' he chided. 'You *have* got money!' He tut-tutted. Then he looked around the room as if searching for something. 'A weight . . .' he said to himself, 'I need a weight . . .' Then his eyes brightened. He was humming as he went through into the room where Claire still lay, unconscious and unheeding, slowly but steadily losing blood from her womb, and reaching up high on the wall, pulled down a length of the chain that hung from the hooks attached to a band of iron driven into it. In days gone by, carcases had been hung there to be preserved through the winter.

'This should do it,' he said on a satisfied sigh. Draping it round his neck – it was heavy, cold and wet and made him shiver – he left Wilkie lying while he made for the short passage that led to the steps. Carefully he opened the trap-door at their top, shivered as the coldness of the air hit him; it was, he thought wrinkling his nose, unpleasantly fuggy down below. I'll leave the trap open, he thought, let in a little fresh air. He unwound the chain from his neck and laid it on the cracked marble of the pavilion floor. Now for Wilkie, he said to himself. Wrapped in that lot he should sink like a stone. And if anyone asks, he is no longer in my employ. He was insolent, even for him, and I simply could not keep him any longer . . . He giggled again, and then, as he inhaled a pleasurable lungful of fresh night air, he choked on it. In the distance, under the light of the moon as it came from behind a cloud, he saw what looked like a rubber dinghy coming towards the island, and in it were some figures. Three of them . . . He dropped from his knees to his belly, only his head above the small parapet.

Poachers? he thought. Come for the trout. Wilkie had caught several and cooked them in oatmeal. They had been delicious. He peered out, trying to distinguish who they could be. Then, as the moon came out once more, it shone on a head of bright blond hair. Rory's breath drew in sharply. Jake Burns! he hissed the name involuntarily. He flattened himself once more; the marble was icy against his flesh but he was high on cocaine and it did not penetrate; it felt only pleasantly cool. Wriggling backwards he closed the trap, then picking up one end of the chain he carefully hefted the other until it was clear of the ground. Holding it off the floor, arm muscles complaining, he wriggled backwards, out of the pavilion and down the short flight of six steps to the bottom of the small hill. There he pushed the chain under what had once been a growth of honeysuckle, careful to make no noise. Once he was satisfied it was out of sight he ran, knowing he could not be seen from the other side of the mound, to where the boat was moored. His heart was pounding but his eyes were glittering with excitement as he untied it, and entering the water, took hold of the rope and began to swim round the island to where a tangle of overgrown hydrangeas overhung the water. There, he pushed the boat under it and out of sight, following it before pulling the branches behind him. Once inside, he climbed into the boat, his head brushing the bare branches, but out of the water and completely hidden. Then he waited, every sense stretched.

He heard someone say in a breath of a voice, 'Beach the dinghy half-in, half-out of the water.' An American accent, but not Jake Burns's voice. He had heard that once when he had watched Jake being interviewed on television. Then he felt rather than heard them above him, for the pavilion was badly cracked and ready to collapse in on itself at any time. The same voice said, 'Trap's open . . . That could mean one of them is out – stay here while I take a look . . .' After that nothing, though he strained his ears. He smothered a giggle. 'The mouse has flown,' he told them in gleeful silence, 'and neither Claire nor Wilkie will be able to tell you where . . .' But he waited, hardly breathing, listening with ears that were always ultra-sensitive when he was high, and heard the delicate tread of feet as the small island was searched. He had to clap a hand over his mouth when he felt a hand carefully prize aside the thick growth and involuntarily ducked, but it was too thick to see through. The searcher went back the way he had come. 'Nobody up top,' he said.

'Maybe they just wanted some fresh air,' another voice said, 'it must be awful shut-in down there.'

'And they must feel pretty confident otherwise they wouldn't have done it.' Jake Burns's voice was on a tight rein, even though it was, like the others, a mere breath of sound.

'Okay, so let's surprise them.'

Rory felt his grin widening under his hand. 'You are the ones who will be surprised,' he told them, wanting to giggle at their stupidity.

Ray went first, seeming to float down the short flight of steps and into the corridor, at the end of which was a square of light. Flattening himself against the wall he eased towards it and then waited. He could hear no sound that was not usual. Even when they were at rest, people made noises: a shift of movement, a sigh, a sniff, a cough. He could hear absolutely nothing but the hiss of a gas fire. Hefting the sap he burst in through the door, only to stop short. The room was empty but for a body lying on the floor near another door. He did not stop to take more than a glance but moved forward towards the further doorway, fairly confident now that he would not meet any opposition. One glance and he knew. 'I've found her,' he called back, and a moment later Jake was there. He took one look and a cry that was a howl left his throat before he dropped on his knees by the bed. Ray went to fetch one of the lamps, saw that Henry was on his knees by the body. 'Wilkie?' he asked.

'It ain't Ballater, and he ain't been dead long. Strangled.' When Ray went back Jake was holding Claire in his arms, his face a mask of pain. 'She's dead,' he groaned, 'I've lost her, she's dead . . .'

'Let me see . . .' Ray placed his fingers against Claire's throat. 'No she isn't,' he said. 'There's a pulse but it's weak. We have to get her to the nearest hospital.'

'Should we move her?' There was a lightening of Jake's voice but fear had replaced the despair.

'We don't have any choice. She'll die if we wait for help. I don't know how long it will take for an ambulance to get here. Best we get her to the car and make for the nearest hospital. Here . . . wrap her in these blankets. I'll call Iain, tell him to bring the Rover down to the water.'

Carefully Jake swathed her in the blankets Ray brought him, his teeth sunk into his lower lip as he absorbed her condition. It was not until he lifted her that the pool of blood in which she had been lying was revealed. 'Jesus Christ! What in God's name has he done to her?' With the greatest of care he settled her in his arms and then Ray said, 'Hold on . . .' and pulling away the blankets placed the wadded towel he had found between Claire's thighs. 'Okay,' he said. Jake needed no second bidding. He was off at a run.

'Can you make it up the stairs?' Henry asked, but Jake was on automatic pilot; he twisted his body so that he was able to carry Claire up the stairs and out through the trap with all the economy of a ballet dancer performing a tricky lift. But as he stepped out on to the floor of the pavilion one of Claire's arms fell from under the blanket to dangle limply. Henry, immediately behind him, picked it up and put it back.

'Careful!' Jake raged. He was as taut as rawhide; his face ashen, his eyes wild. Henry thought he had never seen such suffering on any human face, and he had seen this one the night Stella died.

'She don't feel nothin',' he soothed, as Jake cradled her. 'And that's a mercy.'

'When I get my hands on that bastard he'll beg for it,' Jake snarled. 'Now where's that bloody boat. We have to get her to hospital . . .' Once down the steps he took off at a run.

'You want I should stay here and wait for the police?' Henry asked Ray.

'No. Just leave everything. If they want us to come back with them then we will. No point in you hanging around. Ballater is long gone by now . . . He probably thought Claire was dead too, and at that, if my knowledge is anything to go by, she is in a bad way. I think he ruptured her internally.'

Henry swore softly as he followed Ray down the steps.

Once the voices had faded, Rory cautiously left his hiding place and crept up the mound to peer over the low wall of the pavilion. In the distance he could see the three figures, and on the opposite bank another one standing by the Range Rover. Then the sputtering noise of the outboard shattered the silence as the dinghy made at full speed for the shore. He waited, shivering now, as the dinghy was pulled ashore and left, and when Jake was helped out with his bundle. Not until the red lights of the Rover rapidly disappeared into the distance did he stand up.

So, Claire was not dead. Anger spread its warmth over his now thoroughly chilled body. Well, that would have to be remedied. But first he needed to get dressed . . . He went back down into the icehouse where he found his clothes and dressed rapidly. He also found an unopened bottle of whisky which he drank from in great gulps, felt it set fire to his blood. He pulled on a pair of rubber boots and then, without a backward glance, went to get the boat.

Claire felt very confused. Between nightmare and waking, unable to escape from one to the other; she had a vision of a bottle of blood hanging above her, of tubes being inserted up her nose and down her throat, of hands probing and testing. She hurt everywhere, and kept begging them not to let her baby die. 'Please,' she moaned, 'don't let him kill my baby, please . . . don't let him kill my baby.' At one time, among the faces she thought she saw hovering above her was that of Jake, looking white and distraught. 'Jake?'

'I'm here.'

'Don't let him kill my baby . . .'

'I won't,' he said, but his voice was as fragile as her own. Then she sank into a whirling blackness. When she opened her eyes again she found she seemed to have left her body; she was up by the ceiling, looking down on herself, lying on a bed, as white as it was, only the bottle of blood and her own hair showing up against the whiteness. The bed was flanked by machines and bottles that dripped into tubes inserted into her nose, arm and body. She no longer felt any pain.

Then she saw that Jake was sitting in a chair by her bed, chin sunk on folded hands that were propped on the bed, his eyes fixed on her face. She called his name but he did not hear her. She called again but still he took no notice. She drifted down from the ceiling and looked into his face. Which was when she saw he was crying; silently and steadily, his tears falling on to his hands from where they dripped on to the white coverlet of the bed. The normally light eyes were filled with despair. Once more she said his name but he did not hear, which was when she knew she would have to go back into her body so that she could reassure him that she was all right. When next she opened her eyes she was looking up at him. Her heart contracted at the grief etched deeply into the sun-burned skin. His eyes were so dark with suffering that they looked like black holes.

'Jake . . .' Her voice was so weightless it was almost non-existent but his head snapped up and it was if somebody had flung back his curtains, so that the light inside him streamed out over her.

'Claire!' His voice cracked a joyous relief. 'Oh, God, Claire . . .' He put his face down on the pillow next to hers and she could feel him shaking.

'I'm all right . . . don't cry, please. I'm all right . . . just . . . so tired . . . so very tired . . .' She tried to lift a hand to touch him but the effort was too much. She closed her eyes and drifted away into a deep, healing sleep.

When she regained consciousness again it was daylight and the room was very bright from reflected snow. She no longer felt muzzy but she ached all over. Her ribs felt tight and her stomach was sore. It was very quiet but she could hear someone breathing. Slowly she turned her head. Jake was still sitting by her bed, grey with fatigue, unshaven, head lolling, but one of her hands was clasped by his, fingers entwined. Lovingly she gazed her fill at the reality to whose memory she had clung as tightly as she could while Rory gave vent to his rage and spite, telling herself that he would get her free, that he would make all this wrong right as only he could. Her fingers caressed the ones she had substituted for Rory's before they began to do things Jake had never done, would never do, was not capable of doing. And so looking, knowing for certain that the nightmare was over, her heavy eyelids dropped again, and on a sigh that told of burdens lifted and safety assured, she fell asleep again.

When she awoke again it was to clear-headedness and the warmth of lamplight. The curtains were drawn, the machines were gone, but she still had a tube in her arm. And she was no longer lying flat, while in the chair where Jake had sat, her mother was immersed in a copy of *Vogue*.

'At your devotions?' Claire asked, astonished at the rustiness of her voice.

The magazine slid to the floor as her mother rose to bend over her, her relieved smile broadening to a lighthouse beam when she saw the lucidity and awareness in the sunken eyes. 'Thank God! Welcome back, darling . . .' Her voice broke. 'How do you feel?'

'Like a herd of elephants stampeded over me.'

'You have been a very sick girl.'

'My ribs hurt.'

'They're strapped. Three of them were broken.'

'I also remember tubes and bottles.'

'You lost a lot of blood.'

Claire was silent a moment, then: 'What else did I lose?' she asked.

'Her mother's eyes did not falter. 'Your child.'

Claire turned her face away to stare at the bright chintz curtains. Her mother drew the chair nearer the bed and possessed herself of Claire's hand. 'You haemorrhaged,' she explained gently. 'There was no way it could be saved. I'm sorry, darling.'

A minute or two passed in silence. 'Where's Jake?' Claire finally asked.

'Sleeping. He was dead on his feet. He has spent almost every minute since you came in sitting by your bed.'

'I know, I saw him.' Claire's voice was tender, which Lady Margot recognized as a good sign.

'He's been out of his mind with worry – so have we all.'

'Where am I?'

'In a private room at the Ian Charles in Grantown – it was the nearest hospital. Jake has had every specialist in the business to look at you and you have had round-the-clock nursing – the very best of care, darling.'

'How long?'

'You have been here six days.'

'How?'

'Jake staged a midnight raid on the island. He and Henry

and a friend – Ray – whom he brought over from America and used to be in the American equivalent of the SAS. It was the Iranian Embassy all over again except that when they got there Rory had flown, leaving you behind. They think he thought you were dead.'

Claire said, 'He had good cause.'

'Well, the police are looking for him now. It's only a matter of time.'

'I hope so. He's quite mad, you know. He was halfway there a couple of years ago; now he has completely flipped. Even Wilkie had a hard time controlling him.'

'I'm afraid he can't have been able to at the end. Wilkie is dead. Jake and the others found him when they went looking for you. He had been strangled.'

Claire's face, a study in primary colours crossed by the black lines of her stitches, over her eyes and around her mouth, still showed her shock.

'Thank God Jake refused to wait any longer,' her mother said on a shiver.

'How did he know where I was?'

'That was Ray. They went to take a look at Ballater House and when he found out about the icehouse he went over to spy out the land and confirmed his suspicion that they were holding you there. It was an inspired hunch, as he would say. I would never have thought of looking there.'

'Rory thought it funny,' Claire said tonelessly. 'Right under your noses.'

'That's what Ray said. He is very well up on the psychology of people who abduct other people.'

'I should like to meet him, thank him.'

'You will, darling. Everyone is anxious to visit. Even Mollie is here.'

'Mollie!'

'She heard what was going on. We tried to keep it as quiet as possible but you know what a gossip Kitty Melhuish is . . .'

'Kitty? Oh, yes . . . I remember . . . she tooted at me when we passed just outside Carrbridge.'

'It's thanks to her that we found out where and when you had been taken. Poor Jake, of course, blames himself.'

'Why should he? It wasn't his fault. Rory was in such a state he would have tried anything to get his hands on me. Besides – ' She sat up and winced as her strapped ribs protested. 'I must see Jake, I have something important to tell him . . .'

'You will, darling. He's only just down the corridor. Let him sleep a while longer; he hasn't had above a dozen hours since you disappeared.'

'Oh, my poor love,' Claire murmured in distress.

'Not any more. I never saw such a change in a man once you were pronounced out of danger. He shed twenty years in a moment.'

Claire's eyes met and held those of her mother. 'You *are* sure it was too late for the baby?'

'Yes, much too late, but not to save you, thank God.'

Claire turned her head away. 'I managed to keep it from Rory but – ' Her voice broke.

'You will have others, darling. You have been gone over by the best in the business and the verdict is that in time, there is no reason why you should not have other children.'

'I wanted this one.'

'I know you did.'

'Does Jake know?'

'Yes.'

Claire burst into tears. Her mother sat down on the bed and carefully gathered her into her arms. 'Let it all out, darling. So much better out than in . . .'

When a nurse put her head round the door Lady Margot shook her head and taking in the scene the nurse nodded understandingly and withdrew. Disjointedly, Claire sobbed out how she had tried her best to protect herself, how she had held on to the thought of the baby and Jake, offered Rory no resistance in the hope that he would get tired and bored. 'But he didn't . . . he would go away and I'd hope he'd had enough but he would come back and I'd know he'd been snorting that horrible cocaine and it would start all over again . . . He was like I'd never seen him before, and I thought I had seen him in all the ways there are. But he's gone over the edge; everything about him has gone to extremes.'

'That's the cocaine,' her mother said knowledgeably. 'I have been asking the doctors about that. Evidently, if you are given to extreme behaviour, the cocaine enlarges those extremes to unbelievable boundaries. They found a spilled amount of it on the floor of the icehouse and they think that it may have been the cause of the quarrel between Rory and Wilkie.' She paused. 'You didn't hear them quarrel?'

Claire sniffed, wiped her eyes. 'No . . . but I know Wilkie was angry. I heard him shouting at Rory.'

'Yes, he was the only one who ever had any influence over him. As Henry would say, they were as thick as cold molasses.'

For the first time Claire smiled. 'Dear Henry . . .'

'He sent you these.' Lady Margot laid her daughter back against her pillows then reached into the cupboard at the side of Claire's bed to bring out a cardboard box. 'He made them fresh this morning.'

They were chocolate chip brownies; two-inch-thick squares. Claire burst into tears again. 'I don't know what's the matter with me,' she wept. 'I seem to have turned into a watering pot.'

'It's natural to be emotional at a time like this, and I for one am glad you are. It's a healthy sign. Now then, what about a nice cup of tea and one of these brownies? Could you manage that, do you think?'

Claire nodded. 'I would love a cup of tea.'

'Then we shall both have one.'

'How is she?' Jake asked anxiously, when Lady Margot went to wake him.

'Emotional, but lucid and eager to see you. She says she has something important to tell you.'

'She can tell me anything she wants,' Jake swore fervently. 'I was beginning to think I'd never hear her say anything again.'

When he stood in the doorway of Claire's room, and she saw the look on his face, she held out her arms, ignoring the pain. His embrace was that of a man seizing a lifeline.

'Hold me tight,' Claire begged, her face muffled against his shoulder. 'I need you to hold me, Jake . . . '

'From now on we are *never* going to be apart,' he told her. 'All this is my fault. Forgive me.'

Claire laid fingers across his mouth. 'No . . . you were not meant to think of Rory as being a potential source of danger. All those "accidents" were meant to turn your gaze elsewhere so that Rory would have a clear field.'

'I should have realized all the same.' Then as what she had said registered he said, 'How do you know Rory was involved in my troubles?'

'He let it slip. He knew all about them and something he said – the way he knew so much about you I knew somebody had been feeding him information. I think it was Charlie Whitman.'

'Charlie!'

'Think about it. He hates you, doesn't he? He has been getting at you one way and another ever since Stella died; he did it through women until you met me and when that happened he tried it on with me, only I wasn't having any. I turned him down the night of the Thanksgiving party, don't you remember?'

Jake smiled. 'Often,' he said. 'Lately, all the time.'

'Once he heard that I'd chosen you he probably decided there and then that it wouldn't do. And he knew Rory, remember?'

Jake looked surprised. 'I didn't know that.'

'But – oh, no, I didn't tell you, did I? We weren't – close – then.'

'When?'

'That time on Nico Constantine's yacht; the first time I
ever met Charlie. He told me he knew Rory through Bruno
de Souza – I did tell you about him, didn't I?'

'The drug baron? Yes.'

'Well, Charlie was once Bruno's lawyer until he found out
how he made his money.'

Jake smiled. 'Is that what he told you?' Then: 'There's
something I haven't told you.' Claire waited. 'It wasn't
Charlie who fed Ballater information. It was Cora Sue.'

Claire's jaw dropped. Jake explained how that had been
discovered. Claire was astonished but unconvinced. 'I still
think Charlie Whitman is involved. Cora Sue wasn't there
the night Stella died, was she?'

'No, but she knows how it happened.'

'But she wasn't *there* . . . the way Rory told it to me he
had obviously learned about it from someone who was. I
asked him how he knew and he just gave me one of those
superior smiles of his. The one that meant: 'Wouldn't you
like to know.'

Jake's face had taken on the abstracted look he wore when
his mind was ticking over.

'Somebody is behind all the "accidents" you've been
having,' Claire argued, 'and Charlie Whitman has both the
knowledge and the means. Who better than him to put Rory
up to abducting me?'

'How would they get together?' Jake asked sceptically.

'Charlie would contact Rory. He comes over here all the
time, doesn't he? And he had already met Rory; already
knew he was obsessed by me. He told me so. They're so
alike, don't you see? It was because I spotted it that I
wouldn't trust Charlie. They are both opportunitists, both
self-serving, both self-oriented. Rory wanted to revenge
himself on me, Charlie wanted revenge on you; what was
more natural than that they should get together and plan
how to do it? Charlie would arrange the various "accidents"
with the object of making you think it was somebody back

home, while Rory would pretend to be abroad – establishing an alibi (and I'll bet you a pound to a penny that Charlie will have an alibi too) but in reality coming back secretly and biding his time, waiting for the opportunity to grab me.'

'But what could Ballater hope to gain? He would know you'd blow the whistle on him the moment you were freed, even if he'd demanded I pay for the privilege.'

Claire was silent. 'I think Wilkie believed there would be a ransom demand, but I don't think Rory ever intended to let me go – not alive, anyway.' She shivered. 'He is quite mad. Terrifyingly so, because he sounds so rational even when he's saying the craziest things . . . and Wilkie had to stop him once or twice. They had a row about it; I heard Wilkie telling him he was letting his obsession get the better of his judgement – but I knew Rory had lost that a long time ago. If you could have seen his face sometimes . . .'

Jake held her as she buried her face in his chest. 'I'd dearly love to smash it to a pulp,' he said tightly.

Over Claire's head his face was intent. *Charlie!* Working with Rory Ballater? It was that far-fetched enough to be possible. Charlie never forgot anyone who might be useful to him, and once he found that Jake Burns was involved with Ballater's ex-wife the wheels would have started turning. It fits, Jake thought. You can't even see the join.

But Charlie *wanted* Claire, he reasoned. True, but since when did Charlie ever let a woman get in the way of what he really wanted? He didn't want either of the women he took from you; he did it just because you did. And Claire had a perception that bordered on what the Scots called 'fey'. An uncanny ability to sense things other people did not even register. If Rory knew what had happened the night Stella died, then only Charlie could have told him. Another plus was that Charlie had both the means and the know-how to cause me the kind of trouble I've had. He knows the oil business because he was brought up with it; he is also a lawyer and he must have a hundred names of men willing to do anything for the right price — which he can well afford.

He put Claire away from him and his smile was wry. 'Charlie Whitman,' he said, in a 'Well, I'll be damned' voice. 'Who was it said that sometimes you can't see the wood for the trees?'

'Probably my mother.'

Jake's laugh was exultant as he hugged her to him. 'Now I know you're getting better.'

'You are the only medicine I need.'

His grin faded as their eyes met. 'I'm sorry about the baby,' Jake said simply. 'Now I see why you were, as your mother said, burning a very bright light.' He saw the one that had been shining in her eyes dim.

'I was saving the announcement until you came back to me.' Sadly: 'I wanted your baby very much, Jake. It was conceived in love.'

'We hit the brass ring first try,' Jake whispered, 'but we'll do it again, you'll see. I can stand losing this baby, Claire. What I could never have stood was losing you.'

'You won't,' Claire promised fiercely, remembering the sight of him sitting by her bed in flat despair. 'I need you, Jake, to make me clean and whole again. What Rory did was — dirty; he degraded and denigrated me in as loveless a way as there is. You and I, we make love in the truest sense of the word. Not just the mechanics of sex, as I now know it always was with him — two people engaged in an act that can be as ugly as it can be beautiful. Rory only ever used me as a vessel in which to empty all the hatred he feels for women. It was always a defilement. I need you to give me back the identity he tried to steal, the way you gave it back to me once before.'

'I will, oh I will . . .' He held her tight. 'When you're well enough I am going to take you away to a place I know; it's small and quiet and peaceful and there is a little house on the edge of the sea . . .'

'Sounds lovely,' dreamed Claire.

'It is . . . the sun shines all day and every day and you can see twenty feet down in water as clear as as a saint's conscience.'

'Mmm . . . wonderful . . .'

He longed to kiss her properly, to express the passion she uncovered in him, time after time, but a talk with her doctors had made it plain that he was to be very careful. 'She may seem bright and cheerful but she has been done a great deal of emotional damage as well as the physical kind. Be as loving as you can, but do nothing that she could construe as sexual.' So he only held her now, kissing her closed and bruised eyes, the lines of stitching; lovingly but chastely. Claire's nurse came in to find them locked in each other's arms and whisked herself out again without being seen or heard. She gave them another five minutes, and when she went back she knocked loudly on the door.

'Sorry to turf you out, Mr Burns, but Miss Drummond has to take it slowl .' Her smile showed twin dimples. 'There will be plenty of c ther times from now on . . .'

Two days later Claire was interviewed by the police. A pleasant, soft-spoken woman who wore sergeant's stripes. She was obviously trained for the job because Claire was able to answer her questioning without strain, from the moment her car was forced off the road to the moment she last lost consciousness. She was not able to be of any help concerning Wilkie's murder, but she was able to confirm that there had been raised voices more than once. 'Wilkie was concerned for my value as a ransom demand,' she said sardonically. 'But I don't think Rory had any intention of exchanging me for money. I think all he wanted was to make me pay for what he considered to be my humiliation of him.'

'Is that what they argued about?'

'I think so, because once Rory had finished with me Wilkie would always come in and see how I was and I could see he was angry, then I would hear them arguing. Wilkie was the only one who ever stood up to Rory; just as Wilkie was the only one Rory ever listened to, but by then Rory was so – so irrational that he was not willing to do so any more.'

'Lord Ballater had a violent temper?'

Claire shivered. 'His rages were murderous . . . that was what made him so terrifying, and the cocaine made him worse.'

The sergeant was making notes in her small black book. 'Do you remember what time it was when you last heard raised voices?'

Claire shook her head. 'I had no watch. Rory took it.'

'I see.'

Something in her voice had Claire asking in outrage: 'You don't think Jake had anything to do with Wilkie's death!'

'No. We know that none of the men who rescued you did. The murderer must have been badly scratched during the struggle; skin and blood were found under the dead man's fingernails, enough to indicate that the hands which strangled him were torn by those nails. Neither Mr Burns nor either of his friends had so much as a graze.' On a smile: 'The only thing of which they stand accused is taking the law into their own hands, but I don't think they will spend any time in prison for it.'

'I should think not! They deserve a medal for what they did in rescuing me!'

'I am afraid that lies beyond our powers,' the sergeant said humorously. She folded her notebook. 'You have been very helpful, Miss Drummond. Thank you. I think we have a complete picture of the man we wish to interview in connection with Mr Wilkie's death.'

'It's a picture of Dorian Grey,' warned Claire. 'A picture of evil,' she explained to the sergeant, who had obviously never heard of it. 'He's as mad as a hatter and dangerous.'

'All you have told us will be taken into account,' she was assured. The sergeant rose to her feet, expressed her best wishes for a speedy recovery, and left.

Within minutes Jake came in. 'Okay?'

484

'Yes, she was very nice. She said they know it must have been Rory.'

'Well, it wasn't me.'

'I know that,' Claire said lovingly.

'Not that I couldn't have killed him had I been given the chance.'

'Leave him to the police,' Claire said agitatedly. 'Don't even *think* of tackling Rory.'

'I don't even know where he is. Probably miles away,' he added, as he saw the look on Claire's face. 'Don't worry, my love, there is a policeman outside your door at all times. Everyone has made it quite plain to the police that Rory Ballater is, as your brother forcibly put it, a nutter.'

Claire shivered.

'You've got visitors,' Jake said cheerfully. 'Iain and Moira are here, and Mollie, not to mention Henry. And messages are coming in by the truckload, as well as flowers.'

Claire glanced around her small room, already resembling the window of Constance Spry. 'So kind . . .' she murmured, eyes suffusing again.

'You can have them one at a time or all at once. Which shall it be?'

Claire's smile lit her face. 'Let's have them all in . . . I feel like company.'

CHAPTER EIGHTEEN

Jake faced Cora Sue over the desk in the study that had been the late Sir John Drummond's favourite room. Lady Margot had given Jake the use of it as temporary headquarters for Burns Enterprises. He had seen little of her, said nothing to her, since the momentous disclosures of the past week. She had holed up in her room, brooding on the injustice of things while constructing a monumental edifice of self-justification. By the time Jake sent for her she was confident that she could get him to see things her way. It was all his fault for shutting her out. If he had warned her, put her on the qv, well then . . . things might have been different. But how was she to know Rory Ballater was a crazy? He had seemed okay to her. She was willing to admit that she had been conned, but that was all. The bottom line was that she had been shut out, kept in the dark, badly treated. The minute she entered the study her first words were to that effect.

'You have to understand, Jake, that I was the last person in the world to expect Claire's husband to set his sights on me. If you had thought to put me on my guard, warn me what he was like . . . but you didn't, did you? You and Claire shut me out. Is it any wonder – '

'That is not the issue here,' Jake interrupted curtly, dumping her excuse in the wastebasket. 'What matters is that you allowed your jealousy of Claire to warp your instincts and get the better of your loyalty to me. You danced to every tune Ballater played but it was Claire who had to pay the piper and for that I am not prepared to forgive or forget.' He picked up a long white envelope, gave it to her. 'Six months' severance pay, for which you have Claire to thank.

I would have bounced you out of here without so much as a cent for what you've done.'

'What *I've* done!' Cora Sue gasped.

'Run off at the mouth to a man who – as you just now pointed out – you knew absolutely nothing about, telling him things that were strictly personal and confidential; making him privy to information he used to cause Claire suffering of a kind you can't even begin to comprehend.'

Cora Sue was so shocked that she was, for once in her life, speechless.

'I want you out of this house by tonight,' Jake said flatly, and then, as his anger got the better of him: 'Didn't you stop to wonder for one little minute what the hell he wanted to know so much for? Just *why* he was so curious about Claire and me?' He shook his head disgustedly. 'I trusted you, Cora Sue; you had a job for life, but all you could think of was what you thought Claire was doing to me. You let that spiteful jealousy of yours get the better of your judgement, and why the hell you were jealous in the first place is beyond me. I know for a fact that Claire was never less than pleasant to you, yet she was top of your shitlist from the moment she came to work for me.'

'Because I had her dead to rights, that's why! I knew what she was after – and has succeeded in getting. You!'

'Which shows how little you understand her. You also overlooked another fact; my private life was never any of your business. Nor did I ever give you cause to think that I saw you as anything other than a damned good secretary. I gave you a free hand; you more or less did things your own way, I trusted you with all kinds of information, yet you spilled it all to a man who read you like a book and saw just how green every damned page was. There is no excuse for what you did, and you know it. If that's your idea of loyalty it's a pretty weird one – but then, everything you ever see is only seen from one angle – your own!'

Cora Sue was by now a deep red, her bosom heaving as though having trouble containing feelings which were threatening to explode. 'Why is it *I* always get to play the heavy? I gave you twelve years of loyalty, but the moment she came on the scene it was as though I'd never existed. It was sickening the way you pandered to her. I saw you follow her around with sheep's eyes, sucking up to her just because she has a family that goes back to God knows when and her mother is the daughter of an Earl, which makes her connected to half the aristocracy. I warned you about coming to Europe but did you take any notice? I did my duty as I saw fit. You are the one who is being disloyal – and to your own country!'

'I think you had better go,' Jake said quietly.

'Don't think I'm not glad to. I'm sick and tired of being shoved in a corner while you got on your hands and knees to her. You ought to be ashamed of yourself.'

'I'm not the one with anything to be ashamed of. Claire is the best thing that ever happened to me. If I had listened to you I would never have met her in the first place.'

'And much good has it done you! You're not the Jake Burns I thought I knew.'

'That's because you didn't know me at all.' Jake paused. 'Just as I obviously didn't know you. Not once have you asked how Claire is doing, not once have you visited her in hospital – where she is right now because of you.' He picked up the envelope – she had left it lying – and threw it at her; it fell to the floor. 'Take your thirty pieces of silver and get out of my sight.'

Burning anger at a rate of knots, Cora Sue stooped to pick it up; she was not going away empty-handed, nor was she going to let him get away with a measly six months' severance pay. She would hit him with an unlawful dismissal suit that would have him bleeding money, and she knew just the man to do it. Charlie Whitman. 'I'm glad to be going,' she told him scathingly. 'I'm not taken in by all this high society crap you've been lapping up ever since we came over here to this has-been of a country. Don't you preach to me about loyalty. Where is yours to your own country? *You* are the traitor! And for what? Just to cosy up to *Lady* Margot and *Lady* Balquidder – rotten snobs the both of them. Don't you realize they look down on you?'

Jake shook his head and there was such pity in his voice, that she flinched when he said quietly, 'You believe that only because you think they look down on you.'

His eyes held hers: steady, unforgiving and filled with something else she found she could not face. She fixed her eyes instead on a point beyond his shoulder. 'I can see I'm wasting my time,' she said loftily, 'and I've got much better things to do with it.' She turned on her heel and stalked out, though what she wanted to do was run.

When Henry came in a minute later Jake was standing by the window, staring out at the distant, snow-covered mountains. 'You want I should drive her to the airport?'

'No. I've done my last thing for Cora Sue.' Henry saw there was bafflement on his face. 'I thought I knew her as well as I knew anyone, but I never really knew her at all.'

'Well, you never bothered to try, did you?' He met Jake's widening eyes steadily. 'She was just Cora Sue; always there, but never really seen.'

'You think *I* did *her* wrong?'

'No. But she does, and Cora Sue ain't nobody I'd want as an enemy. You got enough of them already.' Pause. 'I come to tell you the Chief Constable is here and wants to see you.'

'Okay. I'll be right there.'

He frowned after Henry's retreating back. How *was* I supposed to see her? he asked himself. She was always there, just like Henry said, part of the furniture. Bossy, cantankerous, quick to take offence and suspicious of motives but a damned hard worker and as efficient as an IBM. All right, he thought, so she was possessive. She was the same way with my father, would have married him had he said the word, only he wasn't interested in her either. Cora Sue was not the kind of woman to interest any man. Which was why he couldn't understand how come she hadn't – with that suspicious mind of hers – wondered what the hell a man like Rory Ballater was doing bothering with a fifty-year-old overweight amazon who had all the sex appeal of a Sherman tank.

Claire had tried to tell him: 'Cora Sue feels cheated,' she had said. 'I don't think she has ever had anything in her life that she really wanted. The choicest fruits always went to somebody else; all she had were the small, unripe ones. I think she wanted to be more than she was allowed to be, much more. All she had was you.'

'Me!'

'She worked alongside you, had your confidence, but what she wanted was you. She didn't mind the blondes because they weren't permanent, but when I came along . . . and then Rory threw her back on herself by not meaning any of what he did or said.'

'But I never gave her any encouragement!' Jake protested, aghast. 'Cora Sue was – well – Cora Sue . . .'

'Exactly,' Claire had said. 'Don't be too hard on her, Jake.' She had hesitated, he remembered, looked at him searchingly with those lovely violet eyes, sunken and scarred but filled with compassion. Don't – heap your guilt on her shoulders.'

'But she betrayed me – us!'

'Rory knew exactly how to open her up; he can do that, I know. I think Cora Sue was ripe for a little tenderness. I don't think it was something she had much experience of.'

'She shouldn't have told him,' Jake maintained stubbornly. 'She should have known better, been honest with herself – '

'Oh, Jake, how many of us are capable of being really honest with ourselves? All this is down to one man's crazed obsession, and Cora Sue just happened to be grist to that relentless mill of his.'

'I can't forgive her,' Jake had said, low but final. 'I can't even stand to look at her.' Angrily: 'And I'm not piling her with my guilt. I know I'm to blame for leaving you alone – '

She had laid a hand across his mouth to stop the

self-tormenting words. 'No, you mustn't think that. Guilt festers. It took me a long time to come to terms with mine. What you did you did for the best, and that is all any of us can ever do.'

'But you might have died!'

'But I didn't. You rescued me. *You*. You came looking for me, knowing that Rory was dangerous. That we are here together, now, is because of you.'

He had taken her hands, raised them to his lips. 'All I ask is the chance to spend the rest of my life making it up to you.'

'There is nothing to make up for,' Claire had said patiently. 'All I want is what you are . . .' Squeezing his hands: 'Don't let's carry a load of guilt into our future, please.'

On a long sigh: 'Okay, I'll try.' A little-boy grin. 'For you – anything.'

Except working with Cora Sue, he thought now, as he prepared to go and meet the Chief Constable. Guilt or no guilt, I never want to have to see that face again.

'I just wanted to bring you up to date on how things are progressing,' the Chief Constable said.

'No sign of Ballater?' Jake asked.

'None. He has vanished off the face of the earth. We have had his houses searched again – Ballater House and his flat in London – we have interviewed his friends, had airports and mainline stations watched, even the ports. He hasn't been sighted and it's nine days now.'

'But you are still keeping Claire under guard?'

'For the time being, as long as she is in hospital.'

'We're hoping she will be able to come home in a day or two,' Lady Margot said.

'You think he has somehow managed to leave the country?' Jake asked.

'It's possible. Scotland is full of small fishing villages . . . a small boat, a waiting yacht. I believe he was at one time very friendly with a Mr Bruno de Souza.'

491

'Did Claire tell you about that?'

'Yes, and his yacht has been berthed in Southampton, but it left for France a few days ago.'

'And Ballater could be on it?'

'Perhaps. Mr de Souza was interviewed and denied any knowledge of Lord Ballater's whereabouts, as did all his friends, but it may be a repeat of what happened with Lord Lucan.'

'Who is he?'

'He is wanted in connection with the murder of his children's Nanny in mistake for his wife,' Lady Margot explained. 'That was about – oh – ' she turned to the Chief Constable.

'Ten years ago at least – '

'1974,' the Dowager said with relish, 'since which time he has neither been seen or heard from.'

'You think he was helped to get away?' Jake asked.

'Perhaps,' the Chief Constable said neutrally. 'But I think we must now consider the possibility that Lord Ballater is far beyond our jurisdiction.'

Jake frowned. 'I don't like that,' he said.

'Neither do we, but we must face facts. He had powerful and influential friends, and – '

'One never betrays one's friends,' the Dowager said emphatically.

'Exactly, Lady Balquidder.'

'But he is a murderer!'

'Kim Philby was a spy,' the Dowager reminded, 'and even now we do not know who all his friends were.'

'I don't believe it!' Jake was aghast.

'It is known as "the old school tie" syndrome,' Lady Margot explained.

'Even though Rory was expelled from Eton,' cackled the Dowager.

'Hang on a minute – you're telling me that Rory Ballater may have been helped by his friends to get away, in spite of what he's done?'

'It is a possibility.'

'So Claire has to spend the rest of her life looking over her shoulder? No way!'

'There is no question of calling off the search,' the Chief Constable informed him stiffly. 'We will continue with our enquiries, I assure you.'

'I should damned well hope so!'

'I merely thought you should be made aware that our efforts so far have been unsuccessful,' the Chief Constable said.

'Then I shall just have to make some of my own.'

'You are at liberty to do so, of course, provided they in no way conflict with our own.'

'The only conflict that concerns me is the one Claire will have when she knows that bastard is somewhere out there only waiting a second chance.'

'Even Rory would not be so foolish,' soothed Lady Margot. 'He has no doubt taken himself off to where nobody either knows or cares who he is or what he has done.'

'I don't give a damn if he has dug himself a grave – I want him found and dealt with for Claire's peace of mind – not to mention my own!'

'I can't believe it!' Jake exploded to Claire angrily, when he went to visit her that afternoon. 'It's only been nine days and already they are giving up.'

'No they're not, they're just making it plain that Rory has vanished.'

'What kind of friends has he got, that's what I'd like to know!'

'Rory was always careful to misrepresent the truth,' Claire said matter-of-factly, 'and a lot of his friends believed his version of things. I was never quite accepted by a lot of them, you see, I was just not the type to fit into their circle. High-living, high-rolling, high-profile people who thought they were above and beyond any law except that of loyalty to their own kind – Rory's kind. In a situation like this they would close ranks.'

'I'm not prepared to spend the rest of our lives wondering when and where,' Jake said tightly. 'I've got my own resources. I'll find that bastard if it's the last thing I do.'

'I hope it's not,' Claire said in mock-alarm.

'You know what I mean,' Jake grinned reluctantly. 'You told me yourself he never lets things rest, and once he knows you're still alive he's going to want to change that. God knows he's crazy enough to try it.' With firm decisiveness: 'I want you to give Ray a list of the people you think Rory might turn to for help. Be as comprehensive as you can.'

'It would be a waste of time, Jake,' Claire said patiently. 'Nobody will say anything.'

'No matter; Ray has his own methods. Just give him the names and leave the rest to him.'

Claire sighed. 'All right,' she said pacifically. 'If it will make you feel any better.' She paused. 'And Charlie Whitman? What are you going to do about him?'

'It is being done,' Jake said cryptically. 'Now then, what about you? When are they going to let you come back home?'

Cora Sue arrived back in London still in an incandescent state of vengeful fury. That fucking bitch went from strength to strength. It was just not *fair*. Life was a bummer; all it had ever handed Cora Sue Mennenger was the shitty end of the stick. Well, she'll pay, she vowed, as her taxi dropped her off at the mews house. She'll pay if I have to spend the rest of my life figuring out how. There has to be a way. Too bad that her ex-husband didn't finish her off when he had the chance. He's the one who has my sympathy, married to that scheming doll-face. No wonder he went ape; she drove him to it. I'm glad I told him everything, she thought vindictively. I'd do it all again. I hate you, Claire Drummond. I hate you for appearing on the scene. I hate you for being irresistible to Jake. I hate you for ruining my life. I hate you for *being*.

She leafed through the mail. All for Jake. Nothing for her. Nobody even writes to me, she thought self-pityingly. She went through to the kitchen, took bread from the freezer, made herself a tunafish and mayonnaise sandwich which she wolfed hungrily; anger fuelled her appetite. Then she went back into the library and switched on the TV set because it was time for the news. She sat up when Lord Ballater's name was mentioned. There had been a false alarm in Felixstowe, an east coast port. A man had rung in to say that a red-haired man matching his description had been seen on board a small yacht that was berthed there. On investigation the man had turned out to be a visiting Frenchman, at least ten years older and nowhere as good looking. The police were continuing their search, now in its tenth day, as they were anxious to interview Lord Ballater in connection with the suspicious death of his manservant, Angus Wilkie.

'Anxious to interview,' Cora Sue mimicked disgustedly. 'Always the same mealy-mouthed, "mustn't offend" politeness. We all know he's wanted for murder so why the hell don't you say so?' She was so irritated she switched the set off and flung herself back into the easy chair, where she spent the rest of the evening drinking more than half a bottle of Scotch and brooding on the injustice of life, until she fell asleep.

She woke early, to the sound of milk bottles being placed on doorsteps all along the mews; her head was splitting and her mouth felt foul, but her mind was filled with the bright light of realization; something she had stupidly overlooked flashing on and off like neon. Like where Robert James, aka Lord Ballater, was holed up. It was as though her intake of alcohol had burned away everything but the one, salient fact which would enable her to pay back every last one of those sons-of-bitches — and the arch-bitch herself — for treating her like so much garbage.

She was humming as she went into the kitchen to put the

coffee to drip while she showered and changed, and she ate a hearty breakfast. Then she went through to the garage and got into the little red Mini Henry used when he went shopping.

As usual, when she arrived, the little street was lined with parked cars, but she did not want to leave the Mini there anyway. She parked it a couple of streets away, then walked back. Clever, she thought, as she passed the small neighbourhood shops, their fruit and vegetables piled in boxes outside. Not the sort of neighbourhood where you would expect to find a Lord living, but just the right place for a gentleman who had fallen down the ladder a rung or two. Not downmarket exactly, but a long way from upmarket, and on the wrong side of the river, with the enormous chimneys of Battersea Power Station dominating the skyline, even though Robert had told her that the district was undergoing the process of what the British called 'gentrification'.

She came to the small, white-painted house she had come to know, its well-kept appearance giving credence to that same process of gentrification, contrasted to its shabby counterparts on either side. Checking the four brass-bound card-holders she saw that one still bore the name R. James. 4th Floor. Putting her hand in her pocket she took out a ring holding two Yale keys, one of which opened the front door, which gave on to a small lobby and a steep flight of red-carpeted stairs. Quietly she climbed them, and at the top, coming to the plain white door with the numeral 4, paused a moment.

Her heart was thudding and it was not from the climb. She found she was not so certain now of his reaction. After all, he must know by this time that she knew who he really was. But once she told him she had come to help, show him how he could complete the task he had set himself, she was sure she could win him round. What she had to do was get her words in first . . . Drawing a deep breath she put the key in the lock and entered the flat. Sniffing the air, she smiled. Yes, he had been here all right. That after-shave of his was quite pervasive, even if faint, probably not detectable by anyone else, but she was possessed of a sense of smell like a bloodhound.

'Robert,' she called. 'It's me, Cora. Don't be alarmed. I've come to help. I'm on your side, and I'm sure I can give you a lot of useful information . . .'

Silence. Opening fully the slightly ajar sitting-room door she entered it cautiously. Yes, signs of occupation. A cup and saucer on the table by the window; a jacket slung over a chair-back, a newspaper flung carelessly down on the floor. An old one, she saw, as she stopped to pick it up. A week old. He couldn't be out, surely. Not with every cop in the country looking for him. She went into the kitchen, which opened off the sitting-room. Dirty dishes in the sink, pans with the remains of food, empty tins likewise. She wrinkled her nose. The neat and tidy Robert James had been just another part of a fictional character. She shivered, realizing that the flat was cold, and checking the radiators found them turned off. Shit! she thought furiously. He's long gone. Done a runner, as they say over here. But she still checked the bedroom, just in case he was staying in there for warmth. Nothing except more squalor. Her mood getting uglier by the minute because she felt thwarted, she made for the bathroom, where the door stood partly ajar. But the door wouldn't open any further. Something was jamming it. She heaved with her considerable strength and managed to squeeze through, saw it was a fallen towel wedged between door and carpet. Then she saw what was in the bath. She leapt backwards, banging her shoulder painfully on the edge of the half-open door. Rory Ballater lay there in water that was cold and scummy, head back, eyes closed, looking no more than peacefully asleep but in reality very dead. One arm was draped over the bath's edge; exactly underneath, where it had dropped from lax fingers, lay a plastic bag containing white powder.

Oh my God! Cora Sue stared wide-eyed at her last hope of ever wreaking the revenge she needed so badly. 'You stupid bastard!' she hissed between clenched teeth. 'You've ruined everything! Now how am I going to get even! I was going to use you as you used me but you've gone and left me no place to go.' She felt no pity; once the shock ebbed anger took its place, abetted by her powerful sense of self-preservation. Squeezing back she pulled the door almost closed again, wedged the towel once more. She had not taken off her gloves so there was no danger of fingerprints. Best leave as she had come; unseen. But she waited at the top of the stairs just in case. Silence, as always. She had never seen a soul on any one of her visits. She closed the flat door as well as the street entrance by means of her key, then she walked briskly, forcing herself not to run, back to where she had parked her car. There is one good thing about this country, she thought. Everybody makes a fetish of minding their own business.

She stopped her car on the approaches to Battersea Bridge then got out, the keys to the house and flat concealed in one gloved palm. She walked to the middle of the bridge, leaned over the rail as though admiring the boats tied up at Chelsea Reach. Then she let the ring and its two keys slip from her fingers and drop into the water, where they sank at once. He can stay there until they find him, she thought. It meant that her chance of revenge was gone, but better safe than sorry. She smiled to herself as she walked back to where the Mini waited.

She wanted to laugh at the thought of the nervous people back at Castle Drummond, wondering where Rory Ballater was and waiting for him either to be caught or reappear to try a second time. Let them sweat, she thought vindictively. Serves them damned well right! I could set your minds at rest, I could give you peace of mind, especially that fake-saint bitch, but I won't. I've got my revenge after all, she thought. In this cold weather he won't start to stink for a while yet. They could be in for weeks of strung-up wondering and waiting . . . And the thought was so pleasurable that she did laugh. Once back inside the car she sat and laughed her head off. Then she drove back to Kensington to do her packing.

Bruno de Souza swivelled his chair to where he could look out from the wall of windows in his twentieth-floor offices in the Millbank Tower. He had just been apprised of Cora Sue Mennenger's brief visit to the little house in Battersea, which belonged to him, though it would have been impossible to prove it. He owned the conglomerate which owned the corporation which owned the company which owned the firm of estate agents who managed it, and the basement flat was occupied by a man who also worked for him, whose job was to keep an eye on the people Bruno sent there to hide out for as long as was necessary before being spirited away in one of Bruno's container ships to a far country. As Rory Ballater had confidently expected to be.

'I think it would be in both our best interests,' he had said confidently to Bruno, when they had spoken on the telephone. 'After all, I know a great deal about various "operations" of yours and if the information was to get into the wrong hands . . . But of course, I have no intention of telling anybody anything because I know you will help me in my present predicament.'

'Help you, but of course,' Bruno had agreed smoothly.

'After all, I can still be useful to you,' Rory had hinted. 'And if anyone can help me vanish like a raindrop on the Sahara, you can. Then, once I've had my face attended to by your friend in Rio, we can go on with our – as I'm sure you will agree – mutually profitable arrangement.'

'My dear Rory, by the time I have made the necessary arrangements you will be positively non-existent,' Bruno had assured him.

Self-satisfaction had oozed from Rory's voice as he said smugly, 'I knew you would see the – er – ramifications of the situation.'

'Indeed I do. Now then, you stay where you are – it is quite safe and will do for the time being – and very soon someone will be along to escort you to a departure point where you will be able to wait in comfort until such time as all my arrangements are made.'

As they had been. Arrangements to ensure that Rory Ballater would never get to use the dangerous information he possessed, because while he had been useful – contacts, names, blackmail information – he was also as unstable as a dangerous chemical, likely to blow at any time, and Bruno never allowed even the lightest risk to endanger what was, as Rory had pointed out, a highly profitable enterprise. The man was an obsessive, unhinged by his fixation on a woman who had had the good sense – with the help of a clever mother, Bruno had thought admiringly – to escape from him. Kidnapping, Bruno had thought on a regretful head-shake; rape . . . The last things he wished to be associated with. Rory Ballater had become a liability, and Bruno de Souza never kept anything else but scrupulously balanced books – for public consumption, that was.

So Rory Ballater had been dealt with, quietly and ef-ficiently as always, the liability paid in full. Bruno steepled his fingers and gave his mind to the problem of Cora Sue Mennenger. He had been aware from the beginning of her visits to the little house. His basement tenant had recorded, by means of a hidden TV camera, every visitor to the house, just as hidden tape recorders had later revealed every word said. Bruno had listened to the post-coital gush of infor-mation Rory had extracted from Jake Burns's confidential secretary, a great deal of which he had found useful. He had even thought – which was foolish, he now realized regretfully – that Rory was doing it for the eventual profit of them both. I should have known that obsessed as he was by his wife, he was only thinking of himself, Bruno sighed. Which was why Rory had had to go. Women were for pleasure, diversion, no more. Never to be allowed to get in the way of what really mattered: money and power. That reminded him to have a word with his silent partner. He had stirred waters already badly muddied. Fortunately, what lay at the bottom had not been exposed, but it could have been.

As for Cora Sue Mennenger, she would have to be watched. If – though he doubted it from what he knew of her – she decided to take things further then she too would be dealt with – and he knew exactly how. If she did not, well then, he would leave well alone while keeping her under observation. In the meantime, the little house would be vacated and put on the market. At that time, Rory Ballater's body would be discovered, but not Bruno's connection with his death. The estate agents were genuine, an old established firm. The lease to 'Robert James' was perfectly legal; he had provided references, his rent had always been paid on time. It would be just another sad case of an addict succumbing to his habit.

Besides, Bruno thought, I liked Claire Ballater. She was a marvellous hostess. I would have appropriated her myself had it been – had she been – possible. To tell the truth he had been somewhat relieved when she managed to divorce her husband. She had been too sharp. He had not liked the way she had discovered about the non-existent development and he had warned Rory that must never happen again. So of course, the idiot had had to go and try to have her declared incompetent. He would do it *his* way, Bruno thought distastefully. If he had let me do it mine . . . I should have realized then that he was no longer worthwhile.

But she is, he thought. If she knows that the man she fears is dead, she will bury all she knows of him along with the body – including what she knows of me. If, on the other hand, I were to dispose of her husband in such a way that he remains a permanent loose end, who knows what she might unravel? She and that formidable mother of hers, with her powerful connections to people I have no wish to see poking their noses into my affairs. No, he decided, with all the cunning that had made him rich and ensured he kept getting richer, we will give it another week or so. In this cold weather, the late unlamented Baron Ballater will not be 'nosed' until I order it. Smiling to himself, he reached for his private, scrambled telephone.

Claire returned from hospital to a heroine's welcome and a champagne reception. She was also engaged to be married to Jake Burns.

He had come to take her home, found her all ready and waiting, sitting in a chair eyeing the door expectantly.

'Brought your clothes,' he said, handing over a small case. 'Your mother picked them out.'

'Whatever,' Claire said happily, 'just so as I can get out of a hospital gown.'

'What about all these flowers?' her nurse asked, indicating the vases that crowded every surface.

'Give them to the other patients.'

'But they are still coming in, not to mention the phone calls asking how you are.'

'Tell them I am alive and well and living at Castle Drummond,' Claire said sunnily, as she disappeared into the bathroom. When she fastened the skirt of her tweed suit it hung on her. No wonder Henry kept scolding her to eat more, but she was pleased to see that her face was improving daily. The bruises were pale shadows of their former selves, the cuts were all but healed, and the lines of her stitches fading. Jake had told her he knew a top-notch plastic surgeon who would be able to erase any faint traces that were left.

Talk about a battered bride, she thought, as she combed her hair, and then had to admire her ring again as it caught the light. Jake had presented it to her the evening before: 'Just to make it official.' It was a square-cut, solitaire rose diamond, set in a raised cradle of platinum. Claire had been speechless. 'It out-does Elizabeth Taylor!' she had exclaimed. 'It must have cost an arm and a leg.'

'If you look closely you'll see I'm on crutches,' Jake sighed.

She had flung her arms around him. 'Darling, it's gorgeous! I shall be the envy of everyone!'

'And I've started the wedding proceedings – or rather

your mother has. I have to establish residence, fill in the prescribed Notice to the District Registrar and get hold of my birth certificate – I need yours too but your mother is seeing to that. You have to produce your divorce papers and I have to give proof that I am a widower; then I gather he makes an entry in his Marriage Notice Book which is then open for all and sundry to inspect in case they wish to object.'

'Nobody in their right minds would object to me marrying you,' Claire said lovingly, but for a moment a shadow darkened the brightness of her smile.

'He isn't in his right mind, is he?' Jake asked matter-of-factly. 'Nor is he going to be hanging around here waiting for the chance to object.'

'All the same, I wish he was under lock and key.'

'It's only a matter of time,' Jake said confidently, even though he was sure Rory Ballater was long gone and far away. The enquiries he had instituted had produced nothing. Nobody knew anything or, if they did, were prepared to say anything. All the same, he was not going to leave Claire unprotected until the day he could take her away, not only from Castle Drummond but from Scotland, to the other side of the world where nobody would find them.

Now, as Claire declined the wheelchair and insisted on walking out, he was proud of the way all the nurses came to say goodbye. 'A model patient,' they said. 'Come back any time . . .'

'Not if I can help it,' Claire said, 'except to the maternity wing, of course.' They had all seen and admired her ring.

Henry was waiting at the wheel of the red VW. 'Oh, you got it back then!' Claire said in surprise.

'Didn't I tell you? It was found in a parking lot in Nairn. The police went over it and they only handed it back yesterday.'

He felt her hesitate as Henry got out to open the rear door. 'Bite on the bullet,' he said softly. 'It's like falling off a horse; if you don't get straight back on . . .'

Her smile was an excellent imitation, but she got in the back seat and he climbed in beside her. 'Henry gave it a real valet servicing,' he encouraged. 'Clean as a whistle.' He took her hand, felt her fingers interlace with his. The sooner I get you away the better, he thought, wishing he could do it right now, but she had to return to the hospital in six weeks' time for a final check-up, and her ribs were still taped up. 'A few weeks' quiet convalescence in familiar surroundings, among people with whom she feels safe, then she will be able to go wherever you wish to take her,' he had been told. Only, he thought wryly, not in the sense he longed for. No sex, the doctor had told him. 'Not until she is given the all-clear internally.' And he had once more been assured that there should be no problem with having more children. Oh, well, he thought prosaically, they say anticipation is half the fun . . .

Watching him, Claire thought what a great gift she had been given in this tall, thin-faced man with the light eyes and straight-from-the-shoulder personality. It had taken his pure, steadfast flame to burn through the hate that had soldered her to Rory; now she knew a deep longing to have his love cleanse her of the filth Rory had poured into her. Until then, she knew she would feel like a poor leper, whom people avoided, crying 'unclean, unclean'. It had taken all her courage to get into this car, filled as it was with hateful memories, but with Jake's hand warm and firm in hers, Henry's bulk in the driving seat, she found that it was only a car, after all; something to get them from A to B. Which reminded her: 'Where are you taking me on our honey-moon?'

'That's a secret. All I will say is that we're going where the sun shines and the world doesn't have a membership card.'

'Sounds perfect.'

'It is.' He smiled down at her. 'Like everything else right now.'

*

Later that day, once the homecoming celebration was over, the champagne all drunk, the ring seen and admired, the congratulations offered, when Claire went up to her room to rest she asked her mother, 'What happened to Cora Sue?'

'I gather she is no longer in Jake's employ.'

'Where did she go?'

'I have no idea. Back to London, I suppose, to pick up her things before going back to America.'

'Poor Cora Sue.

'She was more than somewhat indiscreet.'

'Yes, but remember to whom. Rory could always charm the heart out of any woman's body.'

'She still breached a great many confidences.'

'But that's just it. It was because she felt left out that she was so resentful.'

'I think resentment forms a large part of Miss Mennenger's character. Such a *difficult* lady; all prickles and barbs. I think Jake had every right to be angry. She more or less placed you in Rory's hands.' Lady Margot stripped the carved brocade counterpane from Claire's bed. 'Now, you are to rest until tea. Doctor's orders.'

As Claire lay down she realized she was exhausted, even though she had let herself be carried along on the stream of Jake's exuberance, content in his so-obvious happiness. When her mother went back at four it was to find her daughter deeply asleep, so she forbore to wake her. That evening, strength restored, and clothed in the happiness that the look in Jake's eyes swathed about her, she ate a good dinner and was once more the life and soul of the party.

Mollie went back next day. 'Work beckons,' she sighed. 'But I'll be back for the wedding.' Her embrace was warm, if mindful of the still-strapped ribs, but she was conscious of a nagging unease. There was something at the back of Claire's eyes. It's that bastard Ballater, she thought. She knows he's still out there somewhere and she's afraid. Why the hell don't the police get off their backsides and lock him away in Broadmoor? Clive had told her that from what

Claire had described of Rory's behaviour, he would almost certainly be pronounced unfit to plead. That would obviate the need for Claire to go into the witness box and tell a packed court what had been done to her, something she regarded with sick shame, along with an agonizing suspicion that her life was in some way inextricably bound to that of a man she feared, hated and despised, so that she would never be free.

'Take care,' Mollie said brightly now, unable to say more because there was something in Claire's attitude which prevented her. 'See you in six weeks.'

'Yes.' Again, the quick, bright smile; again the emptiness behind it. 'Just six, short weeks . . .' But what she meant was forty-two wondering, waiting days.

After a week of nothing but peace and quiet, Claire found that she was becoming restless. She slept a great deal, she took slow, pleasant walks with Jake, she planned her trousseau, she helped her mother with the invitations – not many; this time her wedding would be a quiet, private affair – she dutifully ate all that was put before her but found she was not gaining weight as she should be.

'She's worried,' Henry confided to her mother. 'It's like she's waitin' for somethin' she is resigned to happenin'.'

'It's Rory. He is still at large. She spends ages sitting at the windows, as though expecting to see him coming up the drive.'

And Claire was having nightmares. Lady Margot heard them, because she had thoughtfully equipped Claire's room with a special baby-alarm, the kind Moira had installed in the nursery, to be used on Nanny's days off. One plug was inserted into the wall socket in the nursery, the other wherever you wanted the sound to reach. And without fail, now, every night Claire relived her captivity.

'I think,' Lady Margot said to Jake one morning after a bad night, 'that you ought to take Claire away now. There is too much here to remind her of things better forgotten.

There are doctors elsewhere who can keep an eye on her, perform the six-weekly going over.'

'I'd like nothing better. I've noticed that she's slowly being wound to another breaking point.'

'Take her far away; wherever it was you intended to take her anyway. But keep in touch; if there are any developments I will pass them on.'

'You are a lady with a bottomless well of common-sense,' Jake told her appreciatively.

He took Claire to a small island in the Grenadines, where he had a little house by the sea; just the two of them. He had had it well stocked with food, and Claire was happy to potter around the doll's kitchen, content to lie out in the sun, to swim in the half-moon bay they overlooked. There was just one bedroom, with a huge king-sized bed, but there was a big couch on which Jake was prepared to sleep, until Claire said practically: 'There's no reason why we shouldn't share the bed; all we're going to do is sleep in it after all . . .' And wrapped in Jake's arms she felt safe. For the first couple of nights she woke, thrashing and gasping, her mouth open in a silent scream, her body slippery with sweat, but the fact that Jake was there to soothe her, sponge her fear-fevered body with cool water, then lie back down with her cradled against him, smoothing her hair, demonstrating his concern and love, calmed her fears and eventually led to nights of undisturbed peace, especially after he had her swimming half the day, tiring her physically, sharpening her appetite. He was careful not to be too demonstrative; he had felt her tense once, when he had let his leash slip for a brief moment, noticed how she stayed out of reach for most of the next day.

There was no phone in the cottage, and they had to drive to the nearest town – Claire always going along – to call Scotland, where for the first few times Lady Margot reported no developments or news. But at the end of their first week, when Jake said, 'I'm going to call your mother, coming?'

Claire was able to say languidly, 'No thanks, darling. I'm too comfortable here.' She was lying on one of the deeply cushioned loungers, wearing a bikini that was no more than two strips of black lastex, revealing a body that was noticeably more rounded, the protruding bones once more cushioned in satiny flesh that had been toasted to an apricot gold.

'Sure?'

She did not open her eyes and her voice was placid when she said, 'Quite sure . . .'

Better and better, Jake thought happily, as he went for the small car that came with the cottage. He picked up the mail first, found there was a three-page report from Ray, which he read intently, eyes widening in delight, finally finishing it with a whoop that had people turning to stare and one old man asking, 'You got good news?'

'The best,' Jake grinned, never expecting that he was about to receive his second gift from the gods in one day.

'Oh, Jake, thank heavens!' Lady Margot exclaimed as soon as she heard his voice. 'I've been dying for you to call, I have the most marvellous news!'

'You too!'

'Rory is dead!'

'*What!*'

'Rory is dead – honestly. His body was found in the bath in a flat, the day before yesterday. Evidently he'd been living there under the name of Robert James, but all the tenants were to be given notice to quit because the house was to be sold for redevelopment. When the agent went round to notify the tenants he found Rory in the bath, dead as a doornail – had been for at least a fortnight, chockfull of cocaine. The police were called, naturally, and it was they who recognized him, but he was officially identified by his mother, who just happened to be in town for a visit – she lives in Switzerland now.'

'This was in London?'

'Yes, in Battersea of all places. The search is off and the case is closed. James Dalziel came over to tell us so himself.

Isn't it marvellous? I can't begin to tell you how relieved I am. I never thought to see the day when I would be happy at anyone's death but I am at this one. And I'm so glad for Claire . . . is she there?'

'Not today. For the first time she felt safe enough to stay at the cottage by herself.'

'Thank God. This will only confirm that she has nothing more to worry about where Rory is concerned – ever again.'

Jake drove back to the cottage with his foot down all the way, leapt out before the engine had stopped and ran round to the front of the cottage. Claire was no longer on the terrace.

'Claire!'

'In the kitchen.' She was preparing chunky pork ribs she had earlier taken from the freezer, turning them in their marinade. 'Where's the fire?' she asked, when she saw his face.

'Right here.' He picked her up, whirled her round.

'What is it?' she demanded laughingly. 'You look like you've just acquired Shell, BP, Exxon *and* Texaco!'

'Much better.' He set her down, drew her to a chair where he sat down with her on his knee. Drawing a deep breath he said, 'I have something wonderful to tell you.'

'I can see that!'

He stared into her eyes, filled with laughter and enquiry. 'Rory Ballater is dead.'

She went very still.

'It's true. Your mother just now told me.' Almost word for word he repeated what had been told to him.

Claire seemed to have shut down. She was so still he shook her slightly. 'Don't you understand? Rory is dead. You don't have to worry about him any more.'

'Are you sure it's him?'

'I told you, his mother identified him.'

'How would she know? She saw him so rarely she must have forgotten what he looked like.'

'The police recognized him too.'

'Did he have a crescent-shaped scar behind his left shoulderblade?'

'I don't know.'

'If he didn't, then it isn't Rory.' She was stubborn.

'But he was found in a flat under the name of Robert James, the name he gave Cora. If it isn't him, then who the hell is it?'

'That's what I'd like to know,' Claire said darkly. 'Who told mother about him?'

'Chief Constable Dalziel. He got the information from Scotland Yard.'

'I won't believe it until I see it,' Claire said flatly. 'You don't know him like I do. He's mad but he's also crafty. It could be a ruse to put us off the scent.'

Jake made up his mind quickly, as always. 'Then the only thing to do is for you to see him for yourself. Are you up to that?'

'Yes,' Claire answered without hesitation. 'If Rory is dead I have to see his dead body; *know* it is him.'

'Then that's what we do. You go pack, I'll go back and call your mother, get her to make the arrangements.'

They flew back that night; a small plane to Barbados, a British Airways jumbo from there to Heathrow. They drove straight to Kensington where Jake found a message from Claire's mother on the answering machine, telling them they were expected at the mortuary the following morning at ten o'clock.

'Are you sure you want to do this?' Jake asked, as he drove her there next morning.

'Quite sure. I need to see his body with my own eyes.' She placed a hand on his knee. 'I have to be quite, quite sure, Jake.' He nodded. 'You think I'm being ghoulish, don't you?'

'Well . . .'

'Unless I am absolutely certain I will never know any

peace. Rory is devious enough to do anything that will help him get what he wants. Me.'

'Okay,' Jake agreed. 'It's just that mortuaries are not very pleasant places.'

'I know all about unpleasant places,' Claire dismissed. She was absolutely certain of what she had to do. Calm with the determination of the dedicated. Under the surface fragility there was a titanium steel skeleton.

They were met by the Superintendent – Lady Margot had obviously had one of her 'words' with the powers-that-be – and conducted to a small room where Rory's body lay on a trestle. His face was uncovered, and their first sight of him was his perfect profile. The face was thinner, made gaunt with the use of drugs, but the red-setter hair was bright as ever, the darker red lashes bright against the waxy whiteness of his face. Claire went right up to him and stared hard at the face. Then she said, 'Could I see his left shoulder, please.'

The Superintendent stepped forward to turn the body by the torso. There, just above the armpit, was a small, pink, crescent-shaped scar. Jake heard Claire inhale deeply. 'Yes,' she said. 'That is my former husband. Turning to the Superintendent: 'Thank you,' she said, and her obvious gratitude was such as to throw him off balance. At that, thought Jake, it is as though she has just sloughed off a very ugly chrysalis. And when she asked the Superintendent, 'Have any arrangements been made for the funeral?' Jake knew that she was testing her wings, waiting for them to dry.

'It's to be a cremation – at Golders Green. The body is being collected by the undertakers this afternoon.'

'Thank you,' Claire said again.

In the car: 'You don't have to go, you know,' Jake said.

'Oh, but I do,' Claire replied calmly. 'I have to see this through to the very end.'

And the first thing she did when they got back was call the crematorium. The funeral was set for nine o'clock on the following Thursday morning.

'You don't have to come if you would rather not,' she said, when she saw Jake's face.

'I'm not letting you go there alone.'

The organ was playing softly as they entered the chapel, which was, Jake saw with surprise, quite well-filled, until he realized that almost every mourner was a woman. Claire walked purposefully down to the front, where a solitary figure swathed in sable was sitting just in front of the coffin, which was piled with flowers. The figure turned and when she saw who it was, the woman smiled and moved along the pew, giving Claire the position of chief mourner. Jake was conscious of a rustle of suprise, whispers, craning heads, and it was not, he thought, because Claire was there in the first place; it was because she was not dressed for a funeral, but rather for some kind of celebration. A superbly cut coat of pure wool in deepest parma violet, with a tip-tilted hat of black mink, shoes, handbag and gloves of softest, shiniest black calf. She looked elegant, assured, and the ultimate in poise. Only her face still betrayed the ordeal she had undergone.

The service was brief, no euology, no fulsome tributes. As the coffin slowly moved through heavy velvet curtains which closed behind it, Jake was conscious that Claire never took her eyes from it. and when it was gone he heard her draw a deep breath, release it slowly. Then, head up, looking neither to the left nor the right, she walked out of the chapel, past all the curious eyes, and into the crisp, fresh air.

The woman in the sable, who had followed, approached Claire to say in a husky voice that was vibrant with an odd sort of amusement, 'It seems we are destined only to meet at one sort of ceremony or another where Rory is concerned.' Her eyes went over Jake in frankly surmising examination. 'How do you do, Mr Burns,' she said, holding out a small hand gloved in silky calf. 'I am Davina Carlyon. Rory's mother.' She turned back to Claire. 'I heard what happened,' she said. 'Bad luck.' Her hard blue eyes held something like admiration. 'I told Rory he was taking on more than he was allowing for.'

'It's a pity you never thought to tell me,' Claire said.

Davina shrugged. 'Would it have made any difference at the time? Oh – before I forget . . .' She opened her crocodile handbag, put in one hand which came out holding a watch. 'This was found in Rory's flat. The inscription told me who its owner was.' Claire took the Rolex from her. Jake had had the words 'To Claire – who has given me the time of my life', engraved on its back.

'Thank you,' Claire said, wrapping her own fingers tightly around it.

'I doubt if there are any other mementoes you would like.' Her eyes went over the fading stitch-lines, the very faint remains of deep bruising. 'You already seem to have more than enough.'

She turned as a man in mourning clothes came up to murmur in her ear. 'Ashes! My dear man, what on earth would I want with ashes?'

'I will take them,' Claire said.

Davina raised her exquisitely plucked and shaped eyebrows. 'As you wish.' She was entirely indifferent. She turned to go. 'I doubt if we shall ever see each other again,' she said frankly.

'I hope not,' Claire said.

Jesus! Jake thought as he saw Davina Carlyon smile in amusement. She is pure asbestos. For the first time he began to understand what Claire meant about Rory Ballater and his mother.

'I did tell you that I was born without the slightest vestige of maternal instinct,' Davina returned, unmoved, 'nor am I a hypocrite. Had I known you retained any interest in Rory I would have left all this to you. He and I had long ceased to have any interest in each other.'

'If it suits you to think so, then by all means do so,' Claire said. 'But now I see where he got his belief from that nothing was ever his fault.'

The hard eyes – the coldest and hardest Jake had ever seen on any woman – did not even flicker. 'I repeat, I am not a hypocrite. One cannot mourn something one never loved.'

'That was the root cause of all his problems,' Claire said.

With a graceful inclination of the head Davina acknowledged the cruel barb, but said, 'In that, Rory was indeed my son. Both of us constitutionally unable to love anyone but ourselves.' Her eyes flicked to Jake once more. 'It saves one such an awful lot of trouble.' Her smile was as hard and glittering as her eyes. Then she was moving in the direction of an enormous Rolls-Royce Corniche, which a chauffeur ushered her into before driving it away.

'So that,' Jake said bemusedly, was your ex-mother-in-law.'

'A cat is a better mother than she could ever be,' Claire said, before walking to where Jake had parked the car. She had not acknowledged a single person there; it was as though none of them existed.

There'll be a high old time at dozens of dinner tables tonight, Jake thought, as he followed her, but when they reached the car a man was standing there. Well, well, Jake thought, it seems every last worm has left the woodwork.

Bruno de Souza bowed, because Claire did not offer her hand, his olive-skinned face wearing the appropriate expression.

'A sad occasion,' he said gravely. 'Rory had such possibilities. I would offer condolences, except that I think, considering recent circumstances, they would be misplaced. Permit me to say, however, how happy I am to see you looking so well.' He turned to Jake. 'Mr Burns.'

'Mr de Souza.'

'I have been meaning to contact you. We have not met, but I know of you, of course – '

' – as I know of you,' Jake countered.

Bruno de Souza's mouth smiled. 'Then you would not be averse to my giving you a ring some time concerning various – mutual interests?'

'Feel free,' Jake assured him. Bruno de Souza bowed once more, then moved away.

'I know you swim with sharks,' Claire said crisply, 'but that one is a Great White.'

Jake said nothing, only smiled.

In the car he asked, 'What are you going to do with the ashes?'

'Dispose of them.'

'You won't be satisfied until you have?'

'No. To the very end, I said, remember?'

'Okay. I'm as anxious as you are to dispose of the remains.'

For the first time Claire smiled. 'I knew you would understand,' she said.

Three days later, Rory Ballater's ashes in a plain wooden box resting on her lap, Claire directed Jake as he drove them to what turned out to be a Council refuse dump, where huge skips stood in a row, piled high with the detritus humanity left behind wherever it went. There, carefully toting the box in her hands, Claire mounted the steps to one of them, where she opened it and poured its contents on to the pile of smashed-up furniture, empty bottles and cans, broken electrical appliances and tattered carpets.

'Ashes to ashes, dust to dust,' she said, as the wind took them, tossed them to settle and mingle with other ashes and dust until they became indistinguishable. Then, throwing the box after them she dusted her hands in a final 'that's that' gesture. 'He's gone,' she said. 'Every last vestige.' She lifted her head, drew in a deep breath of air that was malodorous to say the least, but to her it was obviously clean and pure. She turned to Jake: 'Only one last thing and then I am truly cleansed . . .'

She took his hand in hers, and meeting her eyes he saw and recognized the look in them, felt his heart accelerate. 'Let's go home,' she said softly.

*

When she came into the bedroom he saw that she was wearing the rose-red fall of silk she had been wearing the night of the Thanksgiving party. She had unpinned her hair, brushed it till it gleamed like fine old Burgundy through a candle flame, and as she went into his arms his nostrils inhaled the familiar smell of 'Joy'.

'Complete my cure, Jake,' she whispered, her body warm against him, her lips travelling over his face. 'Love me as only you can.'

'But – it's not six weeks yet – '

'I don't care. *I* am ready – oh, I'm more than ready . . .'

'How do you think I feel?' he asked unsteadily. 'That week on the island was a case of so near and yet so far.'

'We have arrived at our destination now, but for the last, all-important step. I'm ready to take it – I need to take it. I need you to perform the one, last rite of exorcism then I am all yours, for ever and ever . . .'

'Amen,' Jake said huskily, before lifting her in his arms and carrying her to the bed, where he proceeded to demonstrate his love for her, his every touch, word and movement so concentrated with feeling as to absorb and obliterate every act of defilement Rory Ballater had inflicted on her unwilling body. He instigated a mutual giving and taking which lit a fire that consumed every last, lingering trace of what had gone before. Gradually he led her up a rising slope of fulfilment until, attuned by now to every quivering response, he let go and they both went over the edge together. Afterwards, he read in her eyes, seemingly huge in the small, heart-shaped face, a brimming gratitude. Wordlessly he gathered her to him; there was no need to speak. He heard her sigh once, then, even as she closed her eyes, she was deeply, satisfyingly, healingly asleep. He settled her more comfortably, feeling the utter relaxation of her body, that of one who knew she was, finally and for ever, safe, and letting his own heavy lids drift, as always, followed her.

EPILOGUE

Consciously making an entrance, Margot Drummond slowly descended the big cantilevered staircase that rose from the huge, window-walled living-room of the remodelled ranch house of the Burns spread some twenty miles from Cimarron. Seeing her coming, Jake halted his nervous pacing in mid-stride, stood waiting as she approached, with a look that was prayerful in its intensity. His mother-in-law's smile was radiant as she transferred the shawl-wrapped bundle she was carrying from her arms to his. 'Allow me to introduce you to your daughter. All of five minutes old and weighing in at seven pounds four ounces.'

Reverently accepting her offering as if being handed the Holy Grail, Jake asked quickly, 'Claire?'

'Dead tired but enormously pleased with herself. You can go up, but my instructions were that you were to see *her* first.' She moved aside the cobweb folds of the silk shawl that the Dowager had crocheted herself. 'Isn't she perfect?'

Jake's awed expression made it plain that he thought her incredible, from the floss of red-gold, cornsilk hair to the darker red lashes that lay on her flower-petal cheeks like feathers. As he gazed those lashes fluttered and his daughter yawned hugely before cautiously raising them to reveal that she had inherited her mother's eyes: large, lustrous and of a deep, pansy purple. 'Wow!' Jake breathed.

'Well done!' his mother-in-law congratulated, bestowing a hug and a kiss. 'She's going to be tall, like you. She measured twenty inches! And a true strawberry blonde. What you have here, my dear Jake, is a potential heart-breaker.'

'She's already done for mine.'

'Then why not go up and tell Claire so.' Fondly she watched him tote his precious bundle back up the stairs, then she went to tell Henry that he could open up the champagne.

Upstairs, Claire was exhausted but happy. The baby had not been due for another week, by which time they should have been back in San Francisco, where the headquarters of Burns Enterprises were now located, and where Jake had made exact arrangements for the birth months before. They had brought her mother to Cimarron to take a look at the alterations and extensions Jake had made to the old ranch-house, she having arrived from Scotland a couple of days earlier.

'You have a genius for calculating ripe times,' Claire had told her thankfully through gritted teeth, as Jake took off at a run to drive into Cimarron for the doctor. 'Jake has made so many checked and double-checked arrangements for this baby; wouldn't you know it would decide to upset every last one of them?'

'Babies do have that tendency,' agreed her mother, calmly taking charge, as usual. Jake had returned with the doctor, in a state of wild-eyed fright, only to be told that everything was proceeding normally, and that if Lady Margot was any judge, it would be some time yet. Claire was fine and he could stay with her if he wanted to. But he could not stand to see her in pain. Claire had refused all and any high-tech aids. 'No drugs, no epidurals – and no caesarian either. Where I come from they are a last resort, not a convenience. Labour, in my books, means exactly that: damned hard work.' So he had retreated downstairs to pace the living-room, drinking pots and pots of the black coffee Henry kept bringing him, becoming progressively more unwound as the hours wore on. 'First babies never hurry,' his mother-in-law had reassured him.

'We shouldn't have come. We should have stayed in San Francisco.'

'Every one of my four children was born at Castle Drummond,' Lady Margot said, 'and look how they turned out.'

Claire's first thought, once she knew she had a healthy child, was for him. 'For God's sake, Mummy, go and put him out of his misery,' she had begged. Now, at the sight of his face as he came into the bedroom – where the new bed had, as Claire put it, been christened too – she felt her throat tighten at the look on his face.

'Well?' she asked.

He placed the sleeping baby on the bed by her, bent over it to kiss the mouth she raised to him. 'The very best anniversary present you could have given me,' he said.

'An unintentional one.'

'I wonder. I think she knew it was one whole year to the day since we got married.'

'Don't forget the whole thing would have been inconceivable without you.'

He laughed. 'Mine was the easiest – and the nicest – part. You are the one who has done all the work.' His look was intent as it went over her; face wiped clean of sweat, damp hair brushed and tidy, colour restored, eyes bright. 'You sure you're okay?'

'Never better. Mind you, if you had asked me thirty minutes ago . . . but on the whole, it was well worth it, don't you think?'

Jake's look as he gazed down at his daughter was one of such bemused happiness that her eyes filled again, but she was saved by the doctor coming out of the bathroom. 'Well, Jake?' He was an old friend. 'I never expected I'd be around to help your daughter into the world. I told your wife you were one of the very first deliveries I made. This makes something like three hundred in all. A nice retirement present.'

'Thank God you were still here. You were the first name that came into my mind.'

'Well now that yours is eased, I'm off to join your mother-in-law in a quaint old Scottish custom she calls "wetting the baby's head" except it's my throat that gets the liquid. You can have five minutes, then Claire has to rest. She's had a long, hard day.'

'Don't I know it!'

The doctor's nurse followed him out.

Still bemused, Jake said wonderingly, 'What have we made, between us?' The light eyes were crystal clear when he said, 'We must do it again.'

'I don't doubt it for a minute.'

'She is so incredibly beautiful – like her mother.'

'Our next will be handsome – like his father.'

The baby stirred, stretched out a hand which opened up, fingers spread. Jake inserted a forefinger and the fingers closed, grasped, clung. 'Will you look at those hands? And those nails? Miniature but flawless! She's an absolute miracle.'

Claire winced. 'Miss Miracle Burns? Even allowing for American names – and that is some allowance, believe me – I don't think that's quite right, do you? I thought perhaps – Stella?'

Jake's head came up, eyes meeting hers. What he saw there made his glitter even more brightly. 'Have I told you lately that I adore you?'

'Yes, but you can always do it again.'

'I mean it, Claire. You changed my life.'

'What about what you did for mine?'

'I thought I'd lost all hope of something like this. You gave me my second chance.'

'Likewise.'

'Nine months I've waited for this and I'm still rocking on my heels.'

'My pleasure.'

'And more to come.' He kissed her again. 'Now you rest, like the doctor says. I'll be back later for longer.'

'With a bottle of champagne, I trust.'

'Henry has had it on ice all day.' He got up from the bed, bent to kiss her yet again. 'Best day's work you ever did for me,' he complimented.

'You don't do so badly yourself on the nightshift.' She could hear him laughing all the way downstairs.

He came back later that evening to find Claire, much rested after a few hours' sleep, feeding their daughter, something else she had insisted she wanted to do herself. 'I don't believe in interfering with nature,' she had said firmly. 'I have the best possible kind of milk on tap and that's what I want for my baby.'

Now, Jake watched in rapt fascination as his daughter suckled greedily, one tiny hand resting proprietorially on Claire's milk-filled breast. 'She's already got quite an appetite,' he exclaimed.

'Which, if the expression on her face is anything to go by, is now satisfied. Here – ' Claire removed the sleepy baby from her breast and handed her over to her father. 'We may as well begin as I mean you to go on. You can bring up her wind.'

'What do I do?'

She was about to ask him if he didn't remember, then decided not to kick that sleeping dog. From what she knew of Stella, it was more than probable that he did not. 'Just pat her back gently, or rub it in a circular motion. Babies haven't any manners; she'll burp like a foghorn but that's what you're aiming for.' Tying the ribbons of her ruffled bedjacket, she asked, 'Is that today's paper you've brought?'

'Nope . . . it's a copy of the *Daily Telegraph* sent on from San Francisco.' He picked it up from the foot of the bed, dropped it on Claire's lap.

'Read and enjoy. It gave the perfect touch to my day, I can tell you.'

Claire picked it up; Jake had folded it so that the headline leapt out at her:

TWELVE YEARS FOR LAWYER WHO HELPED LAUNDER DRUG BARON'S MILLIONS

'A corrupt American lawyer was yesterday jailed for twelve years at the Old Bailey for his part in a five-year-long conspiracy to launder and reinvest what is conservatively estimated to be around £500 million, proceeds of a drug syndicate headed by Bruno de Souza, the Brazilian industrialist, himself under arrest and now awaiting trial in Paris.

Charles Whitman, 38, was described as the syndicate's 'Chancellor of the Exchequer' and originator of the scheme which involved vast amounts of cash, the proceeds of drug dealing, being deposited in foreign banks in London and elsewhere in Europe, later paid to bogus companies set up by him and thus laundered in a complicated series of interlocking financial transactions so that its origins were virtually impossible to trace until such time as it was returned to London for genuine investment.

Whitman, whose address was given as the Savoy Hotel, was found guilty of conspiring to handle the proceeds of the drug syndicate by a 10 to 1 majority.

Judge Arthur de Lisle said that Whitman had been 'grossly dishonest' and had used his status as a foreign national and lawyer of international repute to make a fortune for himself and his partner. It had been his fertile brain and worldwide contacts which had set the whole thing up, starting with an office in London as a specialist in international law, in reality a cover for the laundering of the multi-million pound profits that came from the sale of massive amounts of heroin and cocaine.

He had set up shelf companies in London, Panama, the Cayman Islands, Nassau and Lichtenstein, transferring the cash between them in a maze of deals deliberately designed to obscure its illicit origin. Profits had been paid into a Swiss bank, where he had opened an account under the name of Premium Investments and it was from here that the cash was again transferred to other banks, the enormous amounts spread thin so as to give no cause for comment before being legally invested in reputable companies.

It had taken Scotland Yard a year to follow the tangled skein of deception, culminating in the arrests of Whitman in London and de Souza in Paris and the smashing of the syndicate.'

Claire laid down the paper and looked to where Jake was now crooning what sounded like 'Oh What a Beautiful Morning' to his sleeping daughter.

'How did you do it?' she asked.

'Me! I didn't do anything.'

'Come off it. I have a good memory, remember? I asked you – oh, ages ago when I was in hospital – what you were going to do about Charlie Whitman and your reply was – and I quote: "That is being taken care of." So – how did you do it?'

Jake sighed dolefully. 'Can't I hide anything from you?'

'No.'

He came back to sit on the side of the bed again, still cradling the sleeping baby. 'Well, you know I used to go to Zurich every now and then – '

'You mean every six weeks as regularly as clockwork.'

'Right. Well, that was because I have an – interest – in a certain Swiss Bank.'

Claire said, 'You *own* a Swiss bank?'

'I said an interest.'

'With you that means a controlling one. Go on – no, hang about. It was your bank that Charlie used to deposit his ill-gotten gains! Except, of course, he had no idea it was yours in the first place.'

'Right. It was brought to my attention and when I saw the size of the deposits – well, I began to wonder. And then, from another source – '

' – and you've got more of them than the river Nile.'

' – I heard he was doing the same thing elsewhere. So I decided to do a little checking.'

'I thought Swiss banks were the ultimate in confidential.'

'But I'm a banker . . . And at the same time I had Ray

checking on Charlie's movements, and he came up with the fact that there was a definite connection between Bruno de Souza and a lawyer who was supposed to have done a Pontius Pilate on him. So then I really began to dig, and it seemed to me there was a slight case of overstatement concerning Charlie's hand-washing.'

'A case of the gentleman doth protest too much?'

'You got it.' Jake paused. 'I also came up with the fact that Cora Sue headed straight for Charlie after I fired her.'

Claire's mouth hung open.

'I think she wanted a little revenge of her own. Funny thing, though. Ray had her watched, and he reported to me that somebody else was keeping an eye on her too until she went to work for Charlie in his Tulsa office, where she no doubt told him all he wanted to know about Burns Enterprises – which is why I played along with Bruno de Souza. The information he had on me could only have come from her via Charlie.'

Claire was shaking her head. 'This has more twists and turns than Hampton Court maze!'

'The one thing Cora never knew about – nobody knew about – was my connection with the bank, but all the same, I had to put some pre-arranged contingency plans into operation. Charlie had already cost me one takeover; I couldn't afford to have him spiking any more of my guns.'

'I always knew you were a slippery character,' Claire pronounced.

'I told you something once, remember? Never, but never, keep all your eggs in one basket.'

'Which is why Charlie now has egg all over his face?'

'Precisely. Once I had enough to put two and two together and get the right answer I laid the information where it could do most good.'

'Would that be where I introduced you?'

'Of course. That's why I wanted to be introduced in the first place.'

'My God,' Claire said in amazement, 'I've heard of the

long arm of the law but yours is longer than the Mississippi.'

'I remembered what you told me about believing he had put Ballater up to snatching you; how he seemed to know things he could only have heard from Charlie and I started from there. I still can't prove it was Charlie who arranged all those "accidents" I had, but I know he did, and as soon as all my spade work proved a definite connection between him and de Souza I latched on to that and really went to work. Rory was too quick for me; I never got to deal with him, but I was determined to nail Charlie. What I never expected was that it would be for currency manipulation.'

'Speaking of currency – how much did it cost you?'

'A lot. I had a carefully selected squad of people sifting through everything and anything where both Charlie and de Souza were concerned. I had them turn over every stone we found and then put what was under them through the computer. It took months of checking facts, following trails, tailing people – I tell you, it took the patience of a saint in the end.'

'Oh! Who was he?'

Jake grinned. 'Sassy! You know I can be patient when I have to. I was with you, wasn't I?'

But Claire was thinking. 'Do you think Charlie knows it was you who shopped him?'

'I hope so. They're investigating him over here too; it seems he was steadily transferring huge amounts from London to Chicago.'

'And Cora Sue? What about her?'

'She's out of a job again, isn't she?'

'You don't forgive, do you?'

'Not things such as she did, no. Never.'

He handed over the baby to its nurse, who came to take it away to its brand-new nursery. 'Good night, angel,' he crooned.

'I hope you feel the same way come two a.m. tomorrow morning because that's when I have to feed her again,' Claire warned innocently.

'I would if I could but – '

'You can't. I know the lyric. In which case, the least you can do is pour me a glass of that delicious champagne.'

'Should you? I mean, with you feeding Stella – '

'If she gets the hangover I'll take the pledge.' But her heart had lifted at the easy, perfectly natural way he had said a name that had not been said for so long. She had decided, as soon as she knew for sure she was pregnant again, that if it was a girl she would call her Stella, and when Jake had said to her, 'I think, now, it is time we went back home,' she had agreed at once.

'Yes, I'm curious to see Cimarron.'

'I've sold the house – the one in town that is. I've outgrown Cimarron. It will remain the headquarters of Burns Oil as it has always been, but the rest, Burns Enterprises – well, I've decided to build a new corporate building in San Francisco.'

'Why not New York?'

'I don't want to live in a fortieth-floor chunk of some condominium. I want a house with a yard and – '

'Like those gorgeous Victorian gingerbread confections we saw?'

'Right. That's why I've bought one of them.'

'Angel!'

'I remember how you flipped when you saw that one we visited.'

'Who wouldn't! Is it on a hill? Is there a view?'

'Yes to both. I'm also having the old house done up back at the ranch. God knows it needs it; I thought it could be modernized so we could spend weekends there now and then and I could teach the kids to ride . . .'

'Sounds perfect.'

So, not all ties cut, she had thought. The ranch was some twenty miles outside Cimarron but still considered part of the town where Burns Oil was still the major employer, yet there had been a major reshuffle, as much in Jake's list of priorities as anything else, for he had indeed outgrown Cimarron. He was no longer just the owner of a small, independent oil company. He was an internationally-known entrepreneur and Cimarron was much too small to hold him. Perhaps, Claire thought, had already been that way when his troubles began, because that fact had been part of them. I think Stella must have realized what was happening; that she was losing him too, and it was all more than she could handle. He was capable of growing, expanding, becoming what destiny had planned for him. She was not. She was what my mother shrewdly surmised she was: a nice, small-town girl. But fate has been kind to her after all; Jake's daughter has been born here, in Cimarron, where Stella tried and failed three times. Now, our Stella has brought the wheel full circle. The old Stella can at last be placed where she belongs; in the past. Gone, but not forgotten thanks to her namesake.

'Let's drink a toast,' she said now, taking the glass Jake handed her.

'To what?'

'Us – the Burns family and its future.'

'I'll drink to that – and no heel taps.'

With fond indulgence Claire eyed her husband over the rim of her glass. 'Darling my love,' she said, 'you are a financial genius of the first order; you are the most uxorious of husbands and I have no doubt you will make an ideal father; but one thing you are most definitely not.'

'What's that?'

'Fred Astaire.'